Thaddeus S. Kenderdine

A California Tramp and Later Footprints

Life on the plains and in the Golden state thirty years ago, with miscellaneous

sketches in prose and verse - Vol. 1

Thaddeus S. Kenderdine

A California Tramp and Later Footprints
Life on the plains and in the Golden state thirty years ago, with miscellaneous sketches in prose and verse - Vol. 1

ISBN/EAN: 9783337369576

Printed in Europe, USA, Canada, Australia, Japan

Cover: Foto ©Andreas Hilbeck / pixelio.de

More available books at **www.hansebooks.com**

A
CALIFORNIA TRAMP

AND

LATER FOOTPRINTS;

OR,

LIFE ON THE PLAINS AND IN THE GOLDEN STATE THIRTY YEARS AGO,
WITH MISCELLANEOUS SKETCHES IN PROSE AND VERSE.

ILLUSTRATED WITH THIRTY-NINE WOOD AND PHOTO-ENGRAVINGS.

BY

T. S. KENDERDINE.

NEWTOWN, PA.
1888

PRESS OF GLOBE PRINTING HOUSE,
112 N. 12th St., Philadelphia.

Preface.

THIS book was not written to fill a long-felt want. Neither was it at the "urgent solicitations of my friends," many of whom do not know that I made the journey herein described. Nor was it written to make money, but rather with a reverse expectation. I wrote it partly at the request of my immediate family, partly with the hope that it would interest my friends as well as a portion of the outside public, partly to experience the sensations of authorship.

The title of the work is capable of two constructions—a pedestrian journey, and the nomadic life I led for a time in the likeness of the Ishmaelites which infest our rural districts, with the exception in respect to the last part—and a blessed exception it is—that while an Eastern tramp hunts work, praying he wont find it, his Occidental brother did the contrary. As to the first rendering, it might be open to criticism, inasmuch as two-thirds of the overland journey was by rail and water; but I can plead Mark Twain in his "Tramp Abroad" as an extenuating example; his walking being done on cars and steamboats. But as he was guilty of the hypocrisy of carrying a staff and knapsack, and I did my steam pilgrimage without these deceptions, I think I leave Mark far in the rear in respect to disingenuousness.

The past winter I conceived the idea of placing my writings in a more durable shape than that derived from scrap-books and loose manuscript, and rewrote, excised and added; although occasionally for want of time I was obliged to let them stand as written. This state of things comes in good play, for whenever the critical reader takes exception to the use of flowery language, redundant or rapturous adjectives and prosy description of route or scenery within the volume, I can lay it to the pen of the young ox-driver.

There was a physiological law contemporaneous with my school days, that the human system was changed once in seven years; that all that was there on the first year was expelled through natural causes by the seventh and replaced with new material. If this is in being yet and has not been relegated into mythical nothingness by new and iconoclastic school-books, along with the accounts of the "Maelstrom" and Sea Serpent, and the story of Pocahontas and John Smith, which were established facts as far as descriptive text and wood cuts could make them, I am more than four removes from the young traveler and ranchero of thirty years ago. Therefore should anything be found in the book which makes a favorable impression credit it to his mature successor or evolvent, who is palpable and capable of feeling praise or blame. The other party is away in the shadowy realms of the past, and unsensitive to both. In fact, so disassociated is he from myself, that I can give his portrait, as well as full-length representations of him in connection with other illustrations, with no more feeling of egotism than if I were showing off the features of one of his fellow cowboys of the plains.

Who reads this volume with the impression that it is full of wild hunting adventures and narrations of murders and robberies indigenous to an unsettled country will be disappointed. My mode of travel precluded Nimrodic pursuits, and had it been otherwise I don't imagine the wild animals of the Wild West would have been noticeably reduced in numbers. As for scenes of violence, although there were opportunities to participate therein, I left them for others who saw more fun in them than I did myself. It is true, this book would have been more replete with interest could I have given personal narrations of these; but as participation might have been only another name for annihilation, I don't regret that lack of individual experience has enabled me to be in a position to write an autographical and more commonplace account.

As for the "Later Footprints" following "A California Tramp," I will only say that among the prose sketches the article on John Burns should be worth attention as far as it furnishes facts proving the old man was a real militant in the Battle of Gettysburg; and as to those in rhyme, simply state that some of them had the questionable fame of newspaper republication.

When an author apologizes for literary defects, and airs the difficulties he has labored under, it is generally assumed that he could have done no better under favorable circumstances, and by implication is assured that if the work was so burdensome the reading public would have excused him from its performance. Nevertheless, I will say that the preparation of this volume was made before and after business hours since the preceding winter, and when it is understood what a disadvantage this disconnected procedure has when compared with continuous work, I hope the literary imperfections involved will be overlooked.

The illustrations, while not up to the high art standard, picture scenery and incidents of which I was a part sufficiently well. The most of them are from original sketches redrawn and made available through wood and photo-engraving. In a work of so limited a circulation they involved an outlay hardly warranted, except by my desire to represent and perpetuate what has been heretofore unillustrated and now nonexistent save in memory.

I have now accomplished what until lately I never seriously thought of doing—written a book. This act is what Job wanted his enemy to do; either because he would lose money or be criticized beyond the punishment of personal boils. But hoping that the miseries of authorship only existed in the imagination of that synonym of Patience, and that the perusal of this work will add a mite to the pleasures of my readers, I remain

Their friend,
THE AUTHOR.

Newtown, Pa., 10th mo., 1888.

Contents.

Illustrations.

A California Tramp.

I.

Preliminary.

THE reading of Fremont's Narrative and other works of Western adventure gave me, during the last two or three years of my minority, a great desire to travel over the trans-Mississippi plains and mountains. The departure of a friend and schoolmate for Oregon, on a surveying expedition, still further unsettled me, and showed my prosaic home life in yet more unfavorable contrast with the possibilities which Western travel would furnish; and when, in the spring of 1858, I secured a situation in the interior of Michigan, I concluded I had made one step in the coveted direction, and was partially satisfied.

I never shall forget the night when, having bid farewell to the home circle, I left Philadelphia for the West. The hour was eleven of the clock; darkness all around and the weather stormy; and not knowing a soul on board, or in my prospective home, I sank into a fit of the blues, not of the "deeply, beautifully" sort, but rather, from the sensations I felt, as if tinged

with blue vitriol. In those days the Western trains started
from Eleventh and Market streets, and were drawn by mules
to the suburbs. The drift of the rain on the car windows almost hid the lamp lights as we slowly passed out the drenched
streets; until, when beyond the Schuylkill, a locomotive displaced our long-eared propellers. There were no sleeping-cars
then to mitigate the sorrows of all-night travel, so I had
ample time, in my wakefulness, to think over past deeds and
the future troubles my leaving home might bring. To cheer
myself up I bought a comic book of one of the juvenile fiends
who, even in those times, made travelers miserable; but its
overdrawn humor and stale jokes so increased my unhappy
feeling that I put it away in disgust. Ever since I have had
a horror of books of the alleged "funny" order, a feeling
which extends even to works of the "Mark Twain" class,
books whose humor generally is made at the expense of religion and morality. The night passed at last, and when morning brought a clear sunrise and a view of the beautiful valley
of the Juniata, I began to take a more cheerful view of life.

Around curves, by heavy grades and through gloomy tun-
nels, and the Alleghenies were passed; and at two o'clock in the
afternoon the smoke-plumed chimneys of Pittsburgh came in
sight. The coming night was passed on a Lake Erie steamer,
and the next afternoon found me at my destination.

The party who employed me turned out to be a visionary—
a "crank" he would be termed now. The large tract of land
he was on he was simply superintendent of, instead of owner,
and the business I was to have charge of was simply his mental tenant, without prospect of the remotest materialization.
So in course of a month I discharged my employer; and with
ten dollars and a pair of boots I had earned, I re-obeyed
Greeley's as yet unspoken command to "Go West, young man"
—an order, it will be noticed, I obeyed in instalments.

I stopped one day in Chicago, then on jack-screws and work-

ing its way up. The sight of houses rising Phœnix-like from
the mud, with the people dwelling therein, living and dying
as usual, was an edifying one, but as a canvas of the town
showed it could get along without me, I shook the mud aforesaid from my boots and left it to its fate; certainly not a luckless one, with real estate so rising.

Money being the root of all evil, I felt myself as harmless as
Mary's little lamb when preparing to leave what, from a severe
strain on the imagination, was called the "Garden City." I was
compelled to buy a second-class ticket to Kansas, where destiny
and inclination seemed to call me. My departure was in an
emigrant car at midnight; my only companions two drunken
bandits, armed with guns. The car was dark, and I always
hailed the conductor's advent with his lantern, from my place
in an unobtrusive corner, with silent orisons. In St. Louis I
only stopped long enough to note how similarly the streets
were named to those of Philadelphia. I left there at ten
o'clock on June 2d, and passing over a country of alternate
prairie land and wooded streams, reached Jefferson City late
at night, where I boarded the "Polar Star" steamer; the Western railroad system then not reaching beyond that town.

At that time the only railroads reaching beyond the Mississippi were the Missouri Pacific and the Hannibal and St. Jo.
The latter had not reached the Missouri, so part of the road
was made by stage, and consequently was the least popular
way to Kansas, as by the former route the whole journey could
be made by boat and rail; a great favor in the days of border
ruffianism, when Free State emigration by private conveyance was often checked or turned back by pro-slavery high-
waymen.

Four days I endured the discomforts of deck passage, many
and many a time wishing myself an Astor or Girard that I
might climb out of it to the beatitude of the cabin above, where
amid high living and luxurious surroundings the first-class

passengers' lives slid along. My companions were the lower
order of emigrants, foreign and domestic, and the deck hands
or "roustabouts." Many of the latter were desperadoes, whose
gashed faces showed the effects of personal encounters. My
sleeping places were on bundles of freight, and my provender
the rude fare I bought at the landings. My impression had
been that deck passage simply meant absence of state-room
and dining privileges, but I soon learned that the enjoyment
of the upper deck was fruit forbidden, and that the officer in
charge knew a steerage passenger by a sort of instinct as a
personage who was to be hustled down the gangway on sight.
So I perforce passed my time below, with one eye on my belongings, lest they should be stolen, and the other on the
scenery and surroundings generally. The shriek of the "calliope;" the cough of the exhaust pipe, as that of an asthmatic
giant; the escape of the angry steam; the roar of the mud-
valves, when the sediment of the river water was forced from
the boilers; the cursing of the crew by the mate on duty; the
mutterings and low spoken threats of the former, and the sing-
song call of the leadsmen, as the treacherous channel was
sounded, I still seem to hear. In my vision are the unwashed
passengers; the grimy stokers feeding the fires under the
high-strung boilers; the vile deck hands on duty, or eating
their fried bacon and hard tack, with their feet hanging over
the muddy water, into which they now and then dipped their
tincups for drink; the envied cabin passengers promenading
the upper deck and occasionally coming down to our purga-
tory to see the possibility of endurance; the mile-wide river
with its driftwood and caving banks, its shabby towns and
wood-yards; our wooding up at night in the glare of pine-
knots, when, like fiends in their glare, the aroused crew carried
armloads of billets on a run, under the occasional stimulus of
a kick or blow. All these sights and sounds are bright in my
memory now. I became so disgusted with my surroundings

that I made an effort to exchange my deck for a cabin passage.
Watching my chance, I ascended to the celestial regions to see
the clerk about it, but his manners and figures had such an
altitude that I was fain to retreat before, mistaking my errand,
the mate accelerated my steps. Like all tribulations, mine
passed away, however, and with several dollars saved for future needs by my privations, I at last landed at Leavenworth
on the 7th of June, feeling just as well as if I had fared on the
high living of the upper cabin, instead of on the husks, in the
shape of bread and bolognas, I ate on the lower deck.

I had come these hundreds of miles to hunt work, but with
dull times and no friends to help me, I was sore beset to find
anything to do. I tried around the city, then a place of from
one to two thousand people, but I did not seem necessary to
the growth of the town any more than I was to that of Chicago.
At that time there was one business open to young men of easy
conscience, and that was to go out in the country, take up
claims, make affidavits that they pre-empted them for their own
exclusive use, and then sell out for a stated sum to their employer. The law required that a habitation twelve by twelve
must be built thereon before the claim could be held. This
was accomplished by the erection of a Liliputian residence of
twelve inches square, or by a simple rail pen of the required
dimensions in feet. A young Kentuckian, similarly situated
financially as myself, and I walked a long distance out of town
one day to see a real estate agent who gave men this questionable employment. On this journey I learned how they made
country calls in Kansas thirty years ago, of which I give an
illustration drawn from life. We did not go up to the door
and ring the bell for two reasons: there was no bell to ring,
and we were afraid of the dogs. We just stood out in the road
and shouted "Hello!" If no response were made we would
scream, "Call your dogs off," this soon becoming a necessity
If the party called on had any politeness, they would rush out

with clubs or boot-toes and extricate us, otherwise they would give the dogs aid with their guns in helping the intruders off. This seemed like queer doing to me, but they were natural to my comrade from the "dark and bloody ground," and under his tuition I soon grew familiar with them. We at last found the agent we were after, but on learning there was more or less of perjury connected with the business, although we were as-

A COUNTRY CALL IN KANSAS IN 1858.

sured that custom sanctioned and semi-legalized it, we resolved to touch not the unclean thing, although "there was money in it."

Hearing there were ox-drivers wanted at Kansas City, to take a train to Santa Fé, a place I had a desire to visit, I lugged my trunk down to the steamboat wharf, for I was always my own porter, and when the next packet came along went down the Missouri. This time, as the trip was short, I took cabin passage and enjoyed the privilege of the saloon and "texis" deck and was as good as the best of them. I could see the "calliope" man playing on his instrument of torture; the silk-hatted gamblers playing at cards; I could lounge on a sofa, and do other acts and things lately forbidden. Arrived at my destination I soon hired with a transportation agent to drive team, and forwarded my trunk home. The sending of this, which contained nearly all of my civilized belongings, seemed like burning the bridge behind, and that I had entered on a dangerous, half savage life, from which I might never return. Before leaving the agent, I made some inquiries of him in regard to the scenery on the route, and other matters, which smacked more of the tourist than of the experienced ox-propeller I professed to be. The next morning, rigged out in my roughest clothing, I reported for duty at the wharf, where a train was being made up. What was my mortification when my yesterday's employer told me curtly he did not want me. "Why?" I asked. "Any one who asks such questions as you did, is too smart for an ox-driver," he roughly answered as he turned away. I resolved that next time I would guard well my tongue.

Concluding to return to Leavenworth and again try my luck there, I passed the coming night waiting for an up steamer. A dismal wait it was; till midnight in a foul smelling saloon, and after that was closed, on the dark levee, by the side of the rushing river. Towards morning a boat came along, and on it I returned to the above town. Here I again hired as an ox-driver, trying to look as rough and unkempt as I could, that I might seem worthy the vocation. My destination was Salt Lake. This time I was careful to ask no questions, though I shrank from the rough life before me.

One thing that reconciled me to engaging in this journey

was that a congenial young fellow whom I got acquainted
with at my boarding-house, named Will Finlay, was going
with me; in fact, the enterprise was a mutual affair. I knew
from the class of men I saw about the departing trains, that I
would want some one like him for a comrade, and thought,
from the spirit he showed, he would stick to me. Still, as he
had been brought up to gentle ways and had joined the train
out of a spirit of adventure, I do not wonder that he afterwards
deserted me, weighed down as I was with such surroundings.

Some of the particulars of my campaign life I will tell in a
chapter entitled "A Day on the Plains." For a few days
we were engaged in loading the huge wagons and branding
cattle. The mark was an ox-yoke burned in front of the right
hip. This was the private brand of Russel, Majors and
Waddell, the most extensive freighters who ever crossed the
plains, with whom I had hired. We branded five hundred in
one day. The groans of the struggling oxen and the smell of
their burning flesh sickened me, but the fear of another rebuff
made me hide my emotion and feign that just such work was
what I was suffering for.

The few days we were waiting to start on our journey I
lived at a place called the "Outfit." Our sleeping quarters
were full of vermin, but these were less disgusting than a portion of my human associates, many of whom were merely
waiting for the time for their clothing to be dealt out to
them, when they would run off. Some of them were jailbirds
and other desperadoes, and petty thieving was common. In
their talk they were the vilest of the vile, yet on account of a
few semi-respectable fellows among them, I concluded to not
back down, but to follow out my resolve to go to Utah, to
which place we were to take supplies for the army sent to sub-
due the Mormons, then in rebellion. The soldiers around the
Fort made it a lively place, but their numbers were so small
compared with the million or more who sprung to arms four

MAKING OUR MARK.

years after, that they are unworthy of notice. I think they were not over four thousand men under General Johnston, commanding the Utah army, the most of which had preceded us. Still their white tents among the greenery of grass and trees, with the moving columns of horse, foot and artillery around them, formed a scene to be remembered. -

Before we started each man was given a whip, with a lash ten feet long. These were but toys to what supplanted them when they wore out. With a sort of poetic injustice, from the skins of cattle which died of hardship, lashes were cut and plaited five or six yards long, to facilitate the turning of the hides of other oxen into whip material. These scourges were from an inch and a quarter to an inch and a half in thickness at the " swell," one-fourth the way from the stock, from which they tapered each way, with a buckskin " cracker," and in the hands of an expert they did murderous work.

Each train had a box of medicines which was kept in the train-master's wagon, along with the revolvers and ammunition, which was its proper place. If I remember rightly, the basic matter of the contents was composed of calomel, laudanum and Epsom salts, with a few outlying adjuncts for doing their work. These, in the hands of an ignorant practitioner, were capable of much mischief. I think the quack who had his medicines numbered to suit the ills inherent to flesh, and when he was out of the required number 6, gave numbers 2 and 4 as an equivalent and promptly killed his man, was a wagon-master. I knew I fought as shy of that chest as a fox would of a box-trap. When a little out of sorts or low-spirited, the old professionals would make things worse by telling what became of the teamsters when they died, that is, in this world; for it is pretty easy to tell where most of the " bull-whackers " went, unless orthodox theology is at fault. These Job's comforters told how the translated unfortunates were buried in scant roadside graves, in boxes made from the sideboards of their wagons. I, however, made up my mind not to stay sick or downhearted and patronize the death-trap in the master's wagon, and thereby keep the wagon body as well as my own and soul together. But for all that, I would sometimes think in the dark hours of the night I was lying in a prospective coffin!

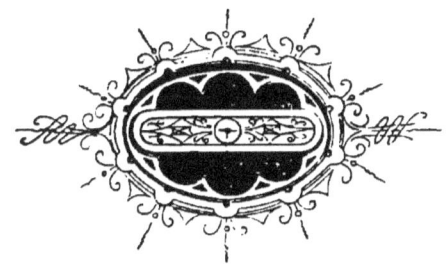

II.

To the Land of the Buffalo.

WE at last got under way, but on account of unbroken teams, ignorant drivers and desertions,
it was several days before we got in working
order. Sometimes the whole night guard, with their outfits,
would decamp in a body, leaving the cattle to wander over the
country. The deserters were replaced by better men obtained
from returning trains, with which we sent back our sick.

After some days of tribulation we crossed the valleys of the
Big and Little Grasshopper, and reached Walnut Creek on the
8th of July. Here we saw our first deer, which our wagon-
master gave chase to on his mule, but with limited success.
On the night of the 17th, when one hundred and twenty miles on
the road, we had the most terrible thunder-storm I ever saw.
I was out all night herding the cattle, and the glare of
lightning and crash of thunder rendered them hard to
manage. They hardly lay down all night, but wandered fit-
fully about, which made it hard for us. However, the sun
rose bright and warm the next morning, when we could
hardly realize what a night we had passed.

Our next night's camp was by the side of the new-made
grave of a teamster, who had been run over by a stampede of
oxen. A mound marked the spot on our arrival, but by
morning the herd had so trampled down the wet earth that no

trace was visible of the resting place of the poor fellow, even the rude headboard, on which was his name, being displaced.

On the 20th we came to Marysville, on the Big Blue. Here was a mission and reservation of the Otto Indians. While descending the bluff one of our oxen died; but the noble red men, when apprised, soon had him skinned, cut up and carried to their village. These Indians shaved their heads and were otherwise as near naked as they could well be. Still, the weather was warm.

The valley of the Big Blue was swarming with mosquitoes, and that night while herding cattle we were badly pestered with them. They bit through our clothing and sang merrily at their work. We wrapped ourselves from head to heels in our blankets to fence them off, though the air was oppressively sultry, but in spite of that they bit us so we were covered with a rash the next morning. To their shrill tenor a band of wolves on the adjacent bluffs howled a blood-curdling baritone. The howl of one wolf is enough, but when a band of this species get down to their work, it is more than that. They commence with a shrill whine, which increases and deepens until it ends in an unearthly yell which you feel in your bones.

We crossed the Blue on a rope ferry, swimming all the oxen except what we wanted to pull the wagons on to the boat. My friend Finlay and I were sent to herd cattle on the other side of the river, where we were kept till night with nothing to eat. When we were relieved, we had to swim the river to our wagons which were not ferried over. The river was swollen, so that we landed far below in the darkness. The next morning we found our shoes stolen as well as some of our clothing, which we had left on the other side.

After crossing the rest of the wagons, the guards were re-arranged, and our rifles and a few rounds of ammunition given us, as we were getting among hostile Indians. There were pistols also in the train arsenal, but for motives of policy they were not given out. Some of our men could punish one another with fist and tooth sufficiently without using these. At noon on the 25th we met a part of the troops sent to Utah, returning. They were artillerymen, with some cavalry or dragoons, as they were then called, and General Harney, still living in 1888, was with them. They had gone four hundred miles before taking a return course.

We reached the valley of the Little Blue on the 26th of June. This was full of mosquitoes, and at night noisy with wolves. While herding that night, a wolf crossed a knoll within twenty yards of where I was lying down, looking in silhouette against the clear sky to my excited fancy as large as a horse.

Our route lay the next day along the valley of the Little Blue in the direction of the Platte River. The road was miry and lined with the carcasses of dead oxen lost by preceding trains, which filled the air with sickening odors. We afterwards left the valley and crossed high ground, from which we had a fine view of the lower country to the south. Broad vistas of verdure, traversed by belts of darker green, marked the timber-lined streams. The main trunk was the Blue, and from this extended short branches.

The 1st of August found us among a range of sand hills which announced our approach to the valley of the Platte. These were a succession of knolls and ridges from thirty to sixty feet high. Amid their defiles our wheels sunk deep in the sand, and we frequently doubled teams in order to get through. From these we came to the broad, level bottom of the river, which was marked by numerous wooded islands. In the distance we saw Fort Kearney, the low buildings of which were just visible above the prairie. When within a mile the train was stopped, and orders given for each man to overhaul his load, and put the flour which was in any way

damaged by rain in the bottom, so as the load would pass
governmental inspection. We were forced to become parties in
this fraud, whether willing or not. We encamped at noon a
few hundred yards beyond the Post.

Fort Kearney is about one hundred and sixty miles from the
Missouri. It was established during the Mexican war, the
intention being to connect the frontiers with the Pacific by a
chain of military posts along the Platte and Columbia rivers.
The buildings consisted of barracks, hospital, sutler store and
cavalry stables. Some were of logs, others of frame, but the
majority were of dried mud and roofed with sods. It was not
a very prepossessing place, but after a journey of three hundred
miles through a wilderness, we welcomed the sight, as we
also did the sound of the bugle that night, and the roll of
drum and the shriek of fife the next morning from the
musicians of the little garrison.

At Kearney Finlay left me. Since the train started he had
been as sick of his profession as the traditional dog of the pro-
verbial broth. He could see no romance in "hollering" at
and beating oxen all day and herding them on alternate nights,
and was disgusted with his associates. Much as he disliked to
leave me, he was determined to quit the train in some way.
One dark and stormy night, when on guard near the sand hills,
he came to camp and, awakening me, tried to persuade me to
desert with him and make our way through three hundred
miles of wilderness to the Missouri by the route we came. I
did not start out with the intention of turning back, and prevailed on him to desist from his intention. He was afterwards
taken sick, and went back with the next return train. He
cried when we parted, and I felt badly enough, for he was my
wagon mate and the only congenial comrade I had in all that
unkempt gang of ox-drivers. I never heard of Finlay afterwards.

We left Fort Kearney the morning after our arrival, and

slowly moved up the valley of the Platte, whose waters we were to follow to the summit of the Rocky Mountains. Our route was about a mile from the shore, which we were unable to approach nearer on account of numerous "sloos," as the "Pikers" call marshy creeks, which extended from the river. The water we could not see for the many islands. Towards night we passed a French trading post, whose owner had grown rich trading with emigrants and Indians. Of course, the item of whisky was the most attractive part of his stock. These traders generally had one or more Indian wives, by which means they ingratiated themselves with the noble red men.

We camped six miles west of the Fort. The next morning we broke corral early, as our wagon-master was anxious to make up for lost time. I never saw birds in freedom as tame as here. They would alight near us as we passed along, and it was sport for the skilled "Pikers" to "pop" them with their whips—the "crackers" being as fatal as bullets. But we were soon to see larger game than birds. About 9 o'clock, while leisurely trudging along, we were startled by a shout which ran from head to rear of the train: "A buffalo! A buffalo!" In the direction indicated, we saw a dark, moving object, a mile off. The wagon-master and his assistant immediately started in pursuit; while we, taking matters in our own hands, stopped the train to enjoy the chase, trusting that the outcome would be a change from our scurvy-producing bacon to buffalo steak. Mounted on little mules, armed with rifles, revolvers and knives, with their heels, which nearly dragged the ground, bristling with huge rattling spurs, our heroes looked like Don Quixote and Sancho Panza, starting out on one of their windmill storming expeditions. The buffalo took the alarm when they were in rifle-shot, and galloped toward the sand hills as fast as his clumsy legs would carry him, closely followed by his pursuers. These fired several shots after him, but he only ran the faster; and, kicking up a cloud of dust which hid him from our sight, he out-distanced his pursuers, and was soon lost from view among the intricate system of hills which bounded our vision on the south. Our sportsmen soon gave up the chase and returned somewhat crestfallen to the train.

An hour before sunset we saw scattered bands of buffaloes to our left, near the sand hills, and willing that we should have some sport, the wagon-master allowed us to halt earlier than common. About a dozen of us shouldered our rifles and with a few rounds of fixed ammunition started on our buffalo hunt. As we neared the bellowing and already excited bands, we parted, each man taking a different route. I picked out a big bull, as a foeman worthy of my gun, and started after him, but he led me a weary race, and before I had a chance to draw on him, we were in the midst of the sand hills. He was a cunning old fellow, and all the time, by adroit management, kept at a respectful distance. I, at last, got within rifle-shot and fired, but the report only frightened him, and he galloped away and was soon lost to view. Although it was now after sunset, and I was a long distance from camp, I was not yet satisfied with the results of the expedition, and ramming home another cartridge, I started after fresh game. Moving on a short distance among the sand hills, I came across a herd of bulls sociably grazing together. Always on the watch for human intruders, as these animals are, they started off in a body upon seeing me, but resting my rifle scientifically on my knee, I took aim and fired. *That* shot told, for while the remainder of the herd dashed madly forward, scared by the report, my buffalo stopped; but, alas! for my skill as a marksman, he did not drop as I wished him to, either because the ball did not enter a vital part, or because he had scruples about giving up the ghost in my presence just then. I fired again and wounded him, but he made no acknowledgment, except to move on a few steps, while I reloaded my rifle. Again and again did the

2

report of my piece ring out on the air, each of which my huge
opponent merely acknowledged by a toss of his shaggy head,
or by slightly changing his position.   I shot on until but one
cartridge was left, and then I stopped, thinking my stubborn
game might eventually conclude to take the part of hunter
himself.   Some stories I had once read of wounded buffaloes
turning upon their pursuers and goring or trampling them to
death, came to my mind at this time, and at last I concluded
that the "world was wide enough for him and me," and to
return to camp.   Suiting the action to the thought, I started
off in what I supposed was the right direction, casting an
occasional look backward towards the buffalo.   I had not gone
far, however, before I found out I was lost.   I had started on a
buffalo trail which I thought led to the river, but instead it
was leading me into difficulties.   I got bewildered at last, and
lost the direction of our camp.   Here was I, a youthful seeker
after adventure, far away from camp, locked amid a maze of
sand hills, surrounded by darkness and in danger every
moment of being run over by the bands of buffaloes, which were
now on their way to water and filling the air with low bellowing.   And what if I should come on to a stray party of
Cheyennes, who might want to play one of their practical
jokes on me?   My heart jumped in my throat at the thought,
but I started on, and with the Polar star as my guide, I endeavored to reach the north side of the range of sand hills,
whence I could find my way across the valley to the Platte.
So I walked on through the yielding sand, in ravines and
over ridges, sometimes following the buffalo trails, but leaving
them when I thought they diverged from a right line.   At
last, to my great joy, I saw I was nearing the edge of the hills,
for the abrupt knolls and ridges began to subside to broad
undulations, which announced the level plain beyond.   But
where was the corral?   I looked through the darkness in
hopes to get a glimpse of our campfire, but saw nothing.   It

gave me the horrors to be thus alone in this gloomy place, listening to the mutterings of moving herds, and not knowing which way to go to find my transient home. I now thought of my remaining cartridge, and concluding to let my comrades know of my whereabouts, with that I loaded and fired. A moment of suspense, and it was answered by two or three shots, and soon a blaze shot up through the darkness, by which I knew my companions were directing my steps. I hurried over the prairie, and soon the circle of the corral arose before me, and I was among my brethren of the plains.

I admit that I was badly frightened while in that labyrinth of sand hills, not knowing where camp was, and invisible monsters bellowing all around me. My companions, who had long since got in camp, knew the import of my rifle-shot and, simularly answering it, built a fire for my guidance.

One of our men, who was an old hunter, had shot a buffalo out towards the sand hills, and asked me to go with him to get some fresh beef for supper. As dark as it was, through a sort of instinct, he led the way straight to where the animal lay. He was so heavy, we could hardly roll him over. Carving a choice cut from his flesh, we lugged it to the camp, much to the delight of the thirty men who had lived on salt pork long enough to get the scurvy. Still we soon got tired of buffalo meat, as it was tough and had a strong musky odor, and some of the men were made sick by the change.

The road was lined with bands of buffaloes, and the whole plain between the river and sand hills was fairly black with them. We saw them not by hundreds or thousands, but by hundreds of acres. The main body was about a quarter of a mile from us, the column near a mile in width, and extending parallel with the river as far either way as the eye could reach. Several were grazing near the road and some came close to our wagons, heedless of danger, and were constant targets for our rifles. I shot one within ten yards of the wagon. How many were killed during the day I don't know; but far too many, and we at last got disgusted with the miserable sport and put our rifles away. To be sure, my first adventure with them was quite exciting, but now so quiet were they that there was no sport in firing at these harmless brutes. Numbers of them, killed by parties in advance, were scattered over the plain, half devoured by wolves; and the inroad made upon them by immigrants and hunters, were in thirty years to drive them out of existence, except where protected. I am ashamed to think that we had any part in this slaughter.

To show how near the outlying members of the large herd of buffaloes which darkened the plain on the east, came to our camp, I will mention that a half-grown specimen jumped over one of our wagon tongues, on its road to water. Its temerity was rewarded with a fatal shot. The bellowing of the main body made the air tremble and frightened our cattle, while a musky odor filled the air.

The hunting of these animals seemed so much like gunning for cows in a barnyard, that I only mention my experience to show how near I became lost while engaged in that misnamed sport.

Buffaloes resemble hogs in liking to wallow in mud and water. With the river in sight, when thirsty we had to drink from the little ponds where they had been disporting, though from its musky odor it was almost unbearable. Still it was better than the alkali water we drank further on.

With the plain full of buffaloes on one side, and the island-filled Platte on the other, we wearily traveled on under an August sun. It was pitiful to see the suffering of the oxen, as with tongues lolling out and eyes turned appealingly to the brutish driver, they slowly moved along. Sometimes they were lashed, beaten and overworked until they fell dead in their tracks. In fifteen miles from our morning's camp we stopped for the night, to the great joy of man and beast.

I was captain of guard No. 4. This meant that I had the most of the work to do and got the blame for what was undone. It was nice to write home that I was a "captain," even if it was over a scurvy crew of four. It did to accompany the other fiction that our employers would hire no one who swore or drank. To be sure, the men were clear of drinking—when they could get none. It pleased me to hear how particular our bosses were, and I so wrote; but I never told my parents that my comrades, with few exceptions, swore like pirates and stole what little there was to steal. At first they stole the best oxen from the weaker drivers, when they found their merits and before each one well knew his cattle; then they would steal pipes and tobacco, tinware and bow-keys, as well as the wood, got with so much labor in readiness for cooking breakfast. They were a nice set, take them all around; but there were three or four, I hope the reader will believe, who did not train with the crowd.

I was routed out by the captain of "No. 3," suppositiously at midnight, although we were sometimes defrauded of our sleep by being prematurely awakened. I would be acquainted with the condition of the herd, when I would awaken the rest of my men and start forth to relieve the old guard. Our predecessors had had a hard night of it to keep the cattle from being incorporated with the buffaloes which were surrounding them. The shaggy brutes were on their way to water from their grazing grounds, and were making the air tremble with their terrible roaring. In the darkness we could not tell one beast from another, and we were often in danger of being run over by the buffaloes which seemed to be trying to stampede our herd. It was claimed that they purposely did that. One of our men, "Dutch Bill," said that while on a return trip from Laramie, in 1857, his train was overtaken by a snow-storm near the junction of the North and South Platte. The oxen were turned out to graze, but the grass was so covered with snow that they half perished by starvation and cold. One day, while the remainder, now scrawny skeletons, were wandering around or browsing on the willows bordering the river, the snow-bound men witnessed a strange sight. A band of buffaloes came floundering through the snow on the road to water, after getting which they went among the oxen. The buffaloes, as if commiserating their bovine neighbors, licked their faces and in other ways showed their good feeling. Suddenly a low bellow was heard, and in a moment the mingled band of buffaloes and oxen were moving from the river and over the sand hill. The whole party disappeared from view, leaving the teamsters in a sad plight: a dreary winter before them, and no fuel but the willows along the river. After much suffering they were relieved in the spring.

Of course we could not divert the course of the buffaloes, the best we could do was to keep our cattle away from them. The continued muttering of the former kept the latter restless, and we were kept busy until morning in preventing the oxen from wandering away. We could hear through the darkness the buffaloes as they jumped down the bank into the river, or their bellowing as they scrambled back. We were glad when the sun rose, when driving our cattle to the corral, we were ready for another weary drive.

Wherever there are buffaloes there are Indians. Hitherto we had only seen the tame variety hanging around the trading posts, some naked from their shaved heads to their bare feet, with the exception of a tribute to modesty in the shape of an apron, a world too scant. In the forenoon we were favored with a sight of the unadulterated article, untainted with civilization, mounted on horses and brave with paint, feathers and silver ornaments. They seemed friendly and shouted the customary salutation of "How! How!" at us. Not to be behind in courtesy we also said "How!" Their chief wants here below were whisky and tobacco, in which they showed a great resemblance to the noble white man. They traveled with us awhile and then galloped away.

III.

A Day on the Plains.

LEVEL valley, miles in width; a broad river, full of wooded islands, and shallows, and rippling currents; in the far distance low ranges of interminable hills; a circle of white covered wagons, with the embers of campfires dimly glowing in their midst. This is the scene, but the central object, our camp, only is visible, for the light of morning has not yet come.

It is the dawn of a warm summer's day. Between the hard bed, the heat and musquitoes, a restless night has been passed, tired and needful of repose as you have been; but as daylight approaches, a deep sleep comes over you. Suddenly you hear a thumping on the side of the sheeted wagon, accompanied with cries of "Roll out! Roll out!" and words unmentionable added thereto. This is the reveille of the plains, and the performer is the assistant wagon-master of the train; the musical instruments are his lungs and a detached ox-bow. The sounds travel around the circle of wagons until not a driver is slighted. Drowsily you roll on your bed of hard bags of flour and try to think you imagine the sounds and can sleep longer, but no, they are reality.

A rushing sound is heard. It is the tread of our herd of over three hundred oxen, just being driven from their night's grazing grounds. There are the blowing of breaths, the clatter

of striking horns, and the petulant cries of the night guard,
weary with loss of sleep and keeping the restless cattle closed
up, that the watchful Indian might not break in and steal.
Persistent drumming on the wagon, and entreaties of the bullies
and cursings of the weaklings of the train, and the evolving
process indicated by the initial cries of the wagon-master is
consummated, and the sleepy drivers stand, ox-yoke on shoulder, a bow in one hand and bow-key in teeth, ready for work.

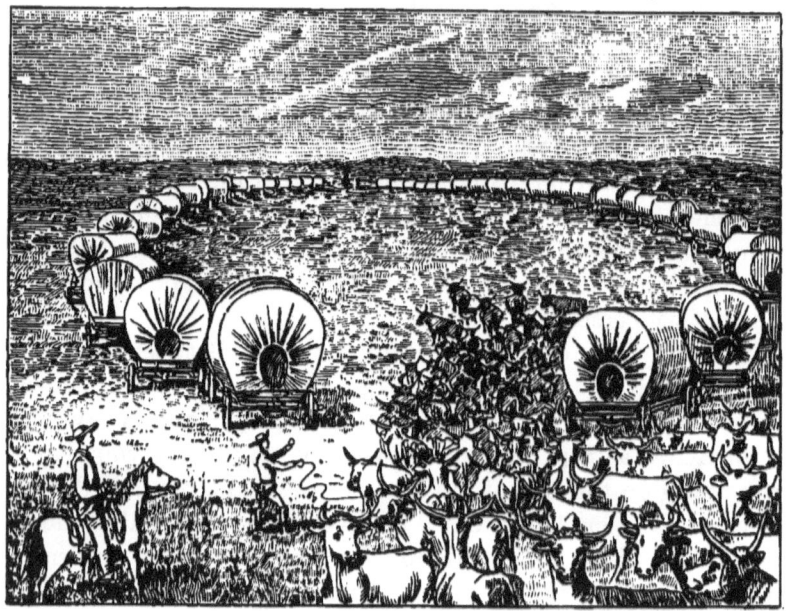

THE CORRAL.

The last of the straggling herd is now in, and the voice of
the wagon-master, hoarse from yesterday's shouting at men
and oxen, yells "Yoke up!" Then comes a scene of noise and
confusion of from ten to thirty minutes, according to the alacrity of the men.

In our train there are a wagon-master, an assistant, two extras, to help in different places, or take the place of sick or in-

jured, and twenty-six drivers—thirty in all. There are three
hundred and twelve oxen, besides some spare ones, often broken
down. There are twenty-six wagons, divided into two wings—
the right and left. As the leading teams have advantages,
these wings alternate in starting. In bad roads the head
wagons get over the difficult spots an hour or two before those
in the rear, and as the drivers often fail to reciprocate favors,
they go on and leave the last to get along the best they can,
with the help of the extras, or those behind. The favorites of
the wagon-masters—neighbors or old comrades of the plains—
get the leadership and the pick of the cattle, while the rest
put up with the leavings. The men are portioned off in four
messes of six or seven, the cooks not having to guard or herd
at night, or at the noon halts. The men are divided in five
guards, so their watches will vary from before to after midnight, as their turns come, though sometimes they stand all
night. The last, though making the duty rarer, was a great
hardship, when after a hard day's work we went supperless to
an all night's guard, after driving the cattle into the river to
drink.

When stopping, the train is placed in two semi-circles, one on
either side of the road, as a protection against Indians and to form
a corral to hold the oxen while yoking them up. The wagons are
narrow tired, weigh eighteen hundred pounds, and carry fifty-
four hundred. They are covered with double sheets and provided with chain-locks. The cook's wagon has a mess-box on
behind to carry our Dutch oven, skillet and tin plates, and remnant of meals. A half-barrel for water is hung on the end of the
guide pole. In the oven is baked saleratus-raised bread, that
comes out of it as yellow as sponge cake and unfit to eat. In
the skillet our bacon is fried, and in the surplus fat dough is
boiled and christened "fat cakes." Our fuel, if we are fortunate
enough to camp by timber, is the dryest branches we can find,
but in certain districts we used "buffalo chips." This last was

not repulsive, only by association, and I have seen "Pikers" roasting hoe cakes in their embers, with mouths a-water. "Pikers" and Missourians were synonymous.

Our train was No. 54; how many followed I do not know. They, as well as hundreds of others, were owned by Russel, Majors and Waddell, government contractors, a part of which firm embezzled hundreds of thousands of dollars of Indian trust funds at the outbreak of the civil war. We were carrying army supplies to Salt.Lake for the soldiers sent out under Albert Sydney Johnston (who was killed at Shiloh) for the suppression of the Mormon Rebellion. Twenty cents per pound was the rate of freight, though when we got out there the troubles were over, and the Government bought all the flour wanted for $5.00 per hundred. Our train, when in close order, was a half mile long, but it often reached from one to three miles. On our way we overtook a train whose. men had mutinied against the wagon-master, and this afterwards traveled with us, making our train twice the above length. The wagon-masters and extras rode horses, the drivers all walked, as it was impossible otherwise to keep the oxen to their work.

The cattle, on account of the immense demand, were mainly unbroken. We aimed to get two good Missouri oxen for wheelers and leaders, size being required for the former and intelligence for the latter. The next grade were the "pointers," which were hooked next the tongue. Between these and the leaders were the "swing," composed of the "scallawags"—the weak, lazy and unbroken. To show how few stood the twelve hundred miles journey, I will state that but two of my twelve got through, the rest having died or given out from time to time. They were replaced by others from returning trains, or by the best in what we called our "calf yard," or loose cattle. This was a corruption of the Spanish word *caballada*, although the "Pikers" did not know it, and, in fact, did not bother themselves about its origin, as "calf yard" seemed the natural term

for a troop of oxen. About half the men were Missourians, the
rest odds and ends of human driftwood, floating around Kansas, waiting for some eddying current to draw them in. Some
of these were lazy and worthless, and imposed additional burdens upon the willing ones. They were paid twenty-six dollars
per month and found, and were furnished with "outfits" of
blankets and clothing at starting, which was charged up to
them. About the first night out the term "found" would not
apply to some of them, for they ran away and were "lost to
sight," though to the memory of their employers dear.

The wagons, on account of unseasoned timber being used in
their make, were a source of much trouble. Only four of our
twenty-six went through. Sometimes we would have to take
the wheels off at our noon rests and soak them in the river.
Those with wooden axles ran easier than those of iron. Many
of the wagons were made East and sent to Kansas by New
Orleans.

I left our men some time back yoking up. At the command
each man starts with a rush for his "off-wheeler." To pick him
out of a herd of over three hundred excited oxen is a difficult job. They must be yoked *seriatim*, so that no matter how
many of the other eleven you see, you must get that particular one. Tearing through the surging mass, for you are sometimes on a race, the " off ox " at last is found, one end of
the yoke attached, with more or less trouble, and he is pulled
and driven to the rear of your wagon which, like all the rest,
is towards the centre of the corral. Then you run around
among the herd after the "nigh-wheeler," which after much
tribulation is found and driven up and yoked to his mate.
These are then taken outside and put to the tongue. The
next to find are the leaders, which, when yoked, are chained
to the wheels, when the rest are brought up in order and the
five yokes chained together, every ox and yoke in its regular
place. The men first mark their oxen that they may know

them, but they soon recognize them all. We once yoked up and were ready to start in five minutes. Sometimes the lasso would have to be used to catch the wild Texas oxen, but they soon were so broken down that they were all tame enough.

Each man furnished himself from the "outfit" house with woolen blankets, clothing and, if he could afford it, a gum blanket or overcoat. The company furnished him with a rifle, revolver and ammunition, which were not given out until we arrived among hostile Indians. I am thankful to add that we never had an excuse to use these for the purpose intended, although a party of hostiles alarmed us one night by coming within a few hundred yards of us and giving some defiant war-whoops. It was so dark we could not see them, and in the morning there was no trace of them, and I was mighty glad of it.

We are now ready to start. Each driver with a cruel whip stands by the side of his wheelers, while the wagon-master and "extras," mounted on mules or horses, revolver at belt and clattering spur at heel, are grouped by the leading wagon. The command of "Roll on" is given, and one after the other the wagons start out and the train is in motion, crawling like a Saurian monster over the prairie. What a half hour ago was a white circle, as silent as death, is now resonant with shouts and oaths and, uncoiled, is leaving its resting place far behind.

The best teams in the train were the first and fourteenth, which alternated in leading. Being picked cattle and having no heavier loads to haul than the poor ones, they generally made a good appearance, so that our line of march was always best foot foremost.

When in a timber country the breaking of an axle or tongue did not much disconcert us, as we could replace them. But when we got out of the hard-wood region along the Platte, it was different. Then we would abandon the broken wagon

THE LEAD TEAM.

and divide the load and team among others. This was only adding more trouble, only to be remedied when an empty train was met, when we made exchanges both of wagons and oxen.

In the journey to Salt Lake we averaged about eight miles a day, which would have been more had we not lost much time by desertions and bad roads at the start. The drivers, on account of so much moving back and forth to keep the lazy oxen up to their work, traveled half as much farther. The free cattle were soon broken down and left dead on the road, or to recuperate in the "calf yard," so that many left behind were lazy and cunning. These would only work when the driver was at their sides, urging them with word and whip.

The oxen were badly used generally. The poor beasts seemed to have a human sense of wrong, and I have seen their sorrowful eyes full of tears under abuse. The old drivers were skilled in the use of their whips—some with lashes over five yards long—and took delight in marking the backs of their cattle ; while others, who were not so accomplished, pounded and kicked them without mercy, and even more cruelly used them. To call these semblances of humanity brutes, would be a libel on the four-footed race. To make the exhausted oxen pull, some of these drivers would not stop short of breaking a tail, staving in a rib, or even gouging out an eye. I grew sick at their heartless doings, but was powerless to avert them. The thousands of carcasses of oxen which lined our trail showed how hard was their usage.

The road for awhile is good, and we are making two miles an hour. On account of the miry places we keep away from the Platte, which, with its many islands, is plainly visible on one side, while on the other is a maze of sand hills. At last we come to a "slough," or swampy creek, and here trouble begins. The wheels sink to their hubs, the team stalls, and

then come lively times. The caravan telegraph is then put
in operation. The driver of the luckless team shouts to the
one ahead, "Hold on !" which in our train is equivalent to
"down brakes." These words are carried from mouth to
mouth, until they reach the head wagon, where the wagon-
master is always riding, looking for bad crossings and fixing
plans for their remedy. This functionary gallops back to the
scene of disaster, while the train halts until further orders.
He gets the "extras," who are experts with the whip, to lash

THE S STRAIGHTENS TO AN I.

the oxen, while strong arms are at the wheels. The men
yell, the oxen pull to their utmost, the whips crack like so
many pistols, and the wagon creaks, but all in vain. Another
team is added and another effort made, but in vain.
Others are supplemented, until twenty yokes are floundering
in the mud in their efforts to move one wagon, but they only
sink it deeper. Finally the last resort is made. A part of

the earth is spaded away front of the wheels, the wagon is partly unloaded, and the long, double file of oxen, almost exhausted by their previous efforts, is placed in the shape of the letter *S.* The wagon must now come or the tongue pull out. Again the whips fly, the wheel men tug, the drivers shout, and the *S* straightens to an *I* with a semblance to a "sickening thud." A moment of suspense and the wheels slowly raise from their deep imbedment, and the wagon moves to dry land. The succeeding wagons move over a more judiciously selected route, and at the shout "Roll on!" the leading wagons are on their way.

From the hardships we went through one would suppose that our noon halts would be wholly for rest, but such would not always be the case. Quarrels would ensue on the drive, or when in difficulties, the lie would be given, or vile epithets used. Then would follow threats of a "licking" at the noon corral. At the latter verbal hostilities would be continued, when cries of "Fight it out!" would come from the unkempt crowd attracted to the spot. The disputants would be two mad Missourians, perhaps, big, dirty and long-haired. Obeying the command, at it they would go like a brace of giants. It was kick and strike—whether above or below the belt, no matter— and gouge and pull hair, until one or the other howled enough. These doings were so natural a sequence to our mode of life that no one was shocked at them, particularly as the contestants soon "made up." Despite their brutishness there was a grotesqueness about the affair, which excites a smile even at this late day. There seemed the necessity of a vent for the combative nature of these rugged fellows, and these fights furnished it.

The fight is over, our dinners finished, and the herds, their appetites satisfied also, driven in and yoked up; we are again on our way. The roads, perhaps, are good, and the afternoon passes monotonously along. The western sun, as it nears the horizon, blinds us with its rays; but as this is an indication that the period of night camp is approaching, we can tolerate it. We anxiously watch the lead team, to see it turn from its course and start the corral. When this comes, how glad we are, and one after the other twenty-six wagons are formed in a protecting circle. And now, all being in readiness, the command "unyoke" is given, and in five minutes three hundred oxen are loosened and, under charge of the night guard, taken to water and grass. The men in camp now prepare for supper. The rations of flour, pork and coffee are got from the cook's wagon, but no sugar, as that has been wasted or stolen to trade to the Indians. The cook begins to mix his flour and water into dough and manipulate the other raw provender; a detail, unwilling albeit, having started off for wood and water. Sometimes the men are so tired that rather then make the exertions necessary to supper, they eat raw meat, or remnants of the day's dinner, and wearily crawl into their beds.

The wood was generally green and a fire difficult to make. To bake bread we needed live coals to put on our Dutch oven, when that was too much trouble, we would fry dough in the salty drippings of bacon—a scurvy dish. Sometimes we would have flapjacks. To turn these required a dexterous twist of the long-handled skillet, whereby the cake could be turned and landed right side up without touching it. The acme of perfection in making this product was for the cook to throw up the "jack" and run around the wagon and catch it —the "jack"—as it came down. I never saw this done. The water was sometimes carried, or "packed," a quarter of a mile. I did not know what to make of the word "pack" at first. My initial job was to help brand cattle at Fort Leavenworth, where I was told to "pack" the red hot irons from the furnace to the "brander." I thought I was to pack the irons

3

in a box, but it did not take the "boss" long to make me
understand what he meant. The half-barrel we used had a
handle to it, through which at first we put a "porter," and two
carried it; but we afterwards got so strong that one would
shoulder it full of water and carry it to camp alone.

At last our rations are getting ready for the "table," the
latter being, in a general way, the ground. The camp kettle,
filled with water for our coffee, is on the fire, which the cook
is swearing at in a very unlady-like way, as, with sleeves rolled
up to the elbow, the tenacious dough is kneaded and a general
supervision extended over the cookery. One of us, with a
coffeemill between his knees, is powdering the fragrant Rio;
another is frying with skill more or less artistic our scurvy-
producing bacon; and the third, whom all save the cook is
continually enjoining to be saving of the fuel, is tending the
stubborn fire, while the rest of the mess are taking alternate
smokes from one pipe owned by the crowd. At last the
coffee is pronounced boiled, the bacon done brown and the
cook has either a lot of saleratus bread, "fat cakes," or "flapjacks" in readiness. Then he warbles "Grub pile," and we all
get to work. Seated like Turks with our table beneath us,
and our motto "fingers were made before forks," we go to
work, dipping our cups in the common kettle and shredding
our meat with our teeth, and dispensing with the effeminacy
of butter-knives for the reason that we have no butter.
Supper over, pipes are relighted for a social smoke, and we try
to enjoy ourselves, while we thank our stars we are not on
guard, as we listen to the cries of the distant herders and
pity the poor fellows from our comfortable situations, hardly
thinking in a few hours we will be routed out to replace them.

Watches, whereby the herders might determine when to call
the next guard, which came on at midnight, were a rarity in
our train. Mine was of the open-face variety and was full-
jeweled. It was the northern sky and the hour hand was the

Great Bear or "Dipper." When I was weary with a hard day's march, how slow it moved around the pivotal North Star? How glad was I when the extreme point of the "Dipper" pointed to midnight's noon, when I would go to the corral, some times a half mile off, and arouse our sleepy successors. These would after a while make their appearance through the dark air, often vowing that my watch was not right and that they had been called too early. I am afraid they were sometimes right in their suspicions.

Our cook was called "Black Bill." He was not a negro, but a dark-featured Caucasian with full lips. He detested the name, but it stuck to him. His duties exempted him from night guard, but his office was a thankless one, for he had to scold the men to make them get wood and water, and was growled at for his cookery. Once or twice he left his work, but his successors did so badly that we coaxed him back and used him better.

Once, after a hard night on guard, I concluded to take the cook's situation myself. The growls of the mess and a haggardness which showed through the tan and dirt shrouding their faces soon, however, relegated me back to my proper place.

For awhile after supper we sit around the embers of our fire, some listlessly dozing, some thinking of the past or speculating on the future, others listening to the talk of more wide-awake comrades, not very edifying at the most.

Just now it is about the buffalo, and how many each one had shot, or what kind of oxen they would make, and whether the herd would stampede our cattle to-night, how they liked the meat, etc. In general, the conversation ran on the day's doings, but sometimes tough yarns, embodying the experience of old teamsters, took up the time.

Let me say something about our motley crew. I did not

have an autograph album along, and, therefore, can do little towards giving the "signs manual" of my comrades, and if I had, it would have been as full of crosses as a penitential monk.

The wagon-master was William Taylor, who was not a bad sort of a fellow, being as good to his men as was practicable under the circumstances. Cy. Conners, his assistant, was abusive and tyrannical until he had his bad points knocked out of him. We found a fellow along the roadside one day, suffering with the chills. He had been, according to his story, heartlessly left there by the wagon-master of a train just ahead, but the chances were he was a deserter. We took charge of him, and he was soon able to work, but was the butt of the corral, and was abused by Conners in particular. One day, after tyrannizing over this man whose name was Donnelly, the assistant gave him a term which he might as well have shortened and called him a dog. It is claimed that a worm will turn when trod on, but Donnelly would do more than this, so he dared Conners to fistic combat in the arena, formed by our corral at noon. The challenge was accepted, and at the time specified the affair came off. It is no credit to our refinement, but we enjoyed the sport, especially when at the supreme moment the assistant, who could only fight in a sort of cat and dog style, went under from a scientific knock from Donnelly. He was much larger than his adversary, but he had to "holler enough," when he was let up. He was cowed down by the humble "bull-whacker's" beating, and had but little authority thereafter, in fact, so much so I pitied the fellow. Donnelly was quite set up by the affair, and bullied around a little in his turn, until one day, on the principle that "fleas have other fleas to bite 'em," a little Irishman, called "U. S.," resented his doings by giving him a punishment he long remembered; for he bit him in the manner of a dog, and in other ways fought him until he was humiliated as much as was poor Conners.

Then there was " Phil "—last name never heard of—one of
the " extras," whose highest ambition was to be a wagon-master
some day. He was a good ox-driver, and could release a
" stuck " team with skill. " Phil " called whip " hoop," and
was a great hand to sit around the campfire of the *elite* mess,
that is where the officials fed, and tell about his day's
experience; how he made a certain team " get up and haul,"
and he would ask the wagon-master if he " minded " how a
certain " off-wheeler " buckled down to it when he began to skin
him with his " hoop," and the action of certain other cattle
when under his leathern stimulant. Then there was Johnson,
a big, fine looking fellow, who was the wheelwright of the
train, and " Kaintuck," and " Yank," a New Yorker. I will
also name " Missouri Bill " as about the greatest swearer I
ever heard. If I could imagined he read, I would class
" Tristram Shandy " among his perusals, for his *maledictus sit*
included nearly every part of the poor ox under dissection, the
" melt " being his particular objective point. When his team
got fast he would stamp and rave and swear until, if there was
a possibility of his bluing the air, his oaths would have
furnished the indigo. All swearers are fools, but he seemed
the king of them. Yet, for all, when in his cool moments he
was a good sort of a chap. Then there was Fisher, a lazy fellow, with a face in a chronic state of grime. He was harmless, so that whenever a coward wanted to show his mettle, he
would provoke him to a retort and then kick him.

Fisher had once lived among the Pottowattomies, where he
had been, in a measure, adopted by the tribe. He would often
sit around the campfire and commence to narrate some of his
experience of Indian life, but he was so lazy that his snoring
voice, which was a soporific of itself, would cease in the middle
of a story through sheer weariness of the vocal chords. Still
we would be so nearly put to sleep ourselves, that we would
hardly notice the cessation. There was another fellow, a

messmate of mine, I am sorry to say, named Bill Casey, who often told us how he had promised his little brother to bring him home an "Injun's skulp." But no one's teeth chattered livelier than his one night when we were given ammunition for an expected attack from a party of Cheyennes. There was "Irish John," with murder in his heart when angry, and an old Indian campaigner with General Harney; and "Dutch John," with a Russian face, a fearful temper and a flow of German oaths; and "Dutch Bill," yet a boy, but who had been on a winter-bound train the year before, when, with cattle frozen or stampeded, the time until spring was passed on the plains. When in his German home, he lived on the borders of the Black Forest, and he sometimes entertained me with narrations of his adventures in that famed wilderness. Another, with the prefix "Dutch," was "Charley"—surname, as usual, unknown—who owned a claim in Kansas, but who joined us when we were short of men when passing his farm. In some of our troublous times, and we had plenty of them, he would doubly curse the day he joined us, and cry like a Banshee for the wife and baby he had left on the shore of the Big Blue. He was a freethinker and argumentator, and when in the mood, he would make the air ring with his excited talk. As he was barely understandable in his calm moments, he spoke no English when excited. Then there was "Whisky Bill," so termed for his fondness for the adjective; there was Bentley, a deserter from the regulars, who hid or disguised himself when near a fort or when nearing a camp of soldiers. Another was "Dutch Joe," formerly a Mississippi steamboatman, in which calling he had learned any amount of profanity and irreligion, and yet at night, around our campfires, he would unctiously sing pathetic songs, the stock specimen being, "When My Old Mother and I Did Part," which, full of good sentiment, got to be as wearisome a song as "The Child in the Grave With Its

Mother," as reiterated by one of Mark Twain's characters. He professed to believe in neither God nor a future existence, and yet the night we forded the Platte, when from exposure he thought he was about to die, he howled like a coward for fear of death. But this was nothing new in my experience on the plains. The greatest blatherskites in sneering at death and religion, were the most grovelling cravens when the last hour seemed imminent. There were others who are still in my memory, but I have mentioned enough to show what manner of men I traveled with. Our mess had a full share of these, among whom I name Fisher, Casey and "Irish John."

The night is wearing on. The men, tired with their day's toil and with listening to the evening talk, are one by one crawling into their wagons to get their needed sleep. Our mess is on guard to-night and should have retired long since. We get into our blankets, and, for awhile kept awake by thoughts of the past or speculations on the future, we are in the mysterious land of dreams.

I have given a sample of our experience on the plains for a period of eighteen weeks, our hardships increasing as we advanced among the mountains and pasture became scarce. Then at nights we would have to drive the oxen across the river to graze, preceding trains having eaten up the pasture on the near side. We would ride the oxen over, if practicable, while the horsemen urged them on, but we would have to spend the night in wet clothing. How we kept our health through it all I cannot understand, but it did not materially suffer.

An incident we occasionally experienced, and which was a pleasing one, was the meeting of the mail stage, or being passed by the same on its western way. The vehicle itself was a cumbrous affair, and was known by the " Pikers" as an " avalanche," which was as near as they could be expected to come to "ambulance." Those who had any sentiment about them could imagine the hopes and fears enveloped in the leathern mail bag on the way to cheer or sadden, unless nipped by the killing frost of train robbery. Plain, matter-of-fact fellows saw a wagon with six mules on the trot, or gallop when possible, clouded with dust or wading in splashing mud.

And now the Kansas prairies, then virgin, over which we so slowly traveled, are covered with farms and villages. The watchful house-dog replaces the howling wolf. The bellowing buffalo, which darkened his pasturage, has made way for herds of cattle, the marauding Indian for the useful farmer. The children of the ignoble red men I saw, instead of practicing with their mimic bows and arrows on rabbits or prairie dogs, or shooting pennies from stakes for the amusement of flush palefaces, are learning agriculture from Eastern farmers, and successfully, too. Where the ox-train moved at the rate of ten or fifteen miles per day, trains of another kind travel six hundred. Where the emigrant plodded his weary way, thousands of excursionists annually flock to California. Colorado, which we traversed a desert wilderness, is now a prosperous state, its seeming barrenness reclaimed by irrigation, and its repulsive mountains teeming with precious metals. The city of Denver had not been located.

With all these changes I can hardly realize what a country I passed through thirty years ago.

IV.

Along the Platte to Fort Laramie.

NTIL the 8th our course was through the buffalo country, but we were now beyond it, though a few outlying stragglers from the main herd might be seen. We encamped at night near the river, which was here a mile in width, and filled with sandy islands covered with a tangled growth of willow and cotton-wood. At midnight our watch was called out to relieve the other which had left the herd to take care of itself. Before we reached the pasturage we heard a noise which came to our ears ominously. It was the herd stampeding for the river. Plunge! Plunge! one after another we heard the oxen dropping into the water from the bank and making for the opposite shore. Splash! Splash! we could hear them, as we pulled off our boots and coats and ran after them. In the water and quicksands, over sand-bars and through tangled islets we labored along, filling the air with yells in our efforts to arrest the progress of the oxen, which, under the guidance of a mischievous Texan, were determinedly moving on. By great efforts we at last so gained on the column as to reach the head oxen, and these we switched on to the back track by severe clubbings. The main herd followed them, and we at last got the runaways back, and in our wet clothes guarded them until morning. One would think that after a hard day's work the cattle would be glad to lie down after eating, but they sometimes seemed endowed with the demon of unrest, and wasted their strength with senseless wanderings, and thus, sleepy and tired as we were, brought us additional hardships.

But there were times when a halo of sentiment covered the surroundings. This was in the small hours of the night, and when the oxen, tired and with their hunger satisfied, lay down in groups around us. The full moon which was high overhead showed the broad island-dotted Platte with its divided channels sparkling in its soft light. From the shore the plain broadened till it met the far-off hills, beyond which there was no trace of civilization, no animal life for hundreds of miles, but of Indians and wild beasts. Dimly gleaming from the prairie was our corral, its circle of sheeted wagons showing like a patriarchal encampment of far away times. The sounds we heard were hushed, the lowing of distant buffaloes, the howling of wolves, the barking of their coyote brethren, or the voices of predatory night birds, coming to us wierdly and faintly. Now and then came a deep sigh from one of the reclining herd, as he, perhaps, thought of the wrongs inflicted on him the previous day. The surroundings induced meditation, and my thoughts would revert to my far-away home and the loved ones there; and I wondered how I ever came to lead such a life among people like my associates, whose ways were so uncongenial and generally repulsive.

My reclining position, the hushed, far-away sounds, the propinquity of so much sleep as was massed in the somnolent beasts about me, the influences of night, one or all, would make me drowsy in spite of the responsibility resting upon me, when I would instinctively arouse with a start to find the late quiescent herd in commotion, and stringing across the plain in the wake of some mischief making leader. The rest of the night guard had been caught napping, and then would be trouble till dawn keeping the cattle together.

THE SLEEPING HERD.

The mile-wide river with its sand-bars, low shores and distant sand hills called to mind a picture I once saw of the river Nile, with the full moon gleaming above it. My unleashed fancy increased the resemblance. The lone cotton-woods were transformed to tufted palms from their positions on shore or island. I evolved the pyramids from the hazy outlines of distant sand hills; the sheeted wagons turned to an Arab encampment, the sleeping oxen to couchant camels, and for Bedouins of the desert I could choose between my comrades and the Indians encamped near by, and present about as Ishmaelitic a gang as the valley of Father Nile was ever afflicted with.

On the 6th of August we came to a timberless reach, and heavy rains having spoiled our *"bois-de-vache"* or buffalo-wood—as the French politely termed our usual fuel—we halted for a half a day to procure some real wood. This we got by wading to neighboring islands, axe in hand, and felling the dryest timber we could find. Cut in convenient lengths, we would "pack" it ashore and through a thicket of matted willows to our wagons. Those who thought this too much trouble, eked out a supply by stealing it from their provident comrades and then boasted about it, as they did of appropriating yokes, bow-keys, cooking utensils and other necessaries of life on the plains.

We reached Grant's Camp at noon on the 12th. This is a fine camping place, near the bluffs, and about three miles from the river, and is supplied with a spring of excellent water gushing out from the bottom of a deep ravine. Hardly had we coralled before a body of mounted Indians rode up, whom we found to be the braves of a Sioux village, now changing its locality, for looking back we saw stretching along the plain and advancing toward our camp a long moving column, which as it neared us, presented a rather grotesque appearance. There were about a hundred persons appertaining to this portable village. The squaws were dragging their heavily laden ponies after them; while the old men, children and dogs were scattered along the line of march, some of the latter drawing loads as well as their equine companions. The Indian mode of transporting baggage from one place to another is to attach the ends of two or three lodge poles to each side of the pony by leathern thongs, leaving the other ends to drag upon the ground. Their provisions, tents, skins, etc., are strapped to these poles, above which we may often see projecting the black heads of the papooses, who appear to enjoy their ride. The dogs with their loads trot along after the ponies, their tongues out, and seemingly in the best possible humor. These have the greatest aversion to the whites, and will fly on them in an instant unless restrained by their owners. As soon as the squaws arrived with the baggage, they commenced unpacking it, after which they pitched their tents, their lazy, dignified lords looking quietly on with pipe in mouth. The squaws are subject to the most abject servitude, and are obliged to perform all the labor.

While we were encamped together at Grant's Camp I employed my leisure time in visiting our neighbors. The lodges, which are some twelve feet in height and ten in diameter, are formed by a number of poles meeting together at the top in the shape of a pyramid, over which is put a covering of buffalo hide; an aperture being left in the top for the purpose of the smoke escaping. In warm weather the cover of the tent is raised to some distance from the ground, so that the air circulating through them makes them pleasant summer habitations. On entering the lodges, which I did *sans cérémonie*, I found them filled with a heterogeneous mixture of squaws, children, papooses and dogs, seated or lying around, the former busily engaged in making moccasons, or in the tanning of skins. The mixed population hardly noticed me, except the dogs, which, from their hiding places into which they had retreated on my entrance, showed their ivory in a menacing manner.

I did not remain long, driven out less by the cool reception I met with than by the rank odor that pervaded the lodges. The "Indian smell," which impregnates everything they have around them, is peculiarly disagreeable; wild animals are particularly sensitive to it and are thrown into the keenest alarm when it is within "nose-shot." Our visits were returned by the Indians with interest, lord and vassal crowding around our campfires, either for the purpose of showing their friendship or stealing bacon (which they all have a failing for), I don't know which. The captains or chiefs would not condescend to notice any but the officers of the train. Squatted around in a circle, the pipe of peace was passed around with great ceremony by the worthy council formed by the officers and the swarthy "chieftains brave and bold." It was amusing to see the Indians drawing the essence from the narcotic stowed away in the bowls of their curiously fashioned pipes. Putting the stems to their lips with all the gravity imaginable they would fill their mouths with smoke, which they would slowly exhale through their well-schooled nostrils, as if bent on extracting all the good qualities it contained from it. While this extempore council was engaged in its solemn sitting, the remaining Indians were lounging around our messes, begging and stealing whenever they were unobserved.

One of our wagons being broken down, we were obliged to repair it here. After taking out the freight, part of which was composed of crackers destined for Laramie, we found the bottom of the body covered with crumbs, mixed with about an equal proportion of dirt. Calling up the squaws and children, who came flocking around like so many hens and chickens, we commenced scattering this rather dubious manna over the ground. Hardly had the mixture reached the earth ere it was surrounded by a group of "anxious seekers," who gobbled it up instanter, and then watched eagerly to see where the next supply would fall. To see this agile pack of wretches running hither and thither, sometimes with faces turned heavenward in anxious expectation, at others, down on their knees scrambling for the precious morsels that fell around them, all screaming and chattering like so many parrots, was a sight to move the risibles of a stoic; and laughter long and deep resounded from the bystanders. The lordly " bucks " standing around seemed to enjoy the scene as much as ourselves, although their manifestations of delight were not so open.

Before we left the camp we had the pleasure of seeing the Indians on a buffalo hunt. While they were lounging around the corral after dinner, a squaw came running up from the village with the information that a buffalo was in sight. The features of the Indians, which a moment before were stolid and vacant, were now full of the liveliest animation, and, springing from the ground, they rushed in a body to where their ponies were picketed; in an instant they were mounted and coursing over the plain in the direction of their victim, which was plainly visible a half a mile distant. The latter soon took the alarm and made for the bluffs, but his pursuers, on their tough little animals, swiftly gained upon him, and in a short time came up with him, when discharging a volley of bullets and arrows at their noble game, he was soon rolling in the dust. It was but a few minutes from the time the alarm was given until the buffalo was killed, and the hunters were on their way to camp, leaving the meat to be cut up and brought home by the squaws. The latter made their appearance at last, each with a heavy load on her back, and they were soon busily engaged in cutting up the flesh preparatory to drying it in the sun for future use. The chase was quite an exciting one, and we watched it with intense interest from first to last.

Leaving our Indian friends behind us, we moved on and encamped at sundown near the river, after a journey of twelve miles. The next day (13th) we passed by the celebrated "Cotton-wood Springs," where, in the midst of a scattered grove of majestic cotton-woods, a clear stream gushes forth, famed for its coolness and purity. We all stopped to get a drink of the delicious water, which tasted like nectar to us who had for so long quenched thirst with the yellow, tepid water of the Platte, and then moved on, encamping at sunset on the summit of O'Fallon's Bluffs, whose steep declivities we climbed with difficulty. These bluffs are opposite the junction of the north and south forks of the Platte, and extend to the edge of the river. Our encampment was on the edge of a pond filled with a villainous fluid, which passed for water by the hardiest, but which we were obliged to drink for want of better. The vegetation on the bluffs was parched and withered, owing to the pervading drought. Thorny plants of almost every description abounded here, making it a painful task to move outside of the beaten track. Near this place a train was snowed under in the autumn of '57, and the whitened bones of its starved and frozen cattle lay scattered around, forming a ghastly spectacle.

The Platte, below the junction, is a mile in width and averages a foot in depth. Between the forks is a low prairie which extends about eighteen miles above the junction, when it reaches the bluffs, ascending to the broad plateau extending between the two rivers farther on. Descending from the bold bluffs on which we were encamped the preceding night, we again rolled over the Platte bottom, the road being bad from the deep and yielding sand. Late in the afternoon of the 14th we reached the celebrated crossing of the South Platte.

At the ford the South Fork, or Padouca, is about a half mile in width, with numerous sand-bars rising above the surface of the water. On account of the difficulty of crossing this stream, from its quicksand bottom, and the heavy freshets which annually fill its banks, this ford is a noted locality on

the great California trail. Luckily for us the river was now
at a low ebb, as it generally is at this time of year. In spite
of the small portion of daylight that was left us, the wagon-
master resolved to attempt to ford the river before morning,
and doubling teams, five of the lead wagons plunged down
the steep shore into the river. But it was impossible to move
them but a short distance over the yielding quicksandy bottom, with so weak a force as we had attached to them, and
after floundering about in the river until after night, we gave
up the attempt for that day, and bringing the exhausted oxen
ashore, we turned the whole herd loose, and left the wagons
until the morning, when the final start was to be made. Sunrise saw us all up and busily engaged in fortifying the inner
man with liberal allowances of pork, bread and coffee, our
standing, unvaried bill of fare, in anticipation of the heavy
day's work before us. After breakfast the herd was hurried
into the corral, when out of the one hundred and fifty-six
yokes, we selected eighty of the strongest. These were divided
into teams of twenty yokes each, our intention being to take
four wagons over at a time, and five or six men were alloted
to each team, to tug at the wheels and belabor the unwilling
oxen. The long, snake-like columns were at last hitched to
their respective wagons, and stood in readiness on the bluff
overlooking the broad river, which lay spread out before us,
sparkling under the rays of a bright sun. The wagons, which
had remained in the river all night, were now deeply
sunken in the quicksand, looking like spots upon the surface
of the water, and as if it would be impossible to awaken them
from their soft beds into consciousness on the opposite shore ;
and all things betokened a day replete with toil and hardship.
The signal being given, our teams began tumbling down the
bank and striking out into the river, each taking a different
course, and soon the excitement commenced. The oxen,
frightened by the broad, glittering expanse of water spreading

4

out before them, refused to pull at first; but a proper amount
of buckskin and yelling being judiciously applied by their
mentors, they were at last induced to change their opinions,
and the wagons slowly began to move. In spite of the
remedies administered, they would soon stop, for the wheels
were continually sinking, and the cattle, from hard driving
and scanty food, were badly broken down. Again, after repeated efforts, we would start, soon to be brought to a full
stop, however; and we were sometimes obliged to unload the
freight and pack it to a neighboring sand-bar until we could
again get under way. And so it went on, until at length,
after laboring tediously and yelling assiduously, the pioneer
wagons of our caravan were across the Platte, and at last stood
dripping on the opposite shore. The teams now started back
for another quartette of wagons, which were got over in due
time. Throughout the day the river was alive with excitement by the shouting of the drivers, the loud cracking of
their terrible whips, the struggling oxen, turning from the
right to the left as they strained every muscle to move the
reluctant wagons, splashing the water all about them in their
mad plunges, and the re-crossing of the long columns after
other wagons. After having made several excursions back
and forth, we at last had the great satisfaction of seeing the
last wagon ascending the northern shore of the South Platte.

Grass being scarce around the ford, we were compelled to
take the herd two miles up the valley, where we found toler-
ably good pasturage. About the middle of the night the
cattle made a stampede for the islands of the river, from which
they were dislodged with much difficulty, some of them not
being found until noon the next day. The day consequently
was far gone before we got under way. We at length began
the ascent of the toilsome steep leading to the broad plateau,
extending between the valleys of the north and south forks of
the Platte. When near the summit we met a small band of

Cheyennes, who were mounted on fine ponies, armed with rifles, shields and lances, and painted and feathered to the last degree of Indian dandyism. Unlike our Sioux friends, who were all exceedingly good-natured and friendly, they did not look at us as they passed by, nor notice the "hows" and "hies" that we shouted at them, and I respected them the more for it.

We had expected to find water on the top of the divide, but after considerable search we found none, and pushing on we

FORDING THE SOUTH PLATTE.

at last came in sight of the bold, uneven bluffs overlooking the valley of the North Platte. Following their rough outlines for about a mile, we came to a steep descent, leading down to the bottom of a deep valley, opening on to the river, some three miles distant. This is known as "Ash Hollow"—a famous landmark on the California trail. We reached the top of the sandy declivity a little after dark, and double rough-locking our wagons, we commenced descending. It was near midnight before the train was all corralled at the foot of the hill, the descent of which was full of danger to both men and animals, for, had a lock-chain broken, the whole team would have tumbled head over heels down a steep whose inclination was some forty-five degrees. Several narrow escapes occurred during the descent, and we were heartily rejoiced when it was accomplished. The oxen had had nothing to eat nor drink since morning, and we were obliged to remain all night in a region destitute of water and grass. We left the famished cattle chained to the wagons, and were under way early the next morning, all hands hungry and thirsty.

Nothing could be more dreary than the region through which we passed. The bottom of the valley down which we were journeying, and which was a bed of sand and gravel, was about one hundred yards in width, almost entirely destitute of vegetation and bounded on either side by gloomy, barren hills, which arose to the height of six or eight hundred feet, terminating in rugged cliffs. It seemed as if some mighty volcano had once been at work here, blasting and desolating everything around in its upheavings. Slowly our weak, hollow oxen drew the cumbrous wagons through the yielding sands, which arose and enveloped us in clouds, as we trudged on our way unrejoicing. At last we emerged from this valley of desolation, and moving about a mile up the river, we encamped near its shore. A rush was soon made for the river by both man and beast, and its warm, yellow waters soon quenched the thirst of all. Near the mouth of Ash Hollow we passed a mail station, near which was encamped a village of Cheyennes. The little naked children crowded around us as we passed by the lodges, whilst the old squaws, squatted around their domiciles, gazed quietly at us through their black, snaky eyes, looking quite as attractive as the fabled dames who guard the portals of the infernal regions. Near this spot a battle was fought a year before

between the Cheyennes and the Americans under General Harney. The fortifications erected by the latter could still be seen
on the flat extending between the bluff and the river. One of
our men who had been an eye-witness of the fight gave us a
graphic description of it. It was a hardly fought contest, but
the skill of the Americans at last prevailed over the superior
numbers of the enemy. The Cheyennes were entirely routed,
with the loss of two hundred of their number and all their
tents and baggage, which were burned in a huge bonfire by
the victors. Their squaws were taken prisoners, and distributed among our gallant soldiers, but were afterwards given up
to their lawful owners. The severe castigation which the Cheyennes here received has humbled them greatly, and they are far
less mischievous now than formerly. Old " Harney " is held
in great detestation among them, and the mere mention of his
name will bring a scowl on the face of a Cheyenne brave.

The scenery along the Plattes begins to change above the
Forks. The broad, level bottoms stretching along the river as
far as the eye can reach, are no longer seen, and the sandy
bluffs often approach to the very edge of the water, rising in
rough, uneven outlines to the height of near a thousand feet.
Among the sharp rocks that cover their desolate sides a few
scrubby cedars are growing, looking from the road like mere
bushes, but several were a foot in diameter, as I found on
clambering up for wood. We no longer see the richly timbered
islands of the lower Platte, the sand-bars being merely fringed
with willows and destitute of trees.

After procuring a supply of cedar-wood from the neighboring hills, we proceeded on our way over a road which
was very heavy on account of the deep sand. Our teams,
weakened by hard driving and starvation, were continually
stalling, so that the day had its usual amount of excitement
to vary the monotony of the journey. A train which had
passed through our corral the preceding night and encamped

by us at noon, came up with us about the middle of the afternoon, and endeavored to pass us. Resolving not to suffer the disgrace of being driven around, without some effort to maintain our dignity, we essayed to inspire with blows and yells fresh energy into our failing oxen. Vain our efforts. As the locomotive dashes by the canalboat, so did our rivals, with their superior teams, glide by us. This was a provoking spectacle, but circumstances obliged us to endure the sight of it. As our rivals had the right of way as soon as they were broadside of us, we stopped and waited until they had moved out of our way, when we humbly followed in their rear. We encamped at night on a broad, well grassed flat, about half a mile from the river, a short distance from our rivals. We endeavored to get the start of the latter the next morning, but we missed it. Our road was sandy enough at starting, but it became worse as we advanced, and as the rays of the sun beat down incessantly and hotly, our oxen were continually giving out. Our route led us over an uneven bluff at some distance from the shore, and tediously working over the deep sand, we came at noon to the top of a precipitous steep leading down to the bottom of the river. After descending this we corralled for the day, in order to rest our weary animals, which we took across the river to graze, the grass on the south shore of the Platte having been eaten off close by trains in advance of us.

(August 19th.) Owing to a heavy rain which fell last night and hardened the sand, our road to-day was considerably better than yesterday, so that we made good progress. While encamped at noon, a homeward bound train from Fort Laramie passed us, stopping long enough, however, to make an exchange of some wagons and oxen. The next day, in the forenoon, we came in sight of the Court House Rock. This natural curiosity is situated about nine miles south of the road, but owing to the dry and pure atmosphere of this region, it does not appear to be more than two or three. It is apparently about three hundred yards long and two hundred in height. It is composed of marl and earthy limestone, and is worn into its peculiar shape by the action of the elements on its soft constituents. Standing alone above the broad plain, its outlines rendered singularly regular by distance, it has an extremely majestic appearance, having much the look of an ancient feudal castle, and the sight of it formed a pleasing variation to the monotony of our journey. Although the land between it and the road is apparently a dead level, it is very uneven, being full of deep gulches which have been washed into its marly soil by the rains of winter. A Mormon told me that while passing this rock one of his party was filled with curiosity to examine it closely, and under the impression that it was but a short distance from the road, he mounted his horse and rode towards it, thinking to regain his comrades in a short time. The plain seemed so level, and the Court House so near that he imagined he was going on a nice little journey of pleasure, but he soon found himself mistaken. Deep ravines were continually obstructing his path, and worse than all, the object he was seeking seemed like the *ignus fatuus* to fly flefore him. But he was a plucky individual, and resolved to attain his object. Perseverance will accomplish anything, and he at last reached this majestic landmark. Having gratified his curiosity, he went on his way, and late in the night came up with his comrades, well wearied and hungered, if not satisfied with his side excursion.

Throughout the 21st the road was bad, sometimes laying across the sandy bluffs which intersected our route, at others, over marshy flats which extended between them. Owing to the severe labor they underwent, the cattle had begun to fail fast, for they were *en route* from early in the morning till late in the evening, over bad roads and under a hot sun. One of our men narrowly escaped being shot in the afternoon. A comrade with a loaded rifle in his hand was walking along by his side, when the trigger somehow caught and the load went off, the bullet just grazing him, and mortally wounding one of his oxen. It was a narrow escape, but the accident furnished us with a supply of fresh beef, which was, however, too tough and gristly for general eating. We came in sight of the celebrated Chimney Rock in the afternoon. This famous landmark, although some thirty miles distant, was plainly visible, owing to the extreme purity of the atmosphere.

Near here we passed an emigrant wagon, the cover of which had been removed and the bows festooned with strips of buffalo meat, which was in process of being dried or "jerked." This gets well covered with dust and as dry and hard as wood. It is soaked and boiled before being eaten.

We nooned on the 23d by Chimney Rock, which is about forty miles west from the Court House and seventy from Ash Hollow. This rock, or rather column, is set upon a semispherically shaped hill, and is about twenty-five feet in diameter at the bottom, gradually tapering to half that at the top. Its summit is about one hundred and fifty feet above the plain, but it was at one time much higher, early travelers say five hundred feet. The winds and rains, acting upon the soft materials of which it is composed, are gradually wearing it away, and the ground around its base is covered with pieces which have fallen from its summit. I cannot account for the formation of this singular object, except by supposing that it was originally a *butte*, or isolated mound, through the centre of which, from its base to its summit, ran a column of harder material than its surroundings, and that the rain and wind, acting on the surface, have worn away its softer constituents and left a column standing. The desert, called the Indian's Enchanted Ground, extending between the North Platte and White River, is in some places covered with bluffs and *buttes*, which the action of the elements has converted in a similar manner into all imaginable shapes. Towers, walls and minarets arise before the eyes of the astonished traveler, in some places, while in others he beholds cities and castles in ruins.

Passing over a dreary country, which barely furnished enough of grass for our famished animals, we arrived at Scott's Bluffs on the afternoon of the 25th. This is a bold escarpment of sand and clay, about a half a mile in length and near a thousand feet in height, extending southward from the river and rising like a gigantic barrier to obstruct our way. It was

CHIMNEY ROCK.

for a long time visible, and at a distance seemed impossible to be surmounted. The road forks before we reach the bluffs, one trail passing around its southern end and re-joining the main road at some distance beyond it, the other passing directly over its summit. The latter is the worse road of the two, but it being the shorter, we chose it. We were detained some time at the foot of the bluff by the breaking of one of our wagons, but we at last got under way, and commenced our toilsome journey over it. The ascent was easy and gradual, until we came to a deep gorge, which intersected our road at the foot of the main bluff. Crossing this at the imminent risk of being run over by the teams as they plunged headlong to the bottom, we came to a series of steep hills and narrow, deep and sandy defiles, through which there was barely room for a wagon to pass. So squarely hewn were some of these passes, that one could hardly believe that art had not a hand in their formation. After a vast deal of exertion we at last reached the summit, when we commenced the still more dangerous descent. Tumbling pell-mell down narrow passages, slowly crawling over abrupt ascents, we at length reached the bottom, and in two miles struck the river and encamped, but not till long after dark. The Platte was here a maze of sloughs and islands, the bed of the river being divided into innumerable channels. On account of the scarcity of grass on the main land, we kept the herd on one of the islands during the night.

On this portion of our journey, and in fact nearly all the way westward of Fort Kearney, we drove early and late. Starting sometimes before sunrise, we would drive on until ten o'clock, when we would stop an hour for breakfast, then we would again start and roll on until after sunset, sometimes until eleven o'clock. These were the times which wore us down. To be wakened from a sound nap early in the morning by the harsh voice of the assistant, as he yelled forth the dreaded reveille, with its accompanying club-thumps on the wagon-body; to go in the tumultuous corral and yoke up while you are so sleepy you can hardly keep your eyes open; to start hungry on a toilsome march; to drive with a short intermission until after night, and then, perhaps, to go on the detested guard, were things to be experienced to be understood.

Our harships began visibly to affect us. While in the early

part of the journey, when our tasks had been comparatively light, the train would have mirthful scenes occasionally. Those were the times when we made short drives; when our diet was composed of something else besides a monotony of bread and pork, and pork and bread; and when, on account of the danger of the men deserting with their "outfits," the train officials were less exacting. But now it was different. Slowly and wearily we walked along by the side of our teams, which were as morose and desponding as their drivers. No sounds are heard as we move over the dreary waste but the dull grating of the wheels, as they grind through the yielding sand, and the sharp crack of the whips, as the teamsters urge on the panting oxen. The miserable animals, exhausted by incessant labor and little to eat, move lifelessly along with heads bowed low, casting their tear-filled eyes imploringly for the mercy they seldom got, and sometimes, completely worn out, they drop in their tracks, to swell the numbers of reeking carcasses and bleached skeletons which line the road. The hearts of all are gladdened at sight of the forming corral, and the oxen quicken their pace when they see it. We unloosen them and they are soon scattering over the sun-burned prairie, seeking to allay their hunger, while we go at our camp duties, getting our wood and water and otherwise preparing for supper. Silently and mechanically we go through our task, a feeling of weariness and sadness, not to say peevishness, pervading all. Our campfires, which of old were the scenes of mirthful horseplay, songs and stories, now see nothing but groups of grimy, care-worn men.

At that time how far distant seemed the Golden State toward which I was traveling! I hardly thought that fate would ever carry me to that glittering bourne!

Besides our returning trains we met, occasionally, other bodies; once, a party of renegade Mormons. When our troops reached Utah and the rebels surrendered, all men and women who wished to go back to the States were allowed permission. This party, a part of whom were females, accepted, and being supplied with teams and provisions, started. They were a hard looking party, the women in particular. With short, travel-stained clothing, and dust-begrimed faces and frowsy hair, they proclaimed the fact that woman, as a foot traveler over the plains, is not a prepossessing object. They were short of food, and we gave them some from our stores.

September 1st. We passed many Indians, who followed us and thronged around us at our noon camp, begging and thieving. They belonged to a village we passed farther on. On an elevation near by we saw a singular burying ground. On scaffolds, six or eight feet high, the corpses, wrapped in robes of the buffalo, were reclining. These stages, rudely built of forked poles and sticks, were the first the deceased took on their journeys to the happy hunting grounds. The sight was very repulsive. A walled sepulchre on the roadside marked the resting place of a "big Injun."

Our road the next morning lay on the bluffs overlooking the river and through sand, in which our teams were continually stalling. From our high ground we had a fine view of the surrounding country, the most prominent object of which was Laramie Peak. To our right extended the valley of the Platte, as far as the eye could reach, walled in and half hidden by high and precipitous hills; while from the distant mountains on the left rolled the sparkling waters of the Laramie River, till they mingled with the waves of the larger stream. Descending the bluffs we moved up the valley, the whole cavalcade enveloped in clouds of dust. We were now nearing Fort Laramie, and soon the many rude buildings and tents of that post were spread before us.

V.

☉o the Great South Pass.

ORT Laramie, with its soldiers and Indians, and the animation around it was pleasant to see, and we were glad to be delayed there a few hours, while our lading underwent government inspection. While here I got hold of a New York *Tribune*. This was such a treat that I went off to myself and had a good time reading. It had been about two months since I had been in communication with the outside world, so that there were many things mentioned whose beginnings I was ignorant of. The Kansas-Nebraska affair was at its height, and the national excitement was well portrayed in the *Tribune*. Then there was the Sepoy rebellion and the laying of the Atlantic Cable, the latter a failure for the time. Editorials and all I eagerly read. We "bullwhackers" were not a very literary set, in fact, I doubt if there were any books in the train but my own. At any rate, I never saw any of my comrades reading. My literary pleasure was of short duration, however, for the remorseless cry of "Yoke up," soon roused me to present duties, and returning my paper to the kind sutler who loaned it, I was on my way towards the realms of sunset.

Fort Laramie is situated on the shores of the Laramie River, about two miles above its junction with the Platte. The numerous and extensive public buildings were neatly built of frame and *adobes*, or sun dried bricks, and to travelers who had been journeying long without seeing civilized habitations, they made a fine appearance. The station was formerly a trading post under charge of the American Fur Company, when it was sometimes known by the title of Fort John. The place was lively from the numerous soldiers stationed there, the workmen and teamsters employed and the Indians encamped in the vicinity, drawn thither for the purpose of trading with the whites. Russel & Co. had a store and smith shop here for the convenience of their trains passing through and stopping at this post. The "store" of this great firm was built of mud and roofed with sods, and stocked with a lot of goods which would be in the States worth not over two hundred dollars, but which was here worth five times as much. We all renewed our "outfits" here, as the supplies we procured at Leavenworth were well nigh exhausted.

We had great difficulty in finding grass for our animals, but finally found some on the opposite side of the Platte, two miles below the Fort, where we drove the herd. We were compelled to ford both rivers on our way, each flowing over a rocky bed with a rapid current. There is a bridge over the Laramie below the Fort, but it is now in a dilapidated condition, and the dingy little toll-house at one end is now tenantless. The lumber used in the construction of this bridge was obtained from the Black Hills, some forty miles distant. Emigrant and freight trains now cross at the ford, opposite the post.

Before leaving the Fort two of our party received their discharges, and one deserted for parts unknown. We procured two others at the post, and then started on the long journey which lay ahead of us; the most of the party in bad spirits, for we had for some time previous to our arrival at Laramie been induced to believe that our stopping place would be there. For my own part, I was willing to proceed in spite of the hard-

ships I had experienced, for I had started on the through journey, and did not wish to back out now, and besides I was
desirous of seeing the interesting country lying between here
and the far distant Pacific. There were but two or three but
who were anxious to turn back, and it is no wonder. The
majority of our men had not joined the train for the purpose
of exploring the country over which they were to pass, but
because they were destitute of means, and saw here a chance to
keep from starving. Arriving at Fort Laramie, wearied and
disgusted with their profession, they wished to retrace their
steps, for they saw on ahead only a repetition of their past toils
and privations. Some of these had families which they were
anxious to return to, others had taken up claims before their
departure, which now needed their attention, and they feared
that it would be so late in the season before they could start
on their homeward voyage from Great Salt Lake, that the narrow gorges of the Rocky Mountains would be filled with deep
and impassable snows, so that they must either remain among
the Mormons till spring, or run the risk of being frozen to
death by returning before. Several applied for their discharges,
but they were refused, for as it was we had not a full comple-
ment of hands.

Crossing the Laramie River at the ford, we passed through
the military establishment and commenced ascending the high,
barren hills which overlook it. Reaching the summit of this
ridge, we descended a dangerous rocky gorge leading to the
river bottom below, which is here about a half a mile in width.
Continuing along this at the base of the hills, the road at
length led us to the top of a bluff from which we descended by
a break-neck declivity to the river. A grove of tall timber
arose from the flat at the foot of the bluff, close by whose shore
we encamped after sunset, the bold, white outlines of which
formed a magnificent background to the scenery. On account
of grass we took the herd to the northern side of the river. So

deep and swift flowing was the Platte here, that we could hardly
get the cattle across, and it was only by riding the mules back
and forth along the rear of the reluctant column, and clubbing
and yelling at the affrighted animals, that we were enabled to
land them on the opposite shore. (4th.) Passing over a dismal flat, the soil of which was in some places white with alkaline efflorescences, with stunted cotton-woods here and there
rising above it, and with a high hill covered with craggy rocks
rising on our left, we came about six miles from our last night's
camp to where the river emerges from a deep gorge, walled on
either side by solid rocks. The road here turns to the left and
ascends a precipitous hill, whose summit we attained with
much difficulty. The characteristic plant of these regions, the
artemisia, now began to make its appearance. This plant, to
which the title of sage-bush is commonly given on the plains,
abounds westward of Fort Laramie. It varies in height from
six inches to as many feet, growing in gnarled, twisted clumps,
and is of a dark gray color, giving the country which it covers
a desolate look. It sometimes grows so thickly that it is a
hard matter to force one's way through it, and it was continually wearing out our clothes and patience. The more elevated
the country, the larger and more abundant it grows, until from
a little weed six inches in height, we find it transformed into a
tree from three to four inches in diameter. Owing to the cold
of the preceding winter, or to the excessive drought, we found
a great portion of the artimisias dead, and the brittle stalks
made excellent fuel. The plant emits a peculiar, but not unpleasant odor, somewhat like that of turpentine or camphor.

We encamped in the afternoon on the shores of a clear,
sparkling stream, shaded by majestic trees, which were scattered along its margin. We found two trains, which had left
Laramie the day of our arrival, and which were under the
command of Messrs. Crissman and Truett, encamped here. A
wagon belonging to one of them, while descending the danger-

ous bluffs overlooking the creek, had upset and rolled over a precipice, scattering its contents in every direction, and the men were busily engaged in repairing damages on our arrival. Leaving our beautiful encampment, we proceeded on our way over a picturesque country, and we corralled after night on the summit of a high hill, after a journey of ten miles.

We had a fine view on the morning of the 5th, from the hill on which we were encamped. Bleak, rocky mountains arose majestically on all sides, covered on some places with pines, whose dark green foliage contrasted well with their dull gray background. Deep gorges in places intersected them, along whose bottoms clear streams were sparkling, as they sped on their way to the Platte. To the north we could discern the high ranges of mountains which walled in the valley of this river, which had now lost its characteristics, being changed from a broad, shallow stream, flowing through a monotonous plain, to a river of the mountains, shut in in some places by high, rocky bluffs, and running with a clear, swift current over a rocky or pebbly bed. I felt a thrill of pleasure as I gazed through the clear, frosty air of the morning upon the wild scenery which surrounded me, looking doubly grand when the sun, as he wheeled above the eastern hills, gilded the summits of the neighboring mountains with his golden light, forming a picture of unsurpassing grandeur and beauty. Descending from our elevated camping place, we came to a large, clear running creek, whose shores were covered with timber, mostly cotton-wood and poplar. This we followed down until we came to a broad valley, which we supposed to be that of the Platte, but it was only one of its tributaries. Proceeding up this for three or four miles, we encamped at noon by a swampy spring, around which our half-starved animals were unable to find but little grass. Proceeding on our way over an excellent road, we encamped about four o'clock on a large branch of the Platte. A trading post, with the

5

usual surroundings of Indian lodges, which was near our corral, gave the thirstier portion of our company a chance to " fire up," and under the influence of the miserable stuff, there dealt out at the rate of twenty-five cents a drink, they were soon forgetting their troubles in this fiery Lethe.

Following up the valley, we at last left it and struck up a long dry cañon which led to the valley of the Platte. The scenery along the route was very striking and picturesque. The Black Hills arose irregularly on our left in huge, black billows, above which towered the cloud-capped summit of Mt. Laramie, which was for a long time visible; but it was at last hid from view by high ridges which arose between us, the whole range enveloped in the hazy atmosphere of the Indian summer. We again reached the valley of the Platte, and at nightfall encamped about a half a mile from the river on a sandy bottom and near a fine grove of cotton-woods.

The next morning we made an early start, and soon reached the first crossing of the Platte about a mile distant. The bed of the river is here about fifteen hundred feet wide, and owing to its deep, sandy banks is in a few places fordable. The stream, which during the spring freshets often fills its banks, was not more than three hundred feet in width now, and by doubling teams we soon crossed it, and proceeded on our way up the valley, the vegetation of which was all dried and withered by the drought. Proceeding over a road filled with deep sand, we came in the afternoon to a group of *buttes*, through which the trail winds, and extricating ourselves from amongst them, we encamped after night on a desolate plateau overlooking the river.

We reached the second crossing of the Platte the next morning. This was a difficult place to ford, the shores being some twenty feet high and exceedingly steep, while the bottom was a bed of yielding sand. After crossing, we stopped a short time to breakfast, when we again started, and passing around a large, sandy bluff which arose across the valley, we followed along the dry bed of a creek, and again struck the river. We commenced to corral at sunset, but owing to the badness of the roads, and the continual giving out of the oxen, our line of march was broken into straggling fragments. Some of the wagons did not get into camp until after night, and one we were obliged to leave a mile back on the road, on account of all its team having given out. The sky was covered with black clouds which portended a stormy night, and we were surrounded by pitchy darkness.

The next morning we were awakened by the usual reveille of "Roll out," but their was a suffix appended to it on this occasion, in which the "awakening spirit" said—*and let's track rabbits*. I could not discern the pith of the suffix, or else was not influenced by the inducements it held out, and thinking that the tolerable comfort I was now experiencing preferable to the pleasure that would accrue from tracking the aforesaid rabbits, which I feared too only existed in imagination, I wrapped the drapery of my couch still closer about me, resolving to not emerge into the outer world yet awhile. A continuation of the reveille, however, at last induced me to "roll out," when, what was my consternation, to see the whole of the surrounding landscape enveloped in snow which was still falling. During the night the rain had turned to snow, and the cotton-woods and their undergrowth of vines and bushes along the river bottom, and the innumerable clumps of wild sage on the surrounding plain, were now surmounted with glittering crowns.

The road having once more become passable, we made a start at noon on the 10th, and rolling over a good road we camped at sunset on the River Fourche Boisee, two miles above its junction with the Platte. This is a clear running stream, ten yards in width, and has a narrow fringe of cotton-woods along its shores. There being no grass around our camp, we took the herd down to the junction of the rivers, where we found a good supply. So great had been the travel over the plains this season, that all the best camping places had been denuded of grass, so that the eleventh-hour caravans were sometimes hard beset to find feed for their animals. The excessive drought which was now blasting these elevated regions, had also tended greatly to dimish the supply of edible vegetation, and from these causes our oxen were continually in a half-famished condition, and their numbers were every day decreasing.

Passing over a broad and desolate ridge, we struck the Platte the next morning, and proceeding along the top of the bluffs overlooking the river, we encamped at noon near its shore. The country passed over was awfully desolate. From the waters of the river to as far as the eye could reach on either side, dreary artemisia-covered plains, with drearier hills arose above them in broken and rugged ridges. The little herbage that appeared above the sterile earth was seen in crisp, sapless bunches, and the want of a sufficiency was telling sadly on our animals, which were daily "falling faint by the wayside," never to rise again. The road was now lined with the carcasses of the oxen of preceding trains, which we were obliged to pass with hermetically sealed nostrils on account of the insufferable stench they emitted. They were in every stage of decomposition, and the sight of these reeking, putrid remains was another disagreeable feature of our journey. We reached Deer Creek, which is one hundred and ten miles west from Fort Laramie, in the afternoon. There was quite a considerable settlement of French traders and Indians here, and it was a pleasant sight to see this village after our long wilderness journey. We had been so long outside the pale of civilization, that the sight of human habitations, however rudely built, with little children, however scantily or duskily hued, playing around their doors, was very refreshing to our minds. These traders had mostly a plurality of wives, which they purchased from their fathers with powder and whisky, and which they put aside at their pleasure as soon as old age has marred their *beauty*. We stopped a short time in this village, but none of the Indians came around us, as they were restrained by the traders from mingling among other whites, of whom they were very jealous. These traders were a rough, hardy set, and but a little better civilized than their bronze-faced allies, whom they had a great influence over. We encamped after nightfall, three miles west of the village, on a broad plain overlooking the river which was about a mile to our right.

On the morning of the 17th, with cattle half dead with hunger and thirst, we slowly drove from our night's camp, and passing over a country rugged and desolate, we moved on a high bluff overlooking the river, which was about a mile distant, and near a clear, sparkling stream which afforded us excellent water. Here we bade a final adieu to the Platte (as the road here left it), a river which I 'for one was heartily tired off. We had encamped on its shores for a month and a half, traveling during that time a distance of over four hundred and fifty miles. When we first saw its dirty face at Fort Kearney it was over a mile in width, lazily flowing between forest-crowned islands and through a dull, monotonous plain. As we ascended it, the hills, which bordered the narrowing valley, began to grow higher and more abrupt, and barren sand-bars to take the place of wooded islands. After a journey of one hundred and fifty miles, we strike the South Fork; in the whole distance not having seen anything worthy the name of tributary; the river decreasing rather than increasing in volume, as the thirsty sands drink in its water. After having crossed the South Fork, quite a change takes place in the appearance of the valley; the river bottoms are often sandy, and occasionally intersected by sandy bluffs. The ranges of hills which bound the valley are now higher and very rocky, and a few stunted cedars make their appearance. As you advance, natural curiosities, like the Court House and Chimney Rock, make their appearance, and the geological features of the country are changing greatly. Continuing farther up the river, it becomes better timbered, and its shores sandier, until you reach Laramie, when another change comes over it, for here it becomes a river of the mountains, and continues so to its native home in the backbone of our Continent. Sometimes between rock-walled cañons, at others through a narrow, desert plain, flanked by desolate hills, we see it rapidly flowing on its way, over pebbly and rocky beds, its volume often increased by the streams which come from the neighboring mountains to join it. Ascending it from Kearney to where the California trail leaves it, we find its width has decreased from over a mile in width to less than three rods; and while witnessing this decrease, I had seen so much hardship and so little pleasure, that it is no wonder that I parted from old Father Platte without tears. Its mosquitoes had lacerated me, its waters had nearly frozen me, its bogs had engulfed me, and its sand had choked me; and it was with heartfelt joy that I caught a last glimpse of its waters, which an intervening bluff soon hid forever from my sight.

From our noon's encampment we passed over a gloomy, God-forsaken country, and corralled at night in a deep and rocky gorge, through which our road led. We had not expected to find water here; but on searching, we found a little brook flowing at the bottom of a deep ravine, near the corral. Thinking ourselves very fortunate, we filled our kegs, but upon trying the water we found it to be so abominably alkaline as to be unfit for drinking. There was not a spear of grass in the vicinity of the corral, so that our miserable, broken down animals were compelled to fast another day.

Owing to hunger, thirst and the bitter coldness of the night, we found several of our oxen lying dead in the corral the next morning, and the rest looked about ready to tumble over. We started on, however, for the longer we remained in this awful place, the worse for us all; but our progress was necessarily slow, and our victims were continually dropping in the yoke. The country grew even more desolate as we advanced, and was covered with beds of sand and gravel, which supported a stunted growth of sage.

The forenoon of the 20th was over a country where desolation reigned supreme. On either side the desert stretched as far as the eye could reach, the dull monotony of its dead level being occasionally broken by abrupt *buttes* which arose above it, in broken outlines, to the height of from one to five hundred feet. We struck the Sweet Water River at noon, here running through a broad valley, the vegetation of which was dried and withered by the fearful drought which was now spreading like a blight over these regions. The river was about three rods in width, with a depth of two feet, and flowed with a rapid current over a stony bed which was very winding. The valley was bounded on the south by a high, broken range of hills, the precipitous sides of which were covered with sharp, craggy rocks, among which there was not a particle of vegetation, and presented a very forbidding appearance indeed. The road in the afternoon was very bad on account of heavy sand through which we moved slowly. We corralled after sunset near the river, where, doubling upon itself, it formed a sort of peninsula, on which we found a scanty plat of grass, on which we drove our animals for the night.

Early the next morning we passed a newly erected trading post, and shortly after we arrived at the celebrated Rock Independence. This is a huge granite rock, somewhat semi-spherical in shape, and is about six hundred feet long and one hundred and fifty feet high, its surface entirely destitute of soil. The outside appears to be covered with sorts of layers or scales of various sizes and from one to two feet in thickness, the whole being of a dark gray color. The surface of the rock is filled with names and dates from base to summit, on the side fronting the road, where ambitious travelers have endeavored to immortalize themselves through the medium of black and red paint, converted into glaring capitals. Thousands of names, known and unknown to fame, are here recorded on a gigantic album which will stand till the crack of doom. Fremont, on his

THE DEVIL'S GATE.

return from his first expedition in 1842, carved a cross on this rock, which, after he became a candidate for the Presidency, became a prominent object: the enemies of the Pathfinder seeing Jesuitism in the act. The rock is situated close to the river, near by where the road crosses it, and as it stands on the edge of a plain, it has a majestic look. About four miles farther on we saw a still greater curiosity. This was the Devil's Gate, where the Sweet Water forces its way through a rugged escarpment between rocks which rise four hundred feet perpendicularly above it, the width of the passage being thirty feet. The bed of the stream is choked up with masses of rock which have fallen from above, among which the river tumbles and foames as it rushes onward through this diabolically named defile. We were obliged to make somewhat of a *detour* to get around the southern gate-post, and we encamped after noon about a mile beyond, on a high, barren bluff, overlooking the Sweet Water, which here flows through a level bottom, a half a mile wide, and covered with a scanty growth of sapless grass. So crooked was the river that it often doubled on itself as it flowed along, looking from our elevated position like a huge serpent crawling over the valley. In our search for grass we found a good supply back of the granite hills, bordering the northern shore of the Sweet Water; and in order that our animals might recruit, we remained all day at our camping place.

The scenery along this river was gloomy and repulsive. The snow-covered mountains gleaming in the far distance, the gray, sage-covered plain, the river-flat, with its yellow, withered grass, gave a cheerless picture, made still more so by the numerous human graves, and carcasses and bones of oxen which strewed the margins of the road and made a vast charnel-house of the valley of the Sweet Water. Near the Devil's Gate we saw where many men, women and children had been buried by the roadside, the victims of a species of plague which had attacked emigrants a few years before. Some of them were unmarked, save by ominous depressions, while others were covered by huge rocks which kindly hands had rolled over them to do double duty for the dead: as monuments and protection from the fangs of wolf and coyote. Their names had been rudely painted on these rocks, but the sun and rain had nearly obliterated them.

My occupation and its surroundings had about driven from

me what sentiment I had, but it came back, temporarily at least, at the sight of the graves of these emigrants, particularly of those of women and children. In fancy I saw the fever-stricken wife and mother borne along through grinding sands or jolting over stony roads or rocky fords, until, the dread hour imminent, the train stops on the Sweet Water. This seems to have been a vale of death, and that the sick who had thus far come, arrived here but to die. In this assemblage of both sexes and ages, ranging from childhood to advanced years, there are affection and kindly feeling, so different from what exists in our rough crowd. The train halts until the last scene in the life of the dying is over. No sick-chamber with rich belongings and comforts are hers. The mildewed wagon-cover makes the walls and ceiling; the hangings, the rough clothing of the family. The doorway is the arched cover, and it looks appropriately toward the west; and the descending sun directs its last glances within on the dying form. Kind hands minister to its wants, and when the life goes out, they perform the last sad rites. Among the less sympathetic of the emigrants there may be impatience at the delay; for behind them are murderous Indians, and the cold wind blowing around them, and the snow on the distant mountains, warns them that the storms of winter may engulf them before the journey is over. A shallow grave is hollowed out, the coffin-less body laid therein, amid the weeping of women and children, and the sad looks of the men who quickly cover the body with earth and protect it with a cairn of rocks. Or it may be a child that dies, when we can imagine the parents' feelings as they lay it away in that desert solitude, and, taking up the burden of their journey, pass on, never to see its resting place again. You who ride by in your palace cars, wining and dining as you go on your profitless excursions, cannot imagine the trials and sufferings of the pioneers who first settled the country where you enjoy your junketing.

The morning of the 26th we crossed the river, and encamped at 10 o'clock on a high bluff on its left shore. We here had a fifteen-mile stretch to cross without water, and allowing our animals three hours to feed, we filled our water kegs and pushed on, our road laying over a desolate, rolling plain covered with sage-brush. In the afternoon we entered a broad, sandy valley, through which ran the dry bed of a stream. Ascending this valley to its upper extremity, we crossed a sandy ridge and corralled about 10 o'clock at night on a waterless plain. We made an early start the next morning, and rolling over a hilly and barren plateau, we descended at noon into the valley of the Sweet Water, which was here about a half a mile in width, and corralled. There being no grass along the river, we drove the herd to the bluffs, which were scantily supplied with bunch-grass. Several of our animals gave out during the forenoon. The river was here fringed by a dense growth of willows, but the characteristic sterility of this valley was manifest in the barren plain and bluffs bordering it. Two miles from our noon's camp we came to where a ridge of rocky hills extended across the valley through which the river forced its way. The road over the bluffs is a difficult one, and we encamped after night on its farther side in a cañon leading down to the river.

Still continuing up the river, we came in the afternoon to where another mountain wall intersects the valley, which, below it, is about a mile in breadth. The river penetrates it by a deep gorge, walled on either side by rocky, perpendicular bluffs. The road leaves the valley by a deep cañon (pronounced *kanyon*, the Spanish for ravine or defile), which turns to the right, and winds to the summit of the ridge, ascending and descending several hills in the way. We encamped at night near its summit. We found a considerable stream of good water, a half a mile from the corral, the shores of which were lined with timber.

The morning of the 30th came upon us with a heavy frost, which whitened the valley and neighboring mountains like a young snow. The whole party were ordered out early to hunt up the oxen, which were interspersed in the jungle bordering the neighboring branch. We broke corral at sunrise, and ascending a rocky hill, stood upon the summit of a succession of barren ridges, which extended as far as the eye could reach in every direction, a rugged depression marking the course of the river. We saw two lakes of considerable size on our left, the shores of which were encrusted with saleratus in nearly a pure state; so much resembling that substance, indeed, that it answered the purpose for raising bread. While on this ridge, a wind-storm came on, which nearly blinded us, as it blew the sharp sand directly in our faces. We were obliged to walk in a bent posture while the storm lasted, which was until we reached the Sweet Water at noon. We encamped on the left bank of the river, near a thicket of willows, which supplied us with fuel, and took the herd a mile down the river to graze. This place is called the Last Crossing. We met here a wagon-master and three teamsters, who had come in advance of a return train which was a few miles back on the road, and they agreed to join our caravan, which was deficient in available men. Draper, the wagon-master, who had been all the way to Camp Floyd and who knew the road well, was to act as pilot to our train over the difficult route which yet remained between us and our destination. We broke corral a little after noon, and crossing the river for the last time, ascended a gravelly bluff, and followed along the right bank of the river. We soon met the returning "outfit," which contained the men belonging to three trains, and some twenty wagons.

The 31st we went but four miles, camping at noon close by the river. Our employers had a herd a short distance up the valley, from which we obtained a supply of fresh oxen, leaving in their stead an equal number of our skeletons. Our night guards were now arranged differently. One of our new hands was to stand guard every night (sleeping in the daytime in one of the wagons), assisted by three others, who were to take their turns every sixth night. This arrangement was quite an improvement over the former system.

On some trains the herders did no driving whatever, which left them fresh for their all-night work, or noon herding. This was not Russel & Co.'s way of doing, as they got all the work out of their men that was possible. We would feel so tired after our day's drive that when our turns came to stand guard we mentally protested; but as this involved silence, it availed nothing when loud-mouthed protests fell flat. So without suppers we would leave camp on a half or all-night guard, depending on something to eat coming out to us by our messmates, and for a nap at our noon-halt the next day. This brought on so much drowsiness that on my next drive I would often find myself turned somnambulist, and driving oxen in my sleep.

VI.

Among the Mountains.

WE reached the South Pass on the 1st of October.
I had thought this was something like the
Devil's Gate on a large scale, a mountain
walled gorge, but it was very different. Imagine a nearly
level desert plain, averaging a mile in width, bounded on
either side by a low range of hills, beyond which extends a
rolling country from ten to twenty miles, until it reaches a
range of lofty bleak mountains—and you can form an idea
of the best Rocky Mountain pass. About two miles to our
right we could see the valley of the Sweet Water, which we
were leaving. The snowy peaks of the Wind River Mountains, which rose far to the north of us, were glittering in the
sun's rays, while to the south, rising like a huge barrier,
we saw Table Mountain. All around, as far as the eye could
reach, was a scene of wild desolation.

We nooned at the Pacific Spring, which is a short distance
west of the culminating point of our route. This is a morass
of twenty acres, vividly green and with a sluggish stream
running through it. When I first saw this meadow I thought
we had a nice corralling place. We camped on the southern
shore. As soon as the oxen were loosened, they broke in a
body for this deceitful meadow, in which many of them were
soon floundering and unable to get out. We dragged them

out by main force, attaching lassos to their horns. In the swamp were many carcasses of oxen, so many, that the water was unfit to drink. We left here in the afternoon, and following along Pacific Creek, a tributary of the Colorado, we camped at night near another swamp. About midnight the hungry cattle got into this, and we worked an hour or more in the cold water and mud getting them out. Some we were obliged to leave there to die.

At sunrise we started, and passing over a desert covered with beds of sand and miry flats and sloughs, white with alkali, we camped at noon by a brackish stream. When we resumed our march, we stirred up clouds of saleratus-impregnated dust which aggravated our thirst, as we could not drink the water where we had camped. Much of the water in this part of the country was the color of weak lye, and tasted similarly. I have known the white hair of oxen to acquire a pink tinge from their continued use of it.

At a place called Deep Hollow we saw three black circles of tires and wagon-irons, where the Mormons had burned as many corrals in the previous fall. There were seventy-eight wagons loaded with provisions for the advance troops of the Utah Expedition, which were two days' march ahead, and which afterwards sorely felt the need of them. The guerilla leader was Lot Smith, a Mormon "Old Put."

As the cold increased, fuel became plentier in the shape of a large growth of sage-brush. Much of this was dry and dead, and at night we made the scenery luminous with bonfires, around which we stood or reclined. On the 9th of October we crossed Green River, the Rio Verde of the old Spaniards. The next day we encamped on Ham's Fork, near where lay the carcasses of five hundred cattle belonging to a supply train of the Utah army. They had perished from hunger and cold the preceding winter. A sickening odor was still around the spot, so that we dared not camp near the ford.

On the 11th we reached Fort Bridger. This had been a trading post, and during the marauding excursions of the Saints, to harass and destroy our supply trains, it was used as a starting point. On the approach of our troops, the Mormons deserted the place after burning it down. General Johnston arrived here at the close of November, and making the place his winter quarters, built a fort and remained here until spring, suffering many hardships from cold and lack of the provisions the Mormons burned. As soon as the snows had sufficiently melted, supplies were sent to the beleagured troops, who were found eating their last rations. They marched on to Salt Lake after recuperating, and accomplished their mission. The commissary here lightened our wagons to the extent of four hundred pounds apiece, which was quite a help to us.

We had now joined with us another train—the same one which had passed us on the Platte. The men had rebelled against their wagon-master, and Russel & Co's. agents had ordered the two trains to run together under our own. There were now in the train fifty wagons, sixty men, and over six hundred oxen. Among the new men were several Mexican Indians. This many men consumed much provision, and our bacon running low, application was made at a cattle station belonging to our employers for some beef cattle, which was refused. That night two expert thieves of our party were sent to the agency and brought home three fine bullocks, which were divided among our men.

Bearing in mind the vast amount of game roaming over the plains and among the mountains, it would naturally be supposed that much of our diet would be from that source. What fresh meat we had outside of the domain of the buffalo, whose flesh, particularly in the summer, is unfit to eat, was mainly from our oxen when accidentally killed. This, of course, was poor eating. We saw deer and antelope frequently, but the only venison we fared on was a fawn one of our men shot on the North Platte, and which, among thirty hearty men, was hardly a taste. Indians sometimes brought deer to sell, but as we had no money to buy with, the result was nothing to our larder. Sage-hens sometimes whirred away in gunshot, but our broken down oxen needed so much stimulus that they parted in peace. A species of hare, called, from its long ears, "jack-rabbit," we met in plenitude among the Rocky Mountains, and we shot many of them. These we made into soup, and as a relief from our bacon were welcome fare. But the proportion of fresh meat was so small that one or two cases of scurvy showed themselves from our diet of salt pork and dough fried in its drippings. We were in poor condition to forage for game. The horses, from galloping from one end of the mile-long train to the other, were too tired for side excursions after deer, and we were too much in the same condition ourselves at our halting places to go hunting. On the Sweet Water we improvised a net out of a wagon cover, and caught a mess of fish, and these were indeed a treat. Once, at a trading post, I was a partaker of beaver meat. It was a dark red in color, and fair eating, but it seemed so like cannibalism to eat of animals so industrious and half human in their providence that I did not enjoy it. In this connection I will mention that at one of our Rocky mountain camps I came across a clearing which at once arrested my attention. It was alongside of a large stream and several rods in extent. The stumps were from two to four inches in diameter and conical. These had all been neatly cut off by four-footed wood-choppers, and the trees and branches floated down to a dam which was seen some distance below. This was the only sign of beavers I saw on the whole journey.

Our implements for the conversion of our few articles of diet into ox-propellers were few at the start, and grew fewer

6

as we progressed. For baking our bread we had what we called a " Dutch oven;" a large skillet with a lid, surrounded with a battlement for holding hot coals. The "rising" was saleratus, and this it took so much of in our hastily got up meals that the loaf, or "pone," as we called it, was as yellow as corn bread and hardly fit to eat. Hot coals, however, were often so scarce that we were fain to fry our dough in fat. The other utensils were a frying pan, camp kettle, and tin pan for kneading trough. A large coffee-pot we had awhile, but it soon got lost or battered beyond use, and then we fell back on the black camp-kettle wherein to brew our Java—when we had any.

On the 17th we were caught in a blinding snow-storm and were detained four days. Our time was spent caring for the oxen, gathering wood and idling around camp. We left here on the 21st, and crossed Bear River, which flows into Salt Lake.

Our road throughout the journey had been a natural one except at the fords, where the banks had been dug away. Whenever a bluff lining a valley came too near a stream, the road would diverge and pass over the hill until the valley became passable. The ascents were generally difficult and required doubling of teams, while the descending slopes were often scenes of serious accidents to men, oxen and wagons. We crossed but one bridge before reaching Utah, and that was built by a trader who charged toll. In the part of the country we were now in, however, we came across an occasional " dug-road," built by the troops the last spring, which enabled us to get along when otherwise it would have been impossible.

By November 1st we had no provisions left but flour; bacon, beans, rice and coffee all gone. Of course, with our wagons loaded with the material for the manufacture of life's staff, we would not want; neither need sailors adrift suffer for lack of water. We had no saleratus, so that our bread was hard and tough. Our beverage, outside of water, was a concoction we called flour soup. On this weak diet we lived a few days, when we were met with a supply of good beef from Salt Lake by agents of our employers, and henceforth we did not want.

There were three ways of entering Salt Lake Valley : by Emigration, Echo and Provo cañons. We took the latter route. The road was built by the Mormon Church at much expense, as at places the rocky walls of the valley came close to the water, when wooden ways would be built over it. Toll was charged us. All the way down Provo Cañon the road was dangerous, in spite of the labor spent upon it. Our long teams had trouble in drawing the wagons around short curves,, as the strain of the leaders had a tendency to drag the "swing" cattle into the gulfs below. One wagon tumbled into the river and spilled its contents. On the plains, when an accident happened, it was the custom for the train to halt until matters were righted. But now that we were continually troubled with breakdowns and upsets, the luckier teams ahead went selfishly on until they, too, were in trouble.

I give a sketch of a part of our road down Provo Cañon. Our artist, in the re-drawing for photo-engraving, has omitted the slope lying between the almost perpendicular rocks and the creek through which the track was cut. Sometimes we would come across expansions of the gorge, but they were so sloping that we could not form corral on them, so that throughout the time we were passing the cañon, we remained in line. Sometimes we would wind around craggy rocks ; then descend to the foaming creek, over which, on a corduroy road, we would go awhile, and then ascend to fresh dangers. If the other passes to Salt Lake were as bad as these I don't wonder that our troops were so long on a stand about entering the valley ; so few defenders could have kept them out.

The reader has a view of our descent of Provo River, but I

can only describe the sounds it gave rise to. I never heard
such a bedlam of swearing and yelling as within the gloom of
its gorges. At Platte crossing and other difficult points I
thought I had heard the acme of malediction; but to Provo
Cañon was reserved the dubious honor of being the scene of
the cap-sheaf of past efforts. To say that the ox-drivers swore
like troopers, or "like our army in Flanders," would be draw-

DOWN PROVO CAÑON.

ing it a world too mild. The air resounded, and the high rocks
echoed with imprecations worthy of pirates. There was the
broad-mouthed oath of the Missourian, the scientific curse of
the Yankee, the guttural imprecation of the German, and the
broguey expletive of him from the Emerald sod. To these
were added the " *carajos*," " *carambos*," " *cozedos* " and arraign-
ments of derelict saints from the tongues of the Mexi-

cans who had come in with our companion train. These all mingled in a sulphurous, polyglot whirlwind and ascended skyward through the deep cañon. Let us hope that when the recording angel charged these things up to the poor ox-drivers, he found something to put to their credit in their after-lives; but, I fear, the chances were small of his doing so. I know that his tears, plenteous as they would be, could not efface the debit entries.

Taking into account the nature of our road, and that there were fifty teamsters, each with twelve oxen to manage, and that our train, when in close order, reached about a mile, it need not be wondered at that there was confusion, with some resultant naughtiness of language.

We had expected to go through the cañon by night, but the continued misfortunes that befell us made it impossible, and we halted as darkness began to arch over the sky-light above us. In our contracted space we could only leave the wagons strung along the gorge, and turn loose the hungry, foot-sore cattle. Here I stood my last guard for "Old Russel," as we called the firm who employed us. The night was bitterly cold, and a fierce wind was blowing down the cañon from the distant valley of Provo. Walking back and forth, over thorny plants and sharp stones, and shivering with cold, I passed a night to be remembered; and I was glad when I saw the morning sun gilding the frost-tipped crests of the cañon walls. Gathering our still hungry and benumbed oxen, we continued down the valley, the scenery of which grew more grand as we proceeded. On the left bank the walls arose almost perpendicularly to the height of a thousand feet, having offsets in places on which were growing tall pines, while at the foot of the gray wall the river leaped and foamed. We passed at one place a frozen cascade which must have been eight hundred feet high. This distorted column of ice was a fine sight, and was an evidence of the coldness of the night we had just passed.

The valley gradually widened, but the road was still danger-ous. We soon met companies of Mormons, men and boys, who were chopping wood and mending roads, and anon we en-countered an aged Samaritan with a wagon load of onions and cabbages for our special use, which he sold to those who had any money, or its equivalent in the shape of transferable goods belonging to our employers. As the most of us were as poor as the turkey allegedly Job's (although his book fails to mention the fact that he ever owned such a bird, either poor or fat) when we hired at Leavenworth, it will be seen that the Mormon hucksters got more bacon and ox-chains than coin of the realm. Those few who had conscience instead of money were obliged to see luxuries, like milk, eggs and vegetables, pass by them like the Priest and the Levite of old, giving them no assistance.

Near the mouth of the widening gorge we came to that evidence of civilization—a toll-gate. Here a saintly keeper slate in hand, kept tally of our wagons as they lumbered past, the toll being one dollar per ton, or $1,250 for our train. The road belonged to the Mormon Church—otherwise Brigham Young. Paying an enemy toll to enter his conquered territory was the height of absurdity. Just below the gate we crossed the river on an excellent bridge, and still following down the cañon we left it by an immense natural gateway, where tower-ing rocks arose perpendicularly from each side of the river.

VII.

In the Valley of the Shadow.

WE were now in the Great Valley, fifty miles below Salt Lake City. We corraled on the edge of a plain extending from the mountain to Lake Utah. The section we were in was oval in shape and surrounded by high mountains covered with snow. In the centre was the Lake, its waters shining brightly in the sun, and from the mouth of its gloomy cañon we could see the Provo River winding through a desolate plain toward the inland sea. The dreary plain, the gleaming lake and rugged surroundings formed a scene of quiet grandeur I never will forget.

On the 5th we continued up the valley. The road was smooth, and we made good time. Evidences that we were approaching civilization were hourly becoming apparent. At first we saw, rising above the plain, an object which proved to be a farm house, but it was so far from us that we could only see its outlines; but further on we came to cultivated grounds enclosed with mud walls and arranged for irrigation. My readers can hardly understand how we felt at seeing the haunts of a civilized people; but if they will recall the time which had elapsed since we left the States, it will not seem strange that these foreign homes of a still more foreign people arose before our eyes like friends long separated. Other farms and cottages came in sight, and sundry of their dwellers began to line the

road and tender to us onions, turnips and other strange vegetables. The country was getting more thickly settled, and soon
the sight of a village greeted us. This was Battle Creek, and
in the heart of it we made our corral. We hardly halted before we were surrounded by men, women and children, dogs,
pigs and chickens, the last hardly realizing their danger in
coming so close to the itching palms of the ox-drivers. The
children had an eye to business and peddled all manner of
things among us; while the men went about, tempting our innocent men, even as did the disguised one of old. They had
the assurance to think that our noble fellows would trade ox-
yokes, bows, chains and other things belonging to our
employers, for whisky, beer, poultry, vegetables and other of
life's necessaries. Some of our men, rather than see the disappointment generated by refusal, made sacrifices resulting in
the coveted exchange; and, to make the Mormons feel more at
ease, even went so far as to drink the liquor at once in
their presence, and soon were laughing and making merry.

One of our Mormon friends invited me to dine with him. I
bought the invitation with a gun-barrel I picked up on the
Platte. At the hour named I repaired to his house, a one-
roomed " adobe," which answered the purpose of parlor, bed-
room and kitchen. He had but one wife and two children,
with whom I was soon seated at table. After grace was said
the man of the house took a quid from his mouth and uttered
the words " pile in," when we all felt at our ease. I " piled in,"
much to the disgust, I fear, of my host, who saw his gun-barrel vanishing in a dissolving view. This mode of dining was
quite a change from sitting on the ground, eating from a common plate, but I soon got used to it. What we had were not
luxuries, but it was relished. There were beef, potatoes, biscuits and butter; and the whole punctuated with a full stop, in
the guise of a disk of good, thick, pumpkin pie! It really did
me good to sit in the warmth of an old-fashioned fire-place,

side by side with a father and mother and their prattling children. To be sure the first was uncouth, but the wife was quite presentable, and I much enjoyed myself.

Dinner eaten, I procured some vegetables for my mess and went back to the corral. It was a pleasure to look on my companions. They all had had good dinners; for those who were without money had the equivalent in the shape of "portable property," which, if not their own, answered the same purpose. Their faces were radiant with smiles, so different from their past woe-begone looks. Some of them, I am sorry to say, were a little drunk. But there was a cessation of their chronic state of swearing, which partially compensated for this.

Among the group of villagers we saw an old man who told me he was from Philadelphia. In this distant land we were acquaintances; in fact, we felt a little related. He seemed to take much interest in me when he found out where I lived, and invited me to his home. "Uncle Job," for so his neighbors called him, dwelt in a little adobe house on the main street, where he lived the anomalous life, in that polygamous land, of a bachelor; for what reason I don't know, unless it was to help reduce the average. He had the patience of his prononym of old, and took me over to his little house and garden and showed me the mammoth vegetables he had raised, and introduced me to his next door neighbor, a fair Mormoness, all the while talking to me in a very voluble manner. Uncle Job had a skeleton in his closet which he showed me. It was a black bottle, and his frequent visits to this was what made him so talkative. He denounced the soldiers for coming among them, praised Brigham Young for his course, and extolled the Mormon heaven as being the true New Jerusalem towards which mankind should travel. He told me his troubles with one of his neighbors, and, in fact, was getting so affectionate and communicative, that I was fain to get away from him and hie me to the corral.

The town had about five hundred people in its borders, mostly of the lower class of English and Danes. There were no Irish, but there was one family of Africans, who seemed to be held in esteem. The foreign element, having come through New York without stopping, had retained their dress and manners. They wore wooden shoes, and were coarsely clad. The houses were on roomy lots, and were mainly of sun-dried bricks, and had few adornments inside or out.

THROUGH THE STREETS OF LEHI.

We left in the afternoon, and after night came to the town of Lehi—a name taken from the Mormon Bible. This was surrounded by a wall twelve feet high. We experienced a strange sensation, driving through streets between lighted houses, but we enjoyed it. The gate-way, as we emerged from the town, was so narrow that I was afraid my wagon might play the part of the rams' horns on Jericho, and send the walls tumbling about my head; but I got through without hubbing.

At midnight we camped on the banks of the Jordan, paying the Bishop of Lehi $50 for the grass. We were awakened the next morning by the crowing of neighboring roosters, a sort of reveille we had not heard for a long, long time. As we would make a dry camp that night, we concluded not to start until noon. The Jordan, which lay in our way, was crossed by a bridge, and was no longer a hard road to travel. The river flows between deep cut banks, and was about twenty yards wide; the water green and somewhat alkaline. As to the origin of the name of this river, allowing Salt Lake, with its bitter water and absence of outlet, to represent the Dead Sea, and Lake Utah to stand for the Sea of Galilee, the appropriateness of the name Jordan to the connecting stream, with its rocky bed and rugged surrounding scenery, is obvious. At the far end of the bridge was a combination of laundry and grocery. The barmaid of the institution was washing at the time, her dishevelled locks hanging around a face not very attractive. Our men being short of money and on the move, and the bar being on the "off side" of the train, but little business was done here.

We encamped at midnight, after a thirty mile drive, the longest day's travel we had ever made, on the edge of Cedar Valley. We were up early in the morning and started on our last drive. We met many return teamsters on foot, and these were eagerly questioned as to how far we had to go, and they gave us all sorts of answers; some rather disrespectful. About the middle of the forenoon the lead teamster reported our destination in sight, and then a shout went up on the desert air which rang all along our mile of wagons. Even the oxen seemed imbued with a subdued enthusiasm.

A few more words about our cattle before we part with them. There is not much sentiment connected with these animals, although when the ancient poet spoke of the "Ox-eyed Juno," the alleged wife of Jupiter, he paid an inferential tribute to

their visual organs, at least when he compared them to those
of the mythological "Queen of Heaven." I have before
alluded to the pathos expressed in their eyes, which under
suffering was almost human and was given vent in tears; a
weakness the rough teamster sometimes contracted: for I have
seen big, bearded fellows crying over a dead ox, as "dying in
the harness," they loosened him from the team and placed his
yoke-fellow in some weakling's place.

Our oxen were too many in number and transient in ownership to merit names, except in certain cases. My wheelers
were "Dodge" and Samson. The propensity of the first to
obey the summons "Whoa!" was such that at the least intima-
tion of it he would surge back and stop the whole team; sometimes splitting his yoke, and once, going into a gully, nearly
getting killed. For this cause I was forced to give the command in subdued tones, and yet so the rest would hear.
"Samson," so named from his strength, broke down from
over-willingness, and at Fort Kearney was substituted by a
bovine giant, which I called Goliath. These names sounded
strange to my un-Biblical companions, who listened to them inquiringly, and who were satisfied with "Texas," "Nig," "Roan"
and other color-giving names; though "Tom and Jerry," from
the name of a favorite tipple, was sometimes given to a yoke.

At Camp Floyd, named after the then Secretary of War,
there were thirty-five hundred troops living in four hundred
adobe houses. There were also commissary houses and cavalry
stables, making a large, well laid-out town. We commenced
unloading at two o'clock, and by four had finished. We then
took the wagons outside the camp where, among acres of
others, we left them to rot down piecemeal. The oxen, except
two teams we kept to haul our provisions and effects to Salt
Lake, were given in charge of Mormon herders. But two of
my own were left of the twelve I started. One was the near
wheeler named "Dodge," from his habit of dropping back as

soon as I went ahead to attend to the forward cattle. His laziness was his salvation. The other was a "pointer" who did his duty faithfully to the end.

Returning to camp we were in time to see the soldiers on dress parade. Their bright arms and prompt movements were pleasant to see, all being regulars. We saw General Albert Sydney Johnston, in command, who in four years was to fall at Shiloh, in arms against the flag which now floated over him. Many of the company's commissioned officers were in the same time to be colonels and generals in either service. Strains of martial music enlivened the scene; among which were the stirring airs of "Yankee Doodle," "Bold Soldier Boy" and the "Girl I Left Behind Me:" airs soon to be familiar to all, north and south. Many of the privates were deserting for California and elsewhere.

This army had many tribulations *en route* to Camp Floyd. It left Fort Laramie the previous September, and from want of supplies (which were intercepted and burned by Mormon guerillas) and deep snows got no farther then Bridger. When spring opened the troops were detained, while Governor Cummings and the Peace Commissioners were parleying with the Mormon leaders, and did not reach Salt Lake until the 26th of June. They found the streets almost deserted, the leading citizens having gone to Provo, fifty miles south. Governor Cummings truckled to the rebels, and to induce them to return they were granted amnesty; and the troops marched to a sterile plain, forty or fifty miles south-east and beyond the Jordan, that their presence might not cause irritation. Thus humored, the people soon came back, and for months reaped a rich harvest selling grain, flour, wood and lumber to the troops. Brigham Young ran his three saw mills in a cañon he claimed as his own, steadily cutting material for soldiers' quarters, each earning one hundred dollars per day. The Mormons had their own fun spoiling the Egyptians in revenge for their humiliations from having to yield to Federal power.

The next morning we retraced our route. Walking in advance of our baggage wagons we waded the Jordan where we crossed it, there being no bridge. Here was another of the "groceries," where whisky was sold at twenty-five cents a drink. We nooned here and again took up the line of march toward Salt Lake City. We soon saw this place, twenty-five miles away, from the divide between the two valleys of Utah and Salt Lake. Near here two remarkable springs gushed forth from the roadside; one hot, the other cold; so close we could almost reach both at once. I could easily say I caught fish in the one and boiled them in the other; but I forbear. When really or practically alone on his journey a traveler is often tempted to amplify his descriptions, as evidenced by the tales of solitary voyages, from Gulliver down; so, thus traveling, let me have due credit for my abnegation in not repeating this fish story; one so justified by modern usage. Both springs were impregnated with sulphur. Many similar ones were in the neighborhood; some with embankments around them formed naturally.

The road we were traveling was a magnificent one; one hundred feet wide, smooth and so straight we could see miles ahead. As we neared the city we saw a few villages inhabited by industrious people. The fields on either hand looked parched and desolate, but the thick set stubble showed that good crops had been raised. They were enclosed with mud walls made by filling board frames with the sticky clay dug from the ditches at the base.

We passed an extensive beet sugar factory on the way. The machinery had been brought at great expense from England, but the enterprise was a failure and the works silent. Further on was the Penitentiary, also still for want of tenants. We reached the city at sunset, and encamped in a vacant lot, which had been prepared for us by furnishing it with plenty of fire-wood and straw. This last was scattered around as if for a herd of cattle. Seeking a thick bunch of it for a bed, and with my worldly goods for a pillow I laid down and wrapped my blankets around me, prepared for such dreams as the circumstances warranted.

VIII.

The Saints' Rest.

GREAT SALT LAKE CITY—the Jerusalem, the Mecca, the Holy of Holies of the Latter Day Saints and the grand centre around which the wheel of Mormonism then revolved; the spot from whence issued all the mandates of the Church and where all the villanies laid to the charge of Brigham Young and his satellites were concocted—is located near the foot-hills of the Wahsatch Mountains and on the eastern edge of the Great Valley. From the base of this range, the tall peaks of which were then white with snow, the town extends towards the lake, which is some twenty miles to the westward; its scattered buildings covering several square miles. Speaking of the place as it was in 1858, each square contained ten acres and was divided into eight lots of one acre and a quarter each, so that it presented quite a suburban and rural appearance. The streets, which were eight rods wide, and from the nature of the soil as hard as an asphaltum pavement, crossed each other at right angles and were shaded by rows of young cotton-woods and locusts; the town in its eleven years of existence not having had time to develop a very large growth of trees. Along the sides of the streets flowed clear and sparkling streams of water, which answered the double purpose of supplying the people with drink and irrigation for their gardens. This water was preserved clean by city ordinances, a fine of five dollars being put on any one caught washing in it. This I found out by experience, for the straw shed in which I passed the first night of my arrival not being supplied with water, as on account of the great rush of guests the waiters had been unable to properly attend to the needs of their rooms, I repaired in the morning to the stream running by our hotel, whose hospitable landlord kept open house, to perform my ablutions. I had got fairly under way when I was hailed by a Mormon and informed that I was subject to a fine, but on my informing him of my ignorance of their laws, he said he would let me go. I felt about as grateful to him for his forbearance as most people do when told of a blunder fraught with risk to the maker, the information of which puts the recipient under obligation—that is, so much so that I forgot to thank him, as in a semi-washed condition I turned and walked away. From the appearance of the rest of our party few of them had been in danger of arrest, for voluntary deprivation from water had made them notorious for their ungodliness since leaving the Missouri, and they were disposed to keep it up.

I give a view of East Temple Street, not to show what the city was like then, for the sketch was made long since, when railroads had made it accessible to tourists and filled it with business enterprise, but to show its position at the foot of the snow-clad Wahsatch Mountains, whence comes the sparkling water which quenches the thirst of its people and irrigates its gardens. The city spreads and rises, but the rugged background gleams from snowy peaks and frowns from shadowy recesses of a lower altitude the same now as then, when thirty years ago I gazed at it from the gateway leading from Utah Valley.

The houses, which were built of adobes, were generally of one story, so that the town presented rather a squatty appearance, which was occasionally relieved, however, by a few houses

7

MAIN STREET, SALT LAKE CITY.

of larger and loftier dimensions, belonging to dignitaries of the Church. These arose above the humble tenements around them, as the worldly positions of their saintly owners towered above those of the vulgar herd. Among these the house, or rather palace, of Brigham Young was conspicuous, both from its elevated position and its architectural beauty. It was located in the highest part of the city and near the base of the mountains, which rose several thousand feet above it in rugged outlines. It consisted of a series of buildings, built apparently at different times—an addition being made, I presume, whenever a fresh victim was added to the spreading establishment of its multi-wived owner—and taking all things into consideration, was quite a respectable looking edifice. The main building was built of adobes, and plastered and painted to an extent which gave it quite a Yankeefied air. West of this and on the same square was the Lion House, a noble building, with its gable fronting the street and with a stone lion *couchant* above its principal entrance. In this was the President's office. The "Tithing Office" and "Home Manufacturers'" establishment were also on the same square, which was surrounded by a stone wall some twelve feet high, and strengthened at regular intervals by abutments. Heber Kimble's square adjoined this, but the buildings within it were very humble specimens of architecture. Temple Block was on the opposite side of the street and west from Brigham's establishment, and was enclosed by massive walls. In the centre of this was the foundation of the Great Temple, which was to be the Eighth Wonder of the World—if it ever got completed. The plan of it was revealed to Brigham in a dream, as well as the identical spot on which it was to be located. The work on this great edifice, which had progressed steadily, was suspended upon the breaking out of the troubles, and had not yet been resumed. Another prominent building was the "Tabernacle," peculiarly shaped and used for theatrical performances and lectures. I give a view of it. Brigham dreamed its plan also.

The "Public Works" was one of the peculiar institutions of the Metropolis. In order to enable the Mormons of foreign countries, who were generally needy, to reach the New Jerusalem a range of workshops were erected in Temple Block, where all manner of avocations were to be carried on, so that the Saint after his arrival at the promised land could refund the money which had been advanced by the Church for his passage, by laboring in these "Public Works" the required length

THE TABERNACLE.

of time for discharging the debt he had contracted. This establishment, in connection with the "Perpetual Emigrating Fund Society," had been the means of bringing numbers of immigrants to Utah, whom a lack of sufficient funds would otherwise have compelled to remain outside the pale of salvation.

The other public buildings were the County Court House

and the Council House. The latter was formerly the place of meeting of the Territorial Legislature, which now meets at Fillmore City.

The business thoroughfare of the city (East Temple Street) runs north and south through it, and was for some distance thickly lined with stores, workshops and hotels. The merchants were doing a splendid business, and their stocks of merchandise were speedily being evaporated by their Mormon customers, who, with their pockets well lined with government gold, were buying at an extravagant rate those foreign luxuries which a lack of the needful had hitherto deprived them of, and which retailed at prices high enough to startle persons fresh from the cheap domain of the East. Sugar and coffee went briskly at 60 and 65 cents per pound, molasses flowed at the rate of $4.00 per gallon, and vinegar was $1.50 per bottle. Calico retailed at from 30 to 40 cents per yard, and clothing of all kinds was proportionately dear. Hardware was enormously high also—a frying pan would not cross the counter for less than $2.50, a coffee-mill would not come down from its abiding place short of a $4.00 bait, and a tin coffee-pot off its nail for less than $3.50. These prices to persons in the States seem fabulous, but from bitter experience I know them to be correct, as our outfits, preparatory for California, were purchased here. As an evidence of how speedily goods were disposed of at these rates, I will state a fact. One house (Gilbert & Co.) disposed of $3,000 worth of goods the first day their stock was exposed for sale—a large transaction when we consider the penurious habits of the denizens of Salt Lake City, and the limited means they had of obtaining hard money, the only kind taken by the merchants in exchange for their goods.

The two hotels, the "Empire" and "New World," were also coining their dimes. Poisonous concoctions, bearing the names of "Pure Old Whisky," "Prime French Brandy," "Superior Port Wine," etc., were here offered to a thirsty public at the rate of two bits (twenty-five cents) a drink, the drinkers little dreaming that they were gulping down a perfect catalogue of poisonous drugs at each potation. Each of these establishments had its gambling hell, where newly arrived greenhorns were scientifically fleeced by experienced blacklegs, who had flocked here from all parts of the Union in anticipation of a windfall. I visited one of them one evening. Ascending a dark stairway in the rear of the building, I entered a low room densely packed with humanity, and reeking with the fumes of tobacco and bad whisky. The players were seated at their tables and busily engaged in solving the mysteries of *monte*, a game peculiar to Mexico and California, but now introduced into the Mormon Zion by its accomplished and unscrupulous votaries. It was a sad sight, to see the self-satisfied composure with which the blackleg drew in his fraudulently obtained gold; while the plucked victim would utter curses loud and deep at his luck, but would again, lured on by the infernal spirit of gambling, venture another stake, which would be certain to follow in the wake of its predecessors to the coffers of the scientific " dealer." It was odd to see what little value money possessed here, where double-eagles were tossed about like coppers by the excited gamesters. The gambling tables were surrounded by eager lookers-on, who seemed almost as much absorbed in the game as the players themselves, and did one of the latter become tired or "broke," there were numbers ready to take his place. Having staid until my curiosity was fully satisfied, I retired from this above-ground Pandemonium, and wending my way to my lodging-house, I moralized, as I trod the gloomy streets, on the frailties of poor human nature.

The tradesmen of Great Salt Lake City were revelling in the present flourishing state of affairs as greatly as the merchants and grog venders. The shoemakers, in particular, wore a look of independence, which spoke of plenty to do and high rates for the doing. These sedentaries unblushingly de-

THE SAINTS' REST. 111

manded $10.00 per pair for coarse boots. The saddlers and
tailors were fat and saucy also, and eke were the sooty sons of
Vulcan!

*   *   *   *   *   *   *

Great Salt Lake City was founded in the summer of 1847
by an advance column of the Mormon emigration, which was
sent to seek some isolated spot in the Far West, where the
Church might locate and prosper, free from the persecution of
their relentless enemies. They were then established at
Nauvoo, in Illinois; a city which they had built up after their
expulsion by a lawless mob from their homes in Jackson
county, Missouri. While at Nauvoo they were granted extra-
ordinary privileges by the Governor of Illinois; one of which
was to raise an armed force whereby they might repel the
assaults of their enemies, for they were believed by their neighbors to be an innocent, persecuted people, deserving of aid and
sympathy. The new settlement grew strong and mighty until
fifteen thousand Saints had gathered around this nucleus;
four thousand of which were well-drilled soldiers. A Temple
was erected on a hill overlooking the city, where the people
might congregate to hear the sublime mysteries of their religion
expounded, and this was the pride and glory of its builders.
Things went on swimmingly for a while; but dark whispers
began to arise at last that the city was becoming a nest of
villainy, a central point for all the thieves and murderers in
the vicinity to seek shelter in, after having transacted their
nefarious crimes, and where, shielded by their aiders and
abettors, they could not be brought to justice. In vain the
Saints endeavored to stay the storm which was gathering over
their heads, by protestations of loyalty and innocence; the ball
was in motion, which was to crush Mormonism in Illinois.
One thing brought on another, until the Saints and Gentiles
were in arms against each other, and scenes of violence occurred, which were a disgrace to the age. Finally the State militia

was called out, and under the command of the Governor they repaired to the scene of the troubles. In order to appease the wrath of the indignant Gentiles, the Prophet, Jo Smith, his brother Hyrum and two others of the head dignitaries of the Church were arrested hy the Governor and his *posse*, and thrown into prison. A guard was placed around the jail to protect the prisoners from the clamorous mob which was thirsting for their blood. This was on the 25th of June, 1844. On the evening of the 27th, a band of two hundred disguised men overpowered the guard, and breaking into the jail, murdered the two Smiths and badly wounded one of the other prisoners. Somewhat appeased by this sacrifice, the tumult of the mob subsided a little, but it was plainly evident that the Mormons would be obliged to vacate Nauvoo. Brigham Young now stood in the shoes of the deceased Prophet, and preparations were soon being made under his directions, for the removal of the Church to some locality where its devotees might follow their peculiar creed, unmolested by the gentile world. Therefore, by the direction of the High Council, "a company of pioneers, consisting mostly of young, hardy men with their families," were sent in advance of the main body, which was to follow in due season. These pioneers were to halt in some valley of the Rocky Mountains and put in grain, and await the arrival of another division, which was to follow in its wake as soon as practicable. They located in the valley of Great Salt Lake, at the period previously stated, and commenced the work of irrigating the soil, and putting in crops, etc., for the proper reception of their comrades, and they laid out Salt Lake City. Emigrants soon flocked into the New Zion from the Old, and the city began to flourish apace, and to send out shoots into different parts of the Territory of Utah, the population of which now numbered well nigh one hundred thousand souls.

After the resignation of Governor Young, and upon the instalment of Governor Cummings, an event occurred whose only parallel was in the desertion of Moscow by its citizens. In Salt Lake City and in all the settlements north of it commenced a human stampede which continued during the months of April and May. Bidding adieu to their houses and lands, the devoted Mormons migrated in large bodies to the southern end of Lake Utah, where in a half-starved condition they dwelt in every manner of abiding places. Twenty-five or thirty thousand people thus migrated from the northern settlements. Of the deserters from Salt Lake City, the more fanatical burned their dwellings, while others were content with tearing the wood-work from them, or otherwise disfiguring them. On the 26th of June the Utah army, which had left Fort Bridger on the 12th, entered the city, which they found silent and deserted. The troops remained here until the 29th, when they removed to Cedar Valley, their present encampment. The deserting Mormons, who were encamped at Provo, gradually returned to their homes during the summer, and by the latter end of August they were all installed in their old quarters, and affairs soon began to move on in the old way.

This is all the author has to say of Salt Lake City, except that the sight of it did not make the impression on him that it has made on other travelers. This was doubtless because he beheld it at an unfavorable season, when the shade trees along the streets were denuded of their foliage, and when the gardens and orchards, which in the summer form the chief attractions of the city, had lost their bloom, blighted by the severe frosts of November; and besides it had not burst at once upon his view, as the way had been paved for beholding it, by the hamlets and villages he had previously seen. But delightful and refreshing in the extreme must be the sight of this city in the month of June, when the dust-begrimed traveler, emerging from the tortuous, gloomy defiles of the Wahsatch, comes in view of it; its gardens in bloom, its trees robed in leafy verdure, and its cool brooks leaping beneath the gleaming sunlight, forming a paradise when contrasted with the gloomy regions over which he has been journeying.

Brigham Young, the Grand Lama of Utah, was invisible at the time of my arrival in his domains. Some said this was because the eyes of Justice were on his trail to make him answer certain charges alleged against him; others, that the Army had offended him in thus entering his domain without leave or license from his royal self, and that he was undertaking to spite Uncle Sam by clinging like a wrathful spider to his den, and refusing to show himself. He had discontinued the weekly gatherings at the Tabernacle, perhaps to show that the conduct of the "outside barbarians" displeased him, and that he would not be a good boy until the Federal troops were withdrawn from his realm and he was left again in power. On the contrary, his more worldly minded or less stubborn subjects, more intent on filling their purses than battling for the interest of the Church, were in high glee at the existing state of things. Heretofore the only means which the Saints had of acquiring money, whereby to purchase their luxuries, was from the produce sold to that portion of the California emigration which passed through their settlements, and by taking surplus cattle to California; the road to which was mainly over deserts, and for a good portion of the year blocked with snow. Now they had a market under their very eyes, which would relieve them of all their surplus produce at prices to suit themselves, for the great army which had come to subjugate them, but which was now to benefit them, was close at hand. Therefore, as soon as peace was established, the lucre-loving Saint might have been seen wending his way toward the great market house at Camp Floyd with his grain, his flour, his vegetables and his lumber, and coming home with his pockets lined with United States gold, and laughing in his sleeves at the bungling way in which Uncle Sam does

up his work. Even Brigham Young, the grand originator of
the difficulties between his subjects and the Gentiles, had a
share of the spoils, and the lion's share by the way, for the
lumber used in the building of Camp Floyd was from his
cañon. Was there ever anything more preposterously absurd?
Brigham Young, the head of a fanatical Church which, owing
to its iniquities, had been driven from place to place till it had
at last established itself among the gloomy valleys of the Rocky
Mountains, a thousand miles from a civilized country, attempts
to set up a government of his own, where he and his brutalized
subjects may enjoy their peculiar institution unmolested by
and independent of the general government. The latter sends
an army to subjugate the rebels, but it is so delayed that it
does not get under way until the season is far advanced.
While in midst of the Rocky Mountains, and on the verge of
winter, three of its supply trains, which have been left negli-
gently unguarded, are burnt by a small band of Mormons,
who after accomplishing their bold design, get off unmolested.
With imminent prospect of being either starved or frozen to
death before they encounter the enemy, the little army moves
onward, but is finally brought to a halt at Fort Bridger, when
cold winter encounters it, and casting an impassable barrier
of snow before it, says with icy tongues, " Thus far shalt thou
go and no farther." Then the half-starved, benumbed soldiers
commence preparing to meet the terrors and hardships which
await them. A dreary winter they pass, shivering with the
intense cold of those elevated regions and barely keeping body
and soul together by the little sustenance they gnaw from the
gristly bones of their broken-down mules and oxen, and unable to withstand their hardships, many poor soldiers sink
beneath them to rise no more. Spring! thrice welcome
spring! at last comes upon them, and with it come supplies
from the far East, how badly needed is well known. Negotia-
tions for peace are in the meantime going on between the

belligerents, but the little army, having been refreshed, goes
on its way and in due time reaches Salt Lake City, which it
finds deserted. Having taken formal possession of the place,
the army moves off to a locality where it can quietly repose
itself after the exploit, it having orders to molest the Saints
no longer. Other troops follow in the wake of this gallant
vanguard, and numerous trains follow these, laden with provisions and munitions of war. They arrive in Utah and find
peace declared and the enemy not only going unpunished, but
as saucy and insulting as ever, and revelling in the pickings
it gleans from the very army which it was so lately in arms
against and with armed impudence defying in the rock-bound
fastness of Echo Cañon.

Still when we remember how the Mormons were persecuted
by the people of Illinois and Missouri, we cannot wonder at
the bitter feeling they bear towards Americans in general,
particularly as the State authorities did so little to check the
persecution. By pitiless mobs they were the victims of murders and other outrages. The memories of these kept alive
the most bitter feelings. Tar forms an attractive background
for feathers, but for the purpose of cementing friendship between the Mormons and Western Americans it proved a dismal
failure.

In regard to the people of Salt Lake City, then regarded in
the East as a set of fanatical brutes, I was agreeably disappointed in them. Though generally ignorant, they were industrious and sober. Intelligence was generally confined to
the leaders, but not altogether. I was an uninvited listener,
one evening, to an argument between a Mormon lady and a
Gentile of the opposite sex. The former was refined in appearance, and her intelligence was manifest in the way she
met the arguments of her opponent. She was the defender
of the Mormon faith, inclusive of polygamy. To see a woman
among these people well dressed and intelligent was startling,

but to hear her defending a religion whose main tendency was to brutalize her own sex, almost took away my breath, eavesdropper that I was.

The Mormons told me that previous to the occupation of Salt Lake City by the troops, women of a certain class were unknown in the Territory; that no liquor was allowed to be sold; that gambling was not tolerated, and that the town was so peaceable that policemen were unnecessary. Now there were nightly disorders from drunken brawls, and the morals were those of a mining camp. The nightly scenes along East Temple Street struck terror into those of us who were "tenderfeet."

Outside of polygamy I saw nothing bad about the Mormons, and I was with them in their settlements and traveling for six weeks. They excelled the old-time Puritans in ignorance, but not in fanaticism. It may be they put "best foot foremost" in their conduct and conversation when in our presence—I simply describe them as I found them. A comparison between the Mormons and Gentiles I saw in Salt Lake was much at the expense of the latter.

Barring the singular people who inhabit it, Great Salt Lake is the curiosity of the Great Basin. Its islands only are visible from the city, but from the table land back we saw its water gleaming in the sun. In the far background arose bleak, gray mountains, the border of immense tracts of desert land extending towards California.

I give a view of the shores of this great inland sea. It is some 130 miles in length by 75 in breadth, Salt Lake City being at its southern extremity. Its waters are intensely saltish, although most of the streams flowing in it are fresh water streams, the principal of which are the Jordan, Bear and Weber rivers. Although the lake cannot be seen from the city, on account of the intervening bluff, the numerous islands which dot its surface are plainly visible at the distance

GREAT SALT LAKE IN THE TWILIGHT.

of twenty miles, their bold, rugged outlines rising like a wall
across the river.   The largest of these, Antelope Island, was the
exclusive property of the Church, which used it as a grazing

range for its cattle. Between this island and the shore the lake is fordable, so that the stock can be driven over in safety. There they were left until the rich grass on the island had put them in good condition, when they were driven across the mountains to California, where they were sold at remunerative prices; the proceeds going into the coffers of the Church, a large portion of whose revenue came from this source. The edge of the lake is shallow and rocky for some distance, when we come to a hard sand bottom, and the color of the water deepens from green to dark blue. In some places along the rocky beach the salt collects in such quantities that it can be shoveled up by the wagon-load and hauled away for domestic use. Saleratus-whitened bottoms abound along the borders of the lake, over which are scattered pools of stagnant water.

IX.

Among the Mormon Settlements.

WE staid in Salt Lake City until the 12th of November. We were paid off on the 10th. It was optional with us whether to take our discharge at $40 per month or make the round trip at $26. I hesitated a while, but a glance at the snowy range to the eastward, and the knowledge that the trip to the Missouri would take two of the coldest of winter months, even if we could make twenty miles a day, soon decided my course. I would go on to California. About half, mainly Missourians, with one or two Kansans, returned and, we heard, underwent much suffering.

Our party of twenty made arrangements with some Mormon freighters, who were going to Southern California for goods, to convey themselves, provisions and baggage to the Pacific. Their charge was $80 a piece. My wages amounted to $140, after my outfit was deducted. Much of this was spent for needed clothing and my share of utensils and provisions for our mess. I also bought a rifle which I thought I would need, but which I had better have left, as I so much needed afterwards the money it cost.

Our means of conveyance were three four-horse springless wagons, in charge of Sydney Tanner, a veteran Mormon. The other teams were owned by the drivers. We got along pleasantly all through the long and trying journey with these men.

We were to go the southern route, which leads through the lower settlements, and then takes across the Great Sandy Desert via the Santa Fe trail, emerging onto the Pacific at San Pedro, which is eight hundred miles southwest from Salt Lake. This route is only traveled in the winter season, as it is nearly impassable during the summer on account of the extreme heat. The northern route, which is far the shorter and more traveled of the two, strikes towards the north from Salt Lake City, along the eastern shore of the lake to its upper extremity, when it runs a westwardly course until it reaches the Humboldt River, which it follows down to its sink; it then crosses over to Carson River and enters Carson Valley, along the western edge of which lies the Sierra Nevada. The road then crosses these mountains, and branches off in different directions towards the various mining camps. This road, which we would otherwise have traveled, was rendered unpassable by snow, so that we were under the necessity of taking the other route. Our departure was to have taken place on the 11th, but on various accounts we did not get under way until the afternoon of the 12th, when, with twenty passengers and their accoutrements closely crammed in our rude conveyances, we gladly turned our backs upon and said farewell to the Salty City. Passing mainly over the same road which we had followed in our march from Camp Floyd, we encamped in the afternoon of the 13th inside the walls of Lehi. In the evening we were treated to a serenade from a juvenile Mormon band. Prominent among the strains of melody which they rolled out upon the still night air was "The Girl I Left Behind Me," an air which had its due effects on the minds of its rough audience, as it brought up old recollections of times gone by. The musicians were stationed in the *plaza*, or public square, and as the music, which was extremely well executed, reached our

8

ears, as we sat around our bright-glowing campfires, it sounded pleasant, especially when compared with the mutterings of the buffalo, the dismal howling of wolves and the shrill notes of the mosquito, which of old had greeted us.

We started the next morning early, and by 9 o'clock reached Battle Creek. I here beheld my enthusiastic friend, Uncle Job, who looked very much as if he had just awakened from a week's spree. As his blood-shot eyes did not recognize me, I did not notice him, being fearful of another affecting scene. After a half hour's halt, we retook our route; the road laying along the eastern shore of Lake Utah, the surrounding mountains of whose valley were white with snow, although it was warm enough on the plain on which we were journeying. In the afternoon we reached Provo City, which contained a population of about fifteen hundred, and was the second city in point of size and importance in Utah. It is built on both sides of Provo River, a few miles below the cañon, the mouth of which is plainly visible from here, seeming like a gigantic gateway cut through the towering mountains which rise on either side. The winds which came howling down this cañon are felt to a considerable distance from where it opens on to the valley; as if some giant, with a pair of bellows in size proportionate to the undertaking, was at work with his engine back of the mountain. As I looked upon the opening of the cañon, the toils and hardships which I had experienced in its depths a few days before, came vividly to my mind, and I was thankful that I had accomplished that journey, and that the one I was now entering on had so much less privation and so much more romance about it.

The Utah Indians, which abound among the Wahsatch Mountains, and which are extremely warlike, were formerly bad neighbors to the Mormons. After having attacked a settlement they would retire with their booty to the fastnesses of this cañon, where for a long time they defied the enraged Saints.

The latter, at last, routed them out of their principal stronghold, which was near the mouth of the cañon, in the following manner, which was related to me by Captain Littel, one of the conductors of our company, who was engaged in the assault. The stronghold was surrounded on all sides by lofty precipitous rocks, except on the side fronting the river, being a sort of a nook cut into the mountain side. For several days the Indians defied their enemies, who had now gathered from all parts of the valley, resolved to avenge the injuries they had received at all hazards. But the besiegers found that without some new mode of attack their efforts would be unavailing, for the besieged had numerous advantages over them, and had already killed several of their number. The Mormons finally planned and executed a species of moveable breastwork, triangular in shape, and made of thick plank, which they sheltered themselves behind, and shoved before them up the mountain gorge, at the farther extremity of which the Utahs were posted, at the same time pouring a deadly fire from their rifles. The Indians, astounded at this mode of warfare and seeing how their ranks were being thinned by the storm of bullets directed against them, soon stampeded in a body, and, rushing toward the mouth of their stronghold, attempted to escape. Repulsed here, they endeavored to scale the rocky walls which surrounded them, but the pale-faced sharpshooters picked them from their slight footholds and tumbled them to the bottom of the defile. So utterly were the Utahs routed in this encounter, that they never attempted to molest their neighbors again.

We remained but a short time in Provo, when we moved on, and, following along the base of the high range of mountains which rises above the eastern limit of the valley, encamped at night at Springville, a village containing about seven hundred inhabitants and appearing quite prosperous. It had the usual quadrangular *plaza*, from the centre of which a tall pole shot

upward. We left this village early the next day, our route
laying over a desolate, unproductive valley, the soil of which
was covered with alkaline efflorescences and supported nothing
but a stunted growth of artemisia. We came at noon to a
low ridge which stretches across between the two mountains
and formed the dividing line between the valleys of Utah and
Juab. Rolling down the latter valley, over a well beaten trail,
we came, before sunset, to the Spanish Fork settlement: one
of the best built and most flourishing towns in the Territory.
It is surrounded by a good adobe wall, pierced on two sides by
gateways about ten feet wide. The Indians around here were
troublesome, and the cattle of the adjoining farms were driven
inside the walls at night, when the gates were closed and barred,
and guard was mounted until morning. The mode of farmers
living in compact villages prevailed then in Utah, where it
had several advantages. Were the people to live in scattered
farms, as in the States, their lives and property would fall easy
prey to the prowling Indians, who are forever on the watch to
commit depredations; but by thus living in walled villages,
they were enabled to withstand the onsets of their enemies,
and besides have a secure place in which to store their grain
and keep their stock. Another thing which made it convenient
for the people of Utah to live in this manner, was that the
farm land all laid along the edges of streams, the strip being
only as wide as could be easily irrigated, so that the farms
were all close together; in fact, this tillable land was sometimes made common property to all the villagers, and surrounded with an enclosure whose erection was participated in
by the whole community. The fences were generally made of
mud. They were formed by digging a ditch and throwing
the contents between board cases, which were set up on its
margin; the frames being two feet apart at the bottom and
inclining to within one foot of each other at the top, and
about three feet in height. The earth was moistened and

thrown in the case, which was left to stand until its contents had the required hardness, when it was moved a length further on to be refilled in the same way. Did rain fall in these regions, these fences would not last a year, and neither would the dwellings; but as it was, I have seen walls twelve or fifteen feet high, of several years' standing, which were apparently as substantial as ever. The lack of rain which would appear in every way disadvantageous to the Utonians, is not altogether a curse.

As there was a municipal law in Spanish Fork against building open fires inside the walls, we were under the necessity of quartering ourselves on the good citizens, who were glad enough to receive us, for the reason we gave them a half-dollar apiece for our meals. My host was the village miller—a clever man by the way—whose demands were so moderate that he had but one better half, while his neighbors' wives indulged in better thirds, fourths, and so on. I spent an agreeable evening chatting with the good people of the house, as we sat around a huge log fire which was burning brightly in the broad, old-fashioned chimney corner. The supper was a good one, although I strongly suspected that the tea was bogus, as that commodity is so dear in Utah that the inhabitants resort to various means to counterfeit it. Coffee is imitated also; the substitutes being scorched wheat and bread-crust compounded, from which a beverage is concocted which is not so much unlike the genuine article.

It was odd to see well constructed saw-mills, grist-mills, threshing machines and other labor-saving machinery in these out-of-the-world regions; but they are quite common. We may say as hard things as we please about the Mormons, but at the same time let us give them due credit for the enterprise and ingenuity they have displayed in the partial overcoming of the great disadvantages of soil, climate and isolation which they experience. Under the necessity of watering their crops continually to prevent them from being destroyed by the intense, all-pervading drought of these regions, and compelled to haul fuel long distances to keep themselves from freezing during the long and bitter winter, they have decidedly a hard life to lead; and when we consider how the mass of the people, who are honest in the opinions they profess, have been harangued and excited by their fanatical leaders, until they have been led to consider themselves a persecuted race, we should be more lenient towards them than what we are, and allow them to peacefully pursue their favorite hobbies until they become disgusted with them, which they ultimately will.

We emerged from the village gate early in the morning of the 16th, and took our way over a region as desolate and dreary as that passed over the preceding day. Our route lay through the middle of a broad, level valley, lined on either side by low mountain ranges, and we encamped towards sunset at a little, isolated ranche, situated on a small stream which wound over the level plain from its source in the contiguous mountains. There were but two families in the settlement, which looked lonely and unprotected, and as if it would fall an easy prey to an Indian attack. In the course of the evening we were treated to a vocal serenade by a couple of precocious Mormon boys; their song being one of the patriotic effusions gotten up by the Saints during the rebellion; and it was to these what the Marseillaise was to the French Revolutionists. The burden of the song was an extolment of the virtues of the Mormons and their ability to crush Federal troops should they be so foolhardy as to enter their domains. Four lines of this defiant ditty ran thus:

> "The Yankees feared our Brigham Young,
> And Heber, his companion;
> They would have liked to crush us out,
> But they thought of Echo Cañon;"

—in allusion to the pretentious cobblestone fortifications which the rebels had erected in that reverberating ravine for resisting the entrance of the United States troops into the Great Valley. The patriotic ardor with which the infantile Saints rolled forth the song was infinitely refreshing, and their efforts were highly applauded by their gentile auditory.

Passing over a country which became more uneven as we advanced, and which consisted of a continuous chain of valleys bounded on each side by elongations of the same two ranges of the Wahsatch Mountains which flank the valleys of Salt and Utah Lakes, we reached the Sevier River on the afternoon of the 18th. This river, which is about eight rods wide, and so deep that it is hardly fordable, rises among the mountains east of our route, and, flowing through a valley so barren and cold that it is unfit for settlement, sinks about thirty miles below where we crossed it. I have seen few sceneries more dreary than that along this river, which runs with a swift, turbid current between high, steep banks, beyond which extends a desolation-cursed tract of uneven country, covered with low, scattered clumps of wild sage. The Sevier was explored some years ago by a party of Mormons for the purpose of seeking some place along its shores whereon to form a settlement, but they returned unsuccessful, after having narrowly escaped being frozen to death for their trouble.

Having remained long enough to fill our water casks, we crossed the river on a narrow and unsubstantial wooden bridge, which threatened at every step to break and drop us in the rushing waters below. We found a party of soldiers encamped on the opposite shore; being stationed there for the purpose of arresting deserters from Camp Floyd, as numbers were leaving that place nightly and starting for California by this route. There was one of these dissatisfied sons of Mars in our company, whose love of liberty was stronger than his desire for playing soldier in an isolated post, or of exchanging black eyes and bloody noses with an enemy. This was Bently, whose heart fluttered with fear when his eyes caught sight of the white, conical tents, which not only called up memories of old times, but reminded him that they contained certain blue-uniformed individuals whose duty it was to exercise a paternal care over his absconding person. He resolved, however, not to despair, and concealing himself as well as he could beneath the baggage in the wagon to which he belonged, he ran the gauntlet in safety, although the inquisitive eyes of one of the soldiers peered into his place of concealment. What visions of "ball and chain," and "drumming out of the regiment," arose in the deserter's mind about this time, the reader can imagine; suffice to say, he safely crossed the Sevier and the Rubicon. Heretofore Bently had been satisfied to borrow my green goggles, for disguise when passing a post, but the close watch here apparent forced greater precautions.

We encamped after night on a cedar-covered bluff overlooking the valley, and as we had plenty of fuel we managed to keep at bay the cold night air which surrounded us, and our well-fed campfires shot out brightly into the surrounding darkness. The cedar boughs spread on the stony ground afforded us excellent couches, and with our feet turned towards the fire, Indian fashion, we rolled up in our blankets, and slept like kings in state; the earth our bed, the star-lit sky our canopy.

There is a pleasure in camp life, which only those can appreciate who have experienced it : a freedom from all those petty cares and anxieties which beset the mind in the midst of civilization. The soul expands and revels in a creation all its own, as it gazes upon the external world, which, if not endowed with the comforts and refinements of civilized life, is at least bare of its deceit and heartlessness, and there is just enough of danger to be apprehended to keep the mind in a lively state of excitement. In a journey like ours, the desolate but interesting country we were passing over; conjectures as to where our night's camp would be formed; the probability of an attack upon us by our Indian neighbors —all formed subjects for thought and conversation during the day, while our nights were enlivened by the brightly blazing campfires, and by well told tales from lips of those who had been participants in the scenes they were describing, and by broad-mouthed jokes more remarkable for point than refinement. To further make our evening camps interesting, discussions would arise between the Saint and Gentile portions of our company in regard to their respective forms of religion; the former contending with a zeal worthy of a better cause that their "peculiar institution" was ordained by God; and the latter battling for the adverse side of the question; and the dispute would sometimes be continued well on to the noon of night, or until the fires had gone down, when the tear-drawing smoke and chilling atmosphere would warn the testy combatants to repair to their respective dormitories.

We encamped on the evening of the 19th at the foot of a long cañon, and about a fourth of a mile from a stream which had a habit of sinking and rising, like many other streams of this singular country. It was an extremely hilly region, covered with occasional groves of stunted cedars, but supporting only a scanty supply of yellow grass, which sprang up in patches between the omnipresent clumps of wild sage. The night was a very cold one, and the ground was covered with a thin coating of snow, which had fallen while we were in a more northern but less elevated locality. We felt the cold sensibly increasing as we advanced (for the country becomes more elevated as we approach the rim of the Great Basin), and we had great difficulty to keep warm while riding in our clumsy stages, so that occasional pedestrian tours became quite fashionable. These walks, while they kept the blood in circulation, greatly gratified the owners of the teams, as the loads were thereby lightened, and a proportionate amount of mule and horse muscle economized. The teamsters, who for the most part owned their teams, were very careful of their animals during the forepart of the journey, that they might be the better enabled to accomplish the latter, which lay wholly over deserts. Our diurnal drives were rarely over twenty miles, and generally ten or fifteen, and besides the grass which the animals would pick during the night, liberal rations of wheat were given them before and after the day's drive. We commenced ascending the cañon by daylight the next morning, and as it was two miles to the summit of the mountain to which it led, and as the road was slippery from the snow which covered it, the ascent was toilsome to the teams as well as to ourselves, who trudged by their sides. Scattered cedars were growing on the sides and summit of the mountain, their verdant foliage comparing agreeably with the snow-whitened earth. Descending the southern slope over a rough road, we entered Cedar Valley—a broad mountain-encircled plain—and crossing another divide, we reached Fillmore Valley. We came to Fillmore City late in the evening, and halted a while to await the coming of some of our delayed wagons. This city is situated one hundred and sixty miles south from Salt Lake and consists of about a dozen hovels overshadowed by a State House. The latter, which has been built but a short time, is one of the finest buildings in the Territory. Uncle Samuel's purse was phlebotomized copiously during its erection, for in this out-of-the-way place the mice could play to their satisfaction during the absence of the cat. The plan of the building is in the shape of a Greek cross, but at present only one wing was completed. This was built of rough-hewn red sandstone, and was the only stone building I saw in the Territory.

One thing could be said of Fillmore City, which could be said of no other Capitol in the Union: that no intoxicating beverages were sold within its limits! There were thirty individuals in our party—men who conscientiously believed that a proper putting down of spirits was good for keeping up the spirits—and that "Mormon lightning" was an excellent article for lightening up the mind as well as the purse—and these had looked forward to the time when they would arrive in Fillmore City with as much pleasure as the sand-choked Arab gazes upon the blooming oasis in advance of him. But lo! when they arrived in the haven of their thoughts they were doomed to bitter disappointment: for a miserable species of beer was the strongest article to be had for love or money. This and pumpkin pies were the staple productions of Fillmore, and a goodly portion of both articles was disposed of during our short sojourn in the place. We left the city about ten o'clock, and encamped at midnight in the midst of a grease-wood-covered plain, eight miles from the city. The night was cloudy and cold, and in order to protect ourselves from the force of the wind, we built a bulwark of bushes in the form of a circle, and making a good fire in the centre, we laid down, rolled up in our blankets, and endeavored to court the drowsy god; but a rain, which soon commenced falling, made our efforts vain for awhile. "Kind nature's sweet restorer, balmy sleep," at length asserted its sway, and with a dreary wind blowing around me, and a driving rain soaking my blankets, I slept—as well as could be expected.

The next morning we were detained by lost horses. We saw Indians riding along the far edge of the valley and we feared they had stolen them, but the Mormons found them by noon. In the afternoon we passed an isolated house occupied by three women, doubtless the wives of the absent proprietor, some children, and an almost naked Indian. The women had repulsive faces, one of them much older than the

rest, and looked haggard and unhappy. The Indian was inso-
lent, and stood warming himself before the fire, holding in his
hand a bow and arrows. As we had been walking ahead of
the teams, we staid here to warm until they came up; but we
gladly left the house, not liking the looks of the inmates.
Beyond here in a valley we came upon a camp of Mexicans,
on whom I aired my Spanish with poor success. You never
know how little you understand a language until you try to
utilize it. They looked like a pack of land-pirates, with their
knives, broad hats, and heads stuck through the centres of
their blankets.

At sunset we came to a new settlement, called Beaver, composed of three or four hundred people. It had been a disappointment, as there had been frosts every month in the
year. At night we went to a religious meeting held in the
schoolhouse. The congregation was rough, and rudely clad,
in homespun, calico and buckskin. I saw here what reminded
me of the old-time Puritan worship: bowie knives and revolvers in church. There was no regular minister; the services being carried on by different members giving in their
"experience." Their language was rough and ungrammatical,
and some of the narrations so comical as to set the audience
to laughing. Some grew pathetic, and their hearers cried, and
on the whole they enjoyed themselves. One told how, when
once afflicted with a plague of grasshoppers, prayers for de-
liverance were made, when flocks of a peculiar bird, strange
to that country, came among them and devoured them all.

We laid up the next day for the purpose of recruiting our
mules and horses, so our conductors said; but I thought that
the real reason was that the Beaver folks might get some of
our gold. Every village we passed through was formed, for
the time, into a toll house, wherein we would be systematically
relieved of our superfluity of evil's root. Our Mormons, knowing the poverty of their isolated brethren, favored them all

they could by delays. Our abstinence so long from vegetables and dairy products made us keen for them, and they were put on to us at high figures. They also knew our failing for pie, and did a fine trade with us in that circular necessity.

We were visited by a small party of Indians in the forenoon. They came from their dens in the neighboring mountains on a begging expedition—enterprises which the sylvan stoics often engaged in—as the scarcity of game kept them in a semi-civilized state. The Mormons satisfied their demands humbly, for should they excite their wrath, they would fare badly. Even if the Indians did not make an attack on the settlement itself, they would make the whites feel their vengeance some other way: by running off their cattle, or by riddling them with arrows. Besides this their long trips over the desert made them dependent on the good will of the savages. It may be, also, that certain enterprises which the Indians and Mormons had in common, such as the massacre of the Mountain Meadows, made the latter humor their swarthy neighbors for fear they might expose them.

There were two characters among the Indians who visited us; one of whom was a chief, called "Injun Tom" by the townsfolk; the other being self-styled "Worky John." The last could talk but little English, and offered us much sport. He would go through the motions of driving a yoke of oxen, at the same time imitating the conversation usually directed towards them by the average teamster, which made our ex-ox-drivers howl with delight. John was almost naked when he came among us, and as a reward for his entertainment we made him up a missionary box, containing a hat, shirt and trousers. I need not say that the hat was of the shocking bad order, and that the other articles were in tatters, for why should we be expected to donate the pick of our wardrobe to the heathen, more than other more pretentious folks. It was comical to see the Indian putting the last on—wrong side foremost and almost upside down. Finally, with our assistance, he was dressed, when he danced and shouted and leaped and laughed, with his hat on one side and the extremity of his linen floating in the breeze through a rent in his breeches. Then he would mock a drunken man; his stagger and reel, his nodding head and leer of eye showing he had seen the effects of fire-water on the human form.

One thing to the credit of these Indians is their disgust of drunkenness; but, no doubt, as civilization encroaches on them they will acquire the habits of their brothers east of the mountains. I think the Mormons were partly the cause of this, through self-interest, if from no higher motive.

Our visitors left us before noon and made their way towards their dens in the mountains. They returned in the afternoon, with several squaws added—hideous beings, by the way. "Worky John" brought a harem of four, all clad in short mantles of rabbit skin. I could have wished the rabbits in that country grew in proportion to their ears, or that the squaws attained a less altitude, though goodness knows they were squatty enough, rarely attaining a height of over four feet. Their faces were hideous, their hair thick and matted, their breasts long and hanging to the waist—altogether they were horrid objects. One of them had a baby hanging to her back, its form lashed in a willow frame and looking contented and sleepy, as all papooses do. "Worky John" took great pleasure in showing his wives, at the same time strongly hinting that presents to them were in order. Our stock of millinery, jewelry and other articles which delight the eye of women just then being low, we were unable to satisfy his insinuations.

"Injun Tom" differed from "Worky John" in disposition, being morose and sullen. He was dreaded by the Beaverians on account of his influence among the Utes. A thoughtless member of our company, to note its effect, told Tom that the

tribes east of the mountains had banded together to exterm-
inate his own, which much excited him. He then angered
him by calling him a "bad Injun," in the assumption that the
good ones were all dead, or doing sentry duty before cigar
stores. The term seemed full of insult, for on hearing it his
whole nature underwent a change. With wild gesticulations
and glistening of his snake-like eyes he commenced yelling
and screaming a string of phrases, half English and half
Indian, at his insulter, who tried to soothe him when the
Mormons told him what might be the result of his imprudence
in the lone journeys ahead. Tom grew so wild that we feared he
might do bodily harm to his enemy; but the Mormons acting
as peacemakers in part allayed the storm, though the fierce
looks remained on his face still. Before leaving us he extended
his hand towards his insulter, but upon the latter preparing
to meet this proffer of forgiveness, Tom dropped his hand, and
spitting on the ground to show his contempt, turned his back
on us, and, followed by the rest of his gang, struck for the
mountains. As we had to travel a long reach inhabited by his
tribe, our Mormons felt uneasy, not so much from direct
attack, but from stealing or killing of our animals.

One of the beauties of Mormonism had lately been exhibited
in Beaver, where a girl of thirteen had just been married, or
"sealed," as they termed it, to a man of forty. The groom
was a tar-maker, and to see this oddly mated couple two of
our boys visited them, ordering a gallon of tar as an excuse.
Having none on hand, he engaged to make some at once; but
I judge he was stuck with it, as the interviewers, having gratified their curiosity, never fulfilled their contract.

In my notes I refer to the above gentleman as an "old man
of forty," which goes to show what a relative term "old" is.
From my then youthful standpoint he seemed well towards
the foot of life's downward slope; now that I have cut my
fiftieth notch on time's reckoning stick, the man of tar appears

young enough to have needed the consent of parents or guardians to his hymeneal venture.

Under various pretexts we were kept at Beaver till the 24th. Time passed slowly, for our provisions were going fast. We spent it lounging around our campfire, practicing with our rifles on imaginary Indians, and in making pumpkin pie raids on the Mormon huts. We at last started on our way. The mountains on the south we passed by a stony cañon, and descended to the valley of Little Salt Lake, where we encamped after dark by a brackish spring in the centre of a green meadow —a real oasis in the desert. The next day we came in sight of the lake itself, which is fifteen miles long and embosomed in a desert valley, and has no visible outlet.

In the afternoon we reached Red Creek settlement, which was built on a plan admirably adapted for resisting Indian attacks. An adobe wall, twenty feet high and pierced by a single gateway, enclosed an area of one hundred feet each way, and formed the rear wall for ranges of dwellings fronting on the hollow square, where cattle and other belongings could be kept at night. We reached Parowan before sunset, and camped within its walls. This town is two hundred and fifty miles south of Salt Lake, is among the oldest of the Mormon settlements and, with one exception, the best-built town I saw in Utah. It is surrounded by a wall twelve feet high and a mile around, and the public square is enclosed by a picket fence and planted with shade trees. Its people numbered about eight hundred.

Three of us visited one of the citizens after supper. As we wanted to buy some provender, we were cordially met and ushered into a common room, in which there was a bed suggestively wide. We spent an entertaining evening talking on matters not remarkably deep. While on the Utah war, of the incidents and causes of which he was profoundly ignorant, my host said, " Uncle Sam's President now, ain't he ? " I thought this was his little joke, until I found he thought that our national uncle and " Jimmy" Buchanan were one and the same, when he asked, " Uncle Sam's a bachelor, ain't he?" I told him he was, and I expect he detested him on account of his lone state still more than he had, for they all hate the Federal authorities. Our host had three wives, all of whom called him "father" when they addressed him. There was a young squaw in the room also, but whether as wife or help I did not ascertain.

A return caravan passed through the town that night, from which we learned that the Indians ahead were getting troublesome; a fight with some emigrants having aroused their anger.

Early on the 28th we reached the walled town of Cedar City —a half in ruins settlement. It was a sad sight to see so many dwellings, once thronged by busy inmates, going to decay; the roofs falling in, the walls crumbling. About half the people had gone to more favored regions. The remainder looked lonesome and owlish amid the desolation, and doubtless the town would soon be wholly deserted.

We waited several hours here for the rest of the wagons to come up. We employed the time in laying in provisions, as this was our last chance before crossing the desert. The people were taking advantage of this to charge us extortionate prices, when Bishop Lee interfered in our behalf, so that flour fell from $12 to $6 per hundred. This Lee was he who afterwards turned informer, and showed the connection of the Mormons and Indians with the massacre of the Mountain Meadows. Though high in the Church, he did not look much like an ecclesiastic. He was a portly gentleman with a red face, which showed that he liked the good things of this earth, and now and then held converse with departing spirits. He was clad in a showy suit, in which a " boiled shirt," satin vest and cloth coat shone conspicuously: so different from his

9

companions, who wore the roughest clothing. He was quite voluble, though the occasional expletives showed him a little profane for a Bishop.

Cedar City boasted the only iron works in Utah; but they were a failure, as the ore could not be made to "flux," and no fire clay could be found to stand the required heat.

The expected teams having come up, we left the settlement. Our road laid for a mile along the large farm which was surrounded by a palisade of jagged cedar logs. We encamped at night in a pass leading up the inner slopes of Fremont's Basin, by a little spring of sulphur, which we could hardly drink. The night was very cold, but with a wind-break of cedar boughs and plenty of fire, we endured it until morning. We reached Panther Creek at noon: the last settlement on the great highway to California.

X.

Along the Desert Border.

A BROAD expanse of wilderness, on which there was not a civilized habitation, now lay before us; the first settlement being four hundred miles distant. Visions of bleached skeletons, parched lips, stinted rations, and all the dismal belongings of desert travel, arose in my mind as we left the little settlement of Panther Creek and resumed our route up the uneven slope of the mountain. We encamped at night on a desolate valley opening onto the Mountain Meadows.

These meadows, which we entered the morning of the 30th, are situated on the summit of the "Rim of the Basin," at the elevation of five thousand feet above the sea, and consist of a level valley a mile in width, and seven miles in length. By the Spaniards it bore the name of Las Vegas de Santa Clara, and was the place where the great caravans bound to New Mexico from California rested to recruit their animals, famished and wearied by their toilsome journey over the Great Desert. Our route lay down the valley over a good, well-beaten trail, and we encamped at noon by a little stream, which barely afforded enough water for ourselves and animals.

Close by our camping place occurred the notorious massacre of the Mountain Meadows, where, in the autumn of 1857, one hundred and nineteen persons were brutally murdered by a party of Indians, and Mormons disguised as such. It was a company of emigrants on their way from Arkansas to California via the Southern Route, who from some cause had aroused the anger of the Saints. With the exception of a few of the children, who were thought too young to ever be able to give an account of the affair, the whole party was destroyed; the children being scattered among the white murderers of their parents, after the massacre. After some time they were sought out by their friends and brought to Salt Lake City, where they remained until the summer of 1859, when they were taken to California by the Government, but not until they had criminated several Mormons among the assassinators of their parents. A cluster of sunken graves, and the remains of a hastily thrown-up fortification, were all that now marked the spot where the unfortunate emigrants perished.

I was not aware at the time that the Mormons were in any way connected with the massacre, further than in burying the victims and taking care of the survivors, and with the rest of the Gentiles drank in as gospel the account of the affair given by our conductors, although I wondered at the time why they had so much aversion to talking on the subject. I give below the Mormon version of the massacre as told me by one of our conductors:

"The emigrants, on arriving at the watering place, were visited by a party of Indians whom the former (pretending friendship towards them) invited to a large feast which they were going to have served up in the afternoon; an ox having been slaughtered for the purpose. In order to rid themselves of the Indians, the flesh of the ox was poisoned by the Americans, as was also the water of the spring; but the Indians found out the stratagem in season to prevent its effects. They took no notice of it at the time, but at daybreak the next morning attacked the camp of the emigrants, which the latter had fortified in anticipation of an assault, and took vengeance on their enemies by murdering all but the younger children.

The Mormons, on hearing of the outrage, immediately repaired to the scene of carnage, where they interred the dead; after which they took the living to their homes, where they were kindly taken care of until their friends came after them."

In spite of the assertions of the Mormons to the contrary, there is no doubt but what they were the principal actors in this fearful tragedy, and that they were closely leagued with the Indians; else why was it that small parties of Saints were enabled to pass through a region infested by savage tribes, which boldly attacked and robbed large bodies of American Gentiles. Bishop Lee, of Beaver, afterwards confessed to being one of the principals of the massacre, and that it was instigated by Mormon officials.

The country became more rough and uneven as we advanced. Filling our casks at a little stream which crossed our path, we made a dry camp at nightfall, on the summit of the rim of the Great Basin. As we were now approaching a region infested by dangerous Indians, a council of war was held in the evening, for the purpose of choosing officers, appointing guards and making regulations for the government of our company. Sydney Tanner, an old mountaineer and veteran Mormon, was unanimously elected captain, and a gentleman who figured in the *New York Clipper* under the *nom de plume* of "Sporty" was chosen sergeant of the camp guard, which was hereafter to be mounted at night; each guard to be composed of two men, and to stand so many hours at a time. The passengers volunteered to stand camp guard, while the more difficult horse guard was to be performed by the teamsters. A short but comprehensive address was made by the captain in regard to our intercourse with the Indians, so that collisions might be avoided, after which the meeting broke up with three loud cheers for the officers elected. Roughly clad, sunburnt, and "bearded like the pard," we formed quite a picturesque group, as we stood encircling a huge campfire, which threw a bright glare over all, and boisterously deliberating on "affairs of great pith and moment." The fact of our being on the culminating point of the ridge dividing the waters flowing into the Pacific from those losing themselves in the Great Basin, was enough to make our camp interesting, while the rugged mountains surrounding us, and the idea of having cast ourselves loose from the bonds of civilization to traverse a region remarkable for its physical features, and the dangers which await the traveler from Indian attack while traversing it, added additional interest to the scene.

I awoke in the morning with a rather peculiar sensation of moisture about my face, and, upon opening my eyes, I was made aware of the disagreeable fact that a snow-storm was raging above us and robing the face of nature, as well as my own, with a mantle of white. The blankets and heads of our party were covered also, and it was amusing to see the sleepers as they awoke from their heavy slumbers (so heavy that they were unaware that Dame Nature in her generosity was furnishing them with an additional coverlet) and brushed the spongy element from their eyes, preparatory to gazing upon the outer world. It was not a very agreeable predicament to be in, but we philosophically arose and shook the accumulated snow from our blankets, and stowing them in our wagons, we were soon absorbed in our breakfast-cooking operations—operations which were carried on in the face of great difficulties, for the fast falling snow, which was accompanied by rain, had a great tendency to extinguish our fires, and consequently our patience. We were detained until near noon by the storm and the difficulty in finding our animals, which had scattered over the neighboring hills, but we at last got under way and commenced our descent of the "Rim of the Basin." Passing down a rough road, particularly dangerous to the wagons on account of the numerous "jump-offs" we encountered, we at last reached the head waters of the Santa Clara, a stream flowing into the Pacific through the Virgin and Colorado. By a route four hundred miles long we had crossed the Great Basin, and we now stood again on the Pacific slope, which we had traveled over five weeks before. We soon reached the valley of the Santa Clara, a rough, sandy flat a half a mile in width, well timbered along the stream with cotton-woods, and flanked by bleak and rugged mountains. Evidences of a tremendous flood, which had swept this valley the preceding spring, were continually visible in the trunks of trees and driftwood that strewed the bottom. The trail had been obliterated by the rushing waters, and we were now traveling over an exceedingly rough road, which had been barely laid out by the few wagons that had passed down the valley since the freshet. These freshets, which occur every spring from the melting of the snows which have accumulated among the mountains during the winter, come pouring down the tributaries of the Santa Clara in torrents, to join their volumes in its valley, between whose rocky bluffs they rush headlong to the Pacific, carrying devastation in their wakes. A rain-storm came on us in the afternoon, and we were obliged to make an early halt, camping at the base of a precipitous steep whose summit arose perpendicularly a thousand feet above us.

About half way up the side a cave was seen. To this I ascended, and found it to be a deserted Indian home, as signs of fire were visible on the floor, and the sides of the chamber were blackened with smoke.

The morning of the second of December dawned upon us clear but cold, and a strong wind was blowing through the dreary valley. We made an early start, and continuing down the river over a trail which offered numerous obstructions to our weary animals, by way of deep sand, rocks and bad fordings, we came upon a party of travelers encamped by a little nook on the roadside. They were in a sorry predicament, indeed, as two of their wagons had broken down, and they would be

obliged to remain until they could get them repaired at a
Mormon settlement the other side of the mountain. They
were surrounded by a gang of naked Indians, of the Santa
Clara tribe, whose impudent demands for provisions they were
thoughtlessly complying with; not thinking that the more
they would give to these beastly wretches, the more they would
ask for. The Santa Claras, which are the most dreaded
Indians on the route, thickly infest the regions around here,
and by murder and robbery lay a heavy toll on the emigration passing through their cheerless domains. The cold
rain of the preceding night had been a godsend to us, as it
had been the means of keeping these Indians within their dens;
had it been otherwise the whole tribe would soon have been
apprized by its scouts of our coming, and our night's camp
would have been thronged by the red scamps, who by begging and stealing would have materially lessened our supply
of provisions, which we were obliged to husband carefully, as
we had scarcely enough to carry us through. Soon after
passing this encampment we met a return exploring party of
Mormons, who had been, as they said, on a search for more
tillable territory whereon the new-comers to the Church of
Latter Day Saints might settle, as the amount of land in Utah
capable of being successfully cultivated is very limited, on
account of the small quantity of water for irrigating purposes
that these rainless regions afford. The party had been absent
some months on their perilous enterprise—perilous on account
of the risks they ran of dying by thirst and starvation in the
desolate country traversed—and showed haggard faces and
tattered garments. Although the explorers had ostensibly
gone for the above purpose, they had doubtlessly been sent to
seek some new abiding place for the Saints, in the event of
their being ousted from their present locations by the Federal
troops. The leaders of the Mormons had for some time been
keeping themselves in readiness for such an event, and I was

informed by one of our conductors, that in the heart of the great desert regions lying west of the Mormon settlements, a fertile valley had been discovered, which, on account of the small quantity of water found along the route leading to it, could only be attained by small companies at a time. Here, should they be driven from their present abodes, they could form a distinct empire of their own, even more isolated than the country they now inhabit, where, revelling in the slough of polygamy to their hearts' content, they might bid defiance to the United States, whose troops could only reach the Mormons in small squads, which could be cut off easily by the "Destroying Angels."

A little after noon we reached a point on the Santa Clara where the trail leaves it to the left, a short distance above its junction with the Rio Virgin. The scenery along the whole of the eighteen miles which we had traveled down the valley was particularly wild and rugged, and extremely interesting to those fond of viewing nature in her roughest aspects. Rocks piled on rocks arose upon the view above a narrow, sandy valley, through the middle of which a small river was dashing and foaming on its oceanward way. Near where we left it, a bold escarpment of rock of a bright vermillion color arose above the left bank of the river, making a pleasing variation to the sombre hue of the surrounding scenery. Filling our water casks, we left the Santa Clara, and climbing a steep, sandy bluff we found ourselves on a desert plateau, in the centre of which arose a mountain two thousand feet in height, and covered from near its base to its summit with a thick covering of snow. Striking across this plain in the direction of a deep gorge in the mountain, we passed, near the roadside, a singular rock, which was about twenty feet in height, length and thickness, being remarkably square. It lay poised upon a pile of other rocks, on to which it had rolled from a neighboring hill, on whose slope were a few more specimens of the same kind, apparently ready to follow in the wake of their cubical comrade. About sunset we entered the defile before referred to, up which we commenced our toilsome ascent of the mountain. The trail was sometimes so shut in by obtruding rocks as to hardly allow the passage of our wagons. We at length reached the snow line, and here the cold grew so intense that our blankets and overcoats were brought into requisition to keep us from freezing. Shortly after entering the cañon we were overtaken by a chief of the Santa Claras, who, enraged that so large a body should pass through his domains without paying the usual toll, had started in pursuit of our caravan, hoping to yet squeeze from it a little tribute. He was very impudent in his demands, which our Mormon friends partially satisfied with presents of flour and clothing, after which he left us. Naked as he was, he went bounding through the snow apparently unconscious of the inclemency of the weather, and was soon out of sight.

It was far into the night when we reached the summit of the mountain, around which a fierce tempest was blowing and chilling us to the bone, as with shivering limbs and chattering teeth we trudged through the snow by the side of the jaded teams. It was near midnight when we reached a point near the foot of the cañon on the far side of the summit, where we encamped after a march of thirty miles, ten of which had been over the mountain. The cutting wind still howled around our heads with unabated fury, and owing to this, together with the darkness of the night and the scarcity of fuel, we were necessitated to go to bed minus our supper, although we had eaten nothing since morning. Our chief thoughts were as to how and where we would pass the remainder of the night. We now regretted more than ever that we had not provided ourselves with tents when starting on our journey, for it was almost unbearable to lie out in the open air on a night like this. An exploring party having found some cedars on the opposite

side of the cañon—which had here expanded to a fourth of a
mile in width—we repaired thither, and building a fire in a
sort of ravine, which broke the force of the wind, we passed a
dismal night. Few had more than one pair of blankets wherewith to fight off the cold, and these were spread on the stony
soil, making a couch that none could sleep upon but weary
travelers like ourselves. The cold had considerably abated
by morning, when we emerged from the cañon into a dreary
desert which lay spread before us, covered with thorny vegetation of all sizes, from the stunted prickly pear to the yucca tree
growing to the height of twenty feet, and a foot in diameter.
The yucca is a singular tree, and gives a peculiar appearance to
the country in which it grows. The wood is soft and spongy,
and the fibres are locked and twisted to an extent rendering it
impossible to separate them. The limbs, which project hori-
zontally, are short, thick and blunt; from their extremities
project circular clumps of bayonet-shaped spines a foot in
length, which are stiff and armed with thorny points. On account of the singular formation of its formidable-looking leaves
the plant is sometimes known as the "Spanish Dagger." These
leaves are of a vivid green color, and are in pleasing contrast
with the few gloomy-hued plants of the desert. The yucca is
short lived, and in localities where it abounds the earth is
thickly strewn with prostrate trunks, which are nearly as light
and porous as so much cotton. It burns freely, but owing to
the sickening odor it emits, is not in much demand for fuel.

The tree is shown in the foreground of the next illustration,
which is sketched from memory.

Traveling for fifteen miles over a plain of sand and gravel,
which abounded with yuccas and other thorny plants, we
halted after noon at a camping place known as the "Beaver
Dam." In the evening a party of fifty or sixty men came up
with us and encamped near, intending to travel with us until
the end of the journey. We now numbered near a hundred

APPROACH TO THE VALLEY OF THE RIO VIRGIN.

and fifty men, a force amply sufficient to withstand a large force of Diggers, for whose appearance we kept a strict watch nightly.

We were under way a little after sunrise the next morning (4th), and crossing a tract of sandy desert, six miles in width, we came upon the valley of the Rio Virgin, and here I cast my eyes on one of the most disagreeable sceneries I saw in my trans-continental trip. Imagine a level, sandy valley, bounded on either side by bluffs of rock and yellow sand, through the centre of which a turbid, crooked river is flowing between steep-cut banks. Imagine the narrow plain covered at intervals with weeds and thorns, and a bright noontide sun pouring upon the glaring sands its dazzling beams, and you can judge of the impression which the sight of the valley of the Rio Virgin made upon me. A few miles above where we struck it the river flows between precipitous rocks, which rise to the height of two thousand feet, forming a gigantic gateway, through which the muddy waters dash and foam on their way to the sandy plain beyond. Shortly after we entered the valley we met a band of Diggers, who accompanied us for some time.

Continuing down the dreary valley, over a road filled with deep sand, through which our horses and mules wearily waded, we camped on the right shore of the river, after a journey of eighteen miles. This camp was in New Mexico, through the northwestern part of which the trail passes. Our evening's camp was enlivened by another cotillon, the participants of which danced to the music of a well-played violin. It was odd to hear sounds of mirth, revelry and music ascending from such a forsaken region. As the Terpsichorean performers moved through the intricate "figures," they would occasionally stumble over the clumps of sage-brush which covered the camp, and considerable confusion was occasioned thereby. A party of Diggers had visited our camp early in the evening. Hearing our shouts and music, they repaired in a body to the spacious ballroom and enjoyed with infinite glee the antics of the obstreperous palefaces. One of the latter having been jilted by his partner, entered the ranks of the dusky aborigines, and, heedless of the consequences that might ensue from the act, dragged one of them (a sort of one-horse chief) out into the cotillon. The Digger took the joke in good part, and capered about in great glee, occasionally giving vent to his feelings in yells of delight, and war-whoops delivered off-hand, as he was pulled and hauled by his not very gentle comrade. His swarthy brethren appeared to enjoy the sport as much as himself, and their gentle guffaws showed them of a less stoical mood than their brethren west of the mountains.

While these saltatory festivities were in progress, our conductors were on nettles for fear the imprudent among us would commit some act provocative of future trouble by their familiarities with the savages. These Indians were the best natured I met on my travels, and the only ones I ever saw enjoy a hearty laugh; but so changeable and treacherous were they by nature, that the least going beyond the mark by our men would anger them in a moment, and set them to concocting some scheme for our injury. The Mormons, being the greatest probable sufferers from any misunderstanding which might arise, did their best to quietly prevent any outbreak; in fact, throughout the journey they showed remarkable tact, both in their dealings with the Indians and our own men.

Bill Bently, our deserter, owned a pup which he had bought of a Mormon at Beaver. He was fat and sleek, but gave little promise of future worth. A bright-looking, skeletonized dog, owned by one of our Indian visitors, took Bently's attention, and he proposed a trade, and not knowing a Digger's predilection, expected to give boot. The Indian gave one look at the fat puppy, and with an affirmative grunt agreed to swap, when the bargain was consummated in mutual satis-

faction. The Indian dog, under protest, was absorbed into
our mess, while the Mormon pup was doubtless soon assimi-
lated into the aboriginal system. The Indians have a penchant
for cooked dog, from the half-civilized tribe bordering the
western frontiers to the brutish wretches who infest the Great
Sandy Desert.

Throughout the forty miles which we traveled along the
valley of the Rio Virgin, the same general features were
presented: a sandy bottom of various width, bordered by
square-cut bluffs which increased in height as we advanced.
We used sparingly of the water of the river, which possesses
deleterious qualities, as its upper tributaries are fed by
poisonous springs. We crossed the river twelve or thirteen
times at rocky or quicksandy fords, where the stream was so
deep that its rushing waters came up to the beds of the
wagons, which were sometimes in danger of being swept down
the current. The road was a bad one the whole distance,
passing over a continuous bed of deep, yielding sand, which
worried our teams so badly that the passengers were obliged
to make pedestrianism a profession a good portion of the way.

At sunset on the 5th we reached that point on the Rio
Virgin where the Santa Fe trail leaves it and strikes south-
westwardly across the Sandy Desert. We encamped on the
shore about a mile from the *mesa*, or plain, which here rises
abruptly to the height of five hundred feet. Hardly had we
halted before the neighboring bluffs were seen alive with
Diggers, who came out of their cavernous habitations in
swarms to look at us. Some descended to the valley and
came running to the camp, where they greeted us with cries
of "*shetcop ashendy!!*" (give us something to eat). They
were grotesque specimens of humanity, especially the old men,
and were nearly naked, what few clothes they had amongst
them being tattered apparel which they had begged or
stolen from passing caravans.

A single garment was the average.   One would have a pair of pantaloons so torn that had there been a background of shirt and any street urchins in the vicinity, he would have been told there was mail matter awaiting call.   Another would have a coat split down the back like a locust shell, a third would have a shirt only, and a fourth only a hat.   Some had quivers of panther skins hung over their shoulders.   These were filled with arrows made of reeds and pointed with sharp flints, bound on with fine sinews.   Their bows were three or four feet long, and made either of wood or from elk-ribs neatly spliced together.   These last must have come from the East, as there is nothing larger than rabbits in this section.   Their bows are powerful, and will send an arrow through the body of an ox or horse, as passing emigrants have often learned to their sorrow.   These Indians had no fire-arms.   The head men knew our conductors well from previous intercourse, and shook hands with them quite ostentatiously ; winding up with the everlasting cry of " *shetcop*," a word which springs as naturally to a Digger's lips as does " *backsheesh* " to those of their near relative, the Egyptian Arab.   Shortly after their arrival in camp they commenced dragging fuel from distant points for our use, for which service they expected liberal pay in food and raiment.   Our animals were given in their charge. The Mormons adopted this plan altogether while traveling in these regions, and were rarely troubled with having stock stolen ; for the Diggers, through interested motives, were true to their trust.

XI.

On the Great Sandy Desert.

WE were now on the borders of a desolate region, extending westward from three to four hundred miles; as truly a desert as the Great Sahara; a land of sand, gravel and rocks; with occasional brackish springs and streams which lost themselves awhile under the surface, again to appear; their courses, when above ground, marked by stretches of salt grass and thorny shrubs and prickly plants. In all this domain there was not an inhabited building, not even a tent for the protection of its savage inhabitants, such as are used by the Indians of the East, for they lived in caves or flimsy hovels made from reeds and mud. A glance eastward over the shores of the Rio Virgin showed mountain after mountain, bare and bleak, rolling backward until lost to view in the hazy distance.

The next morning we intended to have made an early start, as we had a twenty mile desert to cross before reaching water, but we were detained until ten o'clock by being unable to find one of our horses. A party of eight men, who had an outfit of their own, and who had joined us a few days previously for protection, became impatient of the delay and pushed forward, heedless of the consequences. We watched the little party with interest as it slowly moved away from our night's encampment toward the trail which strikes the bluffs some two miles distant.

10   (153)

The most difficult ascent between the frontiers and the Pacific
is up these bluffs. The wagon was drawn by two half-famished
Indian ponies, which seemed hardly able to draw themselves
up the steep, independent of their wagon, and we did not
expect to see them reach the summit. In the dim distance
the men looked like pigmies tugging and toiling at the
wheels, as they aided their equine comrades up the toilsome
ascent. Attaining the summit at last, they fired a volley of
shots and gave exultant shouts, to let us poor, belated fellows
know that they could go as well without us as in our company, little thinking how soon they would need our assistance.

Having lost much precious time searching for the lost
horse, we finally concluded that the Indians had run it off
and eaten it, and resolved to push on. Our cavalcade was
two hours in ascending the bluffs. The passengers were
obliged to put their shoulders to the wheels of their respective
vehicles, in aiding the panting teams up the precipitous, stony
steeps which barred our progress, and we were glad when we
at last stood secure on the top of the dangerous declivity, in
some parts of which the slightest accident would have hurled
wagon and team into defiles hundreds of feet below.

We had an extensive but not inviting prospect from our
elevation of the desolate valley beneath our feet, beyond which
arose a range of bleak and rugged mountains. We did not
stop long to meditate, however, but as soon as the last team
was up, struck across the broad desert plateau which lay
spread before us: a barren tract of sand and gravel, its apparently level outlines occasionally broken by bold, isolated
mountains, which arose in dismal grandeur to the height of
two thousand feet. I say the plain was apparently level, for it
was occasionally broken by yawning chasms where the earth
seemed to have been rent assunder by terrific convulsions of
nature. One of these chasms, around one end of which the trail
passed, was about two hundred feet in width by fifty in depth,

and extended as far as the eye could reach. The bottom was covered with jagged, splintered rocks, which had at one time been subjected to intense heat, and the sides, which arose perpendicularly above it, were rough and uneven and covered with sharp projections. Gulches like this are quite common on the Great Desert, and as it is unreasonable to suppose that they have been hollowed out by floods, as rain rarely if ever falls in these regions, we are forced to conclude that the *underpinning* of the earth's surface has given way in such places and allowed it to sink. The peculiar formation of the earth here to some distance below the surface, which had the appearance of having once been a mass of molten lava, gives rise to the supposition that at some remote time the country had been covered to a considerable depth with the vomitings which made this plain one vast sea of fire.

Our road was exceedingly rough from the bed of stones which covered it, and we traveled slowly. Late in the afternoon we were overtaken by an Indian with the missing horse, which we supposed had long since been disposed of by horse-beef appreciating Diggers and was quietly reposing in their stomachs. But the Indians had been true to their charge, and after a long search for the missing animal had found him. The Mormons wishing to instil into his mind the trite maxim, "Honesty is the best policy," and to further enable him at some future time to resist the temptation of converting live horse into beef, liberally rewarded the conscientious Digger with *shetcop* and clothing, and he retraced his steps rejoicingly and in a brisk canter.

It was near midnight when, having crossed the *jornado*, we descended a steep, sandy bluff and encamped in the midst of pitchy darkness on the shores of the Rio de los Angeles, or rather where it should be, as the river is here subterranean. We procured enough of water, however, in a marsh close at hand, but it was disagreeably brackish. We found encamped near by the eight impatient travelers who had left us in such fine style in the morning. They were in a sorry plight, indeed, for they were surrounded by a pack of yelling Diggers who had them completely in their power. They had stolen their rifles, and were now rummaging their baggage and appropriating such articles, as took their fancy, to themselves, while the humbled eight looked on and trembled. The Diggers desisted from their plundering upon our unexpected appearance, and were finally induced to make restitution from threats of punishment. What would have become of the party had we not seasonably arrived, I can only guess; but it is probable that they would have gone the road of the many others whose uncoffined bones are bleaching on the sands of the desert.

The morning of the 7th dawned upon us clear and bright, and found us encamped on a swampy flat abounding in salt grass, and occasionally covered with thickets of thorny bushes. We were soon visited by hosts of Indians, men, women and children; all clamorously demanding *shetcop*. There were proportionally few squaws, numbers having been carried off by neighboring tribes and sold as slaves in the settlements of New Mexico. What few we saw were extremely ugly. They were low in stature (which was mostly under four feet), thickset and waddling in their gait. They wore scanty mantles, made by sewing several rabbit skins together, which were loosely thrown around them, in "mother Hubbard" style. Their faces were even more repulsive than those of the males, being wrinkled and brutish, and with eyes that glared like those of a beast of prey. They were abject slaves to the men, and while the latter were hanging around our fires and pestering us for *shetcop*, their women and children were squatted in a group by themselves: the picture of humility and abasement. Some of the squaws wore on their heads a sort of bowl made of willow branches closely woven together, which was made to answer the double purpose of head-dress and goblet: a convenient arrangement.

These Indians were of the Pah-Utah tribe, and were similar in physical appearance and attire to their brethren of the Rio Virgin, whom they, however, excelled in impudence. As they were continually and vociferously crying for *shetcop* (something to eat), and as our conductors wished particularly to gain their good will, a call was issued to our company for alms in the shape of flour for the famished Diggers. This was made by the captain and was responded to with right good will by the different messes, so that enough of flour was raised to make three kettles of "hasty pudding." The Diggers, in hopes that they would not be disturbed by the "Americats" in their culinary operations, repaired with their provender to a little distance from our encampment, where they built fires, and placing over them the camp-kettles filled to the brim with an uninviting mixture of flour and water, squatted around them, waiting anxiously for the decoction to come to a boiling point. Two old and withered gentlemen, the patriarchs of the flock, were the appointed *chefs de cérémonie*, their business being to stir the pudding, a task they performed with becoming gravity, while their juniors looked on with mouths watering as they thought of the forthcoming feast. It was as much as the venerable cooks could do to keep the others from pitching pell-mell into the provender before it was half cooked. As soon as it had reached the scalding notch, the famished guests made a rush, and with wild cries crowded around the mess like so many swine each one fearful of not getting his share. Such pushing, scrambling and yelling I never beheld. Some would get their cups full of the beverage and sneak off to some locality where they could enjoy it unobserved, while others would dip their hands into the scalding contents of the kettles and lick them with evident relish. In the uproar about as much was spilled as was eaten,

but the Digger is by no means particular in his diet, and the
mush was scratched from the earth and gobbled down, sand
and all. We were fearful that the "ladies" would fail to get
their just allowance of *shetcop*, as their selfish lords seemed
disposed to appropriate the whole amount to themselves, but
we changed our opinions when we saw a cunning old squaw
step quietly in and take possession of one of the camp-
kettles, while the rest of the porcine group were squabbling
over the others. Returning to a safe distance with her prize,
she seated herself by it, and drawing the drapery of her
mantle around it, secured it from the gaze of prying eyes. It
was mirth-provoking to see the old "Diggeress," as seated by
her prize, she now and then gave us a knowing look. It was
with infinite satisfaction that she at last saw the contentious
crew start for a neighboring thicket, in close pursuit of two
camp-kettles which two enterprising gentlemen had made
bold to bear off for their exclusive benefit. Watching her
opportunity, she called up the squaws and papooses, who
had long been in the background of the scene, and unveiled
to the gaze of watchful eyes her "mess of pottage;" when
with exceeding zest the whole party fell to work and the
beverage disappeared with astonishing rapidity : the ladies
with the bowl-shaped bonnets faring the best, as they could
dip out a goodly portion at a time, while their less fortunate
comrades were constrained to make use of the convenient
goblet of Diogenes—the hollow of the hand. The whole
scene was rife with side-splitting merriment, and the performers were greeted with uproarious laughter by the compact circle of "Americats" which crowded around them, in
spite of the cries of "*Piquee! Piquee!*" (go away! go away!)
which were yelled at them by the annoyed Diggers.

The Pah-Utahs are the poorest and most degraded we saw
of all the Indians east or west of the Rocky Mountains. They
are kept in continual subjection by the powerful tribes of the

Utahs and Parowans, who chase them from their hunting
grounds and confine them to a strip of desert country, which
barely affords them enough sustenance to keep them from starving. Their diet for the most part is such as the ancient witches
were wont to feed on ere starting on their expeditions for tor-
menting mortals: snakes, lizards, toads and frogs, and such other
reptiles which the warmth of the sun draws from beneath the
surface of these cheerless regions. In order to dislodge this
delectable "game" from their lairs, many of the Diggers go
armed with hooked sticks. Some of these animals they swallow raw, merely jerking off the tail by way of "dressing."
Even of this disgusting food they rarely have a sufficiency, and
are mostly in a state of semi-starvation, so that we can partially
excuse them for the begging and thieving which necessity
compels them to resort to as a means of supporting existence.
Some live in caves, while others live in miserable tents. Their
abodes are always in a horrible condition of filth, and those of
us who were venturesome enough to explore their interiors,
found them inhabited by miserable humanity and reeking
with vile odors. They are very cowardly, and will never
attack whites unless they are overwhelmingly in the majority,
and then in the dead of night. They are more dreaded for
their thievish than their warlike habits by travelers, who suffer sometimes severely from the inroads they make upon their
animals. The language of these Indians is composed of but
few words, and those merely relate to their animal wants; the
accent being strikingly similar to that of the Spanish.

It was near 10 o'clock before we left our interesting camping
place; our route lying up a broad, sandy valley, occasionally
varied by miry flats, which were white with alkaline exuda-
tions, and giving forth a sickening odor. We at length
struck the river, which was two rods in width, its tortuous bed
sometimes deepening into holes of unknown depth. Its water
was impregnated with sulphur and very warm. Crossing the

river, we stood on the edge of a *"jornado,"* near sixty miles in
width. Filling our water casks, we left the gloomy valley of
the Rio de los Angeles (river of the angels), and ascending a
broad, square cañon, nine miles in length, and strewn with the
debris of a disruptured world, we reached an uneven desert
plateau, where, from all parts of the compass, the most awful
desolation stared us in the face. Those in the "States," who
imagine the whole of our western territory to be one vast tract
of towering forests and verdant prairies, could hardly be
brought to realize the fact, that within the limits of oúr Republic are regions of such frightful desolation as these. They
read of the sterile, waterless plains covered with beds of moving sands and shattered rocks, which lie spread in desolate
grandeur over the Old World, little thinking of the vast expanse of similar desert region that mars the beauty of our
country. Doomed forever to remain as it is, the abiding place
of those who only in form can lay claim to belong to the
human family, and of loathsome reptiles, deadly in their sting,
its wildness can never be subdued. Desolation sits enthroned
on those cheerless domains, and with a ghastly smile surveys
her awful realm, populated with hosts of distorted specimens of
the animal and vegetable kingdom!

From the time I left the prairies of Nebraska my narrative has contained so many abusive adjectives in reference to
the country traversed, so much disparagement of its soil, rocks,
water and vegetation, that I fear the reader will think it owed
me something it would not pay, and that I was taking a means
to slander it wherein it could not talk back. But my language has been none too strong. The blight on part of the
land may have been caused by an exceptional drought; but the
desolation was mainly normal; so I will let these adjectives remain propped up against their relative nouns, at the risk of bearing them over with too much support. I may have been seemingly too harsh also in my reference to my brother teamsters, the

Mormons and the Indians, particularly the Diggers, but as few of them will get hold of this book, and those who do in all likelihood can't read, I will waste no more apologies on the one than the other.

Over a region like that described our caravan slowly journeyed, after entering the limits of the Great Sandy Desert. The road was so rough from the stones, that strewed it at suitable distances for jolting our corporeal systems to pieces, that we found it about as pleasant to walk as ride in our spring-minus diligences. We halted at sun-down, when about fifteen miles on our journey, to refresh ourselves and animals with food and rest, but only for an hour, when we pushed ahead and continued on our way till midnight. During the latter part of our march the road had been an ascending one, and our encampment was on the summit of a ridge—the culminating point of the *jornado*, or waterless stretch. We had this day traveled about thirty miles.

We made an early start on the morning of the 8th, the sun of which shone on us through the medium of a chilling atmosphere. Owing to the representations of our Mormon conductors, we had expected to find the weather in this region oppressively warm, and consequently many of our party had disposed of their blankets and heavy clothing in the settlements. They now seriously felt the want of these articles, for the weather was for a good part of the time uncomfortably cold, particularly mornings and evenings. We left our elevated camp by a gradually descending road, which passed over a country similar to that on the other side of the divide, and in twenty-five miles reached a broad, level valley, known as "Las Vegas," or the Meadows, where we arrived late in the afternoon. Crossing the valley, which was three miles in width, we came upon the remains of a Mormon settlement. Some years ago a colony was planted here by the Saints; the intention being to form a half-way station between their colonies in Utah and California, where the emigrants might for a while refresh themselves and their jaded animals, after their long and weary desert journey. The existence of valuable lead mines in the vicinity, together with the expectation of deriving great profit by furnishing travelers with supplies, induced five or six families to locate themselves in this wild and dangerous locality, near two hundred miles from any settlement, and surrounded on all sides by fearful deserts, tenanted by hordes of thieving savages. The first business of the colony was to build a fort for its protection, the remains of which were still standing. It consisted of an area of 50 by 100 feet, surrounded by an adobe wall twelve feet high, which was flanked at the corners by square bastions for commanding the face of the wall in case of attack. Around the inner side of this well-planned fortress was an offset in the wall, whereon the besieged might stand while firing on the enemy. The gateway which perforated the western wall was in a dilapidated condition, as were also the dwellings arranged on one side of the hollow square. In one corner was a furnace for smelting lead ore, and pieces of the metal strewn over the floor showed that the attempts of the workmen had been successful. After the erection of the establishment, farming operations were gone into extensively, and a considerable tract was fenced, irrigated and brought under cultivation. The enterprising colonists were in high expectation of reaping a rich reward for their labor, when the Vegas Indians, who were in considerable numbers in this valley, began to give them serious trouble by their thieving propensities, and at last it was as much as the isolated settlers could do to preserve their lives. Matters kept getting worse and worse, and finally the Mormons found themselves obliged to vacate their hard-earned homes and leave them in possession of their savage annoyers; but with a Christian spirit, which hardly seems credible, they bequeathed their houses and lands to their enemies, whom they taught the art of tilling the soil.

The savages tried civilized life for a season, but soon grew disgusted with it and returned to their former modes of living; but not till after they had set on fire all the combustible material of the fort, the roofless domiciles inside of which looked cheerlessly over its gray walls. Sad were the thoughts which the sight of this lone and dismantled fortress raised, as in silent isolation it stood on this once blooming oasis of the desert. Prowling coyotes, venomous reptiles, and those wretched imi-

THE RUINS OF LAS VEGAS.

tations of humanity, the Diggers, now lay claim to those walls which once formed an abiding place for civilized people. Thorns and dry, withered weeds now covered the once verdant fields, which, for want of irrigation, were now returning to their original sterility, and the whole valley presented a scene dismal and desolate in the extreme.

I give a sketch of these ruins, made from memory and my

descriptive notes. Our bivouac was by the side of the walls, which under a bright moon showed wierd and ghastly.

Hosts of Indians came pouring in upon us on our arrival, and pertinaciously stuck to us until our departure. They were very annoying, as, apart from their begging habits, they were inveterate thieves. On account of their scant clothing they could not conceal their plunder about their persons, so when they got hold of a tin plate, knife or cup, they would dexterously twirl it into the neighboring reeds for future quest. I was amused in watching their doings, while with snake-like movements they secured these, their features at the same time wearing the passive appearance of professional pickpockets.

The characteristics of the Vegas Indians were similar to the savages we saw on the Rio Virgin: broad faces, snaky eyes, matted hair hanging over the forehead, and forms low in stature. The clothing of the males mainly consisted of the cast-off apparel of passing emigrants, and was scanty at most; while the garments of the squaws were composed of the skins of rabbits, which had not grown up to the proper requirements. Their language, while resembling the Spanish intonation, came from their lips in such an idiotic way, that I can best term it a lingual slobber.

The nomenclature of the country we were passing through showed we were in what had once been Spanish territory; for all that, such mellifluous names as Santa Clara, Rio Virgin, Los Angeles, Las Animas and the like, seemed unfitted to such streams as we were meeting with, tinctured as they were with alkali until unfit for drink. Terms like "*jornado*," for a day's journey, and "*caballada*," for loose stock, were going out of use, but "*corral*," as an enclosure, and "*cañon*," as a narrow valley, had been incorporated in our language. The substitution of the Spanish "*si*" for "yes," and "*bueno*" for "good," was also common among us travelers.

The next morning a party of us started in advance of the

caravan, anxious to have a bath in the celebrated "Aquada
Caliente de las Vegas," three miles distant. Bidding adieu
to the ruined fortress and the associations and thoughts which
the sight of it called up, we proceeded on our way over a level,
barren plain. We at length came to the Bethsada of the desert:
a circular spring five yards in diameter and of unfathomable
depth, the water of which was at precisely the right temperature for a warm bath. Divesting ourselves of our habiliments
we plunged into the refreshing pool, below whose sparkling
surface it was impossible to sink; not on account of the den-
sity of the water, but of the strong current that boiled up from
the bottom. One of our number, Fisher, the lazy man, who
had not been known to wash since leaving the "States," was
seized and stripped by rude, though well-wishing, comrades,
and cast headlong into the healing and cleansing waters. The
fellow, who could not swim, was afraid for his life; but he
arose like a naiad, if such a comparison is admissible, and
spouting and barking like a seal, paddled ashore. We dis-
ported in this delightful bath until the caravan came up,
when we resumed our journey.

We were now reduced, by those leaving who had joined
us on the Santa Clara, to the three teams and twenty passengers which left Salt Lake in company. While more than a
match for the Diggers who had lately annoyed us, we put up
with their doings, dreading loss of stock. The waterless stretch
reached from thirty to sixty miles sometimes, and we dreaded
being left almost helpless on these desolate journeys.

We had now a thirty mile *jornado* to cross. Passing over a
tract of country almost entirely destitute of vegetation, and
covered with beds of sand, gravel and stone, we reached late
in the night the noted camping place of. Williams' Ranch.
"Old Williams," a hunter celebrated for his daring exploits
and recklessness, once ventured here with a drove of horses
and mules which he stole from the Mexicans, and after him

the camp is called.   A considerable stream here gushes out at
the foot of a rugged wall of rock, which rises precipitously to
the height of one thousand feet above the plain.   We were now
as near as we could tell in the State of California, but as the
boundary lines of the western divisions of our Union are like
the Equinoctial line, purely imaginary, we could form no definite idea as to when we crossed the borders of New Mexico
and California.   It is doubtful if Uncle Sam's surveyors ever
ventured into these wild regions, but I will warrant they were
well paid whether they performed their duties or not.   By way
of parenthesis, I will here mention an instance to show how
government employees get through their undertakings.   When
Utah was surveyed some years since, it was by contract, the
contractor being allowed so much per mile for the ground
traveled over while running the dividing line between the
counties.   This person, who was a genius in his line, conceived a plan whereby he might travel, in imagination, over
the greatest breadth of space with the least possible amount
of labor and wear and tear of shoe-leather.   The ingenious
gentleman and his corps, on arriving at the scene of their
labors, would encamp at some fertile oasis and then, with their
maps spread out before them, and while seated by their blazing
campfires, they would commence their arduous labor of traveling over the deserts surrounding them—on paper.   Growing
weary of one camping place they would move to another,
when another string of "magnificent distances" would be
successfully surveyed; and so on, until the territory was laid
out into counties, after which they returned home and received their reward.   They were paid as much per mile for
their imaginary journeys as if they had really traveled over
and chained the whole distance.   These were told me as facts
by eye-witnesses of the operations.

    The morning of the 10th came upon us clear and cold, and
showed us encamped in a region exceedingly rugged and des-

olate. The clear stream which came dashing by us from its source in the neighboring rocky bluff to its sink in the valley beneath us, was fringed with masses of ice which the cold of the night had formed. The water here is excellent, unlike that found at the few other camping places in the desert, where the springs are more or less tinctured with sulphur. Several of the animals having wandered off during the night, we were detained until the middle of the forenoon searching for them, when, making a retrograde march to regain the trail, which we had left the night before in order to reach water, we followed for a while along a range of mountains which arose as if to bar our progress. We ascended this escarpment at length through a sort of pass, which by a variety of tortuous ascents and descent leads to the summit. The scenery was varied and interesting along our route; the mountain slopes were covered with cedars, and we occasionally passed fantastically shaped rocks. At one place the summit of a steep declivity was surmounted by a rocky pile, which at a distance appeared like a huge watch-tower. The side fronting the road was pierced by a rough-hewn doorway. At another place the side of a rock-faced hill was indented by a cave some ten feet square, which had the appearance of being hewn out by human hands, so correct and regular was it in its outlines. Objects similarly picturesque were continually presenting themselves to us as we slowly trudged up the mountain side. Five miles down the western slope of the mountain, which we descended at a rapid pace, we came to the "Mountain Springs," which are twelve miles from " Williams' Ranch " by the wagon trail, but only six by a Digger path over the mountains. Several of our party came by this "cut-off," under the pilotage of a young Pah-Utah whom we had brought with us from Las Vegas. We found them at the Springs on our arrival, all looking the worse for wear, to judge from the array of toes that we saw protruding from the folds of shoe-leather which had been sadly dilapidated by coming in contact with the sharp volcanic rocks which bestrewed the trail. We found barely enough of water at the Springs for ourselves and animals, and that was disagreeably brackish.

Our provisions now began to run short, and anxious to make them hold out as long as possible, we put ourselves upon allowance; an expedient which, by the way, was suggestive of gloomy forebodings. Upon leaving the settlements we had laid in what we thought was a sufficient quantity, but we found out our mistake when too late to remedy it, and so were obliged to do the best we could; that is, to divide our scanty supply of flour and coffee—all the articles of luxury or necessity we now possessed—into as many parts as there were days between then and the time when we calculated to arrive in San Bernardino; one part, and no more, to be devoured per day. Our future prospects, as may be surmised, were none of the brightest at this stage of the journey, especially when we considered the many accidents which might happen to detain us on the road: such as the giving out of teams, breaking down of wagons and other causes. We allowed for eight days' time to reach San Bernardino.

We left our elevated encampment at the "Mountain Springs" early the next morning, and passing over a rough road which lay through a scattered grove of yuccas, the repulsive aspect of which made the scenery anything but agreeable, we rolled at a brisk trot down the mountain slope. The range which we were crossing was the rim of a gigantic basin of irregular shape and about thirty miles in diameter. Basins like this are often met with in the Great Desert. They are level beds of sand and gravel, supporting no vegetation save scattered and dwarfed specimens of sage, and surrounded by bleak and rugged mountains which afford but few passes. Some ten miles to the north of the trail we saw the bed of an alkaline lake which was white with saleratus, and so in fact was a good portion of the basin, which was of a dead level. It was about sundown when we reached the opposite range of mountains, which, in spite of the distance, had been visible all day, as the same clear atmosphere which covers the plains is found here. After a tedious journey of thirty miles we encamped at midnight on the summit of a ridge which was totally destitute of water, and our only fuel was the detestable yucca, which gave forth such a sickening odor as to almost preclude our using it.

Descending this mountain and crossing a broad waste of yielding sand, we arrived in the afternoon of the 12th at the "Kingston Springs"—the western terminus of the fifty mile *jornado* on which we had been journeying since the morning of the previous day. Here several springs of warm water, strongly tinctured with sulphur, gush from the summit of a mound, rising about four feet above the plain. The scenery here is obstructed on all sides but one by groups of buttes, which rise above the plain with rocky, shattered fronts. These regions are so destitute of anything like ordinary fuel, that had we not brought some along in our wagons we would have eaten an uncooked dinner.

At the foot of one of the high, rocky mounds we found a portion of the skeleton of a poor wretch, who had paid the forfeit of his life in trying to accomplish the feat of crossing the Great Desert alone. Our Mormon friends knew the history of him whose only remains were the whitened bones lying around us. He was a man young in years but of intelligence, who from some cause became deranged. In one of his fits of madness he mounted his horse, and leaving San Bernardino, crossed the Sierra, and alone and unprotected struck out into the bosom of the Great Desert. The next that was heard of him was when a party of travelers found at the Kingston Springs his body pierced with arrows by the side of the fountain. The remains had been buried, but those

11

resurrectionists of the desert, the wolves, had since exhumed them, and the bones now lay scattered around the margins of the shallow grave. The skull was not there, but after some search we found it at a considerable distance, where, tossed about by the foul wolf, it had found its way. The Mormon conductors did not concern themselves in the least about re-burying the bones of their friend, perhaps thinking it was "none of their funeral."

OUR CAMP AT KINGSTON SPRINGS—BENTLY AND HIS DOG.

XII.

From the Kingston Springs to San Bernardino.

FROM its peculiar appearance, surroundings and associations, I give a sketch of the fountain known as the Kingston Springs. The bleached skeleton, with its skull's ironic grin, the splintered rocks, the glaring sands with their repellent vegetation of cacti, thorns and the disagreeable yucca tree made a deep impression on me. Besides, we were now beginning to feel the lack of provisions, and this brings me again to Bently and his dog.

When our provender was divided, no allotment was made for this animal, who was of good size and seemed to have been born hungry, and to have never got over this natal failing. The dog got into thieving habits, resulting in the carrying away of some of our precious rations; his master being caught sometimes assisting him. This, with the dislike their doings engendered in the balance of our mess, made the twain devoted to one another to a degree which, had we not been void of sentiment, would have filled us with pity and admiration. But we were hungry and our hearts were of stone. So two of the mess coaxed the dog from camp and shot him. His master was disconsolate at his loss and the rest of us wondered what had become of his four-footed friend, but, in our then feelings, hoping never to see him again.

Just before sunset we resumed our march and slowly left our late desolate camping place, with its sad associations, in the distance. Our reason for starting at this time was to avoid the Kingston Spring Indians, it being dangerous to halt among them at night. Our Mormons reported them as of large size and differing in appearance from the Diggers generally. They rarely show themselves by day, but watch from behind the desert rocks the movements of travelers, and should they halt at night, steal or kill their stock. The reader can hardly imagine how we dreaded the loss of animals on the waterless stretches of from thirty to sixty miles, and with what anxiety we watched them at night. Their loss almost involved our own lives. But by traveling much after sundown, and by the judicious treatment our conductors pursued toward the Indians, we went through safely. Lack of pasturage was made up with rations of wheat, which for the emergencies of desert travel had been carried from the settlements. This, however, was running short, and our teams were getting thin and weak. The alternations of yielding sand and jolting stones were trying to passengers as well as teams, as much of the way we were obliged to walk.

Our road now lay over a sandy tract, the horizon occasionally broken by rocky "buttes" and sand pillars. Not a tree was visible except an occasional yucca, which, with horizontal, outstretched arms and extended palms, seemed asking for continued curses on this already over-cursed region. Rising to a height of twenty or more feet, with trunks a foot in diameter and of ghostly whiteness, or prone to the ground, decaying in spongy, ill-smelling masses, this nightmare of vegetation gave the landscape a weird look. Grass there was none; but in its place there came from the sand occasional growths of thorny, repulsive plants.

Our journey was growing tiresome. We were getting low in spirits, and everything having been talked out we traveled most of the time in silence. In our springless wagons we could not sleep, so we walked and rode alternately, listening anxiously for Indian approaches, and dreading that at any moment an arrow-pierced horse might fall. But nothing befel us. In the morning, at four o'clock, in pitchy darkness, we halted. The air was cold, and no fuel was to be had for warmth or cooking our scant food. There was not a spear of grass, so instead of hoppling our horses and turning them loose we tied them to the wagons. In prairie travel, when grass was plenty, tethering horses was practicable; but in a country like this it was not; it took so broad a range to feed each. So there being too few teamsters to guard the animals, hopples were used to restrain them. These sometimes got loose, and, in spite of their broken-down condition, the horses would wander out of sight and cause us much vexatious delay. When there was no grass we tied them up and gave them what we could spare of wheat. Our teams were now in such condition we were afraid they would not take us through. Our day's march on the 12th was forty-five miles.

The morning of December 13th dawned upon us bright and clear, and found us encamped in another of these great desert-basins, surrounded by ranges of barren mountains. We broke camp early in the day and continued on our way over the sandy and stony plain in the direction of a gap in the mountain rim, which was indistinctly visible from our camping place. In the course of the forenoon ocular evidence was manifested of our being in the modern El Dorado, for we saw gold-bearing rock scattered over the plain, although in rather limited quantities. Before long our party was scattering over the plain " prospecting " and bringing the results of their searchings to our Mormon friends—the most of whom were versed in aurific lore, which they had acquired during a residence in California—for inspection. The whole of this desert is rich in precious metals, but on account of the lack of water for separating them from the earth and rock in which they are found, they will doubtless, until the advent of railroads, remain where they are. After emerging from the basin through the pass, we came on to a gravelly, rolling plain, occasionally varied by beds of yielding sand. Late in the afternoon we came in sight of what appeared to be a large body of water. Nothing could have seemed more natural. We could see the waves dancing beneath the rays of the sun, now sinking behind the range of mountains which bounded our view on the west, and at the sight of this exhilarating picture both horse and man pressed onward with quickened steps, hoping to soon quench their thirst in the sparkling waters before them. The hopes of all were, however, in a measure disappointed on a nearer view of the imaginary lake, which proved to be a perfectly level plain, a square mile in area, which had been glazed over by water which had once covered it. The reflection of the sun on its glossy surface had given it its watery appearance. This is called "Dry Lake," and is made a halting place whenever water is found in two or three wells on its northern shore. We had not expected to find water at this time of the year, but we found a sufficiency of it at the bottom of the wells; though it was a vile liquid— muddy and alkaline. Having filled our kegs we crossed to the other side of the lake-bed, where we found a little grass scattered among the dwarfed sage brush. To say that the plain was as "smooth as a barn floor" would be altogether within the bounds of truth, so even was its surface, and the hot sun had baked it as hard as a brick. It was quite a treat to ride over such a course as this after having been jolted so long over the rough surface of the desert.

The day was succeeded by a bright moon-lit evening, and as so unparalleled a race-course was at hand, we determined

to make use of it and have a little sport to vary the cheerless-
ness of our journey. Biped nags renowned for fleetness of
foot were selected from our ranks, and surrounded by their
backers they proceeded to the place allotted for the display of
their locomotive powers. Clad in as few habiliments as possible, and with feet encased in light moccasons, the gallant
Olympians would leave the starting point, and with flying
heels and streaming locks they would speed over the level
course toward the speedily nearing goal, amid the cheers and
yells of an admiring and appreciative audience. Bets of
money and of wine—the latter to be forthcoming on our
arrival at San Bernardino—were freely offered and taken on
the result of the races, and the competitors were watched with
the liveliest interest by their friends until they came up to
the score. The whole scene was rife with mirth and excitement, and during the evening's performance the desert soli-
tudes were made to ring with such sounds as had never before
disturbed their silent airs.

Much of our gaiety was forced, however, and we soon settled
down to the normal condition of the past few days. Instead
of a night drive, which the condition of our horses precluded,
we encamped on the shores of the deceitful lake. In the moon-
light of the early evening we could see the yuccas, erect or
fallen, in the semblance of alert or sleeping ghosts, giving the
landscape an uncanny look.

The next morning we saw an object slowly crawling towards
us across the shining bed of the lake. What should it be but
Bently's dog, like Marryatt's "Snarleyow," come back to "visit
the glimpses of the moon." The twain of would-be murderers
announced themselves by their looks when their victim made
his appearance. Bently's emotions were a mixture of anger
and pleasure, while the poor dog wagged his tail to the forgetfulness of his wounds. A reversion of feeling followed, and it
was concluded to tolerate the superfluous member of our mess
a little longer.

At noon on the 14th we reached the Bitter Springs, the water of which was bitter enough indeed. We found a party of traders encamped here, who were *en route* for Salt Lake with merchandise from San Francisco. As we had now a waterless stretch of forty-five miles to cross, we filled our casks at the "Springs," and, passing over a dreary waste of yielding sand, encamped at sunset long enough to cook our scanty suppers, when we drove on. Another long march through the darkness, and we arrived, a little before daybreak, on the shores of the Rio Mojave—the Rio de los Animas of the old Spaniards. Here we refreshed ourselves with quaffs of excellent water, which was in delightful contrast with the revolting liquids we had been obliged to use for the last one hundred and forty miles of our journey.

The Mojave, which takes its rise among the snow-capped peaks of the San Bernardino Mountains, flows through a sandy valley of various widths, beneath whose surface it occasionally sinks for miles. For the most of its course it is fringed with a belt of timber, composed of cotton-wood and willow, amongst which are thickets of thorny underbrush, whose verdant foliage contrasts pleasantly with the barren waste of sand and gravel which extends, on either hand, as far as the eye can reach. The river emerges from its subterranean channel a short distance below where it is crossed by the Spanish trail. Fifty miles lower down the Mojave runs plump against a rocky bluff, which tells it in unmistakable terms, "Thus far shalt thou go and no farther." The Santa Fe trail once followed the river to its sink ; but the route we traveled is now preferred, it being the most direct.

Near our camp we found the head and cleanly picked bones of a horse, which had been killed and eaten by a party of destitute travelers who had left here the day before our arrival. We had not yet come to horse-beef ourselves, but we were in a fair (or rather gloomy) way for it, as we were beginning to

feel keenly the effects of short allowance. We essayed the
expedient of tightening our belts in order to neutralize the
effects brought on by the aching void within; but we found
this plan was better in theory than in practice. Another
mode we had for making a little go a great way was to
drink plentifully of our weak coffee, under the impression
that it would expand the more solid food until it filled up
that vacuum which man, as well as nature, so much abhors.
During the first part of the time we were on allowance we had
our jokes about the predicament we were in, as we endeavored
to drive away the impressions brought on by the gloomy
future that was hanging over us. Having devoured our respective allowances of dry bread, we would lay siege to the
camp-kettle of coffee, and with tincups brimming with the
unsugared, uncreamed and alkaline decoction, we would commence "filling up," as we jestingly termed it, after which
we would tighten our belts another hole and bid defiance to
gaunt famine. These jokes, however, soon became old and
stale, and wearied looks, irritable tempers and listlessness
abounded amid our half-starved company. As may be surmised, our campfires were no longer redolent with the uproarious merriment and practical joking which characterized
those of the forepart of our journey.

Travelers on short allowance are full of selfishness, some
fine writing to the contrary notwithstanding. With us there
was suspicion, accusation and recrimination. One or two
were accused of stealing from the daily allowance, as we
took our turns riding, when there were chances for those
lacking consciences to purloin the bread, which was all we
had and which we would bake to last twenty-four hours.
The most pitiable sight was Bently and his dog. There
was but little sentiment about me; but when I saw the
master secretly getting food for his pet, I had a feeling
which prevented me from interfering. I believe Bently

would have gone still more hungry than he was to have comforted his four-footed companion. The rest of the men watched them like beasts of prey, and would have knocked the man over and re-killed the dog on the least extra provocation. I expected the last would happen, but the watchfulness of Bently prevented it, and the dog went with us to San Bernardino. What afterwards became of the devoted twain I do not know. Both were worthless, and their Ishmaelitish life seemed to bind them together closer and closer. I hope if the soldiers ever got the man, his faithful dog bore him company. The episode of Bently and his dog I will ever remember.

Our route now lay in a westerly direction along the sunken waters of the Mojave. The scenery was uninteresting, as nothing met our gaze save the sandy valley with its barren, rugged boundaries of rocky hills, and the narrow belt of timber traversing it. On the 16th we came in sight of the long-wished-for Sierra Nevada, whose eternally snow-clad summits had loomed up before me ever since I left Salt Lake City. We at last came to where the river flows above the surface of the valley. It was here two rods wide and as many feet in depth. Shortly after nightfall we camped by a little grocery, the first inhabited house we had seen since leaving the Mormon settlement, four hundred miles distant. Here a portion of our company left us on foot for the next settlement, which was thirty miles further on, going by a near cut across the mountains which the wagons could not travel. These individuals had entirely run out of provisions, and as they could not wait until the caravan reached the settlement, they had formed the design of going on foot in advance of us. It was about 10 o'clock when they left us. We watched the progress of the little band with interest as it waded the river, and at a quick pace plunged into the darkness beyond. They were starting on a dangerous expedition, for the route was unknown to them and infested with bad Indians, to say nothing of grizzlies. Poor fellows! We were powerless to aid them, as we had scarcely enough of provisions to keep us from starvation until our arrival in San Bernardino, and our belts were buckled up to the last hole.

The Southern Pacific Railroad follows the course of the Mojave—pronounced *Mohavey*—and reaches the coast by the same pass we went through—the Cajon. Before the descent of this can be made, an elevation of three thousand feet must be reached. This is the only available route through the San Bernardino range of the Sierra Nevada. The Mojave sinks, like many of the desert rivers, near the pass.

Leaving this stream to our right, we proceeded the next morning over a gradually ascending road, which led to the summit of a precipitous range of hills running parallel to the main Sierra. Along the top of a slanting ridge, whose precipitous sides led down to dangerous defiles, we descended to the head of the Cajon Pass of the Sierra Nevada. This ridge, which we christened the " Devil's Back-bone," arose at an angle of forty-five degrees, and on account of its numerous *vertebræ* was dangerous to our wagons. The yucca, which had not intruded its disagreeable presence upon us for several days, made its appearance on the surrounding hills, its repulsive form rising to the height of twenty feet, with its white trunk, and leaves like daggers. We encamped after night in the upper end of the Cajon Pass, in a locality badly infested by grizzlies, the whereabouts of which were made manifest by the restlessness of our animals, which were neighing, braying and scampering hither and thither throughout the night. We spent the evening in polishing up the outer man preparatory to again making our entrance to a civilized region and among a civilized people, as we expected to reach San Bernardino the next day. Razors, scissors and soap were freely administered to portions of the human form sadly needing them, and these were soon followed by a change to

clothing which had long lain in the gloomy recesses of carpet-
bags in anticipation of the time when, to deck the persons of
its owners, it was to be called forth before reaching the settlements. These operations, which somewhat modified the
general piratical appearance of our company, occupied our
time until near midnight. When I at last sought my hard
couch by the side of a faintly glimmering campfire, it was
not to sleep, for the various emotions which thronged through
my mind at the thoughts of the new scenes among which I
was to act my part in life's great drama, alone and friendless,
together with the wild scenery around us and the deep silence
of the night, broken occasionally by the loud cries and furious
tread of the horses and mules as they dashed to and fro along
the gloomy pass, drove sleep from me, much as I courted its
presence.

The morning of the 18th saw us on our road early. The
trail leading along the bottom of the rugged pass was an
exceedingly rough one, lying over beds of rock and stone,
and sometimes in the channel of the stream which it often
crossed. The cañon at length opened into a valley a mile in
width, which was thickly sown with thorny plants, among
which the prickly pear, a branch of the cactus family, held
a prominent place. This plant here grew to the height of
two feet, with oval-shaped leaves an inch in thicknees and
thickly covered with sharp thorns. It bears a bell-shaped
fruit, encased in a purple bulb, which, when ripe, is very
agreeable to the taste, although its surroundings are so full of
minute, barbed thorns, which penetrate the lips, tongue and
hands of the eater, that there is far more pain than pleasure
in eating them. Winding through a thorny chaparral and
over beds of yielding sand, we continued down the widening
pass, which at length opened into the valley of San Bernardino. Descending a gradually sloping bluff, with our teams
at full speed, we reached the level plain stretching beyond;
and passing by the side of fields now green with the starting

grass, our caravan at last filed into the terminus of our present journey—San Bernardino.

This town is situated near the southern extremity of the valley of the same name and a few miles from the foot of a lofty Sierra. The origin of this city is as follows: Shortly after the settlement of Great Salt Lake was founded, a company of Mormons emigrated to California, then a Mexican province, for the purpose of selecting a place whereon to found a colony, as the climate and soil of that region were deemed vastly superior to those of Utah. These pioneers bought a tract of land in the southern end of San Bernardino Valley, for which the sum of $70,000 was paid ; and emigration soon flocking thither, a flourishing colony was founded. This settlement Brigham Young, by an arrangement of his own, incorporated into Utah Territory, which he extended to the Pacific. This arrangement, however, could not stand, and soon after the Mexican war San Bernardino became a portion of the Golden State, much to the disgust of the Prophet, to whom California was a great eye-sore. The settlement continued thriving until the autumn of 1857, when all true believers were summoned to repair immediately to Utah, in order to resist the ingress of the Federal troops, who were now on their way to Utah. The majority obeyed the summons, and selling their property for what they could get, removed to Utah, while the remainder, setting at defiance the thunders of excommunication hurled at them by the head of the Church, resolved to remain. These backsliders were called "Apostates" by their zeal-blinded brethren, who entertained feelings of the greatest contempt towards them. Several of the Mormons of our party had been residents of San Bernardino, and these spoke to us Gentiles in terms of undisguised disgust of those of their fellow colonists who were not devoted enough to the cause of Polygamy to take up the cross and follow them to the realm of Brigham. But even if the Mormons had not left when they did, they would soon have been routed out by

the Americans of Southern California, who saw in this settlement a nest of corruption, an abiding place for all the villains
of the country, and where money was extorted by all manner
of means by unscrupulous Church dignitaries and forwarded
to Salt Lake. Collisions between the Saints and Gentiles
occasionally took place, and there was every appearance of a
renewal of the Nauvoo scenes, when luckily the mandate of
the Prophet came forth to call back the stray Mormon sheep
into their original fold.

Several Americans now lived in San Bernardino; but its
population had greatly decreased since the time when Mormonism sat enthroned there, and tenantless houses gaped sadly
through unglazed windows at the few strangers who visited the
city. The whole place, which contained six or eight hundred
inhabitants, had a tumble-down look; and the fact of the
public business of the city being in the hands of Jews, did
not tend to make San Bernardino prosper. The signs on the
few business places gave the town somewhat of a foreign air:
Tienda Barata taking the place of "Cheap Store."

And now in regard to the condition of our party of twenty,
who left Salt Lake six weeks before in such good heart. A
part had spent all their money, and those who had not, kept
the information for private use. Owing to reasons mentioned,
we were all glad to get to our journey's end and matterless
how soon we parted company. Our discordant mess passed
its last night on the floor of an old adobe house; one of the
many deserted ones of that luckless town, bare of furniture and
cheerless in the extreme. In spite of temptations and theft
our provisions had held out, though we often went hungry to
accomplish this end. We were now to scatter, we knew not
where. Taking our party as a whole, we were about a fair
average of the thousands of ox-drivers who crossed the plains
in 1858, and that is not giving them a very high place. The
best of these was John Galdie, familiarly known as "Scottie,"
a quiet fellow, who shared my fortunes much of the time

while I was in California, and who was a friend to me in time of need. From what the reader knows of my comrades in general, he will not wonder I cared not how soon we parted.

As little as I regretted leaving my messmates, who, I admit, had some good traits woven amid their failings, I felt low-spirited when getting ready to leave San Bernardino.

It is true I had got to California, but I did not know what to do now that I was there, for I was unacquainted with a person along the Pacific Coast. To find work I must get to the northern part of the State, and to reach there required money. When I contracted with the Mormons for my passage I did not think I would be left ninety miles from the coast. Inquiry developed the fact that the steamer plying between San Pedro and San Francisco only ran every twenty days, that its first trip would be on the 23d, and that the fare in the steerage would be $20. Two gold pieces amounting to that was all the money I possessed. I had barely time to reach the coast on foot. Should I miss the steamer, what would I do? So I resolved to start at once.

Speaking in the proper sense, my "California Tramp" began at San Bernardino, for heretofore 1 was either a walking member of an organized body, or alternately walking and riding with the Mormon wagoners. Now I was taking the road in earnest. Here we, who had so long traveled together, separated, some to stay in the town, while those who went on so straggled that there was no comradeship among them. I parted with them with no regret. I don't say but what some of them were good in their way, and that I have seen worse people—in jail; but when I look back on that party, at the end of thirty years, I wonder how I could travel with it for over five months. I suppose it was because I could do no better. It was between the "devil and the deep sea." On the one hand was the desert or prairie with its cruel Indians and wild beasts, on the other our "goodlie companie." As the least evil, I was justified in clinging to the last.

XIII.

Jo Pueblo de Los Angeles.

TO start for the City of Angels on foot was, indeed, a prosaic way of traveling. The steed of Pegasus would have been none too good as a mode of transit to so poetically named a town; but there being no such animal then at livery in San Bernardino, and having not the wherewithal to hire him had there been, I was fain to mount the hack traditionally under the ownership of one Shank and start on my journey. This being without money and without price, I was soon ready for my seaward tramp.

To say that I made a prepossessing appearance would be wrong. I did not resemble the "Views afoot" tourist with his trim suit, his neat knapsack and staff. The most of my worldly goods were in an old carpet-bag, the counterpart of which is only seen nowadays in the hand of bucolic strangers in the city, or on the comic stage. In addition there was a pair of boots as hard as the adamantine heart of Pharoah, and so tight I could only wear them "turn about" with a pair of thin Indian moccasons. They had clung to me with a Damon-and-Pythias-like tenacity, or like "The Old Man of the Sea" to his victim, and were a part of my monthly hire in Michigan. I had borne their infelicities to Salt Lake, when a Mormon cobbler put $2.00 expense on them, after which I could not afford

The Cajon Pass.

MARCHING TO THE SEA.

Mt. San Bernardino.

to throw them away, but took them as thrifty people do over-plus medicine, rather than be guilty of wastefulness. These, when not in use, were slung across my shoulders along with my blankets and an overcoat. Then I had a rifle which I had bought at Salt Lake, and which, as it had nearly drained my purse to the bottom, after I paid my transportation charges, I had regretted buying. It was bought to fight Indians with, but as we found it pleasanter to make our way through hostile territory by firing flour and beef at them, we never harmed an aboriginal hair.

And now with this rifle on my shoulder, my carpet-bag and boots suspended back of the muzzle, the rest of my "duds" otherwise disposed of, and the clothing I wore rent and stained with weeks of open-air travel and lying on the ground, the reader, gentle or otherwise, can imagine my appearance when starting on my tramp, and can be assured I did not improve on further acquaintance during my search for work. I sup-pose I was about an average example of most of the tramps seen on Eastern highways when that class of nomads are in season, except that here my rifle and knife would have lent an additional terror. Of course I wore a belt, to take up or let out as hunger waxed or waned, to which was suspended the above knife. Although this last was in shape piratical, and gleaming with German silver, I am glad to say it was never designed for anything but uses culinary.

This much for externals. Mentally, were cerebral exposure possible, I would not have shown up much better. Worri-ment as to what would be my future, thus cast adrift, put my spirits down towards the zero bulb to keep company with my finances. Besides, the journey ahead was long and lonely, hardly relieved by the grand view of the Sierras, and thoughts of the new scenes I was entering in a country whose romance had not yet been smothered by progress, and which was punctuated with towns, valleys and mountains full of wildness

12

and feudalism, and accented with sonorous Castilian nomenclature. Now, such names as Dog Gulch, Grass Valley and Rogue River are taking the place of the sweet names of a language which could make the most effective oaths sound as lover's mouthings. Even these are being drowned by Yankee substitutes, and the mellifluous "*carambas*," "*carajos*," "*cozedos*" and "*sacramentos*," which to me never sounded more harmful from the tongue of a Mexican than "Dear me" and "Oh! my" from an emotional Eastern woman, are disused by the vile objurgations of the "Americanos." In those days the Mexican "geed" and "hawed" his oxen in Spanish, and "got them up" and "whoaed" them similarly; now his "*anda*," his "*circo*" and other ox-directing synonyms are only heard in out-of-the-way "Sleepy Hollow" ranches.

As to the appearance of the country I was to travel over, it was like this; for although a score and a half of years have elapsed since I was there, it is now plainly before me: Northward stretched, as far as the eye could reach, a nearly level plain, the first part bare of green vegetation and for some distance covered with a chaparral of sage-brush higher than one's head. Beyond the soil grew better, and forty miles from my starting point was green with pasture. The first settlement was twenty-two miles on the road, and after awhile the plain was dotted at intervals of four or five miles with the white walls of ranche buildings. The right of the vista was flanked by a range of the Sierra Nevada as far as I could see; the mountain rising abruptly for thousands of feet, the upper part white with snow. Ten to fifteen miles off to the left a low range of hills bounded the valley, and westward the plain extended to the Pacific, some thirty miles away.

I started about 10 o'clock on the 19th of December, 1858. I cannot say I had no company, for on the road for miles our party was scattered; at long intervals, of course, for there would not be more than two or three in sight at once. A part of the time I would tramp alone, and while I would be resting, perhaps a brother tramp would come up and we would travel together, or "in cahoot," as partnership was called in the plains "argot,"—for all the world like the anarchistic wayfarers on the Bristol Turnpike. Those who had money preferred traveling alone; those who had none, like misery, loved company for the chance it afforded for a "sponge" on the commissary stores of the more fortunate.

My route for awhile lay over the low plain in which San Bernardino is built, amidst fields long since shorn of their harvests, and through scattered thickets which the frost had robbed of their foliage. The day was warm and my load heavy, so I was forced to do as some of my predecessors were doing, cast my superfluous clothing along the road, without hope of it returning in days many or few. Having thus unburdened myself as much as I dared, I went on with a lighter load, but not a lighter heart, for if ever I had what are known as the "dumps," it was when I started on my "march to the sea." I soon reached the shores of a stream which waters this valley, and crossing it climbed a bluff and found myself on a bleak plain. I was now on the beginning of a waterless stretch of twenty miles, and as it was well on towards noon I had small prospect of making the end of the journey before night. In spite of the reduction I had made in my load it was still heavy, and I was glad when, six miles on my way, I met a horseman whom I persuaded to buy my rifle. I let him have it, with the ammunition belonging, for five dollars— one-fourth of what it cost. This was a godsend, for all I had before was the two eagles I had saved and kept from the knowledge of my companions for my passage to San Francisco. The reason I did not take my comrades into my confidence was that I feared some might want to "borrow" them.

The trail soon led into a spreading chaparral, a thicket of gnarled sage-brush, repulsive from a fire which had lately

gone through it. This so hemmed in my vision that I could
only see in advance. I slowly and wearily tramped over the
flinty road, with limbs so chafed and feet so blistered that I
had often to stop to rest. Besides, the sun shone warm, in
spite of December and the snow-covered mountains. I at last
emerged from the chaparral to an open plain.

The day was waning and night came on long before I got
to the stream where I was to pass the night. Mindless of the
saline fate of Lot's wife, I turned to look back and saw the most
beautiful sight imaginable—sunset on Mount San Bernardino.
It seemed as if the sun, with his shadowy lever and the horizon
for a fulcrum, was slowly forcing the light of day heavenward;
the last rays gathering around the summit of that peak of the
Sierras. The gleaming white changed into the most beautiful
purple and gold, and the mountain top remained thus invested
for some time after twilight had mantled the plain below. The
mellow tints grew darker as the sun, in his Archimedean role,
bore down his end of the lever, lower and lower, till, with an
imaginable hiss, he plunged into the sea; while the other
extremity of the phantasmal seesaw climbed the summit and
drove to the cold upper air the last lingering rays of light.
I stopped longer than I could afford to look on this sight.
The thickening gloom warned me to go on, and with a sigh I
retook my weary way over the lonely valley.

I had not gone far into the darkness before I heard the
distant yelping of wolves from the direction of the chaparral.
Those who have heard these demon-dogs know their blood-
curdling howls; those who have not may be thankful. I was
familiar with them on the plains, but I was not alone then;
now their fiend-like voices gave me the shivers, and I hurried
on, hoping to overtake company. I soon found wolves were
not the only animals I had to fear, for I was getting on to a
range of wild cattle—wild in the sense of running at will,
though under ownership by the neighboring rancheros. A

large herd of these animals galloped across the trail just behind me, and I believe that I would have been trampled to death had I been a little later. I now hurried faster, and soon my suspense was ended by the sight of a fire. This was at the stopping place I spoke of, and here I found a few of our men. Just beyond was a stream of water, where I slaked my thirst for the first time in twenty miles. I found I was by the side of some ranch buildings, which were shown by the reflection of a fire in front, around which some Mexicans, who looked like brigands, were toasting their feet, their " *scrapes* " drawn around their shoulders, chattering away with the inevitable " *cigarillos* " in their mouths. I was hungry and was making my way to the ranch for something to eat, as quietly as I could, so as to avoid these men, when the barking of a dog warned me away, and I went back to the shore of the brook, where two or three of our men were lying down. It was cold, and I wished for my cast-away overcoat, but I made the best use of my blanket by wrapping it around me. I sat here awhile, with few pleasant thoughts for my company, watching the Mexicans around their fire, and exchanging an occasional word with my fellows. We were all tired and not in a humor to talk much, and spreading my blankets beneath the boughs of a cottonwood, wrapped them around me and after a while got to sleep. Awakened from my uneasy slumbers by the barking of neighboring dogs, I was glad when morning came. Before the sunlight had reached the foot of the mountain slope I was well on my way from my inhospitable camping place, little rested and much ahungered.

In spite of this feeling, as I trudged along my halting feet involuntarily kept step to a sing-song music, called up by the names of some of the prominent objects which were being brought before me. Most people who were school children in 1850 will remember the " singing geography schools " that spread like an epidemic over the land. They were at first held in the evenings and sometimes by day for a month during vacations. The repetition of the geographical names, with the peculiarity of the rising and falling inflections, were entered into with zeal, and much knowledge of the earth with the appendages thereof was obtained. If there was ever music in "singing geography," it was when chanting objects with Spanish names. So as I walked along I mentally sung "San Bernardino Mountain," "Sierra Nevada Mountains," "Upper California," "Monterey," etc., repeating each with the peculiar change of voice which had been taught me in my school days, until something else drove the subject from my mind.

The country improved as I advanced, and occasional bands of cattle and horses I met showed improved pasturage. Eight miles from my starting place and thirty from St. Bernardino I came to another ranch—the half-way place between Los Angeles and the last town. Here I got something to eat, and stopped long enough to take some mental notes of the place. The houses were of one story and surrounded a courtyard, which was filled with a motley assemblage of people of all sizes, ages and colors. These were the retainers of the proprietor of the ranch, as the rich Dons who lived in this valley had a goodly number of vassals under them. These hangers-on were little better than slaves, but they led an easy life and were contented. Herding cattle and cultivating a little ground to raise the grain and vegetables required, was all they did. The former was done on horseback and was more in the nature of sport than otherwise. One side of the courtyard was strewn with saddles, bridles and lassoes and the rest of the articles a Mexican horseman needs. Large dogs of villainous appearance stalked amid their biped comrades, and paid me such attention that I was fain to leave.

Wealthy Mexicans living on large grants deeded to them by their government were then common in Southern California, and they resisted the invasion of their Yankee neighbors upon their dignified exclusiveness with an old fogy stubbornness. They led the same isolated life at the time I was there as did their ancestors when they came from Mexico. Surrounded by a retinue of dark-faced half-breeds, the patriarchal Don lived in stately pomp on his leagues of domain, unvexed by the doings of the outer world. His chief riches were his flocks and herds of horses, cattle, sheep and goats, which pastured in freedom over his broad acres. The only pure Spanish blood in California was in the veins of this class. These devotees of time-honored customs employed the same simple implements of agriculture as did their forefathers, and contentedly plowed the soil with crooked sticks and harrowed with the branches of trees. Their clumsy carts were made wholly of wood, the wheels being sawed off the ends of logs, and the frame held together by wooden pins. To these carts were hitched, with rawhide ropes, from one to three pairs of half-wild oxen. The yokes were laid behind the horns, to which they were lashed with leather thongs. One reason I heard given for thus attaching them was that advantage was got of the strongest part of the ox, which lay in the neck; that much strength being lost when the yoke rested against the shoulder. It was amusing to see one of these rig-outs in motion. On each side of the column was a "greaser," who, with his goad pointed with a nail, prodded the sides of his victims, accompanying each thrust with a wild cry. Thus equipped the establishment moved on its way, the wheels grinding forth dolorous music, the heartless drivers punching and screaming, the oxen panting under their burden.

The main *forte* of the Mexican is his horsemanship. Such headlong riders I never saw; always on the full jump, they sit their saddles firmly and defy the efforts of their wild animals to throw them. With their lassos they perform wonders. With practiced skill the plaited leathern rope is thrown at full gallop, and a wild bull or horse is floundering in the dust.

These are sometimes broken by the struggling victims, but
the expert "lassero" will pick up the severed end while at full
speed, and with a dexterous coil around the saddle-horn secure
his prey. The horses are trained young as well as their riders,
and as soon as the rope is thrown they will arrest their speed
in a moment, and, throwing themselves back on their haunches,
stand ready to resist the impending shock.

The common answer of a Mexican to a question is " *Quien
sabe ?* " (who knows?). This saves trouble and is not mislead-
ing, for you at least know as much as you did before. So
when I questioned a Mexican, who was standing at the door
of the courtyard, ready for a mount and clad in semi-bandit
costume, broad-rimmed "*sombrero*," "*serape*," leather leggings,
jingling spurs and clumsy wooden stirrups, as to how far it
was to Los Angeles, and he said there were many leagues
'twixt here and there, I was not deceived. Leaving the lonely
ranch, my path still lay along the mountain-bounded plain,
which extends perhaps one hundred miles north of San Bernardino. Over this were scattered herds of wild-looking Spanish cattle and an occasional band of horses. The former were
quite annoying to me, particularly the patriarchs of the flock,
who pawed the ground and made eyes at me from positions
close to the trail. I several times got ready for a foot race, but
nothing serious occurred. The younger stock were less warlike, and a well-emitted yell would scatter them. These cattle
are of a very different breed from the gentle animals pasturing
around our rural homes. They are smaller, generally of a
dun color, and with slender, sharp-pointed horns.

On the whole of the sixty miles of road from San Bernardino to Los Angeles I did not see a single vehicle in motion,
nor horsemen, except the "*vaqueros*" or herders we occasionally met. The trail seemed to be monopolized by our scattered
party; yet it was the mainly traveled road from San Pedro to
San Bernardino and the southern route to Salt Lake, as well
as to New Mexico.

Amid the scenes described I slowly wended my way over the gravelly plains and beneath the rays of a warm sun. My feet were now blistered to a painful extent, and sweltering under the weight of my yet heavy load, I sickened at the thought of the many leagues which lay between me and the next stopping place, which was thirty miles from where I passed the night. Besides, I was chronically hungry and would get no water till night, except by making long *detours* to out-of-the-way ranches. There was not a shade tree along the road; but in the afternoon I was greeted with the sight of a large live-oak rising in solitary grandeur above the level plain to the left of the trail. It seemed so inviting that I went out of my way to rest under its shade, which was near a hundred feet in diameter. As I was anxious to reach El Monte, the first settlement, before dark, I did not remain long. The trail now bore away from the Sierra and towards the coast. Towards sundown I came across some large beds of prickly pears, some as high as six feet and scattered over acres of ground. The leaves were from an inch to two inches in thickness, oval-shaped, six to ten inches long, standing one above the other at right angles, and covered with spines. It bore a purple fruit which stopped my thirst to a certain extent, but left my tongue and lips full of barbed thorns, difficult to dislodge.

Night was approaching, and in company with two or three brother stragglers I hurried on for El Monte, but darkness overtook us before we arrived. The sight of lights in the distance quickened our steps, for we knew we were nearing the end of our journey. Crossing the dry, sandy bed of a narrow river we ascended a bluff and found ourselves in the dark street of a village. Getting a drink at the first house we came to we hunted up a place to stop all night. We found a sort of a hotel, and before an open fire in the bar-room rested awhile. Then we went out to supper. This was spread on a table, and we had benches to sit on and knives and forks to eat with. To

FIELD OF CACTI.

be sure, we lacked napkins and finger bowls, but in view of our other luxuries we pardoned the want of these. Our custom at meals had been to sit on the ground, or, if lazy, to lean on our elbows, while we helped ourselves from the frying-pan in the centre of the group, using our fingers when the temperature of the eatables would admit of it.

Greatly refreshed by my night's rest on the floor I was on my way early the next morning. Passing through the streets of the village, between vine-embowered gardens and scattered shade trees, which looked refreshing to eyes so long used to desert scenery, I emerged to a valley, the most beautiful I ever saw. I was now on the western boundary of the great plain I had been traveling over since leaving San Bernardino, which here arose in sweeping billows as it neared the range of hills on the west. Hitherto it had been semi-desert, naturally so or from drought, but now a covering of herbage, vividly green, spread over the plain from hills to mountains. Pasturing on this were flocks and herds which filled the air with neighing, lowing and bleating. All that was needed were shepherds and tuneful pipes to make this a veritable Arcadia, in which mortals might lead a life of peaceful happiness, undisturbed by the turmoil of the outer world. Near the centre of the valley arose the white walls of a village which gleamed brightly in the rays of the morning sun. Beyond was the mountain, green at the base, and changing to gray and brown as the outlines climbed upwards. Then came patches of snow, and finally an unsullied sheet of whiteness which spread upward and clothed the summit thousands of feet above the plain. Long had I journeyed amid scenes of awful desolation, over black and rugged mountains, amid sandy deserts and by the shores of poisonous creeks and rivers, and now that I had passed all these and reached the borders of civilization, it was infinitely refreshing to look on such a picture as was now spread before me. With my imagination excited by the scenes around, I pursued my way over this pastoral vale, occasionally halting a few moments to enjoy its beauties, for I feared that, like some pleasant dream, it would vanish to nothingness. I was better fitted this morning to enjoy such surroundings, for I had had a good night's rest, and as there were but twelve miles to go that day I traveled leisurely.

Passing through a range of green hills by a winding cañon I came on to a broad plain which extended to the ocean. I was now nearing Los Angeles, and traveling for a while along the foot of a range of hills, I turned to the west and soon came in sight of the "City of Angels," whose white walls gleamed in the noon-day sun.

Note.—The valley extending eastward from San Bernardino, which I found so thinly settled and rarely traveled over, is now traversed by a railroad, along which are many towns. Speculation is rife there in town-lots and suburban lands. San Bernardino itself has a population of six thousand. The name of the mount itself has been vulgarized to "Old Baldy."

XIV.

From Los Angeles to San Francisco.

THE southern half of California was then but sparsely
populated; what few large settlements there were
being near the coast and from fifty to one hundred
miles apart. Among these Los Angeles ranked the largest,
and still stands highest in importance, both on account of its
size and age. One of the first colonies planted by the
Mexicans in California was located here, the site being chosen
on account of the climate and fertile soil. It grew fast and
became the capital of Upper California. It is built on the
shores of the Los Angeles River, near the foot of a range of
mountains which extend in rugged outlines to the Pacific,
which at the port of San Pedro is thirty miles distant. The
architecture of the city is varied, ranging from one-story adobe
houses to large brick stores built by the invading Yankee.
At that time the place was distinctly Mexican, the American
and his style of building being exceptional. The streets
presented a strange appearance in the old part of the town.
The houses were of sun-dried bricks, and the common ones
roofed with reeds and grass, over which was poured a coating
of bitumen, from springs of that material near by. In hot
weather this melted, and running down the walls gave them a
variegated look. Some of the houses extended in large one-
story ranges, at intervals pierced by gateways opening to

(197)

gardens adorned with orange trees and vines. These belonged to the better classes, and were roofed with tiles. A rural, quiet air pervaded the suburbs, but in the business centre was noise and confusion compared with what was known there ten years before, when it was an exclusively Mexican town. Here was to be seen in greatest contrast the varied population of Los Angeles. Plainly attired nuns and fashionably dressed American women were seen together, as well as the swarthy Mexican, in his attire of shirt and drawers, along with the Yankee "dude." Chinese, Indians and negroes abounded ; in fact all the odds and ends of humanity seemed here brought in contact, and, chattering and jabbering in their many tongues, made up strange scenes, rarely witnessed in so small a place. Occasionally an ox-team would come creeping into town, laden with wine casks in transit to the coast, and following after a troop of donkeys with back-loads of wood packed from the neighboring mountains. Now and then the scene would be varied by the appearance of a horseman, who, fully equipped with a Mexican rider's outfit, would gallop by with a rattle of spurs and a stir of dust.

I spent the afternoon of my arrival looking around the town, in the busy centre, the quiet suburbs, and along the shore of the little river flowing by. In the water of this I saw a score of washerwomen with bare feet and in short skirts, pounding the dirt from soiled clothing by means of clubs as it lay in the water. I loitered about the stores, watching the swarthy customers ride up and remain mounted till their purchases were delivered to them, when they would gallop away.

I am speaking of the Puebla of thirty years ago, before it was, as now, a distinctively American town, the Mexican portion a curiosity merely, and speculation wild, and building lots selling at inflated prices. Now a railroad runs by the town and the screech of the locomotive has frightened the little wood-laden "burros" from the streets, and steam washers have driven the swarthy Naiads, who then vexed the clear waters of the Los Angeles with their paddles, to other means of livelihood. I prefer speaking of the town in its quieter days, when the influence of the old Spanish fathers at the Mission Church near by had not lost its sedative restraint, and before all were rushing to get at the head of the financial ladder.

In imagination Los Angeles had been a city of my love. I had read of its beautiful women, its gallant men and its pious priests, who had sacrificed so much for the salvation of the Indians, and a visit to the town made a great impression on me. If I could have shut the innovation of the Yankee quarter from my sight, I might have imagined myself in a town of La Mancha, the tropical courtyards, the horsemen, barbaric in their costume, the water nymphs in the river, and strings of donkeys with their wild drivers to keep up the illusion.

I would have seen more of Los Angeles, its old Mission and other points of interest, but I was so tired and footsore that I was satisfied to rest and prepare for my seaward tramp. So the rest of the day I sat at the corners of the streets, in the old part of the town, and watched the passers-by. Much of the "shopping" here was done on horseback. Buyers from neighboring ranches would gallop in, and suddenly halting before a *tienda barata*, or "cheap store"—as elsewhere, the stores here were all *tiendas baratas*—call for their wants, remaining mounted while the merchant made ready the goods, and after being waited on gallop away with clatter of spur and swish of leather accoutrements.

Throughout the day scattered parties of the adventurers who had started from Salt Lake with such high hopes of the future came straggling into the town, hungry, tired and out of spirits. The first comers got all the situations procurable, while the main part of the adventurers met with disappoint-

ment. Many by their prodigality at Salt Lake, or among the
Mormon settlements, had emptied their purses, and these found
themselves in a sorry plight indeed. The poor fellows might
have been seen at the street corners dolefully discussing their
affairs, present and prospective. Some were going to San Pedro
to take stowaway luck on the steamer to San Francisco;
others to continue their tramp up the coast to the same place,
a journey of five hundred miles over a rough, thinly-settled
country. I never heard how they got through. I am sorry
to say that in those times we did not worry much about what
became of one another.

Shortly after sunset I left Los Angeles, and with one of my
fellow ox-drivers of the plains began a night's march for San
Pedro, thirty miles away. At this time I can hardly say why
I started at that hour, but either because it was pleasanter
traveling by night than by day, or for fear of missing the
steamer, or to save the cost of a night's lodging. I think for
the latter reason, as the five dollar gold piece I got for my
rifle was broken up and the fragments so reduced, that I had
barely enough for my expenses to San Francisco, independent
of my passage money, which I would not touch. My companion was " Dutch Joe," he of the profane tongue and reckless disposition; but the poor fellow was dead broke now and
I pitied him. He had been a Mississippi steamboat man, and
was calculating to " beat" his way up the coast after he once
got on the steamer.

Passing through a street lined with gardens of orange, fig
and other semi-tropical trees, and bordered with hedges of
willow and long extensions of grape-trellises, we left the City
of Angels. Had we the wisdom we afterward possessed, we
would have known these picturesque roadside borders were
screens for expert throwers of the lasso, who practiced on travelers their noted skill and choked and robbed them; and that
the sterile pampas beyond was the haunt of picturesque ban-

dits who annexed murder to their other crimes; Americans and
Spaniards being treated impartially. We soon found ourselves
on a bleak plain, at the commencement of a lonely journey.
As the twilight deepened a depressing stillness came around
us, which was at intervals broken by the barking of dogs of
distant ranches, or the fainter heard howls of wolves on the
Sierra Madra Mountains. Overhead the stars shone brightly,

THE WINE TEAM.

but their glare was as chilling as the winds which at sunset
commenced blowing from the western sea.

I much regret for the reader's comfort that I have not a few
pleasant episodes and reminiscences to string on the thread of
my narrative; but I have not, and must note down things as
they came to me, only too glad that all came out right in the
end.

"Dutch Joe" and I exchanged few words as we plodded

13

along. My comrade was in no humor for singing his old-time songs, or telling his steamboat adventures, or for talking of the times when, a stage driver over a wild Arkansas route, he "beat" his employers out of the midway fares. He was subdued and depressed, and I must admit he had congenial company in me.

About 10 o'clock, through the darkness, we heard the creaking of wheels, the crack of a whip and the familiar talk indulged in by an ox-driver to his team. We soon caught up with an ox-drawn wagon on which was a cask of wine so large that in the dim light it looked as big as the "Heidelberg tun." This was in transit to the coast. The driver was companionable, and for a couple of hours we shared his talk with his oxen. The wine he was hauling was from a vineyard near Los Angeles, and was on its road to San Fransisco, whence it would go to France, thence to New York, where it would masquerade as *Veuve Cliquot* in all probability.

The night air was getting colder, and my blistered feet prevented me walking fast enough to keep warm. I often wished for the overcoat I had thrown away the day before. About midnight we came across a party of travelers who were seated around a fire, and with their permission we sat with them awhile and tried to warm ourselves. We left in an hour, and saying good-bye to our friend the teamster, as well as to Tom and Jerry, his wheelers, and Bill and Barney, his leading oxen—for I heard their names often enough to remember them in connection with threats and entreaties more or less profane—went on our way alone. The wind blew colder and colder, and towards morning we were glad to seek the shelter a friendly bluff afforded, when we built a fire with some coarse weeds and brush we found. With smoke-enforced tears we shivered here until daybreak, when against a wind like a tempest we resumed our way.

A peculiar noise now broke upon our ears, which we rightly

guessed was the surf lashing the shore. Emerging from a maze of ravines and sloughs I climbed a sand hill and to my joy I saw the waters of the Pacific, which the sun was just beginning to silver from his position on the summit of the distant Sierra. I have often thought how I traveled thirty-five hundred miles to see one ocean after living within one hundred miles of another all my life previous to my overland journey.

I could have gone into more extensive raptures over my first sight of the Pacific had I been in a better position to appreciate it. We have heard of Balboa's feelings, when from a "lone peak of Darien" he first glimpsed the same sea; but if he had walked all night lugging a pair of blankets and an unseemly carpet-bag, with nothing to drink and little to eat, and, from wearing tight boots, with blisters on his ankles as big as the quarter-dollars his purse lacked, he would have felt about as I felt. Still I must admit to a thrill of admiration as from the far sea line I saw the waves roll in and lash the miniature "lone peak" on which I stood.

I had struck the coast line at a point on the Bay of San Pedro which was too shallow for anchorage, but which is now near the site of Wilmington, a settlement which has blotted the "town" of San Pedro off the map. I have lately seen a photograph of this part of the Bay, and the sight of the railroad tracks laid under the bluff, the cars thereon, and the piles of lumber and the warehouses, so contrast with the place as I saw it, that I give an illustration of the landing place of 1858. On account of the dangers of this harbor a breakwater has been built to accommodate the increased commerce which the growth of Los Angeles has brought here.

Readers of Dana's "Two Years before the Mast" will remember San Pedro Bay as the scene of the flogging and of innumerable hardships of loading and unloading cargoes. I have often experienced a fellow feeling for the author, as each of our experiences on the California coast developed about the

same amount of fun. The 'town was no larger than on his
visit in 1835, and could not well have been smaller. There
were two adobe houses and a smith shop on the bank, and a
warehouse under the bluff. A steep road ran to the plain
above. There was no water near the place, and the few people
living here depended on a spring some miles inland.

There were but two vessels in the harbor; one the "Senator,"
which was to take us northward, and which I was pleased to

SAN PEDRO IN 1858.

see had not gone, and a sailing vessel, both anchored some
distance off for fear of being driven ashore by sudden winds.
The bay is a dreary sheet of water, surrounded by bleak shores,
bare of trees or verdure. On account of the insecurity of the
harbor and the labor of moving cargoes, in former times, San
Pedro was called by sailors the "Hell of the California coast."

The island in the illustration is known as "Dead Man's
Rock." Here, over twenty years before, a master of a vessel

was buried after a mysterious death, and this has given the place a mournful interest ever since.

We passed nearly the whole day on the shore of this dreary place, sunning ourselves as best we could to keep warm, and dozing away the past night's sleeplessness. How I wanted to get away from here can only be known by those who have been at this desolate port and seen its forbidding shore, with its bleak mountain background, the miserable adobe buildings and the island with its lonely grave, wind-swept, and with scream-ing sea birds circling around it. "Dutch Joe" and I appeared to be the advance guard of our party. The rest, a dozen or so, came straggling in through the day, tired, footsore and hungry. Some of them, who had spent their money, were forlorn looking indeed. To make matters worse, we were hungry and thirsty. Expecting to go directly on board the steamer, we had brought nothing to eat, and water was not pro-curable here, it being literally a "dry town." How such a forsaken place as San Pedro could be the port of a town like Los Angeles, which then had from 15,000 to 20,000 inhabitants, I am at a loss to say. Querulous and weary we spent the time watching the waves rolling in, the sea birds skimming over the water and diving below, and the freight in its tedious transit to the "Senator" from the rickety wharf. Among the latter was the cask of wine of our midnight friend, which came down the steep road leading to the *embarcadero* at the risk of annihilating the driver and oxen, and was laboriously got into a lighter and put on board. I went into a doze calculating the number of "drunks" in the huge tank.

Our resting place was at the foot of the bluff, up whose steep sides Dana and his fellow-sailors of the "Pilgrim," in 1837, carried boxes and bales of freight to the ox-carts waiting above, and down whose declivities they threw the rolls of hides taken in exchange, and which were carried on the heads of sailors to the boats. A wharf now ran a short distance out from shore, but the port accommodations were still very rude.

We were not allowed to go on board the "Senator" till near sun-down. A rope had been run ashore, and back and forward along this a lighter was pulled till the passengers were on board, the freight having been previously loaded. There was a heavy swell on the bay, although the wind had gone down, and I was afraid awhile our rude craft would swamp; but we finally reached the steamer. As the two vessels did not go up and down together, there was some difficulty in getting on board, but with the aid of the down-reaching arms of the sailors we climbed the deck. The "Senator" was on her up trip from San Diego, and for passengers had a motley crowd of dignified Spanish gentlemen, pompous army officers, enterprising Yankee merchants and adventurers of all kinds, seeking a change of scene. I was tired and, having slept none since leaving El Monte, crawled into a rude berth in the steerage and was soon forgetting everything in a deep sleep. When I awoke I found the "Senator" had up anchored and was plowing her way through the darkness, and also that I had missed my supper. However, as the charge was high I was not sorry, as I had saved that much.

That night the Pacific Ocean belied its name. I know of the propensity of travelers who to sea in ships go down to narrate remarkable experiences. They have the quickest or most tedious of voyages from port to port, the most terrible storms and the most quiescent calms. The vessel in question is at the "mercy of waves rolling mountains high," or is a "painted ship upon a painted ocean." Before the storm they note the anxious look of the captain, as he scans the barometer, and the talks among the sailors, who, in hushed voices, tell how they heard the ship's cat give an ominous note of warning the night before, or how the ghost of Tom Bowline, who was lost at sea last trip, appeared to the cabin boy about midnight and gave vent to an expression of similar import. The storm safely over, they hear master and men say they never had such nautical experience. Of course, in this age of steam these romancers cannot get up much excitement in regard to calms, unless they can make out that the captain forgot to take in coal at starting.

So to be in fashion I will tell how the "Senator" rolled and pitched as she sped on through the darkness; how she would mount the waves as if bent on a trip to the moon; how she would give a roll as if intent on spilling her freight and passengers into the sea, and then how we held our breaths when the prow swiftly came down. I will tell how the timbers groaned, the sails flapped; how the wind whistled through the cordage and the way the captain bawled and the sailors swore, and how the passengers wished they were home. It was my first experience on the ocean and I thought then we had a rough royage, but I suppose there was nothing unusual about it. As to the sea-sickness of the passengers I will say nothing; such descriptions are not agreeable. We were nearly two days making the trip, a time of much discomfort to us in the steerage. We stopped at Santa Barbara and Monterey, but between fog and darkness we saw but little of them. During the prevalence of certain winds they are dangerous places to stop at, and as this was the case now we hurried away from both ports. On the afternoon of Christmas Day we arrived in front of the Golden Gate, whose northern post is Punta Bonita, or Pretty Point; whose southern is Punta de los Lobos, or Wolves' Point. My impression had been that the entrance was between two acute headlands, beyond which the Bay of San Francisco expanded, which was erroneous. The passage is five or six miles long, with rugged hills as high as two thousand feet on the north, while those on the south are three or four hundred feet in elevation. The channel is from one to two miles wide. The seaward boundaries of this were bare and repulsive, but as we steamed inland the shores and islands were green and pleasant to look upon. Bearing southward we came in front of San Francisco, where, partly on piles and partly on sand hills, it looked eastwardly toward the magnificent bay of the same name, and beyond to the fertile plains of Contra Costa. We were soon fastened to the wharf and ready to land.

Even when stepping from palace cars to hotel coaches and

ENTRANCE TO THE GOLDEN GATE.

with money in abundance, a traveler experiences peculiar sensations when entering a large city, knowing that among "the whole cityful, friends he has none." How he would feel after the discomforts of a steerage voyage, and but twenty cents in his pocket, would be still more peculiar. I know that when the steamer was fastened to the wharf and preparations made for landing I felt a feeling of "goneness," hardly consistent with an Eastern man's idea of going ashore on the Land of Gold.

The word being given, a rush was made for the gang-plank by the passengers, who, weary of confinement, were glad to leave their ocean home of the two past days. They were welcomed by a motley crowd of cab drivers, hotel runners, young porters, news boys and boot-blacks, who ostentatiously met them as they poured from the decks of the "Senator." Forcing my way through the obstreperous gang, I at last reached the wharf-gates, and passing these I trod the streets of San Francisco—I was almost ready to say, "A stranger in a strange land," but the expression has been used so often I spare the reader its reiteration, and simply say—feeling like a "cat in a strange garret," with a scarcity of mice.

XV.

On the Tramp.

FTER I had started to hunt a place to stay all night I was joined by John Galdie, or "Scottie," as we all called him, who proposed that we should go together. As I knew him to be a quiet, honest fellow I agreed to it. He was nearly as poor as I was, so there was no danger of his taking me to a five-dollar-a-day hotel. We were an uncouth looking pair, and made some sport for the street gamins; used as they were to queer characters. What was known as the "Frazer River bubble," by which thousands had been induced to go up the coast to dig for gold, had lately bursted, and hundreds were coming back ragged and poor. Thinking we were just from the luckless diggings, much interest was taken in us by the boys. They called us "Frazer," asked us how we found the folks and where we proposed investing our money. Paying no attention to such nonsense we trudged over the amphibious streets next the water front; streets lying over what was late the bay. Near the edge of the rising ground on which the solid part of the city is built we came in sight of a sign bearing the words, "Pacific Lodgings, Twenty-five cents." Now the amount of my coin possessions was two ten-cent pieces; but these, on account of a financial reckoning peculiar to California,

amounted to the same as the sum named on the sign.
Thus a dime was the same as a twelve and a half cent
piece. If you bought an article worth ten cents and ten-
dered a quarter they gave you a dime in change. This was
the minimum coin in use. So I felt emboldened to enter the
"lodgings," and with my comrade by my side ascended a
pair of rickety stairs to a set of shabby apartments. We had
hardly reached the landing before the keeper came to meet
us. He turned out to be a good-hearted Irishman, who had
apparently seen better days. On making known our business
he showed us to a sort of a pen about five feet by eight in size,
containing a bed of suspicious appearance. This room we
engaged, and paying for one night's use of it in advance, we
started out to see what we could raise on our watches, each of
us having one. Mine was put on to me at Leavenworth by a
sharper, he getting in exchange a fair silver timepiece. His he
professed to be gold, which metal, he said, was more liked by
the Indians than silver, a fact he knew by experience, and
that they would gladly trade me a pony for a gold watch like
that. So I took it, and the first day I carried it showed it to
be the vilest of brass. I was so tried by the discovery that I
could have thrown it away, thinking I could never realize on
it. "Scottie's" was of silver and worth much more. When
we started out the streets were intensely dark, but as we could
get nothing to eat until we sold these watches we pushed on
till we came to a watchmaker's shop, and entering, made known
our errand to the proprietor. He astonished me with an offer
of three dollars for mine, while to my comrade he offered eight.
We gladly accepted these, and with the proceeds of the transaction in our pockets emerged to the streets, made muddy
from recent rains, and took our way towards our roosting
place. At the first bakery we stopped, and buying two loaves
of bread made a light supper thereon. Arriving at last at
the "Pacific Lodgings" we went to bed. It was long before I

could get to sleep. I thought about my home in the distant East and wondered why I had ever left it for such husks as I now fed on. I compared myself with the Prodigal of old, though, I am glad to say, with exceptions. I mentally traversed my way to the " Pacific." I was again by rail and water traveling to Kansas; then, by the side of my patient, sad-eyed oxen, crossing the plains and mountains to Salt Lake. Then came my trip with the Mormons, my walk to the coast and my voyage to San Francisco. I reversed the line of travel and extracted all the pleasant episodes from it I could, but then there was no sleep for thoughts about my future. "Scottie" was of a more stolid nature and was soon asleep. Our lodgings were of a low grade and frequented by sailors, tramps and others who could not afford the luxuries of a hotel. As these came straggling into their rooms during the night I could tell by their brutal voices and blasphemous talk what manner of men they were. We were separated from them only by thin board partitions, like stalls, which did not run to the ceiling, so that we had a chance for a close acquaintance with the strange bed-fellows we were thrown among. In spite of the racket sleep came at last, and thus ended my first and last Christmas Day in California.

Late the next morning we were awakened by the "sound of the church going bell" as it echoed from the many places of worship in the city, ushering in a day unobserved by me for many a long month. As the sweet chimes came floating to my ears through the morning air memories of the distant land I had so long ago departed from came to me, where the observance of the First day of the week was a rule and not, as here, an exception. During the trip from Leavenworth to San Francisco a single Sabbath had not been observed by our party, and I had not entered a place of worship except a Mormon church, where I had heard the most cranky doctrine.

We laid abed as long as we dared to get the worth of our

lodging money, and when obliged to get up found ourselves in the midst of a dismal, rainy day. We only went out to meals, two of which we indulged in at the "What Cheer House," where we enjoyed the luxury of sitting at a table with a cloth on and waiters to attend to our wants. But it did make a hole in my three dollars, although we indulged sparingly.

Another night in company with beings to whom they with which the Prodigal Son ate husks were blue-blooded gentlemen, and a bright morning dawned upon us. We arose early, as now we must begin hunting for a "job" in earnest, for by the way our watch money was going we found how fleeting was time. We spent a little more of the results of this time at the "What Cheer"—which, by the way, was one of the greatest restaurants in the world and which furnished meals of good quality at a low price and without the aid of liquor sales—and then went hunting for work. The trades and professions we found full of incumbents and even day's work could not be had; so after hunting till we were tired, we resolved to leave San Francisco and travel towards Sacramento, intending to try for work among the farmers, and, failing, then strike for the mines.

My funds were now reduced to one dollar, while probably "Scottie" had three or four, he having run his down in the purchase of a pair of shoes. I could not afford these, although I needed them badly.

With the good wishes of our host of the " Pacific Lodgings " accompanying us we left that vermin-infested dormitory about 10 o'clock on the morning of December 27th. We proceeded directly to the wharf of the San Antonio ferry, where we boarded a little steamer which was soon on its way over the bay. The day was clear and the sun shone brightly, lighting up the surrounding scenery with glowing tints until it was very beautiful. Behind us lay the city with its busy wharves and its roofs and spires gleaming in the meridian sun; before us spread the plains of Contra Costa, and on their margin appeared the pretty vilages of Oakland and San Antonio. On the background arose a range of mountains, whose slopes were green with herbage, with Mount Diablo rising in the distance. Around us was spread an expanse of water, dotted with sailing craft and shining like silver. Everything, around, above, below, was full of beauty, but as I was not in a sentimental mood it went almost unappreciated. The city had absorbed two dollars of my three, the crossing of the beautiful bay had taken twenty-five cents of the remaining dollar, while the plain beyond was simply a hunting ground for work and the mountain an obstacle to surmount in case none was found. We soon reached our landing place at Oakland, but a village at that time, and the home of the artist-traveler J. Ross Browne, a name then spelt without the terminal vowel. Getting ashore we traversed the streets, broad and shaded with the perennial live-oak from which the place takes its name.

Oakland is now a large place—a sort of a Brooklyn to San Francisco—and noted for its beautiful residences and as the terminus for the principal overland railroad. On account of its situation the main city can only be reached by land from the east in a round-about way; so an immense ferryboat has been built for carrying several cars at a time across the bay. The town is many times larger now than when I saw it, and much more beautified, but with all its additions it cannot impress modern tourists more than it did me, when, debarking from an unpretentious ferryboat, I walked its shaded streets with their bordering of well-kept yards and pretty residences. I was hungry, unkempt and out of conceit with my appearance generally, and with spirits down at the heels; but for all that I could not help being impressed with the beauties of the place.

Coming to a baker shop, in imitation of Franklin, we bought two loaves of bread. Except in the matter of soiled clothing, I cannot continue the comparison further, for I have no evidence that there were any Miss Reeds with their interested eyes fixed on us, and the community, as far as I can learn, was never materially impressed with our presence. Bread is not very satisfying, so, to make it durable, we bought

OAKLAND IN 1858—CONTRA COSTA MOUNTAINS IN THE DISTANCE.

some "bolognas," and seating ourselves on a green bank in the suburbs of the town we partook of our homely fare in silence, unquestioning the origin of the solid part of our meal.

And now for another tramp. Formerly I had a definite objective point—San Francisco; now it was where I could strike a job of work, which was a very indefinite point. I thought when I put my luggage on board the "Senator" I

was done packing it around; but here it was like the "Old
Man of the Sea," impossible to shake from my back. There it
lay on the grass, the same old carpet-bag, roll of blankets and
boots. I loathed their sight, but could not do without them.
So I had nothing to do but shoulder them, and between the
Scylla of moccasons with wet feet, and the Charybdis of
tight boots and blistered ankles, go on my way. Our route
lay over a level plain, which the recent rains had rendered

LARGEST FERRYBOAT IN THE WORLD, PLYING BETWEEN SAN FRANCISCO
AND OAKLAND.

impassable by mud and water, and as I now was in the moc-
cason stage of foot-gear I suffered therefrom.

The plain was dotted at various intervals with ranch buildings, but they were generally far from the road, so that we
were obliged to make long *detours* in our search for employment. We had arrived in California at a bad time for work,
as the farmers had all supplied themselves with help. Each
farmer, however, probably to get shut of us, could tell of some

one further on who wanted help, and so we traveled on to be disappointed again.

To make the situation worse towards night it began to rain, and we had both forgotten our umbrellas. Between my leaky moccasons and wet clothing I fared badly. At nightfall we came to a farm-house on whose hospitality we encroached. The owner was away on our arrival, but soon came home and gave us permission to remain till morning, but did not press us to stay to tea. We remained outside in the mist and coming darkness until a look through the window showed the table set and preparations made to partake of its edible trimmings, when, "Scottie" leading the way, we entered the kitchen. Our "cheek" was rewarded with an invitation to a "set-down" supper. Our manners had not shown remarkable refinement, but we were getting well broken in to our enforced life, and did not suffer any loss of self-respect. We were beginning to see how life looked from the tramp's side of the fence.

Our host, now that we had forced ourselves upon him, treated us kindly, and after supper allowed us to sleep in an outbuilding along with the two hired men. It was California style for the help to sleep in the barn, or any other place outside the house, which was often a mere shell of one story, with barely room for the ranch owner and his family. While I was in the State the hired farm-hand had few comforts in this life, and, after he was done with it, was placed without ostentatious ceremony in a fence corner. One of the hands was an Irishman who was extremely patronizing in his way, and, when we told him how unsuccessful we had been in getting work, said it was because we looked so green on account of our dress. He said our caps were enough of themselves to bar us from the pleasures of farm life; we must get hats with wide rims and assume a more free and easy air. As we had not the money to buy hats, nor the wherewithal to raise our spirits, his advice did not amount to much, but I afterwards bore a

14

profound dislike to my particular head-gear, which since leaving Salt Lake had done dual duty as night cap and dress hat. After this I would fain have doffed my cap when applying for work, but as politeness was at a discount, hats on at table even not being a cause for expulsion from dining-rooms where we fed, I abstained from this effeminacy.

Waiting awhile for an invitation to breakfast, which did not evolve, we shouldered our effects with spirits of a downward tendency, and trudged off in the direction of a ranch where lived two bachelors who we heard were in want of people of about our build. These "twin relics," however, cold-shouldered us and sent us on our way. The market for us seemed glutted; the supply for us seemed beyond the demand. This state of things was not very creditable to California, but so it was.

Leaving here, our route lay along a line of telegraph in the direction of a pass in the mountains to the northeast. We soon entered a crooked cañon, down which was laid a narrow wagon road. This was sideling and slippery from the previous night's rain, which was again falling. I traveled as usual in tribulation on account of my feet. Reaching the summit we found it so enveloped in mist we could see but a few paces in any direction. Descending the other side of the mountain by a winding stream we came to a lone inn called the "Walnut Creek House," where we got some bread and pork of a landlady who looked as sour as her bread. The day was cold and wet, and being tired and hungry we stopped at a convenient place and built a fire, where we warmed ourselves and ate our recent purchase. Then we got our pipes and took a smoke. I don't use the weed now, and, in a general way, discountenance it; but when a prohibitory tobacco law is passed I want an exception made in favor of tramps. It cheers them without inebriation. I know that after traveling in all kinds of weather, and being perpetually rebuffed by unappreciating

farmers, a quiet smoke behind a hay rick, or under a shelter-
ing tree, was a great comfort. But I never believed in smoking
in barns. I drew the line there; "Scottie" did not. That
same night we slept in one, and he lit a match in the midst
of straw and smoked away. In my native land I had heard
it called the sin of sins for a tramp to smoke in a barn, but
things were so reversed and my comrade seemed to enjoy it
so, that I said nothing.

It was again shoulder carpet-bags and march! More rain
and no umbrellas! More changes from boots and blisters to
moccasons and misery.

The weather cleared off as we proceeded. We were now
among a maze of vividly green hills through which our road
wound. The land was scatteringly settled, and our chances
for work proportionally limited. State of my financial thermometer, sixty-five cents above zero and falling!

The country began to subside to gentler curves and to become
more settled. Late in the afternoon we came to a little
hamlet and here we made another fruitless effort for work;
but we were told of some further on. At sun-down we came
to a lone ranch whose mistress kindly gave us some biscuits,
which much to our relief she would take no pay for. She let
us dry ourselves by the fire awhile, and when her husband
came home, he allowed us to lie in the barn all night, for
which we were thankful. The sun set brightly, and as its rays
slanted through the dripping live-oaks and broad shadows
crept out from the hills, I was reminded of when, after similar
rain-followed sunsets on the old home farm, I went after the
cows, with the trees glistening with crystal drops and the
swamp-robin's song ringing from the darkening woods which
shaded the waters of the Cuttalossa.

Shaking the straw from our clothing we were again on our
way the next morning, the 29th. Again the green hills arose
and fell before us. From the summit of a range we enjoyed,

as far as stomachic vacuity would allow, the scenery before us—a verdant plain stretching far away and dotted with ranches, with the waters of Suisun Bay in the distance. On the horizon arose Mount Diablo, a landmark which can be seen from San Francisco arising above intervening mountains, although its habitat is near the shore of the Bay of Suisun. This scene of many a weird legend was in view during near all my wanderings around the bay.

A GLANCE AT MONTE DEL DIABLO.

After breakfast time we came to another ranch, whose lady furnished us with breakfast, on our request being made. She seemed kind and had told us if we would wait she would give us something better than cold victuals. We supposed this would be a gratis affair, and when the meal was ready we complained not that the bread was sour, the pork unsavory and the coffee made from old stock, but ate the viands thankfully. Thinking it safe to offer to pay for our fare, I put my hand in my pocket as a preparatory flourish, and asked the extent of our indebtedness. "Oh," said she, "I guess I wont charge you more than seventy-five cents." Taken aback by this extortion we paid the amount, "Scottie" regretting we had not lied and said we had no money. My monetary thermometer now registered twenty cents in the shade, considerably below freezing. I was now as well off as when I debarked from the "Senator," except that I had no watch to hypothecate.

Leaving this ranch which had so raided our funds we trudged through the ever verdant range of hills and descended to a plain bordering a sluggish stream flowing into Suisun Bay. About 4 o'clock we came to the village of Pacheco. On the way we met a man who said there was a fence-builder living there who wanted hands, and him we found at the "grocery," which means a combination of grog-shop and store. He told us if he got a contract he was expecting he would give us work. "Scottie" went with him to see about it, I being too footsore to go along. So I seated myself down on the porch till they got back. The village was mainly Mexican, one of that race keeping the "grocery," or *tienda*. I sat there watching the swarthy customers coming and going on their tough "bronchos," or while they stopped to drink, buy groceries or play cards. The latter, with a gambling attachment, seemed to be their delight. The cards were peculiarly pictured. When off their horses these Mexicans were common looking enough, but when mounted, with ornamented saddles and bridles and jingling spurs, they made a very picturesque appearance.

In an hour "Scottie" and the contractor came back, but with no good news, so we moved on in the direction of Martinez. Just after dark we overtook a man who lived in the latter place. He knew of no work, was poor himself, and if he had room in his little house said he would keep us. Hearing we had no money to pay for lodgings he took us to an empty school house, on the edge of the village, where we could stay all night. He then left us to ourselves in the thickening gloaming doubtless experiencing the same relief we all feel when sending a tramp to a hotel, a proprietor of a brief to the nearest benevolent neighbor, or a book-agent to our worst enemy. We loitered around the door of the empty hall of learning for a while but did not enter, fearing we might not get awake in time for school ; besides, we questioned the right of our departed friend, who had thoughtfully slipped away, to give us the freedom of this hall of learning. We then went on to Martinez, a considerable town and the county seat of Contra Costa

STRAITS OF CARQUINAZ.

County. This is opposite Benicia, on the Straits of Carquinaz, which connect the bays of San Pablo and Suisun, the latter the recipient of the waters of the Sacramento and San Joaquin.

Here we found a liveryman kind enough to let us pass the night in his stable. He sent a hostler with us, and picking out a comfortable stall we secured it by depositing our baggage therein. · It being too cold to sit there, we went to the hotel adjacent, and seated around a warm stove we fired up

our pipes and tried to forget our troubles. The clink of the
two solitary dimes in my pocket reminded me that they would
have to swell to fifty cents before they would take me across
the ferry to Benicia; and we must do that to go on to Sacramento, and I was sore puzzled as to how the difficulty was to
be obviated; besides, we were as hungry as owls. However,
"Scottie" seemed to have a spare dime, with which he bought
a loaf of bread, which, on account of its lightness, contained
about as much nourishment as so much dried fog, and with
this we left the comfortable stove for the stable and took our
places in the stall. We looked so tired out that the hostler did
not think it worth while to put a pole between us, and, so
leaving us, we lay down to sleep along with the other roadsters
in the barn.

The next morning, without any preliminary grooming or
feeding, we left our stable and went to the wharf, where, in an
hour's time, the ferry-boat landed. Willing to run the risk of
being put on shore when the captain found out the condition
of my bank account, I went on board with "Scottie." Luckily
for me that officer did not come around for the fare until the
boat had started. When he came my heart worked up toward
my throat when I had to tell him I had but twenty cents,
which I offered him. "If that is all you have," said he,
"keep it till you can pay me!" Here was a slice of practical
Christianity in a state so covered with mortgages of the Arch-
Enemy!

Our boat was soon over, and stepping ashore I found myself in Benicia, once the capital of California and named after
General Vallejo's daughter, who was dead and lay buried
among the green hills back of the town. Vallejo, a short
distance off, was to have been the capital, and to secure it the
General spent $100,000 on state buildings, which were unused
and went to ruin; a new whim having seized the authorities.
Benicia was then a government post, having extensive bar-

racks. At the wharf we saw a train of Uncle Sam's wagons on the way to San Bernardino. The long line of white sheets looked familiar, and, much as I disliked returning my steps, I would gladly have hired as a teamster. The sight of the train had about the same effect on us as a ship would on a sailor who had turned landsman to better his condition, vowing to never trust the treacherous deep again. We had rough times on the plains, but were having worse now, and were ready to go back to life on a train. So we concluded to make application. To do so I walked a mile to the quartermaster's office, but we were not wanted, so we concluded to tramp on up the valley, still following the telegraph. I had previously invested ten cents in a loaf of bread, which answered for breakfast and dinner. I had now ten cents left; my brother tramp, as it turned out, more.

Striking across a range of green hills we at length came to the road leading to Sacramento. This highway follows the flat land bordering the Bay of Suisun, except where the marshes which fringe it force it to the high ground. Here it was sideling, and my hard boots blistered my feet worse than ever while traversing these slopes. "Scottie," with his comfortable shoes, could easily outwalk me. Conversation on general topics having long since been exhausted, we talked little as we walked along, and as at this season rain was chronic, we had not many pleasant things to say, our wet clothing putting a damper on conversation. The road was a lonely one, and as the ranches were far apart we had few chances for work. The land was marshy and covered with shallow pools. The bay adjacent was broad and shallow, and was the recipient of the waters of the Sacramento and San Joaquin. A sail now and then, or a rare steamer, was all that enlivened its waters, and these were often hidden by mists. We came at sundown to a group of isolated hills, when, turning a point, we came to a lone tavern called the

"Cordelia House." Entering the bar-room we sat down before the fire to dry and warm ourselves, and lighting our pipes prepared, as far as I was concerned, to pass a hungry night. We had walked sixteen miles that day, about forty in all, and still no work. With my sore feet, aching bones and empty pockets I felt about as low down a tramp as runs the

"SCOTTIE" AND I.

road. We sat silently by the fire listening to the talk of the two or three travelers stopping there for the night.

When the landlord came in to see how many of us wanted supper I said nothing, knowing I could not pay for it. When the bell rang I was going to remain and starve it out, but "Scottie" told me to come on and he would pay. Never did his voice sound so pleasant. It appeared he had not been entirely "broke," but this last venture finished him financially.

The supper being on the American plan, and knowing we would now have to beg until we got work, the landlord did not make much out of us. We were allowed to lie on the floor until morning. We failed to work a free breakfast out of our host, but he gave us permission to leave our gripsacks at the hotel until we came for them.

In the midst of a penetrating rain we left the hotel and struck across a range of hills for Napa Valley, where we were told we would find work. I had nothing to carry but my blankets, so I traveled with more comfort. What I had left was of no practical use to me, being a better suit of clothing and some books. One of these was named "Spanish without a Master," which I had studied that I might enjoy conversation with the native Californians. It was aptly named, for if it ever had a master it was without one while I carried it. Arrived in the valley, work was as scarce as ever. We would alternate in making our inquiries. Some would be answered respectfully, others rudely. I well recollect a farmer we came across while he was killing a hog. It was my turn, and in spite of the inauspiciousness of the moment, I humbly asked him if he did not want a couple of good men. Looking up from his gory work in surprise, for he had not seen me before, he spitefully told me he " couldn't raise enough money to pay the men he had, let alone more," and went on with his work. Tired and hungry, as usual, we arrived at a wayside ranch, whose owner was just going to dinner. He had no work for us, but kindly invited us to sit down to the table.

We were now getting into the heart of Napa Valley, one of the greatest grain growing regions around the bay. We came to the little village of Suscol about sunset. Here lived some Bucks Countians, but I did not know it then. Just beyond we came to Napa. Unacquainted with the country over which we were traveling I thought we were going more and more into the wilderness. Imagine my surprise when I saw a large town on a navigable stream in which were some sailing vessels, and from which a daily steamer ran to San Francisco.

The next thing to find out was where to pass the night. The town, covered as it was with the gathering shades of evening, looked inhospitable, which might not have been the case in the broad glare of day. Wandering half aimlessly about the streets and passing groups of merry people—for it was New Year's Eve—who so contrasted with our sorry selves, we again gravitated towards a livery stable. Seeing a light within we entered, and looking around for a comfortable stall humbly asked the proprietor if he could stable us. "No; I will not," said he; "I never allow stragglers in my barn over night." We were leaving when he called us back, and in a kindlier tone told us we might sleep in a shed outside. This we found to be an open place, covered with straw on poles, and here we left our blankets and started out to hunt a fire, for the night air chilled us. We soon found a hotel before whose hearth we made ourselves comfortable. Being hungry we at length sallied out, and striking a bakery invested our joint capital, twenty cents, in two loaves of bread. We were now bankrupt.

Upon coming out we heard music, and going to where it came from we entered a hotel. Here we found an assemblage of young men, who had come from the surrounding country to take part in a New Year's ball; for that day had ushered in the year 1859. Money was flowing freely from these generous young Californians for worse than useless things, while we were suffering for necessities. Things to us seemed out of joint. The dancing soon began, and to see it we went to the hall adjoining the ball-room. Groups of pretty, well-dressed girls came down the stairs and whisked by us, laughing and talking on their way to join the merry-makers. I wondered what they thought of the two tramps looking on, or whether they thought of them at all. The men might have been common rowdies in cheap-store-clothes, and the girls mediocre affairs in shoddy dresses and brass jewelry, but to us, from our humble station, they seemed as of the *elite*.

We looked at this gay scene from our comfortable position as long as we thought it prudent for fear of ejectment, when we left, and wending our way through the noisy streets sought our straw palace. Making our beds on some bales of hay we at last got to sleep. The next morning we were awakened by the crowing of some biddies roosting on the shed. The air was chilling and a thick fog hung over the town and its surroundings. We remained wrapped up until the sun was an hour high, when we rolled up our blankets and resumed our tramp, but with the usual luck. At noon we reached a ranch owned by a retired sea captain, who, on appearing, said: " Well boys! just from the States, are you?" Want work, do you? Got none, but got some dinner for you! Walk right in and help yourselves!" We had a tip-top dinner, winding up with pie.

Here we heard of a ranch a few miles off where hands were wanted. Thanking our entertainer we made a bee line thence, across broad, level fields, and about 4 o'clock got to the boundaries of the ranch. We soon came across two shepherds who were seated by a fire under a wide spreading live-oak and tending some thousands of sheep. Coming to the ranch we were told that the " Patron," Signor Augustina, was not at home, but soon would be. In about an hour he made his appearance, and through an interpreter told us that they had all the help needed, but that a friend, eighteen miles away, wanted him to get him two men, and that if we would stay with him two or three days he would take us over. This information made us exceedingly glad, for it meant something to eat for that length of time.

The Salvador Ranch, which we were now on, belonged to Salvador Vallejo, brother to the General, and was a large tract from the amount of wheat they were putting in—two thousand nine hundred acres. It was worked by one hundred hands, half of whom were Mexicans. Everything was conducted with military precision. At 5 o'clock in the morning the bell on the ranch house was vigorously rung, and at its summons every man was expected to get up, and if he was a driver get his team ready for work. At 6 the bell rang for breakfast. This over, the hands went to their allotted tasks, and under the supervision of a major-domo, or overseer, who on horseback was continually visiting different parts of the ranch, worked on until half-past eleven, when the bell called them to the house in readiness for dinner at 12. At 1 they were signalled to work and at sunset to quit. Everything worked smoothly. The men and animals were hard worked, but all had plenty to eat.

There were fifty plows at work, the motive power being oxen and horses. Most of the former were native cattle and were driven by Mexicans. They pulled by their horns, the yoke being lashed to them. It was an odd sight to see the Mexicans plowing, with sharpened sticks instead of whips, with Spanish oaths instead of English, and with different commands from ours. You could hear the wild cries of the drivers a long distance.

We enjoyed ourselves in a fashion the several days we were on the Salvador Ranch. The reader can hardly appreciate the change from our tramp life to this. We had an easy time, doing what odd jobs we liked, had plenty to eat and a straw-mow to sleep in. The table manners were somewhat primitive, I admit. Hats were worn when desirable. If a piece of bread was wanted no waiter passed it along, neither did the wisher ill-manneredly reach for it. He simply said to the one nearest the edible, " Hello ! pard, heave us a chunk of bread." In a trice it would come, like a quoit. The coffee-pot was passed along that whoso wanted might pour. There was no table-cloth for one to be afraid of soiling, no napkins that might be carried off in lieu of "wipes," no embarrassing finger bowls in danger of doing duty as goblet or wash basin. Everything was plain and unpretentious, free and easy; the latter particularly applying to the conversation. Still I should not criticize or satirize. I was used well, and my life on the Salvador Ranch, following as it did so many hardships, is a pleasant episode in my life.

To make a long story short I left the ranch on the 4th of January, in company with my good friend "Scottie," in a wagon driven by Signor Augustina, and bound for Signor X., who lived in the Valley of Petaluma. The morning was cold and a foggy darkness surrounded us, as drawn by a span of half-broken, half-bred horses we swiftly moved over the flat which extended to a neighboring ridge, beyond which was the Valley of Sonoma. Lightly clad as we were, "Scottie" and I shivered with the cold, and crouching down in the wagon we covered ourselves with our blankets. No talk ensued between us and our conductor for the good reason that it was impossible, from neither knowing the other's language. The ride was unpleasant until the sun rose to partially dispel the mists and warm the air. Like reptiles thawed to activity by the warmth of spring we shook off our blankets and enjoyed ourselves looking around us as we passed the varying scenery. Now we were driving rapidly over a long level stretch, now crossing a rolling divide, through tortuous cañons, along a serpentine road so sideling in places that I was afraid of an upset, and then crossing a break-neck gulch or wading some sticky bog. We passed by scattered ranches and at rare intervals a hotel. At 11 o'clock we came to the old Spanish town of Sonoma, twelve miles from Napa. This is a quaint looking place, with a *plaza* in the centre and built of adobes. Leaving the plains of Sonoma by a crooked cañon winding through a ridge of green hills we came to the valley of Petaluma, and at noon arrived at our destination.

XVI.

Ranch Life.

IGNOR X., an Italian some sixty years old, had been a successful merchant in San Francisco. He had a son named Pedro, who married a native heiress. This lady inherited a tract of one thousand six hundred acres in Sonoma County, and thinking a fortune might be made in farming, the whole party, father, mother, son and his wife and baby left San Francisco and moved to this ranch, on which had previously been built a house and barn. With them were transported all manner of farming implements; among them a subsoil plow for delving in a soil which hardly knew a bottom, some of which was composed of an adobe clay so hard that the coulter point would hardly scratch it. Though Pedro and his wife owned the property they were looked upon as children by the old gentleman, who was the controlling power on the ranch. He scolded his son as if he were a boy in roundabouts, and he in his turn, as if he found consolation in the humiliation of so doing, unnecessarily scolded his employees. Inez, the young wife, was as much of a plaything as was the baby, Ana, or as she was called in the diminuendos of the Spanish language, Anita, and, as far as assisting at household affairs was concerned, was of no more account than the baby. Signor X. did the cooking. He was a singular genius, and cut an odd figure as with head bare, or handkerchief tied around it, and with pantaloons suspenderless and a red sash girt around his loins, he marched about, gun in hand, shooting his enemies, the blackbirds, which in countless numbers lit on his new-sown grain and tore it up. He was extremely passionate, and at times, when stalking around with his gun and wildly shouting, was fearful to behold.

It was here that John Galdie and I began ranch life in the Golden State, January 4th. The only man X. had hired before our coming was an Irishman, named Richard Dobbin, and guided by his feeble directions and the oath-filled broken English of the father and the less bearable interference of the son, who for fear of offending the old man, of whom he was in dread, merely repeated or translated his words, we began operations by breaking up the prairie sod which, unencumbered by bush or tree, spread in abrupt billows all around us.

For drawing our three Yankee plows we had to choose our teams from eleven head of horses, all of which, with one exception, were of mixed native breed. This exception was Old Tom, a bob-tail gray, brought from the States, and which was our main stand-by. He once had a mate, which had departed this life previous to our arrival, poisoned by a discharged hand, so our suspicion-filled master said, but which was more probably killed by overwork. So the whole blunt came on Tom. As far as my experience went, the native horses had but little endurance, and those which were manageable were continually giving out in the team. Some were valueless to plow or wagon, and were only available when spanned with a wooden saddle and bridled with the cruel Spanish bit, and were ridden galloping over the prairie. A few were docile, but these were soon broken down with hard work, so that our plow teams were reduced to one, the centre-piece of which was the faithful Tom. A part of the tract was a deep shale loam and was easy plowing, but a large portion was "adobe," a stiff, brown clay, hard to start the plow in, and when entered difficult to keep there from the roots of a weed called the soap plant. The ranch was quite hilly and inconvenient to work, except where the hills arose like hemispheres, when we began at the bottom and plowed round and round. We worked the horses three abreast but, except in mellow soil, made poor headway. As the horses were mainly unbroken we were in continual turmoil by their kicking, refusing to pull and getting tangled in the harness. The "Patron," or Boss, was constantly on hand, swearing, beating the horses, bearing his heavy weight, for he was six feet high and broad of build, on the plow beam and screaming, "*Mucho terrano! Mucho terrano!*" which meant more ground, in order to make us take a broader furrow and a deeper. At times the team would be completely exhausted, or may be inextricably tangled up, and then the old gentleman would stand angry and overflowing with fearful and unintelligible oaths, gesticulating wildly and with stout staff pounding the poor "*caballos.*" He swore Spanish, Italian and broken English. At such times we cut a comical figure: the struggling horse, the irate master and awe-stricken hired-man. After the teams were reduced to one, a teamless teamster was kept riding the plow-beam, so that the last trio was used up. The whole cavalcade, except Tom and a riding horse, was now turned out to graze and recruit, and our master turned his attention to oxen as plow propellers. First he bought a medium-sized pair of cattle, but under the original dispensation they soon went the way of their equine brethren. Then a new pair were bought, and a fine, big yoke they were. And now, with two span of oxen to a wheel-plow, we might be seen gaily cruising over the prairie. We were all in raptures, particularly the horses, who eyed us from afar on their pasturage, and while we were not interfered with we got along finely. But soon the Patron's evil genius set him to interfering, and the greedy man again screamed

15

"*Mucho terrano!*" and the oxen fell faint in the furrow. We had now broken a hundred acres of land, eleven horses and four oxen, and we thought it time to stop. The wheat had been sown and harrowed in between the blows, and turning the oxen loose to keep the horses company, we turned our attention to fence building. We used redwood for posts and sawed rails of Oregon pine for nailing on them. The posts had been previously sharpened, and were to be driven into the ground. Into the mystery of this I was soon introduced. Mounted on a high, clumsy stool it was my painful duty to pound with a "pepper-wood" maul, the size of a nail keg, on the top of the post, which Don Pedro steadied. This was a little monotonous, not to say tiresome. The good Don Pedro never "spelled" me; instead, he would look inquiringly at me whenever my catapult ceased its vibrations. In fact it was an injured look, and, I am sorry to say, I was sometimes tempted to mistake his head for the post-top. At first he would start a hole with a crowbar, but afterwards, thinking he was humoring me, he stopped that concession. We finished a mile of fence and then quit.

One of my morning duties was to haul water from a spring three hundred yards off, for house use and for soaking barley overnight for the horses. This I accomplished with my faithful companion, Tom, hitched to a wooden sled, on which were placed two barrels; these filled, I drew them up a steep hill. Once I recollect my frail sled pulled apart and set the lading to playing roley-boley to the bottom. I looked at them with unenviable feelings, listening to the tantalizing "glug-glug" the bung gave forth each revolution, Tom looking quietly on.

The Patron always routed us up before daylight after a night which was always too short. I often thought of the miserable negro slaves, who longed all day for night and sighed when the morning came! About an hour before daylight we would hear the voice of the elder Patron penetrating the foggy air with fran-

tic cries for "R-c-e-chard" to "geeta uppa." Dick, I am sorry
to say, often "possumed," when our interlocutor would get so
excited that "Scottie" or I was fain to answer by proxy for the
derelict Dick.

When our eleven horses were all working we divided their
care between us, and generally had them ready for work before
day. We fed them on wild oats, cut green, clover and timothy
hay being unknown, while for solid feed we gave them barley.
This was put to soak twelve hours before using, as it was indi-
gestible otherwise. The horses cleaned and harnessed, we went
to breakfast, which was invariably composed of *galleta Italiana*,
a kind of hard bread and coffee; each of the best quality, but
not a very solid diet for laboring men. This bread, which is
far superior to hard tack, is six inches in diameter and from a
half-inch to an inch in thickness, and one of these disks we
found each morning by our coffee-bowls. Plates and knives
and forks we never had, because we had no use for them. Of
coffee, with the customary trimmings, we had an abundance on
tap in the tea-kettle. The bread we broke up and put to soak,
as we did the barley for the horses; in fact, the two and four-
legged workers on the farm fared pretty much alike, except
the latter got waited on and we did not. The bread puffed up
elegantly, but its staying qualities were poor. One hour's
worrying with the teams or swinging the big maul would turn
it into hired man. Thinking our allowance too small, Dick
explored the kitchen loft one morning with his long arms and
found the source of our bread supply, and after that we did
not want. Our dinners were composed of fresh beef in general,
or cod-fish on fast days, fried in oil, and bread and coffee. Pie
we never saw, but mushrooms we had sometimes. Supper the
same. This was our favorite meal as we were not hurried, and
we often prolonged it rather than go to the gloom of the barn.
We were never in the house except at meal time, and as we
had no village store, with its nail-keg seats held down by gar-

rulous gossips, to hie to for entertainment, we had a dull time outside of working hours; and this kept up for three months and a half!

In justice to Signor X. I must say he was a good cook, and lovingly bending over his stew-pan, he had quite a domestic look, in strong contrast to his appearance when roaming his daughter's broad acres. The family ate in an adjoining room, and, for all I know, fared as we did. We were much edified by the family conversation while at meals—there was but a thin board partition between us—particularly as we could not understand a word they said. They were continually talking; the rough bass of the senior mingling with the soft voice of Inez and the childish treble of baby Anita. Our meals eaten, we would go to our allotted tasks; my morning chore being to hitch Tom to the sled matutinal, when barrel laden we sped merrily to the fountain. After this I would play plow or a tattoo on the redwood posts. Supper over, which was after dusk, we went to our sleeping apartment, which was a room partitioned off in the barn, within hearing of the crunching horses. In our boudoir there were two bunks; one for "Scottie" and I, the other was Dick's Then, if not too tired, we would light a candle and talk on such subjects as came uppermost; Dick, perhaps, about his times before we came with our Patron, how rich he was and what a store he had in "Frisco;" "Scottie," of his life amid the "banks and braes" of Scotland; I, about how much better I was fixed when in the "States." This Dick would doubt, or else cover my narrative over and tuck it in with a more favorable account of his ante-Californian life, so I would wish I had said nothing. Dick was a good-hearted, gabby fellow, head-over-heels, but entertaining withal. During the fifteen weeks we were there we were away but one evening, which we spent with a neighboring farmer, who in a rude shanty kept bachelor's hall, as did most of his class around there. We were always too tired at night to want to run. My life on the ranch, at best, was a cheerless one; of reading matter we had none, and I often wished for the few books I had lugged about me with such tribulation on my tramp, and which now lay in my carpet-bag at the Hotel Cordelia. I don't remember seeing a newspaper while there, and I was almost as much isolated from the world as a hermit.

Besides we three there was a Mexican helper for awhile, named Antonio. He was a good-natured fellow, and I often used him for a lay-figure to try my "Spanish without a Master" on.

In this book was a story I knew by heart, and this I could repeat to him understandingly. It related to three travelers who found a treasure. Being hungry, one of them was sent to buy meat. That he might enjoy the money himself, he poisoned the meat; that the other two might possess it, they resolved to kill him. The result was, all three lay dead by the side of the treasure, much to the profit of a philosopher who opportunely passed by and pocketed the same. The tale, with its burden of gold and murder, was typically Spanish and pleased Antonio, who called it a "*muy buena historia.*" In return he taught me how to "haw," "gee," "get up" and "whoa" our Spanish oxen. In general, however, there were so many "misfits" in our conversational exchanges, that our verbal intercourse was rather unsatisfactory, and I ceased to annoy him.

Antonio was as full of "*Quien sabe*" and "*No Quiero*" as the generality of the Spanish-Indian race. The first, which is literally "who knows," means "I don't know and don't want to," and is a convenient answer for a shiftless, careless person to make. As for "*No Quiero*," it means "I don't want to," also a convenient reply when one is requested to do a thing he objects to doing.

In a few days the Mexican left. Soon after the Patron and

Dick kicked up a quarrel and the latter went, so there were no hired men left on the ranch, but "Scottie" and myself. The duty of milking two or three unruly cows, hitherto Dick's, now devolved on me, as well as that of playing Aquarius.

In March we commenced setting out a vineyard nursery, the ground for which we had previously prepared. There were three acres of it. We made holes in the furrows fifteen inches deep and two feet apart, and in these we stuck the cuttings, pressing the earth close around them and leaving one bud exposed. We set out about three thousand vines. This was done in March, which was the coldest month I experienced in California. The northwest winds prevailed and seemed to penetrate our clothing like needles, but we had but little rain in comparison with the past months. I must say, however, that although I spent the rainy season in California, I lost but few days on account of rain, which mainly came at night, or so light in daytime as not to prevent our working. Setting out this vineyard would hardly be called "temperance work" now, but at that time it was no more than planting out an apple orchard, as far as consequential damages were concerned. Anyhow the wine produced there was probably used for sacramental and mechanical purposes.

We now had little to do. The farm work there came mainly in the winter and summer months, so that in the spring there was much leisure. Our Patron now seemed sore beset to find excuses to get shut of us, as milking, hauling water and chopping wood were all we had to do.

One day, soon after Dick's departure, we had a little variety in the shape of killing a vagabond cow for beef. She was ranging the prairie, when, our meat running low, her fate was sealed; so the X.'s, senior and junior, with "Scottie," myself and the dog Rita, went a hunting. Pedro was mounted on his riding horse, Jim, and with his high saddle, swinging lasso, broad sombrero, leather leggings and jingling spurs was a sight. His father, with his flowing beard and gray locks, capped with a skull cap, his red sash streaming in the wind, with his murderous bird-gun, acted as foot-soldier. Running about, shouting and gesticulating, he made a good companion-piece to his son, while the rest of us took the part of whippers-in for the hunters. Our game was a Spanish cow, roving and fierce in her disposition, so that Pedro had much the safest position among the participants in the *battue*. We had a lively time of it for a while; Pedro, in his *toreador* costume, cavorting over the prairie trying to change the direction of the cow, which, with tail like a banneret and " nostrils all wide," was careering at full gallop; the Patron, gun in hand, running uselessly about, flinging his arms and loudly swearing, " Scottie " and myself pretending to help, but trying hard to keep clear of the cow's horns. At last, more by good luck than otherwise, we got the cow near the barn, when the Patron slipped inside, and through a knot-hole let fly the death hidden in his gun. He then ran with a knife, stuck her and in a tub caught the blood which he stirred as it ran. This was designed for blood-pudding. To see the Patron at his piratical work gave me the shivers. " Scottie " and I " skun " the animal and dressed her as she lay on the ground. For some time after we lived on beef, tripe and blood-puddings. The beef we carried to the house, where much of it was hung up in the open air. In this pure climate it would keep thus for days.

Among the things we did towards the close of our time there was to set out a lot of fruit trees in front of the house. This work was done in those spring fever days, the saddest of the year, and with many anxious glances at the slow moving sun. November days are quoted for their superabundance of melancholia, but, as far as my experience goes, there are a few days in the month which has All Fools' day for its Genesis which lays them under.

While crossing the plains I was called Stephen. Hearing the outrageous nicknames my comrades bore, and thinking my Christian title provocative of something novel and outrageous, from its rareness, I gave my middle name; I regret to say, with unsatisfactory results. The Patron called me Henry, for what reason I don't know. He either thought that "Steve," as "Scottie" called me, sounded like Henry, or, what is more probable, called me Henry indifferently, as we call a Chinaman "John," or a goat "Billy." At any rate, Henry I started, and Henry I remained, even "Scottie" and Dick sliding into the delusion, possibly to save confusion, or, perhaps, thinking our employers might think I was a suspicious character with numerous *aliases*, if they called me otherwise.

Don Pedro was sometimes ridiculous in his reticence. Not condescending to generalize he would give directions on the instalment plan, so that when he began we did not know what the outcome would be. He spoke good English, but as slowly as if there was a dash between each word. For instance, he would say: "Yoke up those oxen! Hitch them to the wagon! Now start! Gee them! Haw them! Now straight ahead! Haw them!" and so on, until one day we found ourselves on the summit of an adjacent mountain, without our knowing from one turn to the next where we were going to, and what was our errand; the Don simply sitting on the wagon and giving directions, as needed. Our business was simply to cut a load of wood from the tops of the live-oaks, trees being too scarce in that section to warrant cutting them down for fuel. As to the desirability of such work, with insecure footing, whacking away at the inferior limbs Don Pedro, from his secure position on the ground, should designate, and at the risk of cutting ourselves, or tumbling to the ground and hurting the Patron, I leave you to imagine.

Let me say here, parenthetically, that on reviewing what I have written I am impressed with the thought of how tame the

narration will fall on the average reader. I know, too, there
are many travelers' tales so full of adventure that they pall the
senses, being too much of a good thing; either because the literary stomach becomes clogged with them, or because the literary
throat is too small to swallow them, which somewhat reconciles
me. I know my hum-drum life in California made a dull
sequel to my journey over the plains. I had thought to get
some congenial employment in San Francisco, or, failing that,
to try the excitement of the gold mines. I missed the first,
when necessity turned me from the line of travel to Sacramento, which was a good thing I know. So fate, luck or circumstances ordered it that I should pass my days in the land
of gold on a lone ranch, where the sun rose and set on a scene
as quiet as the sea; where I saw every day the same fields
rolling away from me in green waves, till they broke in foot-
hills at the base of a distant mountain on one side, or rose in
gentle slopes to the horizon on the other; where the same farm
labors lapped on one another in monotonous succession until,
pecuniarily able, I broke from them.

Antonio had gone; Dick had gone, and now "Scottie," my
only comrade and the last of my companions of the plains,
was to leave also. He and the Patron had a quarrel which
severed the bands which had held them together so long. We
had been in the same mess for four and a half months crossing the plains, and had seen rough times there and on the
road to California. We had been on the tramp two weeks,
wherein he had shared his last dollar with me. But such is
the callousness acquired by leading such a life as ours that we
parted without even a hand-shake. I said " Good-bye, Scottie!"
and he " Good-bye, Steve!" That was all, unless his falling
back to my old name of " Steve " was a concession which indicated a softening of the heart at thoughts of our late vagabond life. With blankets slung over his shoulder he turned
his back on the ranch and started towards Sonoma. He was

hardly out of sight when, in spite of the case-hardening my nature had undergone, my heart swelled within me at the thought of some of his kindly acts during our tramp life, and I was sorry I had not been more lavish of my demonstrations at parting. I never saw nor heard from "Scottie" afterward.

I felt really lonesome and down-hearted that night when I went to sleep in my dingy room in the barn. I was practically alone on the sixteen hundred acre ranch. I longed for the unappreciated company of Dick, with his wild yarns; or his accounts of his heart smashing exploits in his native land— for Richard was something of a Don Juan. I sighed for the quiet company of "Scottie," generally taciturn, but sometimes rising to feats of droll humor. With the exception of Old Tom I had no company now. No sound was heard save what he made crunching his owner's wild oats, (his own he had sown long since) or when, his scanty rations eaten, he gnawed the manger. A steady old boy was Tom, though a little trickey withal. When the barley approached the bottom of the hogs-head we turned him out to grass, and, consequently, I had to catch him every morning to haul water. At such times who so trying as Tom? Hither and thither I ran. Now I had him and now I hadn't! I would pen him in a fence corner and then he would be like the Hibernian flea. At last we would come to a mutual understanding and get to work. Poor Tom! with all his faults I loved him still, particularly when I wanted to catch him. If yet alive, may he get all he wants of his favorite soaked barley; if dead, may he be among the green pastures of the equine Elysian Fields!

I said no noise disturbed me save Tom's jawing. Let me hasten to unsay this. I was afflicted with rats in the worst form, with no "Pied Piper of Hamelin" to come to me with his aid, and whisk them away with the presto! of his tuneful reed. Not in units, twins nor triplets did they come only, but in swarms like the locusts of old. They reserved all their antics for the night and then began. They squealed, they fought and ran foot races over my blankets and face. They dived into my water pail; they eat my candles, my soap even. Over head on a shelf was a Bible, which had belonged to and comforted some former servitor of the ranch, and which comprised my entire library. Under the guidance of the Evil One the rats knocked this into the bucket, and in the morning I found it afloat and hopelessly dissolved. When they had neither candles nor soap to eat they made a raid on Tom's barley. This was touching the Patron in a tender place. So one leisure day, with gun in hand, and myself and Rita for assistants, he gave the rats a regular St. Bartholomew! We routed them from their secret hiding place and exterminated them by the dozen. The old gentleman banged away with tongue and gun, while Rita leaped around barking joyously, and I enjoyed myself more that day than any passed on that lonely ranch. After this thinning out of the rats my nights passed more agreeably.

One day in a good humored mood the Patron asked me for the first time about my family. I did as they usually do under similar circumstances, told him of the better days I had seen, and how I did not have to do as I did now ; just doing it to see the world from different standpoints, etc. He was a poor logician and failed to see my motives, and I had the mortification therefore of seeing he did not believe a word I said.

I was getting uneasy for fear my parents had got none of my letters, some of which had been posted in out-of-the-way places or given in charge of persons who might neglect to post them. I had written two or three times since my arrival, but had not received any since leaving Salt Lake. In the ten months or more since I left home I had no answers. Thinking that perhaps there might be some for me in San Francisco I wrote down, and was gratified in a few days by receiving a pack of letters, which I read eagerly. The one I was most interested in contained a draft on Sathers, Church & Co. (a firm which I think General Sherman was connected with), which amounted to seventy dollars, and with what I had earned was ample to take me home. After this I was contented to stay no longer, for with the means to take me away my surroundings grew unbearable. I, however, had but little to do: milking, hauling water and a daily gallop on Jim to the little landing on the Peteluma River for letters from the absent ones in San Francisco. I told the Patron I would have to leave him. He acquiesced in this, but asked me to remain until his children came back from town. So one evening the Peteluma boat brought up the younger branches of his family, pleased with their sojourn in San Francisco, and I thought rather reluctant to take up their old ranch life with its isolation from society.

The next morning I fixed for my departure. After my solitary breakfast of bread and coffee, Don Pedro called me into the *sanctum sanctorum*—dining-room, sitting-room and parlor combined—a room never seen by the profane eyes of the hired men, save when they received their wages after dismissal. Through its portals went Antonio, Dick and "Scottie" to get their hard-earned gold, afterwards to make exit and seek elsewhere their fortunes. It was not such a grand room; in fact, was partly used as a granary. In the room was the whole family seated, like an inquisitorial conclave, among which was Madam X., the invalid, whom I had not seen since I came on the ranch. Behind a table sat Don Pedro with a pile of gold and silver before him, the amount of my wages. It was correctly computed, at the rate of twenty-six dollars per month, sixty dollars in all, beside what I had received. This he pushed toward me in silence. The only word spoken by any of this weird group was by the aged signor, who, completely relaxed from his old-time ways, spoke kindly, telling me to

take good care of my money and not spend it foolishly. I
thought better of them at parting and bore them no ill will.
Then I left that, to me, singular family, sitting in state; the
pretty, aristocratic Inez, her good-looking husband, the venerable Patron and wife and the little Anita, and with my
blankets slung over my shoulder shook the "adobe" of the
ranch from my feet and turned from it, casting no lingering
look backward.

It was a beautiful day when I left, so different from the
morning I came there. I was different myself. In place of
the seedy tramp with his humble demeanor, and fearing he
could not secure work, I departed erect, in good spirits and clad
respectably. I took the route of "Scottie" and the one over which
Signor Augustina had brought us. It was the 21st of April,
and the hills through which the unfenced road wound were
clothed in the greenest of grass, on which herds of cattle were
pasturing. The range on my left was dotted at intervals with
live-oaks, and with the verdure about them looked like a series
of apple orchards; for at a distance an apple-tree and live-oak
look much alike. At about 9 I came to Sonoma, a town
I had passed through before, but then almost invisible in the
morning fog. This old town possesses historical interest in
connection with the conquest of California, for here Colonel
Fremont proclaimed its independence before he knew of the
war between the United States and Mexico, and hoisted the
"Bear Flag" in the square. It was typical of the towns found
in the province previous to 1847; a bare *plaza* surrounded by
low, adobe structures, whitewashed and glaring, mainly public
buildings, stores and drinking places, before which numerous
saddle-horses were standing. Extending from this at increasing intervals were more adobe buildings, humble enough the
most of them. In spite of this the town had a pleasant look
in its setting of green fields and outlying pasture ranges. I
stopped here but a few minutes, and walking over the level

valley soon reached the range of hills dividing the valleys of
Sonoma and Napa. Just after leaving the town of Sonoma I
came to the "Pike County House," named so as a compliment
to the many "Pikes" in California. In a lonely spot near
here I met two men, a sample of what you were then continually meeting in California. They were "dead broke"
tramps, and a vicious looking lot. They told me they wanted
some money of me, and I gave them a dollar, which they
took as if it were due them. Saying "Good-bye, Charley,"
they went on, and I expect got royally drunk at the "Pike"
on my money. I thought it better to give them one dollar
than to have them "borrow" sixty dollars of me. The last
fate I looked for; but it would have gone tough with me to
have given up my hard earnings on the ranch. But, perhaps,
I wrongly suspected these men. They may have only asked
of me what they had often given others, for the Californian is
noted for his liberality when flush, and his "cheek" for asking of others when luck had turned. Still, in my case it was
a forced loan, and I handed over my dollar with a very unfavorable opinion of the transaction.

I crossed the divide and at last reached the swampy plains
bordering the Napa River. Leaving Napa with its unpleasant recollections to the left, I crossed the river further down,
at Suscol. Here was a hotel where I staid all night, faring
very differently from when last here in this neighborhood,
when my comrade and I slept supperless in a straw-shed. The
next morning I started early and soon struck the trail where
we traveled in such tribulation a few months before. Then
down-hearted, ragged and penniless, foot-sore and limping, I
trudged along, zigzagging from ranch to ranch hunting for
work; often the recipient of snubs and grudgingly offered
meals, and thankful if I could find a comfortable stable to
sleep in. Now I walked cheerfully along, taking in the scenery, with money in plenty, and when tired, "took mine ease

in mine inn," as well as meals and lodging, and was on my
homeward way. I remembered all the localities as I passed,
and their recollections gave me the reverse of pleasure, save
as I contrasted the past with the present. At that ranch we
had sought for work, at this we had intruded at meal time,
and farther on, at yon wayside house, the gory-handed pig-
butcher had rebuffed me. Coming to the divide between the
valleys of Napa and Suisun, I soon reached the plains beyond and started for the "Cordelia House," now a map-marked
town, called Cordelia. It was here that "Scottie" and I had
stopped over night, and where the good soul divided his last
dollar with me and where we left our surplus luggage. The
landlord had forgotten me until I reminded him where he put
our carpet-bags, when, on lifting a trap in the floor, he handed
me mine. "Scottie's" things were there yet; so it appeared
he had not traveled this way. As I saw his familiar carpet-
bag down in the dark, grave-like hole, I could not disconnect
the sight from scenes sepulchral; and when the landlord let
down the narrow trap, it seemed as if he was closing the cof-
fin-lid of poor "Scottie." And here, on the scene of his act
of abnegation, I again felt conscience-smitten that I had not
called him back after his stolid departure from the ranch and
given him a hearty squeeze of the hand and a God-speed, in
memory of past kindnesses and to cheer him on his lonely
way.

I was glad to find my carpet-bag. In it was a suit of clothes
I had carried with me from Kansas, thinking a presentable
appearance would sometimes help me to a situation, and which
before leaving home had been my "best suit." Then there
was a folio-book in which I had transcribed my writings; poor
enough when I look upon them now, but which I then thought
would be a passport to a good position. In it, in pencil, I had
kept the notes of my overland journey. There were other
books which helped weigh me down, all of which I found and

brought home. Their creased backs and bent corners, when I now look at them, remind me that the carpet-bag containing them was long used as a pillow, a hard one albeit.

Now well laden with clothing, bodily and mental, I left the Cordelia House and was soon on my way down the valley towards Benicia, where I arrived at sun-down. After supper I walked out on the wharf to wait for the Sacramento steamer to appear. I would like to have seen my clever ferryboat captain to pay him my ferriage, but I saw nothing of him. I have never paid him yet, but when I go to California I will hunt him up and give him principal and interest. He must be nearing his centennial now.

The steamer soon made its appearance through the gathering night, screaming and asthmatic. It swung to, made a short stop, and I boarded her.

What a medley of passengers! Miners from the mountains and plains; bowie-knived, pistoled and hirsute, but far more peaceable than they looked; merchants from the far inland towns and Sacramento; gamblers, gentlemanly and observant; slant-eyed Chinamen, with their long queues; swarthy "greasers" from the river ranches, and butternut-colored Indians; all talking in their different tongues, and all bound for the centre of the California social and commercial system—San Francisco!

The boat moved slowly from the wind-swept wharf of Benicia, and then plunged with clang of bell, shriek of whistle and escape of steam through the inky waves and increasing gloom. The style of travel I was now indulging in almost took my breath with its luxuriance. This was not working my passage across the plains, shouting myself hoarse at broken-down oxen. It was not jolting over deserts in a springless wagon, or tramping around hunting work and leading a semi-servile life when I found it. Here was richness! Cabin passage in a "palatial" steamer, tinsel and gilding, curtains and mirrors

BIRD'S-EYE VIEW OF SAN FRANCISCO—GOLDEN GATE IN THE DISTANCE.

around me, a genuine ingrain carpet on the floor, and seats
upholstered with real cotton plush! Tramps, such as I had
been, down on deck and not allowed above, and the better sort
of people for my company. I could hardly realize that I was
steaming athwart a ferry which I had lately crossed through
charity, and was opposite a town where I was glad to get a good
horse-stall to sleep in.

Around me the up-river passengers, wearied with their
long passage, were sleepily lounging on sofas and chairs,
while the newly acquired ones sauntered idly around or sat
reading. Soon the hotel-runner, who had boarded our craft
at Benicia, made his appearance. I could tell him in advance
by his gentlemanly dress and address, his dangling watch-
chain on a background of satin vest, his glossy hat and his
smooth tongue, and his peculiar way of introducing his subject. Placidly smiling he accosts you. He takes a random
lingual voyage on the sea of prevailing topics, and by rare and
skilful pilotage brings you by easy stages to the present hotel
system; from that to the way in which San Francisco cara-
vanseries are conducted, and from that to *the* hotel whose
representative and "barker" you are at length made aware
your interlocutor is. Having sown this much he leaves it to
bring forth fruit, and seeks for other victims. Scarcely are you
rid of him when another of the same genus makes his appearance and gives you to understand that his predecessor was a
"Sydney Cove," or escaped convict, and the hotel he represents is entirely beneath the patronage of one of your gentlemanly appearance, and then vaunts the accommodations of
the "Wiggins House." He leaves you at last, only to be followed
by others of the same ilk, whose rear is brought up by the
importunate No. 1. By persistent ding-donging and satis-
factory self-vindication he gets into your confidence, and you
grudgingly promise to patronize his hotel.

Meanwhile, with a persistent, pulmonic cough, properly

belonging to space-consumption, the steamer has been plowing its way through the gloom of air and water towards its destination. The passengers grow still sleepier and less talkative. Finally the scattered lights of a city glimmer through its mounting darkness, and at length, as the clang of the midnight bell comes on our drowsy ears, the boat strikes the wharf with a rebound, and feeling as only those feel who enter a strange city at night's dark noon, you step upon the wharf. And now the " runner" seizes his only victim, and putting you in a sort of convict van, hurries you off to his hotel. He introduces you to the smiling nightclerk, and having bagged his game and got his commission, you need expect no more attention from the gentlemanly " runner."

XVII.

In and around San Francisco.

IT is not of the San Francisco of the present I would
speak. Were I to, in view of the many annual excursionists from the East who bring back oral and
written descriptions thereof, I would be the proper recipient
of the peculiar words of desistance which the supple tongues
of our people lap out of our plastic language. I would speak
of the San Francisco of the past, when a good part of its
foundations were swashed by the waters of the bay they arose
from; before cable cars were thought of, and the "Nobs" had
peopled "Nob Hill;" when the city was badly lighted, and,
for want of works, water was peddled about the town in huge
hogsheads on wheels; when the foreign element was large, and
the vigilantes had just finished purifying the moral atmosphere of the metropolis. Or that more distant time, the
pastoral age of California, when a chain of missions extended
from San Francisco on the north to San Diego on the south,
peopled with converted Indians and surrounded by the flocks
and herds they cared for. Or earlier still, when Drake's
clumsy ship came riding through the Golden Gate, the object
of the attention of groups of deer on the headlands, or dread
of the fleeing natives, while the buccaneer sailors gazed with
rapture on the scene before them.

It is a question whether the Bay of San Francisco was discovered by land or sea travelers, though it is plausibly claimed that the zealous Spanish missionaries who established the missions south were the first Europeans to see this magnificent sheet of water. In a fertile valley, two miles south of the centre of the present site of the city, Father Junipero Serra, in 1769, set up his cross, rang his invitation bells to summon the heathen, and here started the Mission of San Francisco, although it

SAN FRANCISCO BAY IN THE GOOD OLD TIME.

was six years later before it was fairly established. It having been requested that one of the missions should be called after Saint Francis, Father Junipero waited till the 9th of November, 1776, that saint's day, and then, amid his followers and the surrounding wondering Indians, dedicated it the Mission of San Francisco. It was afterwards named the Mission Dolores (Mission of Sorrows). At the dedication sacerdotal music and incense had they none, except what the loaded muskets of the military escort furnished.

Eighteen of these missions were scattered along the coast within twenty miles of the sea. The Fathers were devoted to their work, and at one time (1800) had fifteen thousand converts on the rolls. But they were held by the frail tenure of favor and reward of creature comforts, so that when the missions were denuded of their lands the miserable wretches returned to the ways of their fathers. At its most flourishing time the Mission Dolores had about eight hundred converted Indians connected with it, and eighty thousand cattle, horses and mules, and the same number of sheep. In 1831 the number of the former had gone down to six thousand, while there was no record of the latter. The valleys along the rivers running into the bay made fine pasture ground, and cattle-raising flourished until the Fathers lost their control and their faithful Indians were driven to their late vagabond life. Dana, in his "Two Years Before the Mast," gives an interesting account of his visit to this mission, and the sufferings of the crew while collecting hides and getting wood and water.

The crushing out of the missions through the rapacity of the Mexican government, and the necessity of the Fathers giving up their pious work, and the scattering of their converts, is a painful chapter in the history of California. The Indians, even if held to Christianity by being well fed and clothed, were much better off than when savages, and led comparatively industrious lives, while their religious instructors or masters, if you choose to call them so, though often ignorant monks, led exemplary, self-sacrificing lives, and did the best they knew for the bodily and spiritual welfare of their wards.

While the Mexicans held California there was a struggle between the clerical and secular power over the missions, which at times would attain some of their former power, while at the same time a political conflict was going on between the home government and the provincial, in which latter were living many rebellious Americans. The result was a demoralization which made California an easy conquest by the United States. In fact, as before stated, Colonel Fremont declared the province independent before war between Mexico and this country was known to him.

How they Built the Ships in.

The war over and gold discovered, the Mission Dolores ceased to be the business centre of the region around the bay; for the harbor, where the incoming vessels bringing passengers and supplies must land, was two miles north. This was Yerba Buena Cove, and the deep water opposite was soon alive with shipping, and a few houses on the hillside, built for the necessities of the few trading vessels which had got to coming to this harbor, formed a town named after the Cove. After the gold excitement many of the vessels it brought there were deserted by their crews. The shallow water necessitated the extension of long wharves, and at times the stranded vessels were within their limits. The lack of room on the hillside caused frame buildings to be erected along these wharves and over the water; bisecting causeways enclosed some of the dismantled vessels, which were sometimes used for dwellings or prisons, and the town was becoming a second Rangoon, with houses on stilts. These "water lots" were sold by the State. The space between these wooden streets made a place to dump the sand from the adjacent hills to make building sites there, so that two birds were killed with one stone, or rather the removal of one lot of sand made two building lots. Eventually the water front was filled up to the wharf line and built over. Granite blocks were even erected on this sandy foundation, which settled, leaving yawning crevices in the walls. The wharves, eleven in number, extended from the shore from 300 to 2,000 feet, so that the extent of the water-covered city can be imagined, each wharf representing a street. The stranded vessels, used as dwellings amid this network of wooden streets, with houses building around them, was a singular sight.

The account of the frauds practiced in the sale of these water lots, and the efforts brought to bear on the Legislature to sell more to the detriment of those owning front lots, and to the safety of the harbor on account of forcing the outlying vessels further to the mercy of the swift tides, would furnish interesting reading. Also in regard to one Dr. Peter Smith, who, holding "scrip" which could not be realized on, sued the city and exposed public property for sale. The authorities made proclamation that the purchasers would not get possession of what they bought; but the sale went on, and the properties were sold at merely nominal prices. The result was that, the sales being valid, the city was almost bankrupted and the buyers made immensely wealthy. Then there were the big fires and the actions of the vigilantes. About all these a volume might be written.

Public squares, as we understand them, San Francisco had none, unless two or three open places devoid of grass or ornamentation could be called such. One of these was known

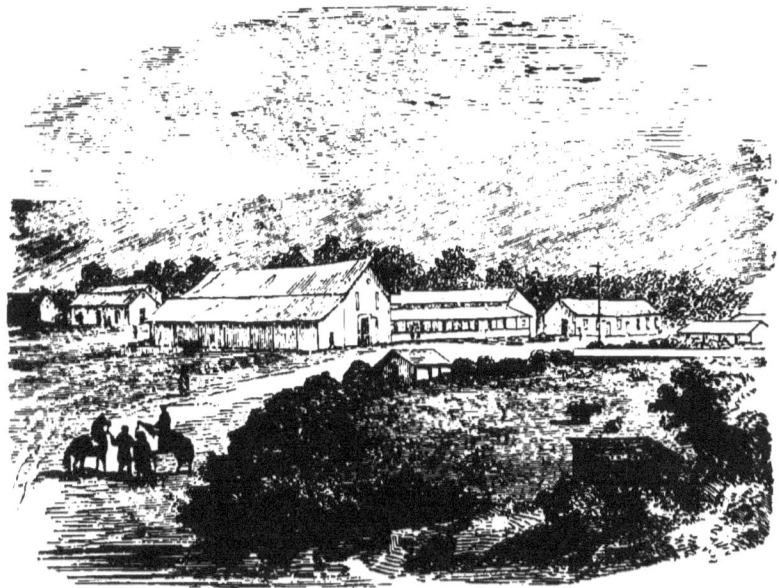

THE OLD MISSION DOLORES.

on the records as Portsmouth Square, but this the people persisted in calling the " Plaza." This was a dismal place, muddy or dusty according to the season, and was the starting place for omnibuses. It also afforded, in past turbulent times, a resort for mobs and hangings by the vigilantes.

At the time of my arrival in California the Mission Dolores

had long since filled its usefulness as a place of Indian conversion, and was more of a curiosity than otherwise. It lay
in a fertile valley, watered by Mission Creek, but which was
surrounded by barren hills covered by stunted shrubs. The
few buildings were in fair repair. The church was built of
adobe and roofed with tiles, the front ·being stuccoed with
some show of ornament, with three bells in the gable. Inside
was a show of tinsel and glitter, and some rude paintings. At
right angles was a rough building with a piazza, which had
perhaps been the home of the Fathers who ministered to the
simple Indians. To the left of the church was a graveyard
full of graves, among which was that of Casey, the man who
slew Wm. Starr King, and who was hung by the vigilantes.
He had a monument with a complimentary inscription on it,
to the effect that he was more sinned against than sinning,
and that he was a martyr in his sudden suspension; which
shows that no matter how bad you live, or how mean your
" shuffle off," there will be kind friends who will go to
considerable expense to lie in your favor. Fifty years ago
this was a rich mission, surrounded by flocks and herds,
and Indian converts by hundreds, who willingly did the
Fathers' bidding. Now it was nothing but a quiet resort for
excursionists.

I give two sketches of this mission. The first was taken in
1854, and represents it with a " lean-to " the whole length,
next to the Campo Santo, or graveyard. A sketch I made of
it four years later shows this " lean-to " removed and the
space occupied by graves. The porticoed building on the
right of the main church was used as a drinking saloon and
hotel at the time of my visit. Since then a sense of shame
has caused this to be done away with, the building torn down,
and in its place arises a towered church which dwarfs the old
mission by its side. I give a representation of the new and
old churches, the former from a photograph.

Thirty years ago a description of the Chinese in San Francisco, their habits, customs and dress, would have made interesting reading; but now, with thousands in our Eastern towns, the case is different. Still I may be excused for saying something about that much-abused race. Shuffling along the streets with their odd countenances and dress, they made a great impression on me. Then as now they were looked upon

MISSION DOLORES AS IT IS NOW.
(From a Photograph by Faber.)

as nuisances, chiefly because they lived on little and were willing to work for low wages. They had been badly abused, cheated, beaten, murdered. They were game for "hoodlums" and people who called themselves respectable. I heard an apparently fair man say that once when out of funds in the mining regions, he sat on the roadside waiting for a Chinaman to come along that he might rob him! He thought no more of it than of knocking over a rabbit to satisfy his hunger. At one time they taxed them seventy dollars per year, but when I was there it was four dollars per month when mining. This induced more of them to work at washing, or as house servants. All the civil Chinese were not at avocations so humble. Some of the wealthiest San Franciscan merchants were from the Flowery Kingdom, and at the large auction sales I saw them in rich silken robes, bidding with the same spirit as their white brethren, and in many cases better able to meet their liabilities. You all know how they are brought over by contractors who farm their services out, and whose main obligation is to take them back to China when dead. You have heard of the "Chinese Quarter" and their theatre, also, so I will say nothing about them. In fact, so many things which I thought were novelties when I came home are now household words, that I may have left out things of interest for fear of duplication.

I have spoken of the "Golden Gate," but I did not say that it was so named before the gold discoveries were made. It is simply a fanciful name. The broad peninsula between San Francisco and the sea is a series of barren ridges, the highest point near the city being called Telegraph Hill. Here was a station formerly used for signaling vessels when they approached the coast; but this had been superseded by a telegraph line. This mode of communication had become common in the thickly settled part of the State, but with the East the overland stage line was the quickest mode of conveying news, unless it was the Nicaraugua route. There was but forty miles of railroad in the State, and this was from Marysville on the Sacramento, northward. The stage and steamboat were as yet the main reliance for travelers. There was no communication with the southern part of the State except by semi-monthly steamer.

On looking back through the vista of the past thirty years I can hardly realize that California was only ten years old on my arrival, and that I came within that time of being a "Forty-niner." But remember, taking into account the fires, the vigilante hangings, the jobbery and corruption of the metropolis, and the murders and Chinese persecutions in the mining districts, with its accompanying music from pistol crack and swish of bowie, California had then passed a century of the life of our more prosy States; hence the time, though seeming long, was brief.

At that time California had no literature. Among its scenery and people there were mines of romance and poetry as rich in their way as even the plains and mountains of gold, and as virgin of efforts at development as they had been so lately. The author of "Ramona" had not risen to so pathetically depict the wrongs of the despised, though semi-civilized Indians. That gifted, though shameless, vagabond, "The Poet of the Sierras," had not woven his poetic warp through the woof of its longitudinal valleys and mountains to draw in its meshes before our eyes his creative imagery from

> "The quail who was piping all day long,
> For the rabbit to dance in the chaparral,"

and that being but little higher in the scale of life, the "Digger" Indian, to the best types of Californian humanity, and from the lowliest valleys to the loftiest mountain peaks. Bret Harte had not come to arrange the rough miner, the polished gambler, the proud Spaniard and humble half-breed, the pious Father, the vulgar new-enriched woman, the respectable though scheming "school-marm" and the Cyprian adventuress, into a grand octave, and play upon it with his deft fingers such tunes as would echo around the world. It is true that the latter tried to make the one good deed of an Oakhurst cover up the vile doings of a life-time, and that he assumed that whoever made a profession was necessarily a hypocrite. But

as a novelist so popular as Dickens set him the example, we
will suppose he did not feel so, but adopted the style for popularity. At that time no occidental Bancroft had come upon
the scene to rival his Eastern namesake in historic research.
But the harvest, though hidden, was there and ready for the
gleaner.

At that time the Indian was considered as a nuisance to be
abated by bullet and starvation; the Chinese as objects of
oppression and robbery; the old-time Spanish aristocracy as
proprietors of stealable lands; and the remnant of mission
priests as pious frauds. A Californian historian said in substance: "The Indians are in the way of State progress; the
sooner they are out of the way the better. Should their pro-
tectors, the Fathers, try to preserve them, well, then sweep the
Fathers away too!" Such was the sentiment of the American-
Californian. Everybody and everything which did not
minister to greed for wealth must be stamped out.

I stayed in San Francisco two weeks waiting for the steamer
for the States. With the Geysers, the Big Trees and the Yo-
semite within my reach (these curiosities which Eastern tourists
now go thousands of miles to see) within a hundred miles or so,
I confined my travels to the boundaries of the city. My humble
way of life in the State had prevented me from hearing of
them, and, had it been different, I was so anxious to go home
on my earnings that I doubt if I would have visited these
noted scenes. I did not even go to Sacramento, although the
competition had reduced the fare to fifty cents. I have many
times regretted that I did not make better use of my opportunities, but 'tis ever thus! But then this neglect of opportunities has its compensation. The reader is spared a reiterated account of the above-named wonders, with a chance of it
being a guide-book rehash of scenery afflicted with lacka-
daisical names, of trees of unbelievable sizes, and so on to the
bitter end. Nowadays these descriptions are generally "skipped,"

so, had I seen and written, it would only have been a waste of
time and ink.   For all this reasoning I wish I had seen these
" chestnuts."   So my time was spent wandering around the
city and suburbs till " steamer day " came.

My first business after coming to San Francisco was to get
my draft cashed.   Sathers & Church, whom it was on, hesitated about paying it, as my signature had failed to come with
it, that it might be compared with my present writing.
Although anxious to go home, I had money in plenty for temporary use, and would rather go to work again than arouse the
bankers' suspicions with persistence.   I was about to tell them
to return the draft, and prepare to hunt permanent employment, when they told me they would pay me, which conclusion they perhaps came to through my indifference.   Taking
the proffered gold I repaired to the hotel, and from its welcoming portals made many a *sortie* to points of interest in and
around the city during my two weeks' sojourn there.

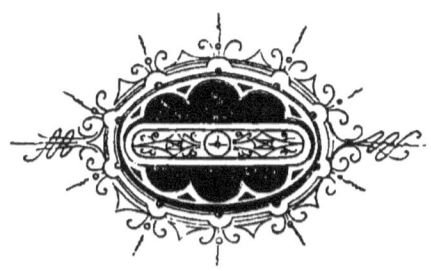

XVIII.

A San Franciscan Day.

QUEEN of the Pacific Coast! Fair city whose changing skies for half the year shower down mist and
rain, and the other half sunbeams of molten brass!
Metropolis of alternate sticky mud and blinding
dust! in spite of these and more thou art a city of my heart,
O Ciudad de San Francisco!

The morning, as befits the month of April in that clime, is
warm and sultry. Breakfast is over, and I sit in front of my
hotel reading the morning paper drowsily, or listlessly watching the surroundings. Along comes the daily waterman, with
his tank on wheels, to serve his customers, for San Francisco
has no water works. The people are supplied in this way, the
indispensable fluid being hauled from distant springs and
furnished at so much per week. The waterman is quick-
motioned and dexterous, and the way he works is quite refreshing to my spring-fevered brain. Close following comes the
brawny butcher and the mealy baker. Then come little accor-
deon and tambourine girls, who sing with precocious voices to
music more or less sweet. They move familiarly among the
loungers, asking for money; young in years, but already old
in sin.

As the sun swings up like a censer, the heat pours from it
faster. To save myself from going to sleep I throw away my

" Bulletin " and start for a stroll, as warm as it is, and move lazily down the pavement. I saunter down towards the wharves and find myself in the clutches of sellers of slop-clothing and " Cheap Johns," who toss me about, one to another, like a foot-ball. Breaking loose from these purse-emptying rogues, I continue on my way over wooden streets and by houses and shops on piles, around whose foundations I hear the low wash of waves, until I reach the end of the wharf.

Sail-furled ships with their net-like shrouds and tapering masts in numbers are riding at anchor in the bay, or are chained, like restive bull-dogs, to the wharves. Clumsy square-rigged craft from the Sacramento, San Joaquin and the lesser tributaries of the bay are rising and falling with the swell, or heavily bumping their slimy sides against the piers. Above me is a huge Panama steamer, slowly shifting with the tide. Far out in the bay is a man-of-war, its deathful guns dia-bolically grinning through many a port. It is the French frigate " Eurydice," lately arrived after a long voyage. A gig is lowered, and as it nears I see in it the captain and some of his under-officers coming to the city. With measured stroke the boat darts into a dock and halts at a clumsy stairway. The officers mount these to the wharf, all glittering in epaulettes and gold lace. There is an American man-of-war's man in the vicinity who, on a furlough, or to suit his convenience, has come down to " Frisco " from his ship at the navy yard at Vallejo. He has been drinking freely, and feels jolly, sarcastic and adventurous. He speaks sneeringly of the French sailors manning the gig, and tells them—only they don't understand him—that his ship can whip a dozen such as theirs. He is bantered to go and shake hands with the French captain, and vows he will do it. Giving the quid in his squirrel-like cheek another roll, he marches forward, his gait combining the roll of the quarter-deck with the stagger of the drunkard. He

17

fronts the dapper captain and, saluting him, grasps his delicate hand with his tar-stained paw, much to the amusement of the Frenchman. Then he turns away with a smile on his lip and a leer in his eye.

I walk over to the San Antonio Ferry. A boat is lying there ready to start. It costs but two bits to cross, and I go aboard. The signal rings and the boat darts out among the waves. How the waters sparkle in the meridian sunlight! A cool breeze is coming through the Golden Gate. It fans my throbbing brow and drives away the *ennui* which has hung over me like an incubus since morning. Little "white caps" are disporting on the crests of the more sedate overgrown waves. The white sails of the river craft are swelled to life from their limber lethargy and flap and bend before the welcome breeze, slowly dragging their cumbrous burdens along. White-breasted sea-gulls, big and little, go flying over the water or suddenly dive below. I am across the bay, and the boat lies moored at Oakland. I remember it as the town from whence I started on my tramp for work. I see the prairie before me and the mountain beyond over which I wearily walked, and I feel thankful that I am not on the same journey again! The plain of Contra Costa, then clouded in mist, is now bright and green, and so is the ridge beyond. The boat doubles on its course and returns and I am again in San Francisco. Here comes John Chinaman, transplanted representative of pig-tailed Orientalism, trigged out in all the oddity of his national clothing. His cap, with its rim turned up at a sharp angle, seems especially adapted for catching rain. His collarless coat of blue hangs loosely about him and eke his short ample breeches. Jealous of his queue is John. Time was when maliciously disposed Americans would slip up behind him and cut it off—the production of a lifetime. Nothing could outrage John's dignity more; sooner would he lose his head. But his rights are better protected than of yore, and these capillary bisections are no longer done with impunity. Still John walks as if in dread of having his fond hopes severed, and carries them snugly coiled under his arms like a cart whip.

My walk brings me to a quarter of the city inhabited by these strange people. I can easily imagine myself on the other side of the Pacific. Chinamen, Chinawomen, boys, girls and babies. Shops filled with Chinese toggery, presided over by a Chinese clerk. Chinese literary depots where books are sold which you begin reading at the back end and read up the page instead of across. Collections of drugs made from all kinds of vile and outlandish sources. Opium dens where groups smoke their worthless lives away.

I go to the Plaza. It bears about as much resemblance to our public squares as does the Sahara Desert to the Grand Prairie. The stunted trees look as if a simoon had been through them, and the yellow grass peeps timidly above the gravel. Unattractive as this promenade is, it is the best our transmundane metropolis affords.

Still hotter glows the sun on this pent-up place. Its brassy beams leap down to the earth, rebound and nearly blind me.

To-day there is a parade. Even now it is passing through the Plaza. There is an orator and poet of the day, who ride at the head of the column in a barouche drawn by four prancing grays. A halo of self-complacency surrounds them. The poet of the day has a poem in his side pocket which is badly rhymed, badly metred and lacking sense. The orator is ready to burst with his suppressed eloquence. There is a brass band with shining horns and stunning drums, and their laborious strains make my head ache. There are horsemen, grenadiers and "citizens generally." On the high side of the Plaza an artillery company is posted which fires off deafening shots. Somehow, owing to the hot sun, the sulphurous condition of the air, the blare of band or din of cannon, I don't appreciate the scene.

I am again at the wharf. The opposition steamers to Sacramento are ready to start. Runners with tickets to sell are capering about buttonholing suppositious passengers and villifying one another. "Sydney coves," "escaped convicts" are amongst the mildest of the names bandied about; while, imitating the quarrels of humanity on shore, numerous seagulls dart and dive, soar and swoop and scream and croak

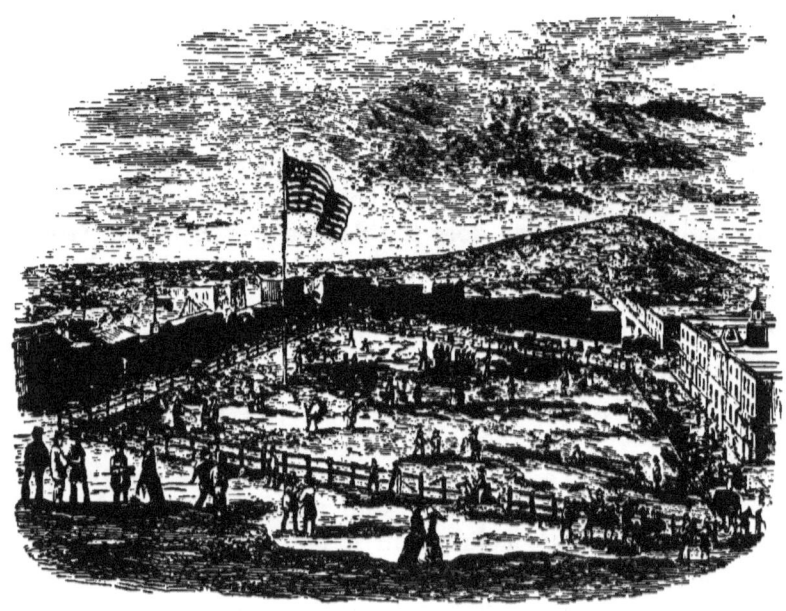

THE PLAZA, SAN FRANCISCO.

as they wrangle over and in the water for edible *flotsam* and *jetsam*. Between these, the cries of the venders of newspapers and small wares, and the escaping steam, the scene is pandemoniac.

It is afternoon; the air is growing cooler, for a sea-breeze is stirring it up. It is reviving, and I stroll to the hills north of the city overlooking the waters leading to the Golden Gate.

Ships sail by me as they make their exits and their entrances. I cannot help comparing the lively times of now with the quietude of twenty years ago, when at rare intervals a vessel came for hides, or to supply the few wants of the Mission.

I return to the wharf. The steamer from the States has been telegraphed and is momentarily expected. It rounds the peninsula and soon bumps against the pier, and the eager passengers tumble pell-mell down the crowded gangway. A crowd of hotel runners, wharf-rats and loungers are crowding around the reporters and the few welcoming friends of the emigrants. Almost suffocated by the yelling, surging crowd, I am glad to get away, leaving the greenhorns to the tender mercies of the sharpers and runners.

I am once more in the heart of the city and on the fashionable promenade. Gaily attired women of varying characters rustle by me in those silks and satins, scarlets and velvets which Franklin notes as kitchen fire extinguishers. To those who have been living for months on a lonely ranch or in an isolated mining camp the sight is a novelty indeed.

Again at the Plaza. An omnibus is about starting on its hourly trip to the Mission Dolores. I am curious to see this venerable reminder of the sway of the Spanish fathers, so I pay my "bit," jump in the coach and am soon rolling over a smooth plank road to the Mission of Sorrows. The two miles intervening are sandy and uninteresting, and I am glad when we arrive in front of the old adobe sanctuary. A quaint old church it is with its unhewn rafters, its three large bells arranged in a triangle in the gable, and its stuccoed columns in *bas relief*. It is the work of the rude Indian converts, who less than a hundred years ago were gathered from heathen barbarism into the folds of the Catholic Church by the preaching and unselfish efforts of the old Spanish *padres*. Adjoining is the Campo Santo, or Holy Field, where lie buried the dead of generations. Here are inscriptions in many tongues, graven on prone slab or stone erectly standing. Here lie side by side pale-faced nun and swarthy Indian girl, pious priest and dark-hued native ranchero. Thickly strewn are the graves; irreverence would say too thick for comfort. But there is no elbowing for precedence in the narrow halls below; there is no jostling to provoke resentment in that world of silence. Granite and marble shafts covered some of the graves, bright sweet smelling flowers grew from others, while some were neglected hollows. The Catholic has a love for the beautiful engrafted in his piety, and you see the homes of his dead ornamented with shrubs, flowers and sea-shells.

The sun slowly sinks below the hills back of the Mission Dolores, and the visitors are departing from the shrine of their pilgrimage. Twilight is mantling the graveyard, and in its shadows one can almost imagine he sees the cowled monks standing rebukingly among the tombs before the representatives of a race whose progress was so antagonistic to their labors. With uncanny thoughts I close the clanging gates and leave the abode of death for the congenial society of the living.

XIX.

𝒯ℌe 𝔅it 𝒯ℌeatre.

AN FRANCISCO is a city of theatres. With but a sixth part of the population (in 1858) of Philadelphia, it can boast of almost as many places of amusement. From Maguire's Opera House down, through intermediate grades to the lowest *cafe chantant*, are a series of entertainments from which fastidious to lax can select a place of evening resort. Occupying a middle rank among these are the " Bit Theatres," so termed from the price of admission, a " bit," or shilling. These are generally conducted by brokendown professionals, and their assistants are amateurs ; their patrons being a medley of those who cannot afford higher priced places of diversion, or who go out of curiosity.

In my walks about the city my attention had often been drawn toward those abodes of the minor drama through the mediums of glaring posters. These, after describing the features of the coming entertainment, short dramas, acrobatic feats, singing and dancing, conspicuously remarked that the best liquors could be had 'for twelve and a half cents ; thus putting the professions of the stage and bar on an equal footing.

In 1858 the part of the city, covering what once had been the bay, had so extended that a view parallel with the front and taking in the upper town made San Francisco resemble a recumbent giantess, a little tipsy, or rather " half seas over," with her feet in the water, and with the contents of her wide-spreading lap in danger of dropping through the fragile apron. Beneath the flat, where now were filth and mud, and the swash of waves as they climbed and fell back from the

SAN FRANCISCO IN 1847.

slimy wharf timbers, once ships were moored, and here, deserted by their gold-greedy crews, some lay rotting, until enclosed by wharf and street they became absorbed in the growing town. The architecture of this built-over portion was shabby enough, and consisted mainly of warehouses, offices connected with shipping, junk shops, Jew clothing stores, Chinese laundries and low groggeries. The hollow square, which these buildings surrounded, was the dumping place for superfluous material from the high ground over-looking the bay, as well as for the odds and ends which commu-nities generally surreptitiously throw into such places. On the planked streets, after the arrival of States' steamers and other craft, drays thundered back and forth, confidence men played their little games on incoming passengers, hotel runners did their work, and bootblacks left their shining marks.

One day in my saunterings over this portion of the city I came across one of the places of amusement heading this chapter. It was of no greater pretension than scores of the rickety buildings surrounding it, except that it was of two stories. The bar-room was as prominent a part of the premises as the liquor announcement was of the posters, as the audience was forced to pass through it to get to the " auditorium."

The manager was Miss Rowena Granice, whether an as-sumed or real name I don't know. I saw her in the trying light of day standing—leaning from a sort of inside balcony above the bar-room—like another Juliet, or rather like the grandmother of that interesting young woman, although on her face paint, powder and paste had done their work, until she looked like a flamboyant fright: an exemplification of the conflict we are warring with time, and of the fact that we may apply pigment and dye, we may pad and bewig, and wrap our forms in the gay robes of youth, only to see what we are trying to fend off come back like a pent-up flood, and, washing off cosmetic and color, and obliterating our other shams, deliver the human humbug to Old Age's grim follower. The Romeo who played to this Juliet was a rotund German, who, from his position on the bar-room floor, invited her to step down from her perch and take a drink with him; a request she coyly agreed to.

Miss Rowena, in spite of this uncomplimentary introduction, seemed like one who had been the possessor of good looks and an actress of note, but who, on account of loss of personal attractions rather than of professional ability, had been obliged to leave more aristocratic boards for this humble theatre. Enterprising, if old and faded, she had managed her " Gaieties " until it was at the head of its class.

Facilis decensus Averni and easy of access was the " Bit Theatre." Passing through the purgatorial bar-room, a place reeking with the fumes of tobacco and liquor, I gave the " open sesame " of a " bit " to a willing recipient, and was ushered into the room adjoining. On entering through a vista of smoke I saw a row of " tallow dips," and behind them the mimic stage. In front of these, on a floor some ten yards square, were rows of tables, around which were the theatrical as well as the vinous guests of the " Gaieties." Before these were placed by attentive waiters the wished-for liquids from the adjoining room. Around three sides of the building was a gallery; the whole building seating about three hundred people.

The view on entering was unique. Enveloped in dense fumes of tobacco, the audience was drinking and talking. It was a *melange* of rough miners, fresh from the mountains and now on their way home to the States, and conspicuous for their shaggy beards and weapons; inoffensive looking gamblers seeking whom they might devour, and curious sight-seers. Mingled among them were a number of boys of various ages and sizes to match.

I secured a seat near the stage. For companion I had a specimen of the genus small boy, the lad who gets familiar and ends by getting impudent. I found him throughout the evening a source of entertainment and general information. As a theatrical critic he was good—for his age. He was well acquainted with the three minor actors, who were young like

himself. As there was no way from the street to the stage
except through the auditorium, the players were obliged to
make ingress among the audience. As they passed us my
little friend addressed them in quite a familiar way, though,
to do him justice, more from a desire to show me his acquaintance with them than from any lack of respect. Not
so with some of his fellows. These spoke to them in words
neither becoming nor complimentary. The young actors bore
these pinthrusts into their dignity with the *nonchalance* of
veteran tragedians when receiving sentient attention from a
demonstrative lobby. Disappearing through a side door they
left the audience anxiously expecting their reappearance. At
length the bell announcing the rising of the curtain was heard,
and simultaneous with its ringing there was a hush in the
ubiquitous conversation and clink of glasses, and soon commenced the performance of "Brigham Young; or, The Prophet's
Dream." This was a mixture of comedy and tragedy, the
former preponderating. The Prophet was represented by a
celebrated acrobat, whose main *forte* was in tying himself up
in bow-knots, but who, in a pinch, could figure in the drama.
His Sultana was the ripe-aged Miss Rowena, his other wives
being represented by three juvenile actors, arrayed in female
garments, and who created a great amount of amusement by
their efforts to adapt themselves to their parts. The only
efforts made to carry dignity into the play were by the two
leading characters, and, to do them justice, they did well
under trying circumstances; but, alas! their efforts were not
appreciated by their listeners, who would loudly laugh at and
guy them during affecting scenes. Unasked-for advice and unseemly remarks would discompose the Sultana while in heroic
attitude she prepared to slay the faithless Prophet, while the
high-tragedy voice and action of the latter were turned into
ridicule. Especially were assaults made on the dignity of poor
Brigham when, after performing in an affecting scene, he

came in front of the curtain in the role of a "supe," to extinguish the footlights, in order that the room might be darkened to the proper consistency while he indulged in his dream. In the face of a battery of uncomplimentary remarks he accomplished his humble mission, and then retired to reappear in his remarkable vision, in which the ghost of his murdered wife was to awaken him to consciousness, remorse and penitence. The only appreciated acting was done by the young actors in female rig, who, at last ignoring the characters in which they were designed to act, seemed only possessed with a desire to amuse the audience; and this they did until the clouds of tobacco swayed to and fro with the shocks of convulsive laughter underlying them.

During the performance of this play my friend, the small boy, rendered me great service. Entertaining me with critiques on the actors and their style, he told me the names of his friends as they came upon the scene. My small boy was of the dignified pattern, and did not join his fellows in their ridicule of the actors, but confined his remarks to me, as also the smoke of a large cigar he was puffing.

Following the play was a series of acrobatic feats by the late Brigham, and then a dance by one of the boys. Next came a song by a little girl of twelve years, who, on account of the homeliness of her last name, was simply known as " Miss Lottie " on the bills. The dance was accomplished to the entire satisfaction of the audience, but, owing to hoarseness, Lottie broke down amid the "Shells of the Ocean." Thrice she essayed the effort and as often failed. The miners, many of whom had known her when among the mountains on a professional tour, sympathized with her condition as much as they wanted to hear her sing, and it was amusing to listen to them in their rough but kind tones encouraging her to go on. At last, getting into a pet at her failure, she ran off the stage amid the applause of her friends. I did not know I would ever hear of this girl again. She became a popular actress; generally, on account of her small stature taking juvenile parts, which she still continues, although over forty years old. Her mother still accompanies her on her tours. Her success has been great, and her fortune is in the hundred thousands. She is called Lotta, and her name of Crabtree is still kept subdued. A beautiful fountain bearing her name—her first name, remember—ornaments the city where she made her successful start in life; a gift from her to the city whence she made her start to fame, if her questionable notoriety can be so called.

The performance was over, and by this time the lights in the vitiated air were burning blue. Odors at variance with those of " Araby the Blest " filled the air from the floor to the ceiling. The attentions of the waiters on their guests had had their natural effect. The drinking part of the audience was getting uproarious. Omens of a continuation of the evening performances were making themselves manifest, and, thinking a bed in a hotel preferable to a muss in a place like this, I left the " Gaietie," and, passing through the thronged bar-room, emerged to the silent and gloomy world without.

Such is a description of an evening's entertainment at a " Bit Theatre," one of the institutions of San Francisco. Conducted and patronized by a class less reputable than those belonging to places of amusement of higher pretensions, I will say that at this particular theatre there was nothing said or acted on the stage of an offensive nature, which is praise, even if of the negative kind. Furnishing amusement to their miscellaneous audiences through their very incompetencies, the actors philosophically bore the indignities heaped upon them, probably finding consolation in the maxim :

A shilling often for a kick atones ;
And what's a drubbing so it breaks no bones ?

XX.

Homeward Bound—Southward.

THE time for my departure for the "States" had come at last. For some days previous to this there had been much unseemly canvassing among prospective passengers by the "runners" of the two opposition steamers which were to sail on the same day for Panama. I thought the sub-agents of the contending river boats were bad enough in the free use of Billingsgate toward one another in their wordy fighting over passengers; but their more pretentious brethren went beyond them by getting up blood-curdling posters, much to the unsettling of the minds of intending travelers. One of these would be headed—over a cut of an old-time casket:—

BEWARE OF THE FLOATING COFFIN!!

followed by some points in the decaying make-up of that vessel. The other poster in a glaring headline would start with something like

LOOK OUT FOR THE OCEAN DEATH-TRAP!!

with the words following similarly grim and savoring of the King of Terrors. These hand-bills so unnerved me, that if I had had a chance to work my passage home on an ox-train I would have taken up with it.

The steamers were the "Golden Gate" and the "Orizaba," on which last I engaged passage. This was known as the

(278)

"Opposition," the former being the "Regular" line, and on the 5th of May lay at Mission Street Wharf awaiting the signal for departure. As was always the case when a "States steamer" left, the dock was crowded with the curious and interested; among whom was a large percentage of sellers of sea-sickness preventives, as well as venders of provocatives of stomachic troubles, and merchants of various kinds of literature, generally novels of the "blood and thunder" variety. There was much rivalry among the passengers of the two steamers, as well as among their owners and crews; so that when the hour came for a mutual start, and the "Orizaba" was found so imbedded in the mud that she was immovable, there came jeers and cheers from the "Golden Gate" as she moved off, and voices of mortification from her fixed rival. By the time the tide had sufficiently risen to let us off we were two hours behind the other, which we saw disappear with flags and streamers flying around the channel leading to the "Gateway of Gold," as Bayard Taylor calls it.

At last we are in a position to move; and now the excitement is at the top notch. Separating friends bestow the parting greeting for the hundredth time, while the book, newspaper and fruit venders unite in one yelling chorus to impress us with the chances we are wasting in seeing such bargains slip away. As our departure becomes additionally imminent the tumult on the wharf increases, and the fruit peddlers, seeing no hope of selling us anything more, are so moved by generous impulses as to sling the more damaged portions of their goods at us as tokens of remembrances, so that we had some decayed specimens of tropical fruitage to eat between meals. The news and medicine venders, and dispensers of bologna sausage and other delicacies, which the steerage passengers may yearn for, make one more effort; friends again send affectionate messages from the lonely wharf to the high deck, and the reverse; the rowdy element shouts;

the dense masses sway to and fro; the bells ring; flags and streamers flap in the breeze; and at last, following a crash of cannon, the machinery is set in motion; and with a parting bombardment of rotten oranges and bananas we are off for the "States."

Soon San Francisco with its memories is far astern, and, sailing through the channel leading to the Golden Gate, we are soon beyond the limits of that rock-strewn portal and out on the bosom of the Pacific. So farewell to the amphibious city of the west coast, to its grand bay and its tributary rivers and their rich valleys, and farewell to the beautiful and quaint towns and lone rancheros I passed in troublous pilgrimage, for I am off to new scenes.

Turning southward we sped down the coast of California, which, for much of the way, was only a faint cloud-bank on our port bow, and afterward not even this was visible, and we lost all sight of land. On the 6th we saw a herd, or a school, or a flock, whichever term is correct, of whales, but we had no time to catch them. On the 9th we came in sight of land. This was the "Marguerites," a group of islands belonging to Mexico. They were barren and rocky, but still a relief to the vision weary with the watery plain around us.

For economical reasons I had taken passage in the steerage. The fare was $52.50, the odd $2.50 being an export tax; that in the cabin was $200, and in the intermediate $150. The "Opposition" had reduced the rate fifty per cent. In the steerage was an unpleasant mode of traveling; but I thought I would feel just as well, after getting to New York, as if I had led the Sybaritic life of those in the first cabin, where they had four meals a day, with a lunch between, gilt mirrors to look into, plush-covered furniture to lounge on by day and cosy state-rooms to sleep in at night. Our sleeping places were the two lower decks, and our beds rude bunks where we slept, from three to seven, side by side, on straw matresses. I was lucky enough to secure a place on the first deck, for from the confined air the hold was almost unbearable. Our eating quarters were between the berths of the first deck, below the main, the tables being narrow and swung by rods so as to accommodate themselves to the motion of the steamer. We eat standing up, once in a while lying down to it when the vessel gave a lurch. Our fare was coffee and tea, in their season, made from a musty base, steeped in water so decayed that it hardly held together; hard tack, which had seen its best days and the traditional sailors' "salt hoss," which had seen its worst. As for dessert, the exhilarating pie had we none, and our ice cream we ate in a sort of Barmecide way, that is, in our minds. But we could not expect to travel for one cent a mile and partake of much edible richness. Then we had many things in common with the nabobs in the upper cabins. We saw the same grand sunsets which they saw, we oftener looked on the day-god as he rolled above the eastern sea to make its waves glitter with his light. We saw the same moon round out and wane, rise out of the midnight waves and pale in the morning sky. We mutually enjoyed the glitter of similar stars, and saw the same constellations move northward, until the Southern Cross replaced the Ursa Major. We partook of the same likes and dislikes toward our fellow passengers; grew hungry and satisfied our appetites as they, although in a different way; yawned and grew sleepy and went to bed. While the first cabin sat around its marble topped card-table and gambled its surplus gold away, the steerage spread a blanket on the salivated deck and worked with the same energy; the changing dross giving forth the same fascinating glitter whether from horny or plebeian palm. Still, through all my optimistic views ran a flavor of sour grapes, and I often envied the more favored passengers who could superciliously come among us without having yelled at them: "Say, you! go to your part of the ship; you don't belong here!"

18

The water-butt, from which throughout the day we quenched our thirst, was near the bow, and access to the contents was through a small hole in the top by letting down a deep, narrow cup with a string. The water was good at first, but grew worse until it got as bad as it could be, when it improved; on the same principle, perhaps, that wine gets better by ocean transit. To be sure the liquid was bad enough from being so warm, but then we had the advantage of the cabin passengers who were obliged to use ice water, which is notoriously hurtful from the bacteria in it. They were also forced to use fresh water to bathe in, while we had nothing but the best of salt water drawn fresh from the sea, per rope and bucket. When it is known what miles the wealthiest of our people will travel for a chance to wash in ocean brine, our position can be appreciated. Then we were ahead of the ship aristocracy in another way, as we in the forward part were always nearer home. So that, taking it all in all, we had the advantage.

I suppose three-fifths or more of the passengers were in the steerage. As there were about one thousand on board, how closely we were packed can be imagined. We slept in rows, and from lack of confidence in my fellows I thought while sleeping. Did one on either side of me shift his position the least I would arouse, finding my hand on my money belt, so that my senses were on the watch whether I was awake or not.

The reader need not think that a steerage passage was a synonym for poverty. There were thousands of dollars in gold or drafts among the forward passengers. I believe there was more money there than about the cabin. The miners, no matter how well off, were more at home among the uncon-ventionalities of steerage life and took it of choice, and though some sported knives and revolvers, I became acquainted with many quiet, worthy men in the steerage.

A noted person in the cabin was General William Walker, a filibuster, who was then on his road to Central America to get shot. He was a short, stout man with a smooth, red face. He left our vessel, I think, at Acapulco to go on the "Oregon" for San Juan del Sur; as when next heard from he was on the opposite side of the Isthmus, where, failing in an insurrection, he was captured, led out in front of a file of half-savage soldiers and shot down like a convict, the victim of not minding his own business.

On the 12th we came in sight of the chain of desolate mountains which fringes the southwestern coast of Mexico. Continuing we came to the harbor of Acapulco, and winding between the rocky islands and promontories which arose around us, we came to anchor at 4 o'clock opposite the town. Here we found our rival, the "Golden Gate," the "Oregon" and a large collier, from which we got a supply of coal before leaving.

We had hardly dropped anchor before a number of natives swam out to us. With their dark features, wild eyes and shaggy hair, they looked like so many sea-imps while disporting around us as we lay three hundred yards from shore. They howled to us to throw "dimeys" and "picayuneys" into the sea, and then see how they would bring them up. Those who were rich enough to invest did so, and following the coins with their sharp eyes, the divers soon brought them to the surface, and shouted for more "dimeys." They stayed in the water hours at a time.

Several boats manned—if this term is admissible in reference to such people—by the wretched looking natives soon put off from shore for the purpose of carrying such of us to land as wanted to go. Many of us went. There was no landing-place; we simply got our boats as near dry land as possible, and jumped ashore on the sandy beach which extends front of the town.

Acapulco makes a picturesque appearance from the bay, with its low, white buildings shaded by tropical trees, and the volcanic mountains rising back of it. The population of three thousand was a mixture of Spaniards, Negroes and Indians, so mixed that you could hardly tell which was the predominant race. And what a set of degenerate beings they were! The men lazy and thievish, the women disgustingly licentious, the children precocious in aping the vices of their parents; all of them bearing the fruits of immoral living in their listless, attenuated frames, which were reeking with scrofulous diseases. These half human wretches get their living mainly from the vessels stopping here for coal and water, and the passengers thereof who venture ashore. The last are annoyed to desperation's brink by troops of beggars, thieves and itinerant merchants, who pester them from their landing to departure.

The *plaza*, or public square, of Acapulco was a lively place in the afternoon. One side was taken up by the stands of venders of all sorts of merchandize, who were shouting forth the merits and cheapness of their wares. They would waylay passengers, and if they could not induce them to buy, they would roll out some sonorous and trilled Spanish oath. At one place an old hag was presiding over a gambling table, where she was dealing "*monte*" to an excited group of natives and passengers, the latter taking to the business quite naturally. Occasionally a dispute would arise between the beldam and the "backers," when the voice of the former would arise to the shrillest pitch and then gradually decline, as her anger subsided. Scantily robed women passed through the square on their way to and from the public fountains, with large earthen jars poised on their heads; and little donkeys, half hidden with loads of vegetables and fruits, slowly worked their way amid the motley group.

When I wrote my notes of travel, or rather, when I amplified them on my arrival home, the temptation was strong and often yielded to, to use foreign terms in my descriptions, and to give the words spoken by Indian or Mexican in their own language. It is the custom of many travelers and becomes natural. It gives one a chance of airing what little he knows; or rather, of ventilating the much he don't know. But when, after thirty years, the writer revises what he wrote in his youth, he notes how tame were his smart expressions, how vapid his attempts at high-flown description, and how silly his efforts to impress his readers with his lingual lore. So now I "put away childish things" and try to expunge all pedantry, and "call a spade a spade." I gathered one piece of information, however, that it is one thing to study a language to what you think is proficiency, and another to put it into practice, but I must admit that a few foreign terms and phrases, mixed in, tone up an article and give the writer a reputation for smartness. So I hope the reader will not meet with many non-understandable words or phrases.

To look at this town, with its low, white buildings, its thatched huts, its tropical vegetation, and its swarthy people, one could easily imagine himself in some country on the Barbary coast, and not in progressive North America and a free republic, and I was much amused and interested in what I saw during my short stay there.

From the *plaza* and its odd sights I ascended the side of a rocky hill overlooking the town, as well as the bay and its shelter of capes and islands. The lower side of the hill was dotted with straw huts, the lazy owners of which were swinging in their hammocks or seated on the ground smoking, while their women were grinding corn and baking the dough therefrom on flat stones set at an angle before an open fire, their naked children the meanwhile rolling in the sand or playing with the gaunt pigs and dogs of the town. Buzzards as big as turkey-gobblers were seated around on projecting rocks, looking pensively on the congenial scenes around, and so tame that they would allow us to come within a few paces, when they would flap their wings, and with a disagreeable croak fly lazily away. They are the scavengers of the town, and, as their throats are used for sewers, are protected from harm.

Crossing over to the fort I passed an open hut containing a stand on which was seated an old, old man with his hands clasped in front of his shins, like those of a Peruvian mummy. His knees were drawn up against his breast, and around him was wrapped an old blanket, above which projected his parchment-colored face. He looked so like exhumed death that I was startled when he feebly nodded to me, and could imagine the dried muscle crackling in the exertion. In fact, taking him for all in all, his cadaverous appearance and sepulchral voice, one might have thought he was inaugurating the resurrection.

The Castillo, or fort, which was situated on a broad knoll commanding the harbor, as well as the town, was quadrangular and surrounded by a walled moat, across which was one of the old-fashioned drawbridges we read about, and which mailed knights clattered merrily over when the besieged did not get it pulled up in season. In these modern times a well-directed cannon shot would have loosened the fastening and sent the fly-trap thundering down. The fort was mounted by some hundred rusty cannon, and garrisoned by a company of what would have been cut-throat soldiers did they not lack energy to do violent deeds. They were uniformed in white pantaloons, ragged shirt and straw hat, and looked as if they would run at the first appearance of an enemy. What I have seen of Spanish-American soldiers makes me think how little we should boast of our victories over the Mexican troops during our disgraceful war with their country, particularly when we take into consideration the factional wars then waging in Mexico. These soldiers were armed with flintlocks, and had plugs in the muzzles to keep out dampness and save cleaning. They were also uniformed with bare feet, which enabled them,

when their guns were thrown down, to be ready for a celeri-
tous run in case an enemy would ever venture into such a
wretched country, a country whose most reliant defense
against an unacclimated foe is the yellow fever. The fort was
built one hundred years ago, and was skilfully constructed.
The chief occupation of the garrison was to guard a chain-
gang, who, on their backs, were carrying sand and lime for
the use of some convict masons who were repairing the fort.
Walking two and two over the sharp stones, with one hand
steadying the sack and the other holding up a rattling chain,
these felons seemed walking exemplifications of the maxim,
"The way of the transgressor is hard." The wretches did not
feel their degradation, but with brutal jest and laugh beguiled
their labor. Just outside the fort was a government smith
shop, the Vulcan of which was chained to his Cyclopian
"beezer" by a chain, and so well was the apprentice "inden-
tured and firmly bound" to his master, that if this plan had
been adopted a generation ago there would have been fewer
advertisements in contemporaneous newspapers of "One
horseshoe-nail reward." When I saw the chances this twain
had for severing the tie which bound them, I thought what a
successful strike they might make for their freedom if they
tried.

" Who would be free himself must strike the blow,"

and if there is a hammer and cold-chisel by, so much the
easier; but, alas for these fellows, the propinquity of two soldiers with loaded muskets prevented them from exercising
their ingenuities.

By the time I came back to the *plaza* the short-lived twilight of the tropics had given way to darkness, and the booths
were lighted up, making the scene quite lively. Two musicians, on violin and flute, were giving the "Orizabians" some
sweet music; but the strains were so short and so often re-

peated, that it clogged the senses, and we were fain to proffer them some of the coin of the realm to stop. The merchants seemed still more lively and persistent by torch-light, and pestered us more than ever to buy their wares, while the women paraded their viciousness with increased boldness. If one town more than another needs to be swallowed up, it is this modern Sodom; but in that event the earth would be pitied for surrounding such a sickening dose.

Fearing that we might be left in this miserable town I moved down to the sandy shore, and, after running the gauntlet between rows of yelling boatmen, I jumped into one of the numerous craft, and shooting out into the darkness, the swarthy Charon, reversing the usual course of that mythological personage, took me from Death to Life. I may be straining a point in the simile, but I will let it stand, as Acapulco was certainly an abode of death, both morally and otherwise, while on the "Orizaba" we had life on the ocean wave—such as it was.

We were nearly all night coaling the steamer. The coal was all carried in sacks on the backs of the men from one vessel to another, and the grimy procession of native carriers, under the glare of torches, made an impressive scene. We hoisted the anchor before sunrise, however, and put to sea, glad that we were once more on our homeward way and leaving such a den of badness behind.

Time passed slowly on board our vessel. Some of us arose by sunrise, although at that time we ran chances of being swamped by the sailors while washing down the decks, as, by accident, they often threw water on those who got in their way. We drew water from the salt, salt sea and washed, a group at a time; until by turns all who cared to wash had pickled themselves, and then been rasped off with a common towel, which operation was in itself a species of dry salting. Then, in season, we went to breakfast, and, standing in rows along swinging tables, drank our coffee whose main strength lay in the water, and ate our salt junk whose main strength lay in its smell, and between the two worried down some hard tack. The sad ceremony over, we lounged away the time until noon, killing it in ways as various as our natures. Some read, some told yarns, some continually got themselves in places where they were sworn out by the mate on duty, many smoked, and several " fought the tiger " in the hopeless task of winning at " *monte.*" At last the dinner hour would come. Then more onslaught—feeble on my part—on the saline hash and " hard tack," while the vessel lurched and the passengers—some of them—swore as they fell against the bunks, or spilt their victuals over themselves or neighbors, while the tables swung like pendulums. This perfunctory meal over, we hied to the deck above to get the fresh air denied us below. More killing of him who cuts down all both great and small, and the time for another meal came, and another return to the comparative pleasure of the deck. The air, which had been sultry and oppressive during the day, would now be stirred by gentle breezes, and, on feeling these to fan their fevered cheeks, the spirits of the travelers would revive from the dreamy listlessness which had per-vaded them during the sun-lit hours. In star-gazing, sing-ing, story-telling, and in another occupation sometimes termed " tripping the light fantastic toe," the evening wore away, and midnight often found the more obstreperous part of our crowd engaged in their revels, much to the annoyance of the early retirers, who could but illy sleep while such a racket was going on overhead.

Thus we spent our days on the ocean, twenty-two in all, and wearisome days they were. The same sea-sights, the same people to look at and talk to, the same recurrence of meals composed of a similarity of unpalatable materials, the same diurnal discomforts from the tropic heat.

On the 14th we entered the Gulf of Tehuautepec, and in crossing it we had a rough passage. As we proceeded, on account of the curve of the coast, we often saw land, some-times in mountain sides, thickly covered with tangled vegeta-tion coming abruptly to the water's edge. The air grew warmer and more oppressive, and the sun as we neared the isthmus was directly overhead at noon, so we stood on our shadows. Heavy showers sometimes kept us below deck.

On the 18th we entered Panama Bay, the shores and islands of which were clothed in the most vivid green. Late in the afternoon we anchored within three miles of Panama.

This old town is in the Republic of Colombia, and occupies a tongue of land reaching out into a bay so shallow that vessels of eighty tons can only come within two miles, while passenger steamers must anchor a mile further out, near an island called Perico. This, like the other islands which make the harbor, was green with rank vegetation to the water's edge; a tangle of vines and mammoth-leaved plants and parasite-clad trees which seemed rife with disease. The little steamer commonly used to carry passengers ashore was out of repair, so we were obliged to make use of small boats, a whole fleet of which put off from shore to meet us. When they came alongside a rush was made for them by the passengers, who looked like a human cataract, as laughing, cursing and yelling they poured down the stairway into the boats which, as fast as loaded, pulled ashore. The boat I was in was one of the first, and was so full that it nearly swamped more than once in the three miles row. When we reached the shore, there being no wharf, we had to ride "pig-a-back" on the shoulders of men in waiting, whom we had to pay. It seemed to me that the boatmen purposely stopped at parts of the shore which would require the services of these marine porters, and thus the thousand, more or less, of humanity which for two weeks had made the "Orizaba" their home got to shore.

XXI.

Homeward Bound—Northward.

ENTERING the city by a picturesque though crumbling gateway which pierced the southern wall, I passed the Grand Cathedral, and, wending my way through some dark, narrow streets, stopped at the "American Hotel," where for two dollars I bought a chance for breakfast —supper being out of the question—and the privilege of sleeping on the floor, which done I took a walk around the city. The walled portion was a half mile square, and in it were fifteen massive churches, besides schools and convents, many of them in ruins. Panama was once the wealthiest city in the New World, as through it passed the trade between Spain and her South American Colonies; but little business is done here now, and many of the grand buildings are tumbling to ruins. The population is but eleven thousand.

The houses which lined the narrow streets in the best part of the town were lofty and faced with balconies, on which were seated the better class of people, chatting in quite a lively sort of way. The soldiers I saw were uniformed gaily, and strutted along as if responsible for much. Itinerant and sedentary merchants of all manner of goods, from whisky to Panama hats, were shrilly enumerating the merits and cheapness of them, and sturdy little donkies, heavily laden with wood, water-casks and vegetables, worked their way through the streets, urged on by their impish drivers—all forming a scene tropical and picturesque in the extreme. But, as if to shadow the lively picture with gloom, directly in front of the hotel arose the high walls of an old convent, now seamed and going to ruin. Nothing was more calculated to call up sad thoughts than this old building, with parasite plants growing from the crevices of its roofless, windowless walls, whose stones they were forcing asunder.

The "American Hotel," from its massiveness, might have been some ecclesiastical building. In the courtyard was a huge tank, and around it several of the ship's passengers, in a state of nature, were taking an upright bath under the manipulations of as many black grooms. Above some wordy warfare among these human hostlers I heard some one say, " I'm no Jamaica nigger; I'm from Bucks County, Pennsylvania, I am." These words so startled me that I went among the splashing bathers, and singling the speaker out found his name to be Robert Grose, and that he had once lived with Stacy Brown, of Brownsburg. He had drifted here, where he was stranded until he could get away. Among the outlandish Jamaica negroes with whom he had been confounded he seemed like a lost black sheep. He was overjoyed to see one from his own native county, and was anxious to get back again.

At 9 o'clock the notes of a bugle rang out upon the air as a signal for all citizens and strangers within the gates to get to their homes, permanent or temporary, or go to the calaboose. Hardly had the tantarara died away before the idlers and street merchants were hurrying home. The day's excitement being ended I betook myself to a large hall in the hotel, where, among a host of others, I lay down ; but sleep was impossible for a long time. The sickly season was beginning; the air was damp and sultry, and it seemed to me as if Death was around picking out victims. The building seemed to swing to and fro in imitation of the motion of the " Orizaba," besides, several of the sleepers around me, who lacked sentiment and nervousness, snored outrageously. So I had a good chance to reflect on the deeds of my past life before sleep came.

Although we had paid for our breakfast in advance, many of us got none through the landlord's rascality, as the train left before half could get to the table, but as it did not look fit to eat, it made little matter. We had been told the night before the cars left at 9 o'clock, when 6 was the hour. Our way to the terminus was through the eastern gate, and then amid the suburbs of thatched huts which lay along the margin of the bay. The half-wild denizens were all ready for us, and with pernicious activity waylaid us with fruits, corals, seashells, whisky, cigars, monkeys, squirrels, parrots and similar goods, dead and alive. We were much amused at a monkey-merchant, whose wares had been captured in the neighboring forest. In his efforts to show the tameness of one of his half-human specimens, that he might the easier sell it, it got away from him and struck a bee-line for its former home. The last we saw of the twain their speed was so nearly matched that we were in doubt as to the result of the race.

The starting of the train rid us of these mercantile pests, and we were soon rolling over the fever-breeding swamp which marks the first section of the Isthmian crossing. The lives lost in building this road were fearfully numerous; but thirty years since they are being more than duplicated in digging the canal. When we came to the ridge we used two locomotives to ascend it, and from its slope we took our last view of the Pacific near where Balboa had his first, and also of the ruined old city on its shore.

Nothing could exceed the denseness, luxuriance and gigantic proportions of the vegetation through which we rode. The surface of the fever-breeding slope was covered with a matting of creeping vines above which rose a growth of mammoth plants, with leaves eight or ten feet long and a foot or more wide. Far above these giants of the lower vegetable kingdom towered the stately mahogany and the slender, tufted palm, the forms of some hidden from view by parasite plants. But this prolific place, where nature has so recklessly showered her bounty, is a vast plague spot, where death stalks silent and ghostly, seeking for victims.

Though since dwarfed by the great enterprise of De Lesseps, the building of this railroad was a great undertaking when we think of the natural obstacles to be surmounted; but when we consider that the placing of each tie severed a human life, we are tempted to wish it had never been built. Thousands died in its construction, but at last the road was built, and now the shrieking locomotive, like the Juggernaut of India, rolls over a road-bed of human corpses, drawing in its wake a living freight, which concerns itself little of the sacrifices made for its convenience.

We frequently stalled in the ascent, although we had but one section of the passengers. At the summit the rear engine was sent back to help up the other half. The descent was quickly made down the valley of the Chagres. On this river we passed some collections of huts, whose people were lounging about them. We cannot expect much snap in a community which can pick its dinners off of trees as wanted, and don't have to build a fire to cook them. Crossing the Chagres on an iron bridge we rolled into the modern built city of Aspinwall. Here we met a ship load of people who were to fill the vacancies we left in California. How they plied us with questions, and how patronizingly we answered these " tenderfeet." How differently were the two portions situated; one having seen the elephant, the other just entering the menagerie !

The people of Aspinwall, like those of Acapulco and Panama, live on the pickings they get from travelers passing

through. We experienced the same vicissitudes as in the last
named places, although the pirates were more villainous looking. Many of these were Jamaica negroes, and a more repulsive set of beings I never saw, unless they were the Diggers on
the Great Desert. Some were giants with feet like those of
" Dandy Jim of Caroline." Many of the venders were females,
who, in their outlandish English, addressed us affectionately
as "Come my lub, buy dis bottle Jamaky rum, brot it from
dar meself;" or, "Here honey, hab one dese big pine-apples."
They looked like scant-frocked gorillas.

Our Atlantic steamer was the "Northern Light," which we
boarded in the afternoon. In San Francisco we had our
berths, such as they were, numbered, so that there was no confusion; but here the earliest bird got the choicest worm; thus
there was much rushing and crowding to get bunks on the first
deck. Each one had to show his ticket, and "stowaways" had
a poor show. There were several of these who beat their way
from San Francisco, and in their impudence boasted of their
doings. But one of these got on to the "Northern Light." He
was a rowdy New York boy, who, when he was refused
passage, watched his opportunity, jumped into the water,
climbed up the paddle wheel and got through an opening to
the deck when he was discovered. The officers were going to
put him ashore, but he pleaded so hard and looked so forlorn
in his drenched clothes that he was allowed to continue on
his way by working his passage heaving coal. He was a
"Bowery Boy," and had been full of his pranks; but now,
when we saw him, he was crestfallen enough, and so remained
until his old haunts on the Battery met his gaze.

Whenever we left a port the people showed the greatest
regret, which was greatly to our credit. At Aspinwall they
crowded on the wharf, and howled and yelled and swore as
they thrust long poison-filled bottles at us, and pine-apples and
bunches of bananas, and so continued until the vessel left.

Aspinwall is underlaid with a coral reef, and the water is so bad that for drinking purposes the people depend on huge cisterns, which are filled in the rainy season. To supply the ship-tank we were obliged to diverge from our homeward course and proceed down the New Grenada coast for twenty-five miles, where we took in water. I was glad of this, as it gave me a chance to see the scene of an exploit I read of in my young school days in " Parley's History;" namely, the capture of Porto Bello by the buccaneer Morgan and his piratical gang.

Had we been under the Equatorial sun the weather could not have been hotter or the scenery more tropical than what we saw and felt while going down the coast. The high mountain shores were covered with a network of vegetation that hid the earth down to the edge of the water which duplicated it in reverse. The stillness was oppressive, even the beautifully plumaged birds flitting among the fever-suggesting shrubbery being silent.

Slowly steaming along we came before sunset to a scene of picturesque quietude, whose equal I never saw. This was Porto Bello, the " beautiful harbor," discovered in 1502 by Columbus, and settled one hundred years after. The ruins of the old town were close to our anchorage, consisting of remains of towers, churches, convents and other buildings, overgrown with tangled vines, and with limbs of trees projecting through the windows, and shrubbery growing from the joints of the stones. How different from two hundred years ago, when the town was the northern terminus of an isthmus highway, paved with stones and extending over the ridge to Panama. Then Porto Bello was the point of exchange where the gold and silver of Peru met the costly merchandize of Spain, when convoyed by armed vessels it was landed here. At stated times fairs were held, to which the merchants of the western coast of South America came to make their purchases which were carried by mules and llamas to the Pacific shore, and thence shipped. Porto Bello grew in wealth so that the buccaneers resolved on its capture, which, in 1668, they effected by surprise.

The church ornaments and wealth of the town, however, were placed in the castle which defied the pirates. Morgan made use of a stratagem by which he thought to accomplish his ends without bloodshed. Collecting the priests and women whom he found in the city, he commanded them to go in advance and plant the scaling ladders, thinking the garrison would not harm them. The heart of the Spanish commander was, however, proof against the prayers of priests or tears of women, and he ordered his men to fire on all who advanced. His scheme failing, Morgan stormed the castle and secured an immense booty. Porto Bello never survived this blow, for Spanish commerce was swept from the neighboring waters by this same bold buccaneer. The fleets which once rode here at anchor are unrepresented now except by the occasional steamers which come here to water. So abrupt is the shore that we anchored within twenty yards of it, the slope being covered with tangled vegetation to the lower edge. The water with which the ships are supplied is from "Columbus' Spring," which, high up the hillside, pours its rich tide from under a mass of rank growing plants, which, through botanic ignorance, I must term mammoth weeds in the likeness of caladiums and ferns. An iron pipe runs to within connecting distance of vessels, to which a hose is attached, and the tanks quickly filled with the best of water.

The deck was covered with the passengers, who, quietly commenting, looked on the surrounding scene. Birds of beautiful plumage, but voiceless, flew from bough to bough, preparing for their night's rest. Among these were brilliant parrots and paroquets and others I did not know. Larger ones, such as pelicans and cranes, flapped their wings clumsily amid the

19

branches of huge lignum vitæ and mahogany trees, whose mossy trunks seemed to grow almost parallel with the steep mountain side. A hut stood near the edge of the water, built of reeds and thatched with broad leaves, a sample of the dwelling 'places of the few mongrel descendants of the old population of Porto Bello. The owner of this was paddling around us in a canoe in which, on its back, lay a huge turtle, whose angry eyes showed that it would turn, like the worm, if it were possible. The owner made no effort to sell his prey. Another boat was loaded down with bananas, which also had to sell themselves or go unsold. Such independent merchants I never saw. At last these mercantile representatives of Porto Bello's vanished glory left us and lazily paddled toward the ruined town, which the setting sun was now gilding with its last rays. As it sank below the hills a mantle of golden light lingered awhile on the vine-covered walls and towers, as if to redeem the place from the loneliness and desolation surrounding it.

The silence about us was really oppressive, and the darkening waters so still that the steamer hardly moved, while the air of that mountain-hedged harbor was sultry beyond endurance. These, with the sight of the ruins, which looked ghastly in the twilight, and as if some of the old Castilian knights and priests, friars and nuns which once dwelt in its castle and convents might crawl out of their former haunts, and, mistaking us for buccaneers, smite us with ancient engines of warfare and harry us with exorcisms and consignments to pits bottomless, gave us such feelings that we grew impatient of delay and glad to leave what had been such a picturesque place, but which now was getting unbearable.

From some unexplained cause we did not leave till midnight, and when we awoke in the morning we were gaily steaming over the Sea of the Caribs. On the 23d we passed between Cuba and Hayti, and on the 25th entered the warm waters of the Gulf Stream—a river flowing through an ocean. Soon we were plowing waters afterwards familiar to me in 1862 and 1863; but who could have dreamed that in ten years our country would experience the horrors of a Civil War. On the 26th we passed Cape Hatteras, and the 28th brought us in sight of land, which was the coast of New Jersey.

In the years before I left home I heard a great many satirical things said of the State east of the Delaware. Would-be smart folks called it Spain and a sand-bank, and its people Spaniards, and sand-pipers, and other cutting names were prevalent. Perhaps I thought these sayings smart, and in a modest way indulged in them myself. But when I saw its shores for the first time, after my year of journeying, I was in no mood to indulge in or tolerate the cheap wit of former days. It was the verge of my native land, and I welcomed its unpicturesque, low-lying shores as the threshold of my home.

Soon the shores of Long Island came in view, and, passing by Governor's Island, we steered through a labyrinth of shipping, and at last the "Northern Light" was moored at her dock, just above the Battery. Now came the hurry and confusion of landing, after which, forcing themselves through a noisy array of hackmen, runners and porters, my thousand shipmates scattered and parted forever.

XXII.

In New York.

A RED-LETTER day in the annals of New York sharpers is the advent of a California steamer. Hardly is the vessel telegraphed before a fleet of pilot boats start out to meet her, each anxious to be the lucky one which is to act as her escort and be the recipient of her pilotage fee. The boats are furnished with packages of circulars, mainly of hotels, boarding houses and clothing stores, and these are scattered broadcast over the steamer as soon as opportunity offers, and are eagerly read by a community whose literature has been so rare as that on our vessel. Solomon Levi's statements in regard to the merits and cheapness of his clothing are absorbed, without their truth being questioned, by people who look upon them more as a mental entertainment than as schemes for entrapping the unwary into shoddy dispensaries. Peter Hash's account of his luxurious parlors, Sybaritic dining halls and gorgeous dormitories are enjoyed like romances, and so are the descriptions of the Oriental accommodations of the Occidental Hotel. Weakened by such mental pabulum the passengers go on their way, weary with their long journey and full of excitement at the prospect of landing. Wistful are the looks which they cast upon the city, with its scenes of busy life, as the steamer nears the wharves; but glances more eager meet theirs from the crowd of human hyenas and vultures which line the docks ready to pounce upon their prey as soon as it is within reach. Hardly is the vessel made fast before the anxious seekers for whom they may devour, despite the efforts made by officers to prevent them, are mounting the deck, and with insidious smile and lying tongue plying their vocations. The hotel runners are the first to greet you, and these keep up a sort of guerilla warfare until you emerge from the wharf on to the street. Running the gauntlet of these worthies you are next set upon by a fierce and noisy array of cab drivers. These assail you from all sides with whip and tongue, and you may thank your lucky stars if you pass this ordeal without being impressed into one of their flaming chariots, in which you are carried one square, all for the sum of four York shillings. The feelings of one of these sons of Jehu were so outraged by my not accepting a ride in his phæton, along with some deprecatory remarks I made, that he offered to "lick me for a quarter," which coin not being to spare I was let off. Passing these characters you next come on to a legion of young porters who, for fees as small as themselves, agree to carry your luggage to any part of the city. These, the light infantry of the army of sharpers, are very tenacious, and grabbing your gripsack will only leave you on threats of summary punishment.

Passing successfully these inner defenses of the city you at last reach your hotel. Now, you think, "I have passed the troubles incident to the invasion of an enemy's country, and 'I will take mine ease in mine inn!'"

Innocent man that you are, don't you know that the steps of the returned Californian are dogged by persistent mercenaries from the time he sets foot on the soil of Gotham till he leaves it, lightened in purse and spirits! Hug no delusive fancies. Hardly have you emerged from the bath-room and barber-shop before you are met by a gentlemanly-looking

man, with a winning address and an elaborate necktie, who
has seen your exit and patiently awaits your entrance. He is
a Count D'Orsay in manners and appearance, and is well
calculated to come the confidence game. Endowed with a
deep knowledge of human nature, he has noticed your greenness, and he will profit thereby. Meeting you with a bland
smile, he will grasp your hand like an old acquaintance and
tenderly inquire after his friends in California; for, in nine
cases out of ten, your confidence man has been to the land of
gold, and such is his knowledge of localities there and your
greenness that his lies are credited. Getting much interested
in your welfare, and seeing your somewhat shabby attire, he
makes you the recipient of gratuitous warning and advice.
He cautions you against numerous clothing store agents, who,
taking advantage of the condition of your wardrobe, and appealing to your pride to get it replaced by an array of their
cheap but elegant wares, will try to decoy you off to their
Fulton Street dens, there to take you in and swindle you.
With a face beaming with benevolence and urbanity he warns
you to keep out of their clutches, and, self-sacrificing proto-
type of the good Samaritan that he is, he offers to conduct
you to where you will get your money's worth. He is not at
all interested in the clothing emporium ; oh no, not he; he is
interested in you and does not want to see you swindled as he
was when *he* returned from California. Being much taken
by his Christian deportment you accompany him, for it would
be ungrateful to repay his kindness with mistrust; so, arm-in-
arm—walking exemplification of the fact that new-made
friendships are as strong as old-established ones—you pass
from the hotel. As you proceed you meet scattered units of
the clothing agent gang, and these, true to the predictions of
your Damon, wantonly assail you with their business cards
and offers of safe conduct to their respective stores. Keeping
you close under his protecting wing, your friend scowls

fiercely at the skirmishers on your flank, whom he severely anathematizes. The latter, also growing interested in you, return his compliments and give you the assurance that you are in the hands of a noted swindler, who will not leave you until he gets your last penny. Your friend shakes his fist and breathes defiance and devotion till your admiration is unbounded. Being clad in verdure as well as in seedy clothing you do not observe Damon exchanging sly winks with his apparent foes between his expletives. As yet you do not know that they are all of one family. Boldly rescuing you from the hands of your tormentors, Damon triumphantly bears you onward, discoursing familiarly on surrounding objects. The building is closed or he would take you through the *Tribune* office. Why, did he know Horace Greeley? Intimate with him; queer man was Old Greeley! Anon, we pass the *Tribune's* antipode, the *Herald*. He knows "Old Bennett," too. We would go through there if it was'nt shut up; so we will have to forego the pleasure. You soon emerge into Fulton Street, that paradise of cheap clothing stores. Elbowing yourselves through the rival merchants thereof, your escort takes you to *the* store and introduces you to the proprietor. They have a private conversation which, in all probability, has reference to your innocence and how far the merchant can swindle you without exciting suspicions. Having been away from the East so long that you hardly know what honest prices should be, you do not know how much you have been financially bled, neither do you observe your companion getting his "price of blood" in the shape of a heavy per cent. on the goods you have been buying. Gathering up your purchases you depart for your hotel, pleased with the deportment of New Yorkers in general toward strangers, and of your friend in particular.

Speaking in the first person, I will say this is no fancy sketch, and that when I came to look over the purchases I

had made, that I might look like a civilized being on my
arrival home, I felt disgusted with myself that, after all my
worldly experience these sharpers could throw such a glamour
about themselves that I could not recognize them in their
true characters. I have come to the conclusion that to see the
world which I saw, while a person may gain in some kinds
of experience, he is the more easily made the dupe of those
who stay at home and study human nature for what they
can work out of it. These rogues seem to exert a magnetic
influence over those who come in contact with them, for in
my case I had read enough about the "Peter Funks" to have
not been imposed upon.

There is another personage pursuing the same calling
whom you will be apt to come in contact with. This is a
venerable gentleman with a placid countenance, who comes
the benevolent dodge also. He, of course, has a son in California—they all have sons or brothers there—a good son, who
sends him a remittance by every steamer. He says he is in
easy circumstances and keeps a clothing store, where he can
exercise his benevolent propensities by selling raiment to
returned Californians at less than cost. Charmed with your
kind old friend, you accompany him to his den, where you
are sold with what you buy.

The thimblerigger, the pocket-book dropper and swindlers
of other kinds should receive passing notices, but I pass over
their claims, though they were always with us, to treat of
an adventure two of us had with some "Peter Funk" watch
dealers.

My comrade had been some years in California, where he
had gone through the varied experiences befalling mining
life, finally graduating at Fraser River, so that he was anything but a greenhorn. For myself, if I had not seen any
of the doings of New York sharpers I had read and heard of
them, and both of us considered ourselves invulnerable to

their attacks. At the gullibility of " Peter Funk's " victims
we had marveled much.

During a promenade on the Battery—where we had seen
the pocket-book dropping and other games played with
mingled feelings of pity and contempt for the victims, and
with much respect for our ability to withstand the seductive
wiles of New York sharpers—we took a stroll up Broadway.
When opposite the City Park our attention was arrested by
the loud cries of an auctioneer who was selling watches at a
great sacrifice.

" Here," I said to my friend, "is a ' Peter Funk ' shop in
full blast. Let us go in and see how the simple-minded
country people are swindled."

My remark was overheard by a man standing at my elbow,
and a remarkably honest-looking person he was, too.

" You are mistaken, sir," said the latter. " The Peter Funks
have all been cleaned out by the police. These gentlemen
do a perfectly legitimate business."

This, of course, was sufficient. It would not do to impugn
the motives of a man like our informant. His whole manner
betokened what is known as God's noblest work. His gray
hairs, his mild eyes, his general appearance stamped him as
a man of probity.

The bidding, now that our attention was drawn towards
the shop, grew fiercer and louder. Watches were rapidly
knocked off to innocent-looking gentlemen who had a mania
for them. They seemed a good thing which they could
not get enough of. Our new-found friend at last caught the
infection and made spirited bids at what the auctioneer
called " a splendid, full-jeweled, gold hunting watch," one of
an imported lot which had just been sold at a great sacrifice
by the custom-house officials to pay duties. Our man soon
ran it up to twenty dollars, at which price he got it. He then
went up to the clerk to pay for it, but could only raise fifteen

dollars. The clerk assumed a particularly angry look and said, with an oath, to the buyer who seemed ready to sink in his boots with fear:

"What did you bid on that watch for when you knew you could not pay for it and when we might have sold it to the next lowest bidder and got the cash. Get out of the way, hay-seeds, and give me that watch."

The buyer was taken all aback by this rude rebuff. He humbly returned the time-piece and begged pardon. But he was inconsolable for the loss of his bargain, which was again put up and bid on with renewed interest. I never saw people so crazy for a watch. As each bid was put on our new acquaintance acted as if he was having a tooth pulled. Coming up to my shipmate he said :

"Come, won't you buy it? I'm a watchmaker myself and live in Jersey City. I am putting up at the Astor House, where I left the rest of my money. The watch will go for twenty dollars, buy it and come over with me and I will give you thirty for it. Oh, it's too bad they wont let me have it."

He then turned to the clerk and implored him to wait until he could get his money. The actuary told him not to bother him with his foolishness, while the auctioneer went on with his intonations. Thus shabbily treated the case of the would-be buyer was becoming pitiable. The contortions of his face betokened a man in the first stages of colic. We felt sympathy for him and detestation for the others. My shipmate was at last induced to buy the watch, being assured by the auctioneer that if it was not all he represented it the money would be refunded, and was the possessor of it for twenty dollars. I need hardly say that, wrapped up as I was in the transaction, I envied him his bargain, on which he would soon make ten dollars. On looking around for the watchmaker he was gone; his appealing face no longer met our eyes. The amount of the matter was, he was a "Peter Funk," and my friend had been swindled.

But he had his remedy, for did not the auctioneer say that if the watch was not all he represented he would refund the money? We inspected the thing and found its odor as brazen as the face of its late owner; so we went back to the shop, which was almost deserted, the auctioneer and four or five persons being all that remained. One of these, a staid, portly old gentleman, with gold glasses, cane and shiny hat, who said he was a jeweler, asked to see the watch.

Taking us to one side he said it was worth but a few dollars, and that we would never see the Jersey City man again. My shipmate, in wrath, went to the auctioneer, who had stopped his noise while trouble was impending, and demanded that he should redeem his promise, as the watch was not what he represented it to be.

"Aha!" said Peter Funk, who was now coming out in his real character, "you won't catch me asleep. I said, '*if it's not all I represent it.*' But I took good care not to represent it at all. So, my friend, you had better keep quiet and leave the store." Our last acquaintance now came forward to our rescue and said:

"Gentlemen, take my advice; these rascals have swindled you and you will never get your money back. The best thing you can do is to exchange your watch for a good common silver one, and make no fuss about it. I am a judge of watches and will see that you are not cheated this time. So don't make fools of yourselves again by calling in the police, as no one will believe your story." So here was another "Peter Funk."

Turning from him we renewed our talk with the auctioneer, who would not notice us. Angry for allowing ourselves to be so duped we, for I was standing by my friend in his trouble, resolved to checkmate the swindlers, even if our stay in the city should be delayed by bringing the matter before a police court; so, giving the watch into my keeping, my shipmate started for an officer. Thinking he was only feigning, Peter told him to go ahead, but, seeing him in earnest, he called him back and agreed to refund the money. He was going to deduct the "usual commission of two dollars and a half," but threats of another sally after the police brought him to his senses, and he gave back the whole amount and ordered us away.

Repassing in a few moments we saw the machine in full running order again, stool-pigeons and all, and with the requisite amount of raw material lying around for working up. They seem to separate and get together by magic.

Such is the experience of two persons who prided themselves on their knowledge of the world. The truth was that we were completely under the influence of the Peter Funks, as was shown by the sequel. If those cognizant of their tricks are thus swindled, why wonder at the number of uninformed strangers who are duped by these knaves? A kind of spell seems thrown around you, and forgetting all former advice and experience you unconsciously allow yourselves to be drawn into the snares set for you, to come out shamefully swindled.

＊　　　　＊　　　　＊　　　　＊

Enjoying the hospitality of New York for two nights and a day, as I could not leave sooner, I left on the morning of May 30th, and before noon came in sight of the Delaware River— a stream familiar to me from my earliest recollections, but which I had not seen for thirteen months. A ride of twenty-three miles and old landmarks around Lumberton became visible, and with the depressed feeling, which we sometimes experience more when nearing home after a long absence in distant lands than when leaving it, I came in sight of the old mill, river-landing, lumber-yard and quarry, and all which made up the little village where I passed my life. Soon traversing the winding valley of the Cuttalossa, which the sinking sun was fast throwing in shadow, my old home

came in view from its forest setting, and here I found the
home-circle intact and well, and glad to see the sun-burnt,
rough-clad wanderer back; while our Irish handmaid voiced
a generous welcome, and Nero, the dog, who unlike his proto-
type of ancient Greece had not forgotten his Ulysses, gave
him the freedom of the house with bark and whine and
demonstrative wag of tail. I also learned how easy a thing it
is to compass sea and land, thinking of the wonder and
admiration you will create, and then, when returning to your
starting place, find what a transient splash you make when dropping in the social sea. For awhile the questioning conversational billows meet answering waves, which ebb and flow and
bear you into prominence on their surges; then, through
familiarity, weariness or lack of curiosity, these subside to the
faintest ripples, until the returned traveler finds himself of no
more nor less account than those who remained at home satisfied with the contentments which every-day life brings forth.
And this is as it should be. If the expectations of all would
be realized who seek prominence, there would be so much
commotion in the world that any other than a hum-drum
existence would be suppressed by penal enactment.

XXIII.

Conclusion.

A "CONCLUSION" naturally belonging to a book as much as a "Preface," I hitch one on to *A California Tramp*. It is a little like a rear locomotive on a difficult grade, placed there to help take the train-like chapters through, although in this case the hind engine is ahead!

These travels involved a journey of seven thousand miles by steam, thirteen hundred on foot and eight hundred of alternate riding and walking, and a period of something over a year. As far as the accumulation of what moths corrupt and thieves break in and steal are concerned, they were a failure; but otherwise, in spite of what I passed through, I would not have missed my experience for all I might have gained in the most prosperous venture in the time employed.

Thirty years ago, with the exception of a few settlements in Eastern Kansas and the Mormons living in Utah, in the country between the Missouri and the gold regions of California, independent of the Indians, who were either wild and murderous nomads or under the influence of white traders, who brutalized them further with "civilized" ways, there were no inhabitants but the soldiers, traders and hunters, and the outlaws which had been driven thence from the States for their crimes. Many of these last were with the Indians, and were the cause of much

(310)

of the trouble between them and the whites, whether as settlers or emigrants. On our school maps the great bulk of the land was marked desert or mountain, and a journey amid its savagery and that of the two and four-footed animals which roamed over it could not fail to interest an observant traveler.

Then game was abundant. The buffalo in countless numbers traveled north and south, as the seasons came and went and pasturage invited them to greener and richer fields, and deer and other animals were in plenty. Now, except in the National Park, the bison is unseen and other game is rarely met. Their Indian hunters, then untrammeled by reservations, in war-paint and fully armed, roamed free, and trading-posts were scattered over what are now farm lands and mining camps. Such is the country I traveled over, and whose description I have tried to make interesting to my readers.

In a foot-note I alluded to the valley extending from San Bernardino towards the coast, then a lonely mountain-walled plain, where patches of chaparral alternated with semi-desert and rich prairie, so sparsely inhabited that in forty-five miles I saw but two ranches, but now traversed by a railroad and dotted with towns, whose people are crazy over speculation in town lots. I will add two other changes: one is the passing of the land along the forks of the Platte from apparent sterility to productive farm land; the other, the transformation of the south branch of the river, from its appearance as shown on page 59, to a bed of sand and stagnant pools in summer. Of course, during the melting of the mountain snows the river is as wild as ever, but at the same time of year that we crossed it the change is as stated. This is caused by the irrigating ditches leading from it to water the ranches on the flats above. To think of the river we splashed through, sometimes up to our waists, in 1858, capable of being crossed dry-shod in thirty years seems unreal. There are other changes less striking which I will pass over.

I would like to say something more of my comrades of the plains; those rough, unsympathetic fellows whose toils and hardships I shared so many eventful months. After our separation I never heard of one of them, although our numbers ranged from thirty to sixty—doubling after our second train was coupled on. On my arrival home, a half year from the time we parted in Salt Lake, I wrote to one or two Missourians whose localities I knew, but, either from their inability to "read writing" or disinclination to start a correspondence, they never replied. The addresses of the only two I was interested in, "Scottie" and Finlay, I did not know. The former I have sufficiently alluded to ; of the last I will say a word or two more. He was a Canadian by birth, a fact he wished concealed from his companions, for fear of their prejudice, although his sensitiveness soon gave way to contempt. He was a youth of intelligence and should have known better than to have started on such a journey, lacking the ability as he did to bring himself down to the circumstances around him in the way of associating with his mates and adapting himself to rough work. Gentle in appearance he was plucky to the verge of science. His brother ox-drivers, who were disposed to criticize his mode of handling a whip and managing his cattle, he could not tolerate, holding himself aloof from them ; yet at times I have known him to unbend until he was quite familiar. I remember one time in particular when he put his arm in an affectionate manner around a " Piker's " neck, and getting his head in a vise-like grip, gave the " bull-whacker " such a pounding for an unseemly remark he made that he bawled for mercy. I mention Finlay now, as I have before, as being the only congenial friend I had in the train, and when through sickness he turned back at Fort Kearney, I felt a loneliness and isolation the rest of the journey which can only be understood through a knowledge of my surroundings.

An overland journey to California now cannot be compared

to what it was thirty years ago, when the traveler and his friends bade farewell, doubting if they would ever meet again. Now, in the comforts of sleeping and drawing-room cars, with all his wants prepared for in advance, his itinerary marked out and his hotel bills and carriage hire paid, he smilingly starts on his way and in a week is at its end. Then, if an emigrant, for two months it was an alternation of march and guard duty, or, if he traveled as I did, a journey of six months when every day in the week was utilized, and when those of an inquiring turn had no chance of satisfying their minds of the doings of the great world outside except what they saw in stale papers at forts and trading-posts, or heard from chance travelers they met. Owing to my limited chances I could not keep a continuous diary on my travels. On the route to Salt Lake we suffered so much from daily hardship and nightly loss of sleep that, in my short vacations, I felt more like resting than writing, so would have to wait and fill them up wholesale when storms or accident gave me a chance. On my arrival home I re-wrote and amplified these notes and published, all up to my California experience, in a local paper, not feeling able to place the result in book-form, as I wished.

Does the present work have that necessary adjunct, a Moral? True, many readers do not care for such, but are satisfied to skim over their readings, careless whether their morals are good or bad. In my tender youth, when I read Æsop's Fables, I always "skipped" the Morals as too ponderous for my understanding, being satisfied to revel in the talks and actions of apes and foxes, wolves and lambs, lions and asses and other impossible conversationalists. But some readers look for results independent of the pleasures of transient perusal: some good to humanity coming from the author's experience.

When "Two Years Before the Mast" was written the author obtained more than the popularity it created, although it is as

20

much of a modern classic as Robinson Crusoe. His narrative of a sailor's hardships and helplessness when in foreign lands, under a tyrannical master, resulted in the passage of laws for the protection of poor Jack. So I have faith of greater bulk than a mustard seed that some good may come out of this literary Nazareth; not from the book generally, but from the part devoted to my California experience. May not those who have been fortunate enough to read this narrative look on a tramp as something more than an absorbent of odors, more or less Arabian, a lodgment for dirt, and an incipient incendiary in case his wants are not supplied? May not ruralists, who are in a position to employ help, change their views in regard to them? When in the stables the alternate thrums in the milk-pails cease; when the plowman musingly halts at the shady end of the furrow, and in the kitchen the rattle of dish-washing stops under your Abigail's manipulations, may not the imminent chiding words be withheld? Will not such favored readers reflect that these helpers may be employing their borrowed, begrudged intervals in studying up points for some forthcoming book in which their employers' virtues or demerits will be aired in the coldest of type? Will they not, in awe, remember that the tramp may be an embryotic author— a "chiel amang them ta'en notes," to be printed for their pleasure or misery in proportion as they treat him?

So, with the hope that at least this much good may result from my literary venture, I close. But I hope for more: that the foregoing recital of my travels over a country so changed since I made my pilgrimage, a generation ago, may have an interest created by the narration alone, and that the reader will be wiser when he comes to the

END OF A CALIFORNIA TRAMP.

LATER FOOTPRINTS;

OR,

MISCELLANEOUS SKETCHES

—IN—

PROSE AND VERSE

ROBERT KENDERDINE,
From a Photograph taken in 1863, before leaving hospital
for the front at Fredericksburg.

Sketches in Prose.

Robert Kenderdine.

AS FAR as the writer can learn, this young soldier was the only native of Bucks County who lost his life in the battle of Gettysburg. This, irrespective of considerations of kin and friendship, makes his short career entitled to record; and there are other reasons for writing this. Thousands of the voters of to-day were born since the war. They know nothing of this terrible time, save as they hear of it through the survivors of the struggle. They who were opposed to the war, and those seekers for office who are anxious to keep from their number such claimants for popular favor as men who had saved their country from ruin, are telling these young men that the war being over, the issues that brought it on are dead, and recollections of the animosities of the strife should be buried with it. This involves the forgetfulness of the participants in that strife. The survivors of these are getting fewer and fewer. Their deeds should not be hidden by plausible platitudes. Three hundred thousand of their comrades went down to death, without hope of reward, that we might have a united country. Typical of these was Robert Kenderdine.

He was born in 1841. In his school days, as well as afterward, he was a diligent student and reader. Before the age of nineteen he was a writer of verses and descriptive prose, and a participant in those debates which of old were common at the cross-roads school houses, and in which, for his age and

experience, he showed rare argumentative ability. At nineteen he commenced teaching, which he followed until he
was twenty-one years old, with the exception of two terms
at institutions, were he went to better fit himself for that
work. When a lad at school he was noted for his peaceful
disposition and for his avoidance of those disputes which the
average juvenile covets to show his prowess. In a school
where the children of Friends formed a small per cent. he
used the plain language to all, his *thee* and *thy* being addressed
impartially to canal boy and to his more refined playmates.
As he grew to manhood and the clouds of Civil War were
breaking over the land, his friends little dreamed that he
would ever be part and parcel of the bloody strife. He was
admired by his acquaintances and reigned in the social circles
around him. He was apparently enjoying life, and it was not
thought by the unobservant that his patriotism would go
beyond the lip service, with which so many lovers of their
country served it. But as the trouble deepened and it became
more and more apparent that the fighting done was but the
preliminary skirmish of a prolonged and deadly war for physical
mastery, wherein one of the sections must go down; when
they who enlisted for a holiday were getting appalled at the
work before them; when stay-at-home advocates of the war
became timorous lest they might be called on to practice their
preachings, and were trying to make themselves believe they
could serve their country best at home; when opponents of
the war were chuckling at their little gatherings, over the disasters that followed one another through the spring and fall
of 1862—then they who knew Robert Kenderdine knew that it
was only a question of time, and that a brief time, when he
would lay aside his peaceful ways and congenial studies and
join in body as well as in mind the soldiers who were fighting
for their country. He debated the matter long and well. There
was the unwillingness of his family that he should enter a

career so fraught with danger, as well as hardship, which his health would not be likely to encompass; there were the pangs he felt to part with his loved pursuits and the society of his friends. On the other hand, he argued that his life was worth no more than another's; that they who talked should act; that while men with families were going to the front he should not hesitate. While he reasoned, there came the reverses to the Union armies before Richmond.

Those were dark days. We hear of the discouraging outlook for the Union cause just before the victories of Vicksburg and Gettysburg. But it could not have been more gloomy than during the days following the defeats of McClellan and Pope in '62, nor result in more depression among the loyal. Faith in the Army of the Potomac was near gone, and enlistments were slow. The heyday of the war was over. Many of the soldiers were returning, but not from expiration of term of service. Some were sick from the malaria of the Chickahominy. Some had lost an arm, others a leg, and once in a while, by express, would come an ominously shaped box with "Honor the Brave" stencilled on the top. It was a grand exhortation, but the inanimate form within was poor capital for a recruiting-officer. So also were the empty sleeves and trouser-legs, and fever-wasted forms of the others. But these times, while they depressed the many, made the few resolve to consecrate the lives, which they had hitherto withheld from the sacrifice, to the service of the country.

At that time patriotism meant more than advocating the war, willingness to bear a share of its costs, encouraging enlistments, or even enlisting expecting only to help garrison forts around Washington, or to repel State invasion. Serving the country meant not standing up for it alone; it meant standing up in line of battle as a mark for Confederate riflemen or cannoniers, with the questionable compensating privilege of making targets of these rebellious marksmen. Many said when the Capital was in danger, they'd go; others, that they'd prove their zeal when the State was threatened. But when they saw Washington escape impending danger, these people guessed the State would get along all right without their aid; besides, it wasn't right for just the loyal people to go. Let the Government order a draft, and make all do their duty; then they'd go sure. Many wouldn't hesitate a moment if it were not for their families. Wives who in ante-bellum times were without control in the doings of their husbands, had suddenly became possessed of restraining influences; sons became dutiful, and swains yielded to the solicitations of their sweethearts when requested to keep out of the cruel war. It's no fun to die for one's country, in spite of the Latin maxim, and those who in the sober, second thought hesitated, were excusable. But they knew some must go; and now that it is all over and the country saved, they should honor and appre-ciate those who saved it.

Among those who enlisted in those troublous times was Robert Kenderdine. His arguments for and against the neces-sity of personal service were drowned in the appeals made by the imperiled Nation. Through bad management, jealousy among officers high in command, or weakness of numbers, our armies were reeling back towards Washington, and it was time for those who had hesitated to enlist to do so now. So one day while he was spending his vacation in a distant State pre-paratory to teaching again in the fall, and when it was thought he had given up the intention of enlisting, a letter came stat-ing that he had joined Collis' Zouaves. In a few days he came home, when his family, finding opposition no longer availing, did what they could to make his departure pleasant. One thing to make them better reconciled was that Captain Elliot, whose company he joined, was a man to inspire confidence, while the company itself was composed of exceptionally good material. Besides, three of his home acquaintances soon joined

him, which was evidence that he would have friends in time of
need. Unfortunately, through discharge and death, he was
soon bereft of these, but he made many friends in the company
and regiment to take their places. General Pope had been
defeated, and his demoralized army was moving northward,
endeavoring to screen Washington from Lee's flanking army.
It was a time of the most intense anxiety to the National
authorities, and all of the available troops in the North were
hurried to the Capital. Among these were the Zouaves, though
their organization had not been perfected.

They broke camp at Nicetown on the night of the 31st of
August, 1862, and reached the Volunteer Refreshment Saloon
in the morning. From here they marched to the Baltimore
Depot. Like the rest, Company F occupied a box car, fitted up
with rough board seats. Leave-taking from accompanying
friends was over, and with the depression which fills the hearts
of departing soldiers, no matter about the outward appearance
of unconcern, the Zouaves were soon on their way to the seat
of war. At Newark, Delaware, an accident occurred, resulting
in the death of Mordecai Ryan, one of the group of Bucks
County boys who tented together, the others being Thaddeus
and Joseph A. Paxson,* Robert Kenderdine and Pierson
Kitchen. In reckless or forced merriment the soldiers were
loudly singing their camp songs. Mordecai, a tall, good-
natured youth, was sitting in the doorway, his long legs
swinging in time to the noisy song he was shouting. Suddenly
he was thrown from the car, his feet having been struck by a
coal-bin they were passing. There being no bell-rope, a young
Zouave was lifted to the top of the jolting car, and by running
along the tops of the cars he reached the engine, and the train
was stopped some three or four miles from the scene of the
accident. Reversing the engine, they found the poor fellow on

---

* Dr. Paxson, of Philadelphia, who died in the Spring of 1888.

the track dying from his injuries. So the first violent death of the 114th was not to have the fiery romance of battle to surround it, but was to result from contact with a prosaic coal-bin. The dead soldier was the son of a widowed mother, and to her home, as his friend and tent-mate, Robert Kenderdine bore the mortal remains of poor Mordecai, while the rest went sadly on their southward way.

Until after the invasion and retreat of Lee in September the Zouaves lay around Washington. When Stuart made his raid through Maryland to Chambersburg, and near to Gettysburg, in October, they were marched back and forth along the shore of the Potomac, in a vain attempt to intercept the retreat of that successful cavalry leader. To reach one ford they marched thirty miles, and retraced their route after guarding it thirty minutes. This service was hard on these raw troops. One night Robert's company of eighty-nine men got into camp with but sixteen, but he wrote proudly back that he was one of them, nor did he discard his knapsack, as did many. With chafed limbs and blistered feet, the rest had sunk exhausted by the way. Still the remainder got in before morning. When the march was ordered again the men thought they could not move, but sixty-four got in line and started on their hopeless search for Stuart. Hither and yon they dragged their wearied limbs, through dust and mud, in sun and rain; hard usage for a boy whose life had been a succession of study and teaching, and which was unacquainted with hardship. Still he wrote home cheerfully, and speaking for himself and two home comrades, the third having been discharged, said they were in good spirits. But the last march was more than he could bear. After an exhausting day marching in the rain he laid down at night in his drenched clothes. In a few days word came from Poolsville he was down sick. His father and brother-in-law, Eastburn Reeder, at once started for Maryland, that they might bring him home, but when they arrived at Poolsville the army had crossed to Virginia, taking the sick along. Fearful of rebel raids the whole country was in a ferment, so the two were sore beset to get anywhere. The farmers whom they induced to carry them to different fording points did so reluctantly, fearful of the capture of themselves or teams. They finally effected a crossing near Edward's Ferry, where they followed the route of the Federals. At Leesburg, in four miles, they came up with the sick, and under an orchard tree they at last found Robert, wrapped in a blanket, on the bare ground and unable to rise.

The hospital tents soon came up and were pitched, when hay was spread on the ground and the sick carried thither, and made as comfortable as possible. They were afterward removed to the public buildings. These had been used by the Confederates for the sick and wounded. They were in a filthy state, and the sick removed there fared worse than when in the open air. The surgeons were without proper medicine and food for the sick, who were dying daily for want of them. Strong efforts were made to get permission to remove Robert to Philadelphia, but with the unreasoning perverseness which officials clothed in a minimum of red tape often show, they were unnoticed. E—— then made a journey to the Friends' settlement at Goose Creek, six miles from Leesburg, to find a home for Robert, as he was not likely to live where he was. He was successful, and the invalid, with permission of the medical director of the hospital, was removed to the hospitable home of Rachel Hoag. Under changed circumstances, Robert was soon past danger. While here rebel raids were imminent, and thinking it prudent to leave for fear of capture, E. at once started north. He was refused a pass by our authorities and forbidden to leave, but he made his way into Maryland, unmolested by either of the combatants, and got home safely. The day after the rebels made their appearance at the Friends' settlement, and made inquiries for the new-comers at Hoag's;

in particular for E. Reeder, and were chagrined to find him gone. They then asked if there was not a Federal soldier in the house. They were taken to where Robert was lying in bed. They remarked he was a very sick man, but made him prisoner, and paroled him. A parole for a sick man meant a chance to get home and exemption from service until exchanged; but Robert protested and demanded the officer's authority. He, however, signed the necessary papers and the rebels left. They were surly at first, but in the main acted kindly, as did several of the Leesburg people, Secessionists though they were. Many kindnesses did the sick soldier and his friends receive at their hands, when the hospital people were powerless to help. Robert, in less than two weeks, was able to be removed from his kind Virginia home, and was brought to Philadelphia, where he arrived on the 19th of November. Here he remained in the hospital, with the exception of a short time spent among his friends, until the 10th of February, 1863, when he was exchanged, and his health being in a measure restored, he was again ready for service in the field.

There were excuses for his remaining behind. Through a medical friend in the hospital he could have been detailed as clerk where he was. For this there were plenty of precedents. Many scholarly patriots joined the Union forces, only to find after they had tasted the danger of army life a while that they might be valuable adjuncts to some quartermaster, commissarist or medical director. Sometimes they were detailed in the War Department. They got what they thought themselves fitted for when they could command the required influence; in such cases they kept out of harm's way till the close of the war. Robert had their chances, but he took no advantage of them. He was too proud to retrace one step. He had joined the army to fight, or he would have remained in the better position of hospital clerk. And if he did not appreciate the hardships of a soldier's life when he enlisted, he knew them now, when they had brought him nigh to death's door. He knew the change from a dainty diet to the rough and sometimes scanty fare of the soldier; from a life of ease to a series of long marches, followed often by picket duty, and the drudgery of life in camp or in the trenches. He knew what it was to be sick, without the care we give our dumb animals at home. So when one night, at 11 o'clock, with his squad of convalescents he heard the hospital gates clang behind him, and marched through the dark streets and chilling air to take the cars and rejoin his old comrades, he knew what was before him. His description of his "March to the Regiment" was at times pathetic, although his army letters were full of noble resolve, of hope for the future, and scorn for those who at home were making rear attacks on the defenders of the Union. As the little band marched through the cheerlees streets on their way to fresh devotion and sacrifices for their country they were watched like convicts. A friend accompanied Robert until the surly guard warned him away. At the station the group sat on the curbstone until the train should leave. Travelers descended from carriages and sought the warmth of the depot. The ladies, as they glided by the Boys in Blue, gathered their skirts closer that they might not be defiled by contact, while their escorts glanced sidewise as if they were looking at beings of a different race from themselves. And they were not wrong if they thought so. Better the humblest private than the citizen, no matter what his talent, wealth, station or profession of godliness, who would pass him by without an encouraging word or sympathetic thought.

Boarding the train the ride to Washington was made partly in a box car. Some of the soldiers were drunk, and Robert spent much of his time in endeavors to keep them from falling out of the car. He stopped awhile in the Capital to visit some friends. One of these was as the comforters of Job. He was an intense patriot at the beginning of the war and joined the

army. Battle and march had taken off the keen edge of his
devotion to country. He got detailed to a clerkship. When
he saw Robert after his experience going to the front again,
he laughed at him for his verdancy in not getting out of the
army when he had a chance. Robert felt contempt for such
an expression from one who had professed so much in his time,
but for all that it made him feel badly.

He passed down the Potomac to Acquia Creek, and thence
by rail to Falmouth, opposite Fredericksburg, where he found
his regiment; but not his tent-mates. By death and discharge
they were gone. While he was away the battle of Fredericksburg had been fought. It was a dull winter day, snow was on
the ground, and the company streets were swamps of mud
when he arrived. The sight was not one to raise his spirits,
but he entered into his duties with a firm resolve to serve his
imperiled country to the bitter end.

He missed the assault on the height of St. Marye and the
glory thereto attached, but there was plenty of work yet to do;
and glory, for that matter. On the 3d of May came the battle
of Chancellorsville. It was a sad day for the 114th; from the
screening thickets came bullet and shell, till one hundred and
seventy-three of their number went down—all their officers but
eight. Captain Elliot, the loved commander of company F,
here died a patriot's death. Robert was grazed by a bullet,
but he came out of the fight safe.

Another defeat to add to the rest of its disasters for the
Army of the Potomac. More chuckling among the opponents
of the war; more satisfaction among deposed generals and
their friends; more worriment for Lincoln; more weeping and
wailing for the dead, and the end of it all hidden by gloomy
clouds. But there were brave hearts left, and the Army of
the Potomac would yet fulfil its mission. The thinned bat-
talions, after a short rest, were again in motion. This time to
the North, for Lee was marching on Pennsylvania.

After the disaster at Chancellorsville the Third Corps had returned to Roscobel, near Falmouth, where they lay when the order to march came. With it went the 114th, its ranks depleted, but the soldiers not discouraged. On the 11th of June this regiment reached Hartwood Church; on the 12th, Bealton; on the 14th, Manassas Junction; on the 17th, Centreville; on the 19th, Gum Springs. On the 25th the regiment crossed the Potomac at Edward's Ferry, which was familiar ground. On the 26th they reached Point of Rocks. On the 28th, Woodsboro, where General Sickles joined them. On the 29th, Taneytown, and the 30th, a point near Emmettsburg.

The weather was warm, and from the passage of such an army the road was deep with dust, which choked the men and horses and made marching difficult, but the army bore up well. Robert kept up with the best of them. He could not be surpassed on a march. He had become a hardy soldier. The battle he had been in had tested his courage and he had borne it well. He was inspired with confidence. His health and spirits were good. He was on his way to his native State, on whose soil he was ready to offer up his life a sacrifice, and he felt ready to do and dare to the utmost.

There was not much variation in the series of alternate marches and halts, for in the time between Falmouth and Gettysburg the Third Corps marched, on an average, but one day in two. The watching for Lee, whose destination was not manifest, and the effort to cover Washington from his attack, made Hooker's progress slow and cautious. The monotony of the day's march was relieved by the sight of camps they passed by, as the corps moved alternately, or by the galloping by of cavalry or artillery seeking the whereabouts of the enemy. Then there was the fording of streams, the camping when the day's tramp was over, the camp duties and the weary night on picket. It took from the 5th till the 30th of June to reach Gettysburg.

Captain Given, of Manayunk, gave me the following concerning the action of the regiment after the 1st of July. From his position he saw but little of Robert in the fight, being on the non-commissioned staff. He was an intimate friend, and had served in the same company until promoted:

"On the afternoon of July 1st, 1863, we reached Emmettsburg, Maryland, from Bridgeport; halted for a rest, when it began to rain. This continued until near dark. Soon word came to fall in, which we obeyed in quick order, and proceeded through the town. A mile outside we began to hear the firing of a cannon. This came from the fight between Oak Ridge and Cemetery Hill, as our men were falling back to the protection of Steinwehr's guns. We were then hurried faster. Our overcoats, which many of us carried, became heavy, and we began throwing them away. A farmer was driving rapidly from the battlefield with his family in an open farm wagon. I asked him if he wanted an overcoat? He said ' No! but I will keep it for you.' It being a good one I threw it to him. Robert disposed of his the same way, and we hurried on toward the sound of battle. We were in good spirits, laughing and joking, although wet to the skin. I remember Robert was as cheerful as any. It was about sundown when we reached the point on the Emmettsburg road where we fought next day—little knowing that here so many of our boys would fall. This was at the Sherfey House, then of no more note than any one of the many farm-houses around, and at the next house beyond turned to the right. In this, then a low, one-storied log structure, lived a man who was sitting in the doorway nursing a baby as we marched hurriedly by. I thought how soon he would be getting out of that. The next day that log-house was a fort, and I don't think that man and baby was part of the garrison. We marched across the fields and were posted on the Ridge north of Round Top. The firing had now ceased. The remnants of the

1st and 11th Corps, which since morning had battled the greater
part of the rebel army on Seminary Ridge, were now lying
tired and bleeding on the hills south of the town, which was
full of the enemy and the prisoners they had captured in
the side streets of the town. It was now dark. The day's
battle was over and we were getting ready for the morrow.
Before daylight we were moved from the Ridge to a point near
the Emmettsburg road. [This movement forward of the 3d
Corps is what General Sickles is blamed for.] Here we lay,
face to the earth, until afternoon, supporting Randolph's battery, subjected to a fearful cannonade. At first the shells
went far beyond, but the gunners shortened the fuses and they
dropped in front and over us. Robert lay with us during this
terrible time, but was not hurt. We had several wounded here
from bursting shells. While we lay there Lieutenant Buck-
lyn, who commanded the battery, came among us. He asked
who had charge of that regiment? As is often the case at
such times, there was no especial one ready to answer; but
when he said, 'If you expect to save my guns, you must charge
now,' we were all ready. The pioneers were sent ahead to
cut down the fence along the Emmettsburg road, and they
went at it with a will, but before they accomplished their mission the enemy was upon them. James Priest was whacking
away at a post when a bullet struck it. He thought that
maybe the men could climb the fence that was yet up and
went back. A pioneer's lot is not a very happy one. It is
not so bad to be shot at when you can reply in the same language, but to be a target for riflemen and nothing to defend
yourself with but a weapon as short-ranged as a common axe,
is not very exhilarating fun, neither is after-service in the
hospital. There seemed to be no order given, but we advanced with a cheer, and double-quicked to the Emmettsburg
road. Through the fence where down, and tumbling over it
anyhow where the pioneers had left their work unfinished,

21

we reached the road and were in the thick of the fight. This was in front of the Sherfey House.

"How long we fought here I cannot tell. In battle a person has no real conception of time. We crossed the road, and I remember myself standing in the path leading to the house directing some of the men what to do. Of course, all was excitement. I remember that in many cases the fighting was hand to hand. It was a desperate battle. Men never fought with so much determination as did our little band. Robert fell not far from here, just to the left of the Sherfey House. The boys were falling all around me. I was almost beside myself as I beheld my comrades' vain efforts to rally. We had to fall back, although very reluctantly. Night came on, and with it came the 5th Corps, when we, a little band of sixty-five men, all that was left out of four hundred and seventy-three who went into the fight, gathered near the foot of Round Top where we lay until morning. We were afterward posted near the Devil's Den, when we were served with rations, the first in forty-eight hours, except a barrel of flour we bought of a farmer on the morning of the 2d. We were soon hurried to the support of the 2d Corps, on the Ridge, who were getting ready for the coming assault of Lee. We were posted in the rear of the Philadelphia Brigade. Pickett's charge was in our front. We helped repel it, but lost no men there. On the night following, our pickets advanced to the Emmettsburg road whence we were driven the day before, leaving the dead and wounded behind. I took a detail of men and reported to a captain in the 26th Pennsylvania, who had charge of the burial squad. I will here mention a curious circumstance. While he and I were talking near the road, he stopped and picked up something which proved to be two musket balls—one a Union, the other a rebel. They had met in mid-air and welded together. We could distinguish them by the rings, the former having three, the latter two. If the captain is alive he has them yet, no doubt. At any rate the statement is correct.

" There are many things I could relate that come to me only when my mind dwells upon that battle, or when persons seek from me information concerning it.

" I remember a circumstance which impressed itself on my mind very forcibly, particularly as I had never seen women assisting amid the horrors of a battle-field before; neither have I since, for that matter. The remnant of our regiment, in coming off the field at the Sherfey House, became detached from the brigade (Graham's). About 3 in the morning I was sent to look for it. I saw a light in a large barn, went to it, inquired and found it a hospital. And such a sight. In the centre was the amputation table. Under and around lay arms, hands, legs and feet, till it looked liked a human slaughter house. Blood covered the table, the floor was slippery with it; the dim flicker of candles cast a sickly glare on the surroundings, making the sight the ghastliest I ever saw. To this was added the agonizing moans and cries of the wounded and dying; while over this was the roar of cannon and shriek of shell, occasioned by an advance of our lines. I turned away and entered the yard. On a stretcher lay an officer in his last agonies; two companions knelt by his side; while the enclosure was full of dead and dying. I turned from these and saw two ladies, evidently a mother and daughter, administering to the wounded. All night long these faithful women bathed and bandaged their wounds, fed and cheered the poor fellows, or soothed their dying moments. I do not believe they deserted their posts, though shot and shell were beginning to fall and burst around. I did not have long to stay. I hastened away from the awful sight; took the little remnant of the Zouaves to the brigade, and was soon again in the heat of battle.

" Early on the morning of the 4th I went out to our picket

line with a detail to bury the dead. Just as I reached the Sherfey House I saw two men, not Zouaves, carrying Robert out of it on a stretcher. He looked badly and was suffering much from his wound. His clothing was torn, and he seemed to have had no care taken of him since the battle, near two days before. I asked him if he was wounded badly. He said, 'Oh, yes; I am very badly wounded.' That was all he said; for they were carrying him off, and I was busy with my awful duties; but the look he gave me I will never forget, it was so sad.

"Sergeant DeHaven, who was killed by my side with a ball through his heart, and who was a neighbor of mine, lay dead in the pathway. I sat down and cut his name on a shingle, and put it at his grave, where he was buried with five Confederates, and sent word to his sorrowing wife. His body was removed, and with six others of our company now lies in our village cemetery. The rude headboard seems to have been wrongly placed, for when the removal took place it was at the head of a buried rebel. The dead sergeant was, however, found at his side. From the conflict of battle they were sleeping the peaceful sleep of death together.

"Robert was a man who was much liked and respected; very kind and always willing to do a good act; to sacrifice himself for the good of others. I have always looked upon him as an ideal American soldier, brave, intelligent and a gentleman in word and deed; ready to fight for his country without hope of reward, save the consciousness of having done his duty."

Sergeant H. H. Snyder, now of New York, was with Robert when he fell; both being in the color guard. The line—if such a confused mass could be called a line, when, without a head, some in the house, some in the yard, some back of the barn— the regiment was fighting, had fallen back to the road. The guard was in advance of the colors, defending them to their utmost. The enemy was working around to the Emmettsburg road and were flanking the left of the line at the peach orchard. Snyder saw one of Barksdale's Mississippians, known by their broad felt hats, taking aim at him from the corner of the barn, for the little band around the flag was so thinned and scattered that preferences could be distinguished. The rebel fired, and Robert fell mortally wounded. Snyder fired at the Mississippian at once, but missed him; a comrade drew on him with better luck, for the rebel fell apparently dead. All was confusion now. The enemy was swarming around the house and in front of the Zouaves; two of their cannons were run into the road and were raking our troops with an enfilading fire, and the last of them were retreating. Robert, who was left lying in the road close by where the monument now is, called to one of his comrades, but he had gone. Sergeant Snyder answered for him, and bidding him good-bye retreated with the rest. This was about 6 o'clock.

Until the morning of the 4th the enemy held this ground, so that there was no chance for the Federals to aid their wounded until then. The latter were taken to the field hospital on Rock Creek, east of Round Top; Robert among the rest. His wound was necessarily mortal. We were fortunate in meeting a comrade, James H. Priest, who was with him to the last, and did all he could to make him comfortable. His father, after making two attempts, at last reached Gettysburg early on the morning of the 10th. After much difficulty, he found him in a tent with a number of wounded. Robert recognized him for the moment, but soon wandered off in the delirium which had clouded his mind since his arrival from the battle-field. It had been thought by his friends that had proper care been taken of him he might have lived, but the best of care could not have saved him. He died on the 10th of July.

His mission was accomplished. He had offered his life to

his country, and it had gone out in the whirlwind of battle. As he lay dying, the enemy were fleeing from the pursuing Federals. The meadows and hills they had fought to conquer were ridged with their graves. Thousands of his countrymen were yet to die and suffer, but the turning point had come. The Union he fought for was to be saved.

The curtain had dropped; the tragedy was over. He who had lain so long, suffering and in delirium, in sight of that rocky height which he had defended, now slept his last sleep in his death-tent under the shadow of Round Top. Those eyes were no more to reflect the fire of battle; those lips to give forth cheering words to faltering comrades; those limbs to move in the execution of the dread duties of a soldier. That mind, that form, those features had found rest. No more the morning bugle call would arouse him to his daily duties, nor nightly tattoo close them. With so much to live and hope for, alas! that it should be so!

He died a common soldier; in his case a symbol of disinterested patriotism. From his shoulder gleamed no star, nor eagle, nor leaf; neither double nor single bar. He bore not even the insignia of a sergeant. He had campaigned and fought for a year. He was loyal, brave and intelligent; but when they bore him from his last fight, the sleeve of his torn and battle-stained Zouave jacket showed only the chevrons of a corporal. But better this humble token of rank than the triple stars of those generals who, with jealousy and envy, sulked in their tents, mute to the appeals of their sore pressed comrades.

A common soldier! All praise to the man who carried the musket. He reaped scant comfort while living; he had no separate monument when dead. From the grave of the colonel or general sprang a shaft blazoned with his deeds. The private soldier had, as far as public recognition went, a hundredth part or so of one of those granite columns which in

the North arose from city square or village green. 'Tis true
he had, when through some fortuitous circumstances his
battle-gashed body reached home, a stone at his head in the
graveyard of his native village which his comrades could
annually decorate. But more than that, and better than
mural marks were the memories of the gallant deeds done in
his devotion to country, which perennially bloomed in the souls
of those who saw him go forth to the sacrifice. In the words
of that beautiful poem, "The Man with a Musket,"

> "I knew him! By all that is noble I knew
> This commonplace hero I name!
> I've camped with him, marched with him, fought with him too
> In the swirl of the fierce battle flame!
>
> * * * *
>
> I knew him I tell you! And, also, I knew
> When he fell on the battle-swept ridge,
> That the poor battered body that lay there in blue
> Was only a plank in the bridge
> Over which some one should pass to a fame
> That shall shine while the high stars shall shine.
> Your hero is known by an echoing name,
> But the man of the musket is mine!"

The body of the young soldier was brought home and buried
in the beautiful yard fronting the Friends' meeting-house
where he attended in his peaceful days. He died a soldier's
death. He was buried in the ways of the peaceful sect which
looks upon war with abhorrence. No battle-flag draped his
coffin, nor soft bugle notes nor muffled drum played a funeral
march to his grave. No platoon, with reversed muskets, went
before him; no parting volley closed the scene. An aged
ministering Friend spoke a few consoling words over his remains, and Robert Kenderdine was laid to rest amid the sorrow of all who knew him, and now,

> "After life's fitful fever, he sleeps well!"

John Burns of Gettysburg.

IT has been shown that William Tell was a myth, and the shooting of an apple from a son's head to save a father's life a thread-bare reiteration, handed down through generations of story-tellers. It has been demonstrated that the account of the rescue of John Smith by the daughter of Powhatan, which went undisputed for two centuries, existed only in the mind of the narrator. It has been proven that Whittier's poem of Barbara Frietchie was based on an act of patriotic defiance which history does not corroborate. It is, therefore, no wonder that John Burns, of Gettysburg, is regarded by those who look into the matter superficially, as a fanciful creation, particularly when we reflect that it required a poem to make his actions famous, and that there was a probability of its being based on as unsubstantial a foundation as was the story of the aged heroine of Frederick. That he was not the "baseless fabric of a vision," but of as real flesh and blood as a feeble man of seventy could be, and that Bret Harte rather understated than overdrew the facts which connected him with the Gettysburg battle, can easily be shown. Being shown, let us remember, while honoring the memory of the titled dead or living, who had such incentives to brave death on the hills and in the meadows around that historic town, that old John Burns, past the fighting age, and while his neighbors were seeking subterranean seclusion from the gathering storm, left his peaceful work, went amid our fighting lines, whose movements were visible from his little home not a half mile distant, and insisted on sharing the danger with veteran soldiers, and who fought until wounded past fighting.

The greater stress should be laid on the actions of John Burns on that eventful day, because his was an isolated case.

In all the raids and invasions north of the Potomac and the Ohio we have no similar instance of a civilian leaving his home to join our troops to fight the invaders. Even in the pugnacious South such resistance, if it ever occurred, has not been given prominence. That the act was Quixotic is not to the point, and if it were, so were the actions of hundreds of thousands who left wealth and comfort to risk hardships, wounds and death, who owed no more to their country than their stay-at-home neighbors. Apologetic spokesmen for his townsmen, on the day of the fight, emphasize the fact that ununiformed men found about a battle-field are liable to be treated as spies if captured, and at any rate would be only in the way; that if wounded they would draw no pension, and if killed their heirs would not be benefited. If so, and assuming that Burns took this into account, all the more credit is due him. That he was cranky and unsociable goes for nothing. He was boastful, and his unrepressed satisfaction at the part he played would produce ill-natured remarks from his fellows. This would create resentment and isolate him from the rest of his neighbors. In fact, the people of Gettysburg seem very sensitive to the non-fulfilment of the expectations of unpractical persons, in that every able-bodied man did not grasp his musket from the hooks over the fireplace and rush out to meet the invaders, while their wives moulded bullets and scraped lint. Mindful of this feeling, the guide tells visitors that all men capable of fighting had already enlisted, and if it were not so, and they had had the bravery to fight among our uniformed soldiers, they would have been shot by the enemy if captured. The truth of the matter is, that the capture of the town was not the object of either army, but the destruction of its antagonist was. Gettysburg, by accident of situation, was where the collision occurred, and its men were no more obliged to turn out in mass than those of Doylestown or Bristol one hundred and fifty miles distant. They did go to the front

about as much as the men of those two towns and no more.
While the shells bursted and the cannon thundered, the people
stayed in the cellars, and when the battle was over did all
they could to take care of the wounded. Still, I was sorry to see
a disposition among the people of the town to undervalue the
heroism of the only two citizens who risked their lives for our
cause—John Burns and Jennie Wade. In their humble ways
they were the hero and heroine of the fight, and epics might
be written on them, but their fellowmen and women, veritable
cave-dwellers as they were in that age, seeing how their exalta-
tion belittles themselves, persist in acting iconoclastic parts and
sneer at or tear to pieces the stories of the young girl and old
Scotchman. Some of these, knowing Burns is too dead to tell
his side of the story, say he was no more in the fight than
they were, which is making a very lamb of him, and what
scratches he had were self-inflicted; that if he did get into the
fight it was either while he was drunk or else while he was out
hunting his cow. It struck me that the most Texan cow-boy
would not have dared the latter feat, and that a man who
would go cow-hunting on Seminary Ridge on the first day of
July, 1863, needed no further eulogy. As an instance of how
little some of the people knew of Burns, I will state that while
on the way from Carlisle I came across a hotel-keeper who had
lived in Gettysburg two years and had never heard of him.
To make the matter worse, this landlord kept a livery-stable
and furnished guides to show its patrons over the battle-field.
    The home of

> "The only man who wouldn't back down
> When the rebels rode through his native town,
> But held his own in the fight next day
> When all his townsfolk ran away,"

was a story and a-half house with a basement, over which hung
a platform reached by a flight of steps running up the front of
the house. It is on the extreme western edge of the town,

where the streets slope down to the meadows, reaching to the foot of Seminary Ridge, a half mile distant. Eight miles westward is a wooded range, a part of the Blue Ridge, known as South Mountain, beyond which is the Cumberland Valley. Between this and the town is a rolling, diversified country, dotted by farms and woods. Before the war we can fancy the old Scotchman, in his hours of rest, looking from his cottage across this peaceful stretch of country and enjoying its beauties, but it is doubtful if he bothered his practical mind much about them. After the invasion we can imagine, with a conviction that our surmisings were realized, how he felt when he saw Early's dust-begrimed veterans take possession of the town on the 26th of June, and begin levying tribute on the startled citizens; how he met the sneers of his neighbors after the horde passed through for not carrying out his warlike threats; how he felt on the memorable 1st of July, when the vanguard of the Federal army marched by his door to meet the enemy thronging from the north and through the mountain-pass on the west, and how his old soldier-blood fired his heart as he saw the combat open; how, leaving his work, he hurried to the front, while his subterranean neighbors gazed wonderingly at him from their seclusion.

On the morning of July 1st, 1863, the greatest excitement was developing in Gettysburg, on Seminary Ridge and the valley of Willoughby Run beyond. The enemy's point of concentration was discovered, and it was known that his advance was in such force that the impending conflict between the armies of Lee and Meade must necessarily take place near the town. The preliminary skirmish had begun, and, knowing its import, the commanding general was sending reinforcements as fast as the exhausted condition of the troops would permit. Here John Burns first comes on the scene. At this time he was sixty-nine years old. In his younger days he had been given to drink, and some of his townspeople, who admit that he fought the enemy on Seminary Ridge, claim that he did it while he was so drunk he did not know a Union soldier from a rebel. He was a patriot and had been a soldier, and maddened by the sight of the preparation for the strife, and the efforts of the citizens to avoid it by flight or concealment, he got down his old flint-lock, and putting his powder-horn and some bullets in his pockets, prepared to take the field. Always bold and determined, he was now full of passion. One who saw him told me he would never forget him as he was that morning, when, with rifle on his shoulder, he cursed every male non-combat-ant he found above ground, calling them squaws, cowards and " chicken-hearts," and similar names, and urging them to go home and melt up their pewter into bullets and go and defend their homes and firesides, but ceasing his unavailing oaths and entreaties he joined the troops now hurried to the front.

The scenes and sounds around were intensely impressive. There was the distant booming of cannon and rattle of musketry, the smoke curling above the Ridge, the frightened country-men fleeing to the dubious protection of the town, the cattle, wild with terror, running and bellowing across the fields until shot down by interrupting missiles, and the waves on waves of infantry and artillery rolling toward the scene of battle and meeting and almost burying the influx billows of wounded and demoralized men. Toward where the noises of battle smote the air the loudest, with set teeth and furrowed brow, marched old John Burns, neither looking to the left nor right, unless to cast a professional eye on the worn foot-gear of the tired soldiers, and, jostled by the armed throngs who crowded by him, he slowly worked his way to the summit of the Ridge.

The Seventh Wisconsin Regiment was a part of the " Iron Brigade," an organization which has a good record in the campaign of the Army of the Potomac. In that brigade there were two other Wisconsin regiments, and the three re-enlisted almost to a man at the end of their three years' service, the thinned ranks being filled up by Indians from the same State.

The commander of the Seventh Wisconsin in the first day's fight at Gettysburg was John B. Callis, then Lieutenant-Colonel, but afterwards made a Brigadier-General. He had previously commanded his regiment in the battle of Antietam, Second Bull Run and Brandy Station, and many minor engagements. He was Southern born, and when, after the commencement of hostilities, he offered to raise a company of volunteers, his proposition was looked upon rather coldly by his countrymen. His bravery during some of the heaviest fighting in the East showed how unjust were the suspicions. In Confederate General Hill's account of the battle of South Mountain, in the *Century* magazine's war papers, I see mention of General Callis' name and the severe losses of his command. He was badly wounded at Gettysburg by a ball through the lungs, and was left for a day on the field from which our army had been driven during the first day's fight. He is still almost helpless from this wound, partial paralysis resulting therefrom. He is now living in Lancaster, Grant County, Wisconsin. It is from him I got the particulars of the part John Burns took in the battle of Gettysburg, my acquaintance with him coming through one of his men I met on the field during a recent visit.

"On the 1st of July the 'Iron Brigade' marched to the crest of Seminary Ridge, south of the Seminary, where it drew the unexpected fire of Archer's Confederate Brigade, this being the first infantry firing of the battle, the previous fighting having been by dismounted cavalry. Our brigade, not having their muskets loaded, charged and captured the opposing force with the bayonet, which took place at Willoughby's Run. After sending the prisoners to the rear we re-formed parallel with the Run and sent our skirmishers to the front, where continuous firing was kept up, with shot and shell whistling and bursting around the main line. At this time, about 11 A.M., I saw an object approaching from the rear, and I think the oddest looking person I saw during the war. He wore a bell-crown hat, a swallow-tail coat, with rolling collar and brass buttons, and a buff vest. He had on his shoulder an old rifle with which he came to a 'present arms,' and then said:

"'Colonel, is this your regiment?'

"'Yes,' I said.

"Then he brought his rifle to an order and said:

"'Can I fight in your regiment?'

"I answered, 'Old man, you had better go to the rear or you'll get hurt.'

"And he replied, just as a shell burst near him:

"'Tut! tut! tut! I've heard this sort of thing before.'

"These words were spoken in a tremulous voice. I again ordered him to the rear, when he replied, 'No, sir. If you won't let me fight in your regiment I will fight alone.' I asked him where his cartridge box was. He patted his trousers' pocket, and said, 'Here's my bullets,' and, taking an old-fashioned powder-horn from his pocket, 'Here's my powder, and I know how to use them. There are three hundred cowards back in that town who ought to come out of their cellars and fight, and I will show you that there is one man in Gettysburg who is not afraid.' Just then some of the boys began to joke him about his hat and to insist that he should have a chance to fight. Sergeant George Eustis added, 'Fix him up, boys. He'll soon get tired of it and go home.' I at last yielded, and with the sergeant's help fixed him up with a rifle we had just captured from Archer's sharpshooters, and leaned his old squirrel rifle up against a tree. He was given a cartridge box and belt, but declined to use them, and instead filled his pockets with fixed ammunition, after which he went into the ranks. He soon grew restless, as the general engagement had not begun, and advanced to the front towards our skirmishers before he could see a rebel to shoot at. Pretty soon I saw a Confederate officer riding towards their advanced line, mounted on a white horse. Burns drew on him and the horse galloped through our lines without a rider. Whether the officer was killed or not I do not know. The old man loaded and fired away until I called in my skirmishers and ordered my men back to the Seminary. In making this movement I was wounded, mortally as I thought, and left behind, our troops being gradually forced back. Consequently that is all I know personally of Burns at Gettysburg."

Sergeant George Eustis, above referred to, is living in Gilroy, California. I wrote to him for further corroborating informa-tion in regard to John Burns. He says: " If any of those who think that the old man took no part in the battle of Gettys-burg had seen him on the 1st of July, 1863, they would change their opinion. I can't tell just what time he came up to us, having left my watch at home on the bureau that morning, but it was after we had captured Archer's Brigade, and while we were lying down in the timber to protect ourselves from the shot and shell flying around, about noon, say, that I saw a little old man coming up in the rear of our company, F. I remember him well. He had on a swallow-tail coat, with smooth brass buttons. We boys commenced to poke fun at him, thinking him a fool to come up where there was so much danger. I wanted to put a cartridge box on him to make him look like a soldier, telling him he couldn't fight without that. His reply was, slapping his pockets, ' I can get my hands in here quicker than in the box; I am not used to them new-fangled things.' In answer to a question as to what made him come up there, he said the rebels had either milked his cows or driven them away, and he was going to be even with them. All this while the shells were screaming and bursting over the protecting timber. About this time the "rebs" began to advance. Bullets were whistling around pretty lively. We hugged the ground closer and the old man got behind a tree. He surprised us all by not taking a double-quick to the rear, but he was just as cool as any veteran among us. We soon had orders to move a hundred yards to the right, and were shortly engaged in one of the hottest fights I was ever in. Foot by foot we were driven back. We made our last stand at the Seminary, where we did good work for a while and then retreated through the town to Cemetery Ridge. I never saw John Burns after we moved to the right. From some cause he did not follow, and we left him with his gun behind the tree. I learned afterward he was wounded in three places. General Callis was wounded and left for dead on the field.

"On our retreat through Gettysburg I saw but one citizen. This was an old man who brought a washtub out to his pump on the sidewalk, and then pumped water for the boys as they passed along. God bless his old soul; I wish I knew who he was that, if alive, I might thank him for his bravery and kindness."

Dr. Horner, of the town, dressed the old man's wounds. He informed me he was struck in the arm, ankle and breast, the latter a trifling flesh wound. The assertions of some of his townspeople that he "merely got scratched among the briars," therefore, will hardly stand.

Another incident in the life of the old hero I came across recently. On the evening of November 9th, 1863, the day on which Lincoln delivered his memorable words at the dedication of the Gettysburg monument, the President, accompanied by his brother-in-law, General Todd, and a few other noted men, attended a lecture. As the party entered the church in which it was given, and were passing to the seats assigned them, it was noticed that a feeble, gray-haired man was following them, as if disposed to intrude. As Lincoln and Todd entered their pew the old man followed. Todd, noticing this, said, "Old man, this pew is reserved for the President and his party." This remark caused Lincoln to look around. Seeing Burns, whom he knew, the President quickly said, "Why, Todd, this is old John Burns, of Gettysburg. He fought all day for the Union, for which you never fired a shot in your life. Come here, John, and sit down by me." And there, side by side to the close of the lecture, sat the greatest man America has produced and the humble hero of its greatest battle!

Why Bret Harte, who is needlessly exaggerative, did not work up the fact of the wounding of Burns, is hard to tell. The poet seemed to have simply seized hold of the main fact and elaborated it regardless of chronology. He says when the fight was over,

      "He shouldered his rifle, unbent his brows,
      And then went home to his bees and cows."

As he fought on the first day it was not until two days after that the enemy "Backward pressed, broke at the final charge and ran." In fact, things looked pretty blue for the Union cause for some time after Burns left the field on a stretcher after turning the command over to General Meade. "The clerks the Home Guards mustered in" were mythical, as he himself intimates when he says Burns was "the only man who would'nt back down."

The field on which John Burns fought is on the left as you near the "Springs Hotel," about a mile and a-half west of the town, and close by the grove where General Reynolds fell. After he was wounded he was carried to his home, which was the first house but one in Gettysburg as you enter by the Chambersburg Pike. He was laid on a lounge in the front

22

room until other arrangements could be made. While lying here a rebel bullet passed over him and went through the partition four feet from the floor. This hole is closed up by pasting a piece of rag over it, but shows clearly how near Burns got his fourth, and, in all likelihood, his *coup de grace*. It was fired from a house filled with rebel sharpshooters near the town, and was doubtless a stray shot, although Burns, who had some conceit, always thought the rebels had a spite against him for his defense of the town. He brooded over this so long that he at last settled it as a fact that one of his neighbors, whom he thought bore him malice, had told his enemies where he lay, that a sure shot might be made. In spite of his wounds Burns was not long in getting about. He traveled around the country as an attraction to different gatherings, where the attention shown greatly tickled his vanity, for which he was hardly accountable, as second childhood was coming over him. After his wife's death he sold his house and went to live with one of his friends, but he often returned, thankful if the new owner would keep him a day or two at a time. His mind was finally set on coming back to his old home to there end his days, for which privilege he offered the landlord all his pension money. The offer was not accepted, and he died away from his little home from which he made his sortie on the enemies of his country.

On the top of Cemetery Hill, in the graveyard adjoining the National Cemetery, are two marble slabs. On the one is:

JOHN L. BURNS,

The Hero of Gettysburg,

Died February 4th, 1872,

Aged 78 years.

On the other:

BARBARA,

Wife of John L. Burns,

Born June 15th, 1797,

Died July 1st, 1868.

" Thy word is as a lamp unto my feet
And a light unto my path."

It will be noticed that Barbara died on the anniversary of the fight her husband made himself famous in. They had no children, but left an adopted daughter, Jennie, who lives with a family by the name of Martin, on the " Diamond," as the central square of Gettysburg is called. She was but two years old at the time of the battle.

*   *   *   *

I have since re-visited Gettysburg and found additional evidence that Burns was the patriot his admirers claimed him to have been. I also saw the same disposition among some of his neighbors to belittle him to strangers. They can scarcely speak a good word for him, and it is the utterance of these which make visitors believe he was what they term him—a drunken braggart. As I have before said, he was at one time addicted to drink, but he reformed, and the later years of his life was a sober man. He had made effort to enlist at the beginning of the war, but the recruiting-officer would not take him, as he was then sixty-seven years old. I was told that he served in the Mexican war, but it being afterwards contradicted, as John led a double life in Gettysburg, it is hard to say whether it is true or not. In gathering information about Burns, it was a common thing for the second informant to nullify what the first said. It is very evident he had been a soldier at some previous time. He received a pension from the Government for his day's work at Gettysburg up to the time of his death.

Shorn of all exaggeration the story of old John Burns, gray
with age, standing on Seminary Ridge among the veterans of
the Army of the Potomac, loading and firing with the best of
them, is a thrilling episode of the late war.   By correspondence
with those with whom he fought, and who would naturally
recollect the particulars of an incident so unique, and by personal inquiry of those who knew him, I have obtained the
details of the deed which made him famous.

If what I have written will do anything towards perpetuat-
ing the memory of the citizen-hero of Gettysburg, and render
him less a mythical personage and more the gallant patriot
he was, it is all I ask.

The Village Store.

CHANGE is written on all things mundane. Speaking in a particular way of man, we see a series of
ever-varying changes, from red-faced infancy to
wrinkled old age.   Noting the human race in general, we see
with what ceaseless mutations it has advanced, from the
grinning pre-historic ape of Darwin to the self-complacent,
self-assumedly perfect man of to-day.   The seasons follow one
another in one endless, shifting succession.   Empires grow,
flourish and decay.   Kingdoms arise from the ashes of past
governmental conflagrations, flap their confident wings into
futurity, knock their heads against the rock of popular will,
and die.   Republics—those synonyms of ingratitude—run
their too brief existence, pass away, and emerge in some

other form. The arts and sciences are continually varying, their course being onward and upward. In manner of locomotion we have gone from the pack-horse to the lightning train; in modes of transmitting news, from the plodding mail coach to the electric telegraph. In our habitations we have advanced from the colonial log hut to magnificent residences, with their wen-like bay windows, their mansard roofs, their towers and their mortgages. The plain public buildings of the olden time are succeeded by massive piles, which cost piles as massive, and which an unconsulted posterity must pay for. As before intimated, change and advancement are accompaniments of all things sublunary, with one exception, and that is the Village Store. I have known this institution for over forty years, and in that period there has been little alteration in its outward and inward appearance, the mode of conducting it, and the *personnel* of its conductor and his patrons.

There was the hitching post with its well gnawed top; the porch filled up with dry goods, soap and candle boxes, and the rakes, shovels and hoes piled up around the outside of the door as of old. On entering the door there was the same trim array of nail kegs to greet the eye. In them were the different gradations, from the festive " three-penny-fine " to the lordly "spike." Not so prominent to me now, but standing out then in bold relief, my first recollections of the grocery store are in connection with the candy jars. Short-necked, apoplectic fellows that they are, with their brass-capped heads; there they stand, just as they stood in my boyhood's days, the centre of attraction for juvenile eyes. Their contents don't seem to have been disturbed. The one on the left is shotted with " sour-balls," the next with mint stick, the next with lemon candy, and then came a jar with " lickerish," followed by another containing " secrets." These latter had printed mottoes around them, as now, and were much affected by the youthful swains at school. These passed them over to the big girls, who received them with the conventional giggle. I don't think the confectionery of the present age is equal to the old-time article on the score of purity; there is so much more chalk in its composition now. Among the eccentricities of my childhood was a partiality for candy. When my parents went to store my last request was for mint stick; my first inquiry after they returned was if they had got it. In vain was the sanitary advice about its being unwholesome for children; vanity of vanities was it to try to curb the appetite for it by the solemn assurance that it would rot out every tooth in my head. That row of jars brings to my recollection a singular conceit that took possession of my callow mind during the Millerite excitement. Several of my schoolfellows, whose parents were firm believers in Millerism, had impressed my mental faculties with the idea that the end of the world was nigh, and that on a certain fixed day the human race was to be extinct on earth. The speculation as to what manner of means was to accomplish this filled my young mind with terror, but I at last gathered consolation from the possibility that one person might be left as a sample of what was, and furthermore, that that person might be me. My impression was that the earth would remain as it was, only uninhabited; the houses stand as they were, only tenantless; the stores—they were the prominent features—without storekeepers; and then, with no one to say nay, I would go for the confectionery! No thoughts of my loneliness, or the fearful silence which would prevail over the land in the suppression of all animated nature, with my single exception, entered into my philosophy. Neither did I draw comparisons between my possible condition and the similar one of Macaulay's New Zealander in depopulated London. The simple possibility of a free range of the candy shelves of a deserted store absorbed all other considerations.

On my right, as I enter, is the counter devoted to groceries and sundry other articles. At its end, next the street, is the powder and shot department. The sight of the powder-can always inspired me with awe, and its possible explosion, coupled with carelessness on the part of the boyish clerk, gave me visions of flying tea canisters, paint jars, mouse traps, clothes lines and the rest of the odds and ends usually found in connection with the grocery department of a "well kept country store." "A quarter o' powder, pound of shot," was the sentiment generally given in by those seeking ordnance stores, and was responded to by the storekeeper with the gravity befitting a dispenser of those death-dealing articles. The scales for weighing these were also used to balance tea, which was proper, as one variety of the nerve-destroying herb was known as "Gunpowder." Close by stand the balances which test the weight of groceries, mackerel and nails. Over these the customer of an inquiring mind leaned while his purchases were tried in the balance. I could always estimate a man's intrinsic moral worth by his actions at such times. Were he unduly thrifty he would appropriate a piece of cheese before the weight of it was announced; if an "all, all honorable man," he would wait till after and then gorge himself with saccharine sweetness or that other production, the use of which would make his breath smell like that of the lord-mayor of Limburg. Mackerel, I always noticed, were never interfered with by either class, but the former would generally inquire if due allowance was made for the brown paper in which the salty fish were wrapped. The considerate questioning of the merchant sounds in my ears as it did in days gone by. "Do you like a sharp cheese or a mild?" "Will you have the mild Rio or the strong?" "How did that last tea suit?" were the stock questions. When I was a boy the coffee was always sold raw. Before being roasted it had to be picked of all foreign matter. I have in my mind an old lady, of an economical turn, who used to save up all this waste and return it to the store along with her old rags, which was not so bad. There is the cellar door leading to the subterranean store house, where were stored mackerel, butter, oil, molasses and other moist goods. Into this cavern, and when he had no clerk, the genius of the store went with reluctance, whenever his customer was morally shaky. The tidiness of the house-keeper was generally reflected in the molasses jug; were it streaky, she was a slattern; if clean, a model housewife. In old times "wallets" were in vogue, but I don't see them any more. Many a time have I gone to the store with one of those double-ended bags thrown over my shoulders, with a jug in one or each end. Once, when quite a lad, I went on horse-back, with a wallet before me containing a molasses and a vinegar jug, in which situation I did not make a bad repre-sentation of a Tartar horseman on his road from the wars, with his enemies' heads at his saddle bow. Arriving at the store I laid them on the ground while I tied my steed, which suddenly shied, and planting his feet on the frail receptacles of those antipodal commodities, crushed them to atoms. The only witness, beside my horse or myself, was an old lady standing on the store porch, who aggravated me beyond endurance by showing me a countenance wreathed in smiles —for I was blubbering at a great rate over my trouble—but I forgave her after my arrival home, when mother told me that the apparent smile was nothing more than a chronic contrac-tion of the facial muscles, which showed the same through sunshine and sorrow; and such I afterwards saw for myself to be the case. The storekeeper soon came to my assistance, and with a cheerfulness heightened by the sale of two new jugs, soon had me straightened up.

There is the medicine closet as it stood of yore, but not filled as then. Where stand the stupefying "Mrs. Winslow," "Pain Killer," "Consumption Cures," and other compounds, was an array of good old Thompsonian medicines; there was the biting " No. 6," the fiery " Kian Pepper," the gingery " Composition," the nauseating " Lobelia," and other beverages. I know them all by heart, for I have gone through the whole course, and a terrible ordeal to my young mind and body it was. These preparations would often drive away disease without being administered at all. Often, when expressing myself as too sick to go to school, miraculous cures have been effected by a mere look at the burning drinks being prepared for my recovery. Not that I loved to go to school more, but that I liked " composition " less !

And there is the show case, the contents a mercantile museum, and its glazed lid still inviting guileless youth to rest its elbows on it and break through. It didn't used to be thought worth while to putty the panes of glass, so frequently were they broken, and I observe they are still only tacked in. As an inducement to the over-confiding and morally delinquent to invest in a grab, I see a ten-cent note pasted on the under side of one of the panes. The standard mercantile joke in specie times was to nail a counterfeit quarter to the counter and thus tempt erring human nature with illusory hopes. Varied the contents of the show case. Here the hired girl got the bows, the ribbons and " balm of a thousand flowers " wherewith to ensnare the village youths ; and here the latter got the " galone " to besprinkle his handkerchief, and the " bear's oil " to anoint his locks, both of which were to make him irresistible in the eyes of the aforesaid. There were eyes for the blind in the shape of German silver spectacles, razors for the unshaven, soap for the unclean and fish-hooks for the fisher of fish. But what took my attention, when a lad, was the knife department of the show case. First and foremost among the collection was that *vade mecum*—the knife with a dozen blades and other appliances, among which were a corkscrew, toothpick, file and gimlet. This, while it bewildered me, was beyond my aspirations. There were knives of six blades, knives of four blades, three-bladed knives, two-bladed knives and so on by easy stages to that single-bladed affair, the "Barlow"—why so called it is not known, probably because Billy of that surname was the inventor. I don't see them any more. They used to sell for ten and twelve cents, and had blades of such villainous temper that a turnip would almost turn their edges. They were, however, considered good enough for little boys to lose, and were often bought for them by thrifty parents in preference to lending them their own .more valuable whittlers. I've not forgotten with what consummate innocence a knife with a recently broken blade was placed in the parental trousers by the youthful delinquent, the ruptured ends carefully placed together, and the damage not discovered until the knife would be next used. The Barlow handle had a peculiar smell caused by the varnish or stain with which the bone was covered, which I well remember. In order to test the temper of the blades we used to blow our breaths on them, and note the length of time it took for them to evaporate. I recollect that once, while in the Barlow stage of existence, and having just lost one of those "toad stickers," as we called them at school, I was flattening my nose on the show case of our store, looking wistfully at some nice two-bladed knives, when the storekeeper asked me if I didn't want to buy one. I told him yes, but "pappy" wouldn't let me. "Ah," said he, shrewdly, "take it home and show it to him and I guess he will." On getting there I found the suggestion had been a good one, for my father could not resist my importunities, and, besides, possession was always nine points of the law. I recollect getting our man of all work, Aaron White, to grind it for me, and my mother calling excitedly to him not to make it too sharp. I also remember his replying that he understood his business, and have not forgotten that he made the knife so dull that the softest pine was as seasoned oak.

I skip to the dry goods department, where the odorous corduroy, the Kentucky jeans, which faded as a flower, the flashy calicoes, whose colors were fast only in the sense of speedily leaving the goods, and the muslins of more or less bleachedness are stored. I pass under the array of dangling boots, which hang like a cloud of leathery manna, ready to descend on an unshod world whenever it should be deemed worthy. I will say nothing of the part devoted to school books, the shelves of which in my younger days were filled with those time-honored works—Comly's spelling book and grammar, Pike's arithmetic, Olney's geography, Parley's histories, etc.—but hasten on to that part of the store where evidences of our nationality sit enthroned in the post-office department. True, there is some change here, for in old times envelopes were not thought of, and the postage was rarely prepaid; but the general appearance is just as it was then. People who have no reason to expect letters make daily inquiries for them, just as they used to, and the wearied postmaster answers them as courteously as he can. The village miss, who is lucky enough to get a letter, makes the most of it, and after trying to find out who it is from by looking at the post-mark, carefully opens it and reads it as she saunters homeward on the public highway—the envy of the less fortunate maids. The business man, to whom letters are no novelty, runs his forefinger into the envelope and rips it open without ceremony. The man who don't take a country paper begs one of his neighbor's out of the pack, and does his best to get through with it before it is called for.

I pass from the stock of the store to the stock company, which there plays its daily and nightly parts—from the inanimate to the animate fixtures. First comes the head-centre of the institution, the storekeeper himself. He is gray of hair and whisker, but he looks no older to-day than when, a third of a century ago, with my eyes on a level with the counter, he gave me my cent's worth of candy. Following so many years behind his wake in the voyage of life I note few changes. When I see new comers in the neighborhood buying goods I see the same hesitancy apparent on his countenance as to whether he should urge goods on them in anticipation of sure pay, or whether to hang back from so doing in apprehension of being eventually victimized. I see with what alacrity the burly, well-to-do farmer—the man who, as he drives the fat oxen of Shrewdness and Contentment, is fat in both purse and figure—is waited on, till the counter is full of packages of dry goods and groceries. I observe how the poor ne'er-do-well, who is always asking to have his purchases "just marked down," is avoided. I still hear "there is nothing made in groceries," and still wonder how the venders of them live.

Then there were the boys who regularly graduated in that store. From mere sweepers of the floor and dusters of counters, from fishers of mackerel and drawers of molasses and bungling wrappers-up of packages, they have become adepts in their business, and left the humble scenes of their tutelage for positions in the city, or, having capital at command, started stores of their own. They were generally composed of lads who were too lazy to work on a farm, and were the envy of their agricultural brethren. Among us school boys a desire to 'tend store was rampant within our souls. The duties of that vocation, in comparison with our farm labors, loomed up so pleasantly before us that it is no wonder we longed for a change of pasture on which our young lives might feed. Often when engaged in the detested occupation of stone picking, with the "spine of my back" (query: is there any other spine?) bent double, and with legs aweary with gathering our annual mural harvest, and my system burning with spring fever, I have looked across the fields toward the neighboring village and envied the new boy that the storekeeper had just got. Not but what a yearning toward the medical and dental professions occasionally took possession of me, but a desire to 'tend store was uppermost in my juvenile mind. The department devoted to the mackerel and pork fisheries, the drawing of molasses and extracting of oil from their respective casks—so detested by the novice before he is half through his probationary exercises and is a full-fledged clerk—had no terrors for me. Even the clawing among the contents of the nail kegs, with its attendant annoyances of getting splinters of nails under your own, and tearing your coat sleeves with the points of the "three-penny-fines," which, after piercing the hoops and staves, come through on the inside, was as naught. The desire to be installed on the other side of the counter, where I would be in a position to say to the customers as they entered, "Well, what can I do for you to-day?" to weigh out the toothsome sugar and mouth an occasional lump, to poise the fragrant tea, to balance the rattling coffee, to recklessly serve out the black gunpowder and bright globules of shot, to wield the murderous cheese knife, to sway the yard-stick sceptre over a prostrate array of rolls of cloths, cassimeres and vestings, of muslins and calicoes, tapes and laces; to dispense the goods in the show case, to hand out the contents of the post-office, and, above all, to sit on the stool at the desk and "just charge it"—the desire, I say, to do these things pervaded my being. Besides, the free run of the candy jars was not to be lost sight of.

I recollect well when Bob Beeser, the son of a farmer neighbor and about my own age, was promoted to a vacancy in our store. The position had been for some time vacant, and I had longed for it like L for the apple pie in the old nursery book. I teased my father for the coveted position, but in vain. He had higher aspirations for me, and Bob got the place. At school I was not behind him: in truth, I was his superior, both mentally and physically. Whether it was a "rassle" on the school grounds or in the spelling class, I could lay Bob on his back. But as store-tender he seemed a head and shoulder above me. When kind fate plucked him from the thorny path of agriculture the jagged surroundings seemed to have torn off and retained his rough exterior, so that when she landed him behind the counter he was etherialized, so to re-mark, and, after being reclad in store-clothes, was in a world beyond me. I remember, about two weeks after his instal-ment in his new position, I was sent to the store after a load of mackerel and molasses. It was during my regular noon-spell and in stone-picking time. A warm April sun showered his rays upon me as I trudged along on foot, with the recep-tacles for the above mentioned luxuries swinging at my side, and my heart rebelled that the time for sending me had not been delayed until after working hours. When I entered the store I was not in a joyous mood. Bob, who was waiting on a village miss, vouchsafed me a condescending nod, which spoke volumes in showing the difference in our present positions in society. Putting my jug and dish-pan on the counter I sat down disconsolately on a hard nail keg and read the hand bills until I could be waited on, as the storekeeper was away. How I envied Bob! My clothing was coarse and untidy, and my feet were bare. My hands were rough and sore and my skin tanned. Bob's clothes were neat and stylish, his hands white and soft, and his face a putty-colored hue, which was my envy; but above all these there was an easiness and famili-arity of manner about him that smote me sorely. But to see him—him who, when he had hitherto come in contact with me, was always the under dog—pretending to be oblivious of my presence, just because he "'tended store," was insupport-able. You wouldn't have thought that a short two weeks ago he was picking stones, cutting wood, feeding pigs and milking cows! To see him when he weighed out the white sugar (how well he had got to know the dividing line between giving

good weight and not too much draft), how generously he
gave the girl a lump after he had struck the balance; to see
him, when it came to cheese, how neatly he gave her a piece
to taste on the point of his cheese knife—a rusty old imple-
ment it was, but to my eyes it was as a blade of Damascus!—
and with what vigor and grace he clave the yellow segment;
to behold him pause—on the road from the grocery counter to
the dry goods department—at the candy shelf to give her a
"secret;" to see her unwrap the confection and put it in her
mouth, and, as she rolled it from cheek to cheek as a sweet
morsel, hear her read the couplet on the "secret" paper:

> " If you love me as I love you,
> No knife can cut our love in two "—

to hear their mutual tittering thereat; to see how dexterously
Bob threw down calicoes and muslins, ribbons and tape on the
dry goods counter; to see their whispered confidences after
the purchases were made and wrapped; how Bob, under pre-
tence to say something in her ear, suddenly shifted his mouth
and gave her a rousing smack on the lips ; the pretended
anger and attempts to box his ears; to see what a time they
had when they got to the post-office department; how he
tried to make her believe there was a letter for her, which,
when produced, turned out to be a lottery policy circular for
her father; how they parted at the door with mysterious hints
and winks intended for my benefit—all this was aggravating
in the extreme; but what drove me nearly wild was Bob's pretended obliviousness of my presence. I was never intended
for a pirate, but when I saw, heard and felt all this, with that
cheese-knife lying in easy reach, I felt as much like Captain
Kidd did " when he sailed, when he sailed," as any good little
boy ought to feel.

When Bob became aware of my presence he turned patronizingly and said, " Well, young man, what can I do for you

to-day," in tones that cut me to the quick. In a sullen voice I told him a gallon of New Orleans and a pan of his best No. 1 mackerel was what I was after, and to stir his stumps, as I was in a hurry; not that I was, but I thought a little bravado was in order. But it was all assumed, for I stood in awe of him. As I saw him turn his nose up at the disagreeable task before him I experienced a secret joy until he appeared from the lower regions. He seemed so disgusted with the moist-grocery part of his duties that I would like to have given him another similar order for the sake of having him get his delicate hands soiled again.

And then the airs he took on when off duty! To see him on a Sabbath morning, when he should have been at Sunday-school, standing in front of the store talking to the hotel-keeper's daughter, was a sight. Languidly leaning against the porch he would be seen smoking what I will be bound was a cigar of the Spanish brand—costing five cents; a fabulous price in those days, when you could get four for a penny—and which I will be further bound, in any reasonable recognizance, was not paid for, unless taking a five-cent piece out of the till and dropping it in again could be called compensation. His hat would be stuck rakishly on the side of his head and his fingers thrust in his pants' pockets, with the thumbs pointing outward in the way still affected by sprigs older than he. This habit, I may remark, dates so far back that I can fancy Adam's little boys standing in that position; that is, if I could imagine them in trousers—which I cannot. As we drove by, Bob would take his "five-center" from his lips, blow a cloud, and bestowing a patronizing nod on father go on talking to Miss Boniface. Young store-tenders didn't wear paper collars in those days nor part their hair in the middle, yet they possessed an irresistible charm in the eyes of the village maids that must have been due to their vocation. But I know one thing, and that is that he became unbearable to me in proportion as I longed to be in his place. I expect you will imagine that with Excelsior and Eureka for his watchwords he eventually turned out to be an embryotic John Wanamaker, but he didn't. He is at present tending bar in a down-town saloon ; his face is as red as it used to be white, and he wears carbuncles on his nose.

At this period of my existence I recollect that for the ostensible purpose of advancing the cause of education, but, I fear, more with an eye to trade, the opposition store started a night school for the education of the village youth. If with the former idea it was a delusion and a snare. With the storekeeper acting the role of teacher we did sums on our slates and finished our "studies" by spelling. I remember getting above several by spelling the word "twelfth." Among the number who took side-steps to the rear was a large boy, who, while I was on my way home, waylaid me from behind a board pile, and told me he'd soon show me how to spell. In my temerity I remarked "he'd have to spell able first," but before he was done with me I felt, physically speaking, as if he had left me with the mark of Cain! I bit the dust a martyr to orthography and "science;" but that way of being "spelled down" I never liked. Another boy, whom I had also got above, told me afterward it was good for me ; but I could not see how it was. But I was young then.

I pass on to the other regular *habitues* of the "country store." Through the daytime the number was few and generally of the genus "loafer." These passed the time in smoking, chewing, spitting at the stove to hear it "siz," and eying the customers, particularly the female portion, while they made their purchases. Much herding together had used up and dwarfed their conversational powers, and they dwelt in a dreamy state —probably wondering why they had ever been created. Occasionally one would start up, as if seized with an original idea, and ask if there was anything in the office for him, and then,

23

overcome with the effort, lapse into lethargic silence. As the custom of these gentry never amounted to anything, the store-keeper always felt aggrieved by their presence, and doubtless often wished they were in some other building—say the opposition store, for instance—with a successful Guy Fawkes running a gunpowder plot in the basement! And yet he was not to blame for wishing it; for what more suitable food for powder than a store loafer?

But at the nightly *soirees* the house was crowded. Then came the patrons of the store far and near. Some came for goods, some for the mail, some to talk and some to hear others talk, and all more or less to loaf. There is the sturdy 'Squire, whose word, as befitted his office, was law; the shrewd farmer, and thrifty mechanic. There is the hen-pecked husband, who fled from his home as the shades of night drew on apace to the congenial society at the store. (That is he among the forks and shovels in a gloomy corner, smoking a mild cigar.) There are the butcher, the baker and, if the trade were not an extinct one, the candlestick maker, the lively apprentice and farmer lads of various ages. The married members of this nightly-meeting *coterie* have left their homes as soon as the evening meal was gulped down, to just "slip down to the corner to hear the news." Their day's work over they leave the wife, whose work is never done, to wash the supper dishes, soothe the cross children and put them to bed, and then pass the evening darning stockings and pondering on those long-passed days when it would have been rank heresy to have believed that John would ever desert her for the coarse attractions of the society found at night at the cross-roads store.

Mark those two lads on the grocery counter, in rather too close propinquity to the powder magazine, considering they are smoking. One of them is the son of the village doctor, who has sent him to the store for some groceries, with strict injunctions to hurry back. He is now making himself sick on a "half-Spanish," for it is his first attempt at using the weed. He has a confiding mother, and she must needs be when, after scenting his coat in the morning, he tells her it was all done by his being in such a crowd of smokers at the store, and she believes it. The other lad, a Daniel Lambert in obesity, is the son of a deacon of the church, also sent on a hasty errand. He is a modern edition of the Prodigal Son, bound in a roundabout and tight trousers. He robbed a hen's nest of its fruit before he left home, and has spent the value of it in riotous living in the shape of a penny cigar. Viewing this as a symbol of pleasure, he has drained it to the dregs, for he is now chewing the stump. So, like the Prodigal, he has come to the husk which even swine would not eat; and I am certain that, knowing all things, if his father had him at home he would at least half kill the fatted calf.

The lucky one of the nocturnal fixtures being seated in the only arm chair, the rest on bench, counter or with their pantaloons patched with nail kegs, the scene is interesting and instructive. Behold the venerable loafer whose back has become bowed, his locks a snowy white and whose tongue has become slightly palsied in the service of his nightly audience. Grown hardened in his sin of telling incredible stories, he has got to believe them himself. There is the other nuisance who tells pointless yarns full of "I tell you what's," "you know's," "you see's," "says I's" and "says he's" until he becomes unendurable, except to his regular listeners. There is the man who is so devoted to fishing that his mouth has grown like a sucker's, his eyes as of a catfish, and in getting out of paying his debts has become as an eel in slipperiness. His tales are of the fish, fishy. There is the sportsman with hunting proclivities, who will lie by the hour if he can have listeners. Too lazy to work, he will trudge from morning till night o'er hill and valley tracking rabbits or hunting squirrels, and then wonder why he can't make a living. His society, too valuable for one single community, alternates between the store and tavern. There is also the man who chatters everlastingly and whom no one listens to. A good portion of the talk is the essence of vulgarity, some of it from the lips of hoary sinners, and especially relished by the more tender youth, whose legs are swinging from the counter and benches.

The night wears on apace. The crowd, in numbers, remains about the same, occasionally varying in *personnel* by exchanges with the hotel opposite. But at last it begins to dwindle. One gathers up a jug, one a coal-oil can, another a basket, and another a bundle and departs. Then follow some of the less inveterate loafers, and lastly, after several pointed hints from the storekeeper or his boy, the sticking-plasters vanish into darkness. The shutters are closed, the doors are barred, the lights put out, and simmering in a stale atmosphere of tobacco smoke, the store is deserted till morning.

My Tramp.

BY JOHN SMITH.

ONLY a Tramp!

He stood before me dressed in a hat of the plug variety, which, by continued dinting, looked like the bellows of a lopsided accordion; and a coat whose sleeve cuffs showed by their silken glossiness that if he kept a pocket-handkerchief it was very derelict in performing its duty.

When this unghostly apparition thrust itself into my presence I was in my store drawing off my last year's account.
Sandwiched between the good bills, like spoiled ham between
fresh baker's bread, were several bad ones. Here was John Doe,
who, by paying cash at the start, had got into my good graces
until I opened an account with him, when, by paying a little
on the old score and buying more on·a new, he had so run
in my debt that I had refused him further credit, and he now
went to the new opposition store, where he paid cash. John had
just gone by with a string of mackerel in one hand and a jug
of molasses in the other, which he carried with a defiant
swing. There was Richard Roe, whom I had nursed, speaking
in a mercantile way, for some time, in the hope that he would
receive a stroke of conscience and pay me like a man, but who,
I had just learned, had run away between two days. There
were others of the same stamp who were making themselves
apparent as I ran over the contents of my ledger, and I con-
fess I was in rather an irritable mood when my tramp
appeared before me, and I felt like inviting him to retire until
I had more leisure to entertain him. It is thus we often make
the innocent the victims of the spleen which others have
engendered.

But then he was only a tramp!

So was Franklin, when landing in Philadelphia, with his
clothing sticking out of his pockets, he stood munching his
roll of bread. In this day and time he would have been
avoided by man, while the dogs would have been invited to
give him their special attention.

Only a tramp?

So was Homer, when, wandering through those seven noble
cities of Greece, each of which afterward contended for the
honor of being his birthplace, he begged his unwillingly-given
bread. In our prejudice how many Franklins and Homers
we kick from our doors!

I knew my interviewer was a tramp, but I pretended not. When he pulled some business-like papers from his coat pocket, I, in return, accused him with being a census man, a book agent and a church-subscription man. But he denied these impeachments. I reached hard-pan by hinting that he was a lightning rod agent, his coolness and impudence so amazed me. At this he laughed outright, telling me in good English, for a Polander, that he had not come that low yet.

My tramp's mouth was a broad one, and when he emitted this laugh he showed his white teeth to that extent that they looked as if they might be the ivory keys belonging to the accordion whose bellows his wrinkled hat represented. This conceit took such possession of me that I felt tempted to mash down that hat to see if there was any music in his soul, but I didn't, for he carried a knotty stick under his arm.

At his earnest request I took his proffered document. It was about the color of a coffee-colored naturalization paper, but what it lacked in cleanliness it made up by unsavory odors. Opening it and holding it at arm's length, I read:

" To the Benevolent:

" This is to certify that the bearer, Signor Vermi Celli, is a truthful, worthy man, but a man of misery. He is a son of Italy ; a dweller in the Valley of the Po. On an island in that river is his estate. During a fearful inundation, the past season, the floods enveloped it, so that he and his family were forced to its highest summits. In order to procure support for them until the subsidence of the waters, he formed the resolution of swimming ashore and coming to America, where he trusts the charitable will pity the sorrows of a poor old man and give out of their abundance; and he will ever pray, etc.

" Signed, SIGNOR MACA RONI."

Having been a tramp, in a small way, once myself, I have an undue amount of pity for these houseless wanderers who are now devastating this country; these sturdy varlets, who, at an expense to the county of a dollar and a-half a night, get their lodgings and two more or less square meals, and then complain of their victuals and the quality of tobacco handed out to them; these lusty beggars who terrify our households and turn up their noses at the best cuts of mince pie. I was melted by the pitiful tale of this poor nobleman, who, far away from his suffering family, was endeavoring to raise funds for their relief. I forgave him the odor of gin which tinctured his breath, knowing he had imbibed that stimulant merely to drown trouble. So that when I handed him back his statement with a present of ten cents, which he insisted I should mark down on his brief that he might properly account for the funds collected, I could not resist his request to partake of my hospitality for the night. Acting on the impulse of the moment, I took my tramp to the house and seated him in the kitchen, much to the annoyance of Mrs. Smith and the disgust of Bridget, our maid of all work, and then went back to the task I was at when my foreign friend interrupted me. It was now nearing night, and going to the house to supper I found the household in somewhat of an uproar. When I introduced my tramp, in answer to my wife's inquiry as to ways and means for lodging him, I had jocularly remarked that he might be put in the girl's room. This my oldest, who had just arrived at the " irrepressible small boy " age, had carried to Bridget's ears, with such additions as the case seemed to demand, when that jewel, red-faced and irate, gave warning on the spot, in spite of all promises of increased wages and a nearly new silk dress. The innocent cause of this disturbance was quietly seated by the kitchen stove, placidly filling the apartment with smoke, and unmindful of the banging and knocking around of pots and kettles by the angry serving-maid. He had conversed but little, merely inquiring from time to time of the progress of the evening meal. When that was ready, he showed some feeling when he saw preparations were making for his eating alone in the kitchen; mildly re-

monstrating against it as being something out of the usual
way, and that he was used to being treated as if he was half
white.   Much experimenting on the cookery of the various
households he had invaded had made him quite a connoisseur
in victuals.   He knew the proper time to turn up his nose at
a cup of coffee, and he was aware when "tramp butter" was
placed before him.   He mildly remonstrated against this
oleaginous compound—an article we generally keep on hand
in cases of emergency, much as your tobacco-beggar's victim
keeps an inferior article of "plug" for his many friends.   It
was buckwheat cake season, and he showed much discrimina-
tion in feasting on those luxuries.   These grew "sicklied o'er
with a pale cast" during the progress of the meal, when our
guest intimated to my wife (who, of course, is the cake-baker,
Bridget disliking the business on account of the cold cakes
falling to the follower of that profession) that he believed he
was done; but his appetite returned, however, when the
proper golden-brown hue was again attained, when, like
Oliver the hungry, he asked for more.   After closing up the
store and returning to the house, I found the vexed question
of how our boarder was to be lodged for the night still uppermost in the female mind, and unsettled.   Objections being
made to any more luxurious mode for his passing the nocturnal hours, he was sentenced to sleep on the sitting-room
floor, from which there was no respite.   A horse blanket and
rocking-chair cushion were the comforts assigned him, after
which we retired; I with an undiminished confidence in
human nature; my wife full of dark forebodings of robbery and
perhaps assassination, and Bridget with a full determination
of packing up and going to her "cousin's" in Lambertville
the next morning.   As to how we spent the time until morning, each of us could have said with him of Gloucester, "Oh!
I have passed a miserable night."   If let alone I would have
slept the sleep of the just; but every half hour Mrs. Smith

with a shake would tell me, " I'd better go down and see if all was right." Once, when I went down on hearing an unusual commotion, I found my tramp taking the table-cloth from its place in the dish closet to do duty as a sheet, the horse blanket being too rough for his delicate system. Pitying the poor wretch, I did not report this to my wife, knowing it would only make a fuss. About midnight I was awakened by the announcement that the house was full of smoke, when, rushing down stairs without inquiring as to what manner of smoke it was, I found my traveling friend sitting in the middle of the room surrounded with a dense vapor, which a pipe, charged with jail tobacco, was giving forth. This he put by at my urgent request, when I again retired, to be again disturbed at various intervals until morning. When my wife did not hear suspicious noises, Bridget did ; so that between them both I made more trips than did Mother Hubbard in the interest of her dog of wonderful abilities. In the dawn's early light I saw him peacefully slumbering in his chair, with his hat down over his eyes, doubtlessly dreaming of the loved ones of his far-off home on the Po.

When I came down stairs preparatory to stirring up the matinal fires and setting the day's work going generally, what a sight met my sleep-robbed eyes! Where I had left a complete realization of the materialization of the genus *tramp* I found his disembodied clothes. These, sometime during the night, he had so stuffed with cushions and other appliances as to much resemble the natural man as seen in the dim light of the stove, while his hat hung rakishly on a broom-handle which stood back of his chair. It was this object I had seen when I had last come down stairs, and hence the quiet that afterward reigned. The same day on which my tramp made his appearance my wife had gone to the city and bought me a complete suit of best clothes, which she had shown me in the evening, and then laid them away in a cupboard in the sitting-room.

My first thought was of them ; but a search for them told me they were gone. On looking at the hat-rack in the hall, a new silk hat and an overcoat, with some business papers in it, were also found missing. Calling up my startled family and telling them the news, we were soon busily engaged, with rueful aspects, albeit, in ascertaining the damage done by our tramp, which were annoying if not serious. The pair of boots the Signor Vermi Celli had worn, which had made night hideous with their Stygian aroma, and which still lent a gamey flavor to the tobacco-scented room, were found inserted in the legs of the dummy, and in their stead he had taken a pair of my French calf-skins. Our three children each had one of those respectable begging machines called "money-banks" sitting on the mantel, all of which had been well filled by considerate friends, but they were now found empty. On learning this our offspring howled like Rome. A sponge cake which had been expressly made for some company we were expecting next day had been taken, and the stand drawers rummaged. Wishing to know no more at present I rushed away from the harrowing scene to see if I could learn anything of the whereabouts of the Signor. An hour's search around the village amounted to nothing; my inquiries being generally met with such unsympathizing remarks as "You might have known better," or, "It served you right." I, however, learned that a through freight train that passed by our village at an early hour in the morning had stopped to drop a car, and this I felt sure had been the means of my tramp's escape. On arriving home I found a far more cheerful feeling prevailing there than I could have expected. The donation of the coveted silk dress, if she would only stay, had exorcised the " laving " demon from Bridget's soul, and she was now merrily rotating the handle of the coffee-mill. My wife, with an I-told-you-so air, was getting breakfast with a cheerfulness of manner which could only be accounted for by the fact that

her rejoicings at my discomfiture had, together with the conclusion to stay of her hand-maiden, outweighed her regret at
the losses from the depredations of our lodger. A merry peal
of laughter from the front room showed that our children had
also experienced a change of heart. On hearing John, my
oldest boy, exclaim, "Goodey, that's the hardest lick it's got
yet," and my youngest, that "he'd bet his toe-nail'd come off,"
I went in to see what caused this merry-making, and was
greeted by a violent pounding at the front door. Opening it
I found Jo Sipes, one of my best customers, standing on one
foot and holding the other in his hand, and swearing at such
a rate that I really felt hurt. On asking an explanation, he
told me that if I was going to allow my young ones to play
such tricks on innocent people I might, but he'd bought
his last cent's worth of me; and turning around he limped off.
It appeared that after my departure little John had been
seized with a bright idea, which had dried up his sorrow at
the loss of his pennies, on seeing the tramp's hat reposing on
its perch. This he had placed on the pavement in front of
the store and ballasted with a brick. Several guileless people
had bestowed kicks upon it, much to their regret and the
enjoyment of my children, who, in witnessing the sport, had
forgotten their recent trouble. Informing the latter that I
would "make them laugh on the other side of their mouths," I
administered the needed correctives, and, amid their wailings,
I sat down to rather a late breakfast. The hat I had ordered
removed promptly from its tempting position; but not until it
had caused me much loss in custom, as several of those who had
attempted to propel it were my patrons, who thought I was in
some way connected with its being placed there. I at last
got to the store, and barring the fact that several customers
had been there for goods and had gone away empty-handed,
and that my tramp had been the indirect means of losing me
some custom, things were soon going on smoothly again. The

loss of my clothing, my wife said, was more than made up by
the carpet rags she got out of the tramp's clothes. These latter,
which had originally been wrathfully carried out with the tongs
at arms length and thrown back of the pig-pen, had been, on
second thought, tenderly gathered up, disinfected and washed,
and made ready to do duty in a new carpet we were about
making. For my part, I comforted myself with one reflection, and that was, if ever a well-dressed man left our town
my tramp was he.

One day while busily engaged in the grocery department of
my store, shortly after the events narrated, my wife came
in with a troubled look on her face and an opened letter in
her hand. It was addressed to her, and read as follows:

MUDDLETON, Jan. 6th, 1876.

Dear Mrs. Smith.—Fearing the subject of the within local
item, which I clip from the pages of the *Muddleton Gaslight*,
may have got into his dissipated habits on account of the worriment of mind a Scolding Wife always occasions, I write to
warn you, if such is the case, to be more considerate with him
in the future. When the prodigal returns home, on money
loaned him by entire *strangers*, who, according to the poor
man's story, are *angels* by the side of his own household (I
mean you), kill the fatted calf for him. I conclude with my
best regards, and by saying that when I looked upon the linen
of your husband—the man you swore to love, honor, obey and
do his washing—I thought that while Charity covers a multi-
tude of sins, it is Vanity to think of trying to hide a dirty
shirt with a two-cent Paper Collar. Yours in Pity,

REBECCA SHARP,
President Muddleton Sewing Society.

The following is the Local:

Another Victim of the Demon Alcohol.—This morning a sad
sight was witnessed in front of Van Splutter's Lager Beer
saloon, in the shape of what was once a respectably dressed
man, lying in the gutter in a beastly state of intoxication.

He was so stupefied that he was unable to give any account of himself. He was at last brought around by the kindly offices of several small boys, who gathered about him and threw water in his face and pelted him with mud. In searching his pockets for matches they came across several handfuls of pennies, which, for fear he might spend them for more rum, they generously agreed to take care of. They ran off after throwing away the papers they found on him. These latter were picked up by a grocery drummer, who was temporarily in the town, and were the means of his recognition. From memoranda found in his pockets it would appear that he was on his return home from buying goods; but according to his own confused statements he left home on account of family troubles, and sought to drown them in the *flowing bowl.* He told a sorrowful tale. It is a sad case, and should be a warning to wives to be more considerate, and always meet their husbands with a smile, etc. The drummer, having an eye to business, loaned the poor man money to return home on, for which he was profuse in his thanks. We would not wish to be invidious, and will mention no names, merely observing that, in his sober moments, if you called him John Smith he would answer to it, and that his store is not far from ——town, Bucks County. We will conclude by saying that, by a substitution of names, the old song would be appropriate for the occasion:

> "Schmidt Johannes is his name,
> America his nation;
> ——town his dwelling-place,
> And brandy his damnation!"

I threw down the paper in disgust. "If ever I extend hospitality to another Bedouin of civilized life," said I, "may I—— Excuse me, ma'am, did you say you wanted the mild Rio or the strong?"

Company Trials.

THERE is a time in her housekeeping experience when a woman wishes she were either a man or dead: a brace of alternatives not so dissimilar when you reflect upon the future punishment that awaits man's selfishness in this life, and the quiet repose of death, and the reward in store for those who have been "weary and heavy laden." This time is when after doing a hard day's work and the hired girl gone she has seen a market wagon load of unexpected company unloaded and settled down, and then beheld how light the burden of entertaining visitors falls on the alleged head of the household. The first thing the latter does after ordering the hired man to put away the strange horses is to take the men folks—the whole load is "his folks," by the way —part of the company to the pig pen, and leaning over the trough discuss the relative merits of Berkshire and Chester Whites, until it is supposed that "Mother" has the parlor fire made. Then they adjourn to the house, and with chairs tipped back at an angle of forty-five degrees, at the imminent risk of cutting through the new parlor carpet, discuss politics or whatever comes uppermost. They find the female guests already here, and engaged in looking over the autograph and photograph albums, and with a tight grip on the other end of the sympathetic chord which connects the two parties in the matter of the expected supper. But while this party are enjoying themselves where is mother? She is down in the kitchen wondering what she will get for supper. She is done wondering whether or not the company will stay all night, for she cunningly got her boy to ask the little company girl how long they were going to stay. The little lad took an inopportune time to propound the inquiry, and made it before the parlor crowd; when he suffered rebuke from his father for his lack of manners, and retaliated by saying that "mother told him to ask!" So the latter has now but one thing to trouble her, and that is provender for her hungry guests. Shall it be ham? The last one is worn to the bone. Shall it be those other stand-bys, dried or frizzled beef? Alas! the places which knew them once are as bare as Mother Hubbard's cupboard. Trips to the parlor door are taken, that consolation and aid may be had from the helpmate (?) there entertaining the company; but winks and beckonings through the door-crack meet with but tardy response. At last the husband comes out into the hall, in a huff, and asks his wife what she means interrupting them and breaking the chain of the argument, and when the case is mildly stated, says it's always the way when "his folks" come visiting; nothing to eat, and he must be pestered about it. 'Tain't the way when "her folks" come. Then there's no end of sponge cake and good things. When she provokingly tells him that what she wants are the very things that she told him to get the other day when at election, he says, she ought to have known better than to have bothered him at such a time, when he had so much on his mind; anyhow, he's heard enough. Finally, the little boy is hoisted on the sharp backbone of the old family horse and started off to the village sausage-shop for carnal food. He is enjoined to also bring some necessary groceries, but, of course, forgets them, and has to go back again. After much tribulation and many paternal visits from the parlor to the kitchen, to see what is making supper so late, that meal is at last ready, and at the announcement of the same the group in the parlor comes pouring into the dining room like ravening wolves. One of the guests having said that "buckwheat cakes would not go bad, but so many women hated to bake 'em," mother, by the aid of some baking powder had hastily gotten up a basis of the same, and spends the time between pouring

out coffee and waiting on children (as father is too busy talking to attend to the latter), in baking cakes and in trotting
back and forth from table to stove. Occasionally she is stimu-
lated to further exertion by remarks such as, the cakes are
getting pale, or they are as heavy as lead, or cold as ice; or,
what ails the coffee; it won't kill anybody with strength; or,
it would bear an iron wedge, point downward; or, that it took
his mother to make buckwheat cakes or good coffee. Almost
fagged out, she sees sausage gravy spilled on the new table-
cloth; the children visitors upset coffee on the same, or drop
victuals on the floor, and vary the sport by breaking two or
three gilt-edged china cups and saucers. With a sigh of relief
she sees the appetites of the guests show signs of being
satiated, and finally their jaws stop wagging. They arise and
seek that haven of refuge, the parlor, leaving the cook alone
with the dirty dishes and cold cakes. She eats a few of these—
the cakes, not the dishes—and after an hour spent washing up
the latter, and getting three or four beds ready, she hastily
spruces herself up and enters the parlor. She casts envious
looks at the sofa rocking chair, in which father is seated, but
he is poor at taking hints, and only leaves it long enough to
go to the coal scuttle to spit, as he is a dear lover of the weed,
it being good for the teeth. The company is engaged in a
spirited conversation, and mother makes desperate efforts to
throw in a few remarks, to show, if for nothing else, that she
is not the hired girl, but they fall on unsympathetic ears, or,
if noticed at all, it is for the correction of some error of statement or grammar. As it is soon bedtime, she remarks that
the folks must be tired and would like to go to bed; so she
puts them all to rest for the night, giving up her own goose-
feather bed, as she expects to take the floor. After this father
gives her a little lecture about bothering him about the
victuals when he was wanting to talk, and looking so cross and
"huffy" at supper-time, when she ought to have been doing

her best to let "his folks" know they were welcome, and also in relation to her looking so "slomicky" when company was about. After receiving the proper amount of rebuke she goes to bed, or to floor, rather, to dream about the days before she was married, when she was so afraid she would die an old maid! She gets up the next morning, makes the fire, and goes through the ordeal of the preceding evening and amid other tribulations till "his folks" depart. Alas! taking one consideration with another, a woman's lot is not a happy one.

Sketches in Rhyme.

In the Shadow of Round Top.

FROM the wooded crest of Round Top, north to Seminary Ridge,
From its sulphur-shrouded ramparts east to Wolf Hill's rocky ledge
Rolls the thunder of the conflict to the far horizon's edge;
  Echoing loud from ridge to ridge.

Crimson horrors mar their outlines; seething vapors veil the sky;
Cannon-booming, musket-rattle, yells and wailing mount on high;
Ushered in with drum and trumpet march the birthdays of July,
  While the death-mist veils the sky.

Back and forth fly iron shuttles, warps phantasmal mark their way
Through a woof of lines of battle, tangled threads of Blue and Gray.
Freedom's shroud or shroud of Treason weaves a thunderous loom to-day
  From the woof of Blue and Gray

How the loyal Nation trembles through that bloody battle-week!
How the fates of sons and brothers kindred pale and trembling seek!
As bewildering, wire-borne voices from the dinning conflict speak,
  Through that dreadful battle-week.

Telling how the Nation's heroes 'neath that bright midsummer's sun,
In their grand self-sacrificing suffering, bleeding struggled on,
Till our banners waved triumphant: Gettysburg was lost and won,
  Just as set the shrouded sun.

*   *   *,   *

From the bristling height of Round Top to the rebel-peopled plain
Comes a sound of crashing thunder ; comes a sheet of leaden rain ;
As red Death, with arms Briarean, starts his Sickles in the grain,
    On the rebel-peopled plain.

Was that leader simply reckless that he thus destruction wooed ?
Did he disobey his orders, or were they misunderstood ?
Profitless the queries, for he paid the forfeit with his blood ;
    That is not misunderstood.

Elbow touching, centre dressing, on its colors rent and scarred,
See that bright-hued line advancing, its allignment yet unmarred !
See that Zouave battling fearless in the thinning color-guard !
    Round the flag so rent and scarred.

He, our hero, leaving kindred, leaving friends behind him far,
Cared for naught beside his country, sought no gleaming shoulder-bar ;
But, beside the humblest private, marched enlisted for the war.
    Friends and kin behind afar.

Reigning in the social circle, glowing with poetic fire
Was his mind and stored with knowledge, yet expanding, broader
    higher,
Sore must be that Nation's sufferings, that such sacrifice require,
    Myriad lives through blood and fire.

Home affection sought to stay him ; love of country urged him on.
Duty warred on inclination ; short the struggle—duty won.
And a letter, wrote in sorrow, came to tell that he had gone.
    Short the struggle—duty won !

Nobly done that duty, whether 'neath the annalled conflicts roar,
Or the unwritten picket skirmish, march or bivouac, he bore
In his soul a glow flamboyant as the tortured martyrs wore
    In the dreadful days of yore.

Now the rage and grim of battle mask his glowing countenance,
As he charges with his comrades, with the colors in advance,
War's dread horrors all around him pass unheeded to his glance,
    So the flag was in advance.

Vain those sacrificial offerings ; for like vultures on their prey
Swoop the gathering hosts of Treason ; now the Patriots stand at bay ;
Now fall backward as they vainly strive the fierce advance to stay,
       Vainly strive to save the day.

Slowly, sullenly retreating from the horrors gathering round,
Him, our hero, they are leaving writhing on the reeking ground,
Grasping still his heated musket, smitten by a mortal wound,
       While the horrors gather round.

Oh, the anguish dire which fills him as he hears the foemen's yell,
When he sees them rush victorious up the highway where he fell.
Agonized in flesh and spirit, how he suffers, who can tell,
       While his foes victorious yell ?

Now he sees behind South Mountain smoke-veiled sink the reddening sun,
And the moon from out the east hills has her arching course begun ;
While the stars in fear and trembling peer through heaven one by one ;
       Sadly gleaming one by one.

Growing fainter in the distance, still he hears the tireless strife ;
Hears the far-off cannon pounding, sees the air with meteors rife.
Countless furies seem to mutter, "Blow for blow, and life for life!"
       Mid the yet unended strife.

Sees the stubborn foemen slowly up the slopes of Round Top creep ;
Hears them as with shouts exultant rock and crag and wall they leap,
Till the brave " Reserves " of Crawford hurl them headlong from the
     steep.
       Hard-won heights they could not keep.

Hears their still more distant onset, strong in numbers, fierce of will,
Echoing from the graveyard-mantled heights of Cemetery Hill,
Till they turn back torn and shattered. Hushed the tumult, all is still.
       Silence covers vale and hill.

Still unsuccored lies that hero, while the full moon high o'erhead
Shows the writhing forms about him ; shows the gaping, palled dead ;
Murmuring not, although the bullet burns within as molten lead,
       Murmuring not, though hope had fled.

Living all his young life over, back his wandering thoughts are sent,
With his kin his thrilling heart-chords in a loving maze are blent;
To the scenes beside the river, where his school-boy days were spent,
    Back his wandering thoughts are sent.

Forward to the speculative future soon unveiled to be,
Longing for the dread transition in his helpless agony,
That would tear aside the veiling of a life-long mystery,
    Which alone the dead can see.

Now his thoughts ring out harmonious to the distant battle's chime.
Now they well from out his bosom in a weird and mournful rhyme,
As the golden grains of memory trickle through the sieve of time,
    Full of weird and mournful rhyme.

Still the invader holds possession; still the wounded plaintive moan;
Still the rigid, staring corpses look straight up with eyes of stone
At the moon which calm, unpitying, stalks her star-lit path alone,
    Heedless as those eyes of stone.

Now the glowing hands of morning tear the shimmering veil of night
From the earth's red riven bosom; and at noon, from height to height,
Rings again the clash of armies as they grapple in their might,
    In the war of Wrong and Right.

And again the spiteful rifle spits its fire from left to right;
Yet again the yawning cannon gives its hidden devil flight,
Till the war fiend, gorged to fulness, grants unwillingly respite,
    In the fight 'twixt Wrong and Right.

Baffled is the dread invasion. Echoing now from hill to hill,
Hoarsely sounding Jubilates all the smoking welkin fill,
Till again the moonbeams shimmer, and the earth is hushed and still.
    Silence covers vale and hill.

Still the rebels hold that outpost; still the thirsty wounded moan;
Still those calm, unpassioned corpses glare straight up with eyes of
    stone;
Still the moon, so phantom-ship-like, sails unheeding slowly on,
    Heedless as those eyes of stone.

Still ungathered lies that harvest swathed by death with reaper keen,
Ripe and ready for the garner long neglected hath it been,
But the harvesters are busy, they have other fields to glean,
    Swathed by death with reaper keen.

Now beneath South Mountain's shadows, southward the invaders go
Through the slanting rain and darkness in a fierce tumultuous flow;
And give back the hard won acres with their harvest to the foe;
    Dead and dying lying low.

And the gleaners come together, gather up the trampled sheaves,
And they lay them in the garner; dust to dust the earth receives.
O the thorns among the roses in the wreath which Victory weaves,
    Blood stains dull its laurel leaves!

Well alligned down in the trenches, blankets muffled in a row,
Like a sleeping line of battle waiting for the trumpet's blow.
Shoulder touching comrade shoulder, as in life they faced the foe—
    Blanket muffled, lying low.

And they gather up the living fragments of that festal day,
And the jolting ambulances, o'er the late plowed fields away,
Bear those maimed, neglected wounded, sad mementos of the fray—
    Fragments of war's festal day.

Bear them fainting o'er the meadows which they late exultant trod,
Up the slopes where late their lines in billows bayonet-crested flowed,
To the hospitals beyond them, gleaming from the trampled sod,
    Slowly ebbed which fiercely flowed.

Days and nights of suffering followed, when one day at early morn
To that tented shrine there came a pilgrim old and travel-worn,
With his staff and heavy burden—burden, he full long had borne,
    Came one day at early morn.

And his plain attire bespoke him follower of that noble creed
Taught of old by Penn and Barclay—born of persecution's seed.
Mindful of the Light within him ever he in word and deed;
    Follower of a peaceful creed.

His the lot to bear and suffer, though a soul of highest worth,
Toiling ever, baffled often, still his genial smile came forth.
Sad exemplar of the passage, " Our rewards are not of earth,
　　Though with soul of highest worth."

And among those tents he wandered, patriarch like of olden time,
Seeking in their sad recesses him who in his manhood's prime,
In that valley heard his death-knell ringing in the batteries' chime,
　　Heard it in his manhood's prime.

And at last his weary vision rests on a familiar face,
Staring forth with wistful glances from that suffering-haunted place;
And the seeker and the sought-for joyful, agonized embrace,
　　In that suffering-haunted place.

Now the lost was found, but succor want, neglect had made in vain,
And the stream of life was ebbing slowly to its fount again;
While delirium's weird, wild fancies o'er him had begun their reign.
　　Want, neglect made help in vain.

Now amid the social triumphs of his former life they dwell,
Now his songs, his pupils chanting, in a soothing cadence swell,
Now, above the crash of battle, comes the foeman's demon yell ;
　　Comes, alas ! to break the spell.

And he hears his comrades answering with defiant, ringing shout,
Till the scenes and sounds commingle which encompass him about,
And they die to softest murmurs and his lamp of light goes out—
　　Darkens to illumine doubt !

Now afar that hero-martyr bears that pilgrim in his woe,
To the vale where passed his childhood by the river's murmuring flow,
Where the remnant of a household—wide war-scattered—lay him low
　　Near the river's murmuring flow.

No funeral pomp surrounds him, o'er his grave fires no platoon,
No bright flags enfold his coffin, drum nor trumpet ring no tune,
As they lay him with his brothers on that summer's afternoon.
　　Drum nor trumpet ring no tune.

Lay him there and part in sorrow; but, ere many years have flown,
Comes that pilgrim, life aweary, there to lay his burden down.
Comes to reap a life-sown harvest, from the Cross to take the Crown,
When he'd lain his burden down.

John Burns Again.

After Bret Harte—Several Years.

Who hasn't heard of old John Burns?
The man so praised and slandered by turns;
Till some, as the stories to mind they recall,
Much doubt if he ever lived at all.
For who ever led such a double life
As he, when the Boys in Blue held strife
With the rebs in gray and butternut brown
On the hills o'erlooking Gettysburg town?

For he saw no fight, yet he bravely fought—
Was badly wounded, yet he was not
A valiant soldier, a cowardly brag,
A crusty crank, a comical wag,
A poor shoemaker in rented house,
A thrifty farmer with "bees and cows!"

Why such contrariness, when, forsooth,
'Tis so much easier to tell the truth?

Where the quiet streets come sloping down
The sun-set side of Gettysburg town,
And shady suburb to meadow turns
You'll find the house of old John Burns.

A rustic cottage I'd like to paint;
Many-gabled and mossy and quaint;

With ivied walls and a floral arch
Bridging the front of the latticed porch;
With flower-lined paths, and nooks with ferns,
Surroundings for which the soulful yearns,
But not the surroundings of brave John Burns.
I would fain give rein to the vain æsthetic,
But I'd rather be truthful than poetic;
So I must come down to language tame
And show a "story and a half of frame,"
With whitewash painted, a flowerless lawn—
'Tis not the picture I counted on.
But I care not who from the canvas turns;
It shows you the home of old John Burns.

And here he lived from year to year,
The sort of fellow who some call queer.
For he paid his debts, but to make amends
Minded his business and stuck to his friends,
Like the wax with which he shaped his ends!

For as to the trade of old John Burns,
He made and mended shoes by turns;
So he sewed and pegged away, and here
Life's stream ran smoothly for many a year.

In the summer days, when his work was done,
He would sit on his steps, while the slanting sun
Sent its beams on his little house of frame
Till the gable windows danced aflame,
And look on scenes in the glowing west,
With peaceful thoughts in his thankful breast.

And truly it was a goodly sight,
Did he look to the front or left or right,
Where the vista spread for many a rood,
Dotted with farm-house, orchard and wood.

Just in front was the famed Oak Ridge,
While on the far horizon's edge,
Lifting it up on either hand,
Arose South Mountain rugged and grand,
Hiding the Valley of Cumberland.

Peaceful the time, but it soon passed o'er,
And the cruel demon of civil war
Had plowed the land and the harvest made
For the reaper Death with his crescent blade.

Throbbings of hope and fear by turns
Pulsed through the heart of old John Burns.
For the "canny Scot" was a patriot true,
Who longed to fight in the ranks of Blue.
But gathering years had bowed him down,
And he needs must stay in Gettysburg town.
So he fretted and fumed day after day,
Though he pegged and stitched and hammered away.
For there needs to be soling and heeling of shoes
Though the war eagle screeches or peace dove cooes;
Though nations go tottering to luckless fate,
Shoemakers must work and customers wait.

One day through the streets of the startled town
An army of horsemen came riding down,
Rebels in gray and butternut brown.

Streaming with tatters their dusty clothes,
Full of vermin, as they with oaths,
Georgia "crackers," "tar-heel" toughs,
Texas cow-boys, Arkansaw roughs;
But plucky in battle as well as defeat,
These ragged fellows were hard to beat,
As with rattle of spur and jingle of sword,
Like a noisy dream, swept the hungry horde

On their Northward road. In another day
Came Buford and Reynolds the selfsame way,
With their Yankee troops, with marching worn,
But their shot-riven flags were proudly borne,
As 'mid clangor and shouts they galloped down
The sloping streets of Gettysburg town.

And where was Burns that fateful day,
When our boys were gathering for the fray?
The man who had said he was ready to fight
As soon as the rebels came in sight?
Down in his shoe shop mending shoes,
Pegging away, but full of the Blues
As the town that morn, for he wanted to fight,
But he'd promised some work that was not done quite;
For I'd have you know the doubtingest Thomas
Ne'er said John Burns went back on a promise!

On the floor was his work in a tidy row,
From coarsest brogan to baby's shoe,
Alligned as if on dress parade;
And on his shoe bench lately made,
A present from old John Burns 'tis said,
Were the wedding slippers of Jennie Wade.
Poor girl! in another day to fall,
Shot dead by a rebel rifle ball,
While, laying aside all girlish fears,
She was baking bread for our cannoniers!

He hears a cannon; he quickly turns
His face to the north, does old John Burns,
And he sees a sight from his house of frame
That sets his tingling blood aflame;
For foemen are gathering to bring renown
And tears and sorrow to Gettysburg town.

In vain for him is that signal gun,
For the promised shoes are not yet done.

Nor he the man from duty to shirk;
So he goes on finishing up his work.

Boom! Boom! Again the cannon's clamor
Plays base to the tenor of his hammer,
As he works away with his stubborn will,
To get through so as to go on the hill.
But now his senses seemed spell-bound,
When a change came o'er all things around.

He saw himself an avenging knight,
Predestined to set the wrong things right.
His garments changed from their cut so queer
To the courtly dress of a cavalier.
From its peg on the side of the dingy room
His napless white hat seemed to bloom
To a Highland bonnet with nodding plume.
His shoe-knife grew to a bright claymore,
As heavy as Bruce or Wallace bore.
While his hammer changed to the sledge of Thor,
Pounding the brazen gong of war.
His awls to hilted daggers grew,
Seeking the hearts of Treason's crew.
The shoe-pegs, ranged in their little stalls,
Grew and hardened to Minnie balls.
While his ink—in a horn—seemed like a flood
Of bubbling, seething, traitor's blood.
Each coil from his ball of thread let loose
Twisted and curled to a hangman's noose,
Ready to give the rebs their dues.
While the muffled stroke on the leathered stone
Seemed "sickening thuds" for traitors gone.
And each dubious bill on his little slate,
A repudiated Southern debt!
But this last gave such a twinge of pain,
He aroused and went to work again.

Testily rasping the sole of his shoe,
He pared the edge and blackened them too.
Marked on the shining face the price,
Then said, as he shut his mouth like a vise:
" I've kept my promise," and then he laughed,
When he added: " I'll never disgrace my craft!"

Thus John, and he stiffly rose to his feet,
Folded his apron tidy and neat.
Then he called to his good wife Barbara,
" I've a job of work on the Ridge to-day.
If young and able-bodied fellers
Choose to hide like rats in the cellars,
I'll show my colors and go the front
And share with the boys the battle's brunt."

He shows her the row of customers' shoes;
Tells whom to trust and whom to refuse ;
Then her toil-worn hands he tightly grips,
Till they tingle to their finger tips.
And looking around that no one saw,
He frightened the weeping Barbara
With a smacking kiss on her puckered lips—
For he wasn't one of the kissing kind,
Though a tenderer man you couldn't find—
And blushing and trembling standing there,
To him she was as young and fair
As when he bore her a bonnie bride
In far off days from the banks of Clyde.

From his heart there seems a lifted load,
As he moves along the dusty road ;
And his halting gait works up to the stride
Of a soldier filled with martial pride ;
While he lifts his head with a pose severe
That would please the eye of a grenadier,
As he hears the sounds and sees the sight
That tells the opening of the fight.

Sections of batteries thundered by,
Followed by squadrons of cavalry;
And limping on with blistered feet,
The tired foot-soldiers filled the street;
While on the hill top, smoke enplumed,
The hot breathed cannon ceaseless boomed;
And underneath was heard the whir
Of the random ball of the skirmisher;
But neither to right nor left he turns,
But on like fate stalks old John Burns,
With soul aflame and teeth on edge,
And never stops till he mounts the Ridge.

And here he sees, in the rising din,
The Seventh Wisconsin going in;
And he says to the Colonel, "Give us a gun,
And I'll help you to make the rebels run!"
Just then a shell tore up the dirt—
"Run home, old fellow, or you'll get hurt,"
Said the Colonel. But John roared back in wrath,
As he stood unflinched in the fiery bath,
"There's no room there, for all the cellars
Are full to the joists with home-guard fellers,
So give us a gun." And the Colonel said,
Under the orders he roared o'erhead,
"There's none to spare," and he said with a smile,
"There'll be plenty if you'll wait awhile,"
As he changed the order to "Fire by file."

Just then came the "zip" of a Minnie ball,
And a tall file-closer was seen to fall,
And when to his side John quickly sped,
No thought had he of robbing the dead,
But rather that of grafting his life
To this one laid low in the battle's strife,
And to finish the work he'd just begun.—
With short apology fighting John

Grasped from the tight-clenched hand the gun,
Smoking and warm ; nor pangs he felt
As he took the cartridge-box and belt
From the dying man, and buckled them on,
For the blood was hot in fighting John.
And he stepped in line with an iron will,
And not forgetting his old-time skill,
When he gunned for squirrels on yonder hill,
And which in his eyes yet seemed to lurk,
He spat on his hands and went to work.

How he and the boys had another spat
About his clothes and bell-crowned hat,
Bret Harte has told you all of that !
No matter if some his story doubt—
So I'll just narrate what he left out.

Not caring a peg for Hardee's drill,
John's plan was to "load and fire at will ;"
And as he blazed to left and right
Each shot gave vent to a special spite.
This for Sumpter.   That Bull Run—
And here he double-shotted his gun ;
This Fredericksburg.   That Chancellorsville—
For each he shot with a will to kill.
This for the time he kept away
From the ranks of the Blue in front of the Gray.
That for the dead Wisconsin man,
Whose record ended when his began.
Mute but appealing lying there—
And here he "loaded his gun for bear,"
This for his colonel wounded sore—
'Twas then as he banged away he swore.
Till with this for that and that for this,
Firing away with seldom a miss,
His cartridge-box was emptied quite
Before he had shot away his spite.

How many were killed, or wounded fell,
From piercing bullet and gashing shell,
He never noticed, but with the rest
His only thought was doing his best!

Thus Gettysburg's patriot grim and lone,
With a borrowed gun but a will of his own,
Loading, aiming, firing away;
So full of life was he that day
From his acts you'd scarce the inference draw
He was dead in the Psalmist's Scriptural law.

He got more bullets—this man of pluck,
Unarmed as yet; but changed his luck
When a low aimed shot his ankle struck.
But still he could fire; when another one
Crippled the arm that steadied his gun;
Another, and Burns fell prone to the ground,
One added to plenty lying around;
And they bore him off as the sun went down
Over the hill and into the town.

And there he lay while the battle surged
Till the fiery day into night had merged,
While the men in Gray pushed the boys in Blue
The streets of Gettysburg through and through,
Capturing some and driving the rest
Till they wearied dropped on the graveyard crest,
When the guns of Steinwehr, grim and black,
Pelted their fierce pursuers back.

And another day, while the rebel right
Was fighting our left for Round Top's height,
Till the famed Peach Orchard ground was filled
With fallen soldiers maimed and killed,
And horses dead by the burst caissons
Just in rear of the useless guns.

Till the trees which in April bloomed with pearl,
Blushed red with the rain of that tempest whirl.
While the smoke-grimed imps in the " Devil's Den "
Were rifling the lives of our Round Top men,
And each rock on the slope of " Granite Spur "
Blazed with the fire of a skirmisher.
While round-shot, shell and musket ball
Were threshing the wheat so yellow and tall,
That gleamed in the valley far below
Alive with the charge of the coming foe,
Till the tangled straw seemed from the heights
Dotted all over with gruesome sights.

And yet he lay while roared and raved
The fight and the rent flags drooped or waved,
Till the twilight shades came quivering down
Over the sulphur waves of brown,
When the fiery rebels of Hoke and Hays ;
Were charging the Federal battle-blaze,
When the gunners were tickling with rammer and swab
Their gun-throats till with retch and throb
They vomited hells of iron and fire
On the torn waves rising higher and higher,
Till they made them turn and backward pour
With their wreckage crowding the sloping shore ;
Flotsam and jetsam high and dry
For the wreckers to gather by and by.

And there he lay that terrible day,
That final day when the grim array ;
The storming column of Pickett stood
Enmassed behind the screening wood,
Left flanked and charged the meadow slopes,
Of hopes forlon, forlornest of hopes !

   *   *   *   *   *   *
The cannon which an hour or more
Had vexed the air have ceased their roar.

The Federals, ranged from height to height,
In awe-struck silence view the sight
As onward the Confederate braves
Come marching o'er their future graves,
And as they cross the meadow's marge
They double-quick the final charge.

Now roar the Federal guns again,
Now flash their hundred fires amain,
The graveyard frees its hidden death
And Round Top blows its poisoned breath,
While the long, low ridge which lies between
Seething with fire and smoke is seen.

The torn lines break but charge again ;
Behind a broadening trail of slain,
In front a narrowing sea of gray,
On the famed Stone Wall breaks away,
Reddening the surface with its spray.

And still he heard from the lonely ward
The battle above as it surged and roared,
While the bursting shells wove a fiery bridge
Of arches which sprang from ridge to ridge.
Spanning the reeking battle mist,
Over which they shrieked and hissed ;
Spanning the swaying noisy sea
Of demonized humanity
With its under current flowing red,
Wounded and dying among the dead.

The sun rose twice, and twice went down,
Back of the mountains dim and brown ;
Twice the moon with softened glare
Rode through the sulphur-laden air,
And the fight was over.   Ah ! who can tell
How many were sleeping where they fell.

The fight was over, but victory
Didn't perch on the banners of General Lee,
Who holstered his pistols and sheathed his sword,
And getting ahead of his rebel horde
They stole—'twas a way they had—away
Through the mountain pass of Monterey,
And off to the South-land skurried down,
Sick and tired of Gettysburg town.

And still Burns lay in his lonely ward,
Tho' hushed were the guns which so lately roared,
Still o'er him the Hither and Yon held strife
On the skirmish ground 'twixt death and life,
For the wounding bullets the probe withstood,
And fever was firing his meagre blood,
The rebels around him—the burning pain—
The battle echoes had turned his brain.

He was fighting still in the sultry sun,
Down by the banks of Willoughby Run,
Swathing the rebels with his gun—
The borrowed gun which this honest man
Was worrying how to return again—
In the gathering smoke and rising noise,
In the line with the brave Wisconsin boys,
Again was he coaxing left and right
His neighbors to get their guns and fight;
Again these subterranean dwellers
Who served their country down in their cellars,
Rang in his ears their senseless prate,
" They also serve who watch and wait."
While this was the loud refrain of some,
" What would be done if we all left home?

Again was he calling them rats and moles,
And telling them all to come out of their holes
As he did before.   And that is why
When you talk of Burns they look so shy.

Instead of giving him votes of thanks,
As they would have done in the elder Rome,
They vote him a crusty king of cranks,
They call him a bug of the genus *hum;*
And this is the local fame one earns
Who does his duty like old John Burns.

One day in his ears these words were lipped,
"The battle is over, the rebs are whipped!"
His wandering mind to the words caught on,
The fever quick from his brain was gone;
The bullets which had so stubborn proved
To the probing steel like magnets moved;
And getting one of his cranky turns,
He soon got well, did old John Burns,
In spite of all the doctor's rules,
And hobbled back to his bench and tools,
And stitched and pegged and hammered away
As he did of old, until one day
Death came along with his manner rough—
As he handles his victims tender or tough—
Gathered him in and bore him off
With the neighbors' help, and laid him away
By the bones of his old wife, Barbara,
On the hill o'erlooking his house of frame,
And the field where he won his deathless fame.

Now this is the last of old John Burns,
Gashed by bullets and rhymes by turns;
The rebels commenced, and Bret and I
Have finished their work successfully,
And laid him to rest on the hills that frown
On the peaceful homes of Gettysburg town.

Jennie Wade.

Killed at Gettysburg, July, 1863.

HAVE you heard the story of Jennie Wade
And Corporal Skelly, her Boy in Blue?
Gettysburg's "Saragossa Maid"
And his country's soldier brave and true?

When the shells burst over spire and roof,
And the balls hissed up and down the street,
And people, from danger to keep aloof,
Hid in the cellar's safe retreat,
Brave Jennie the dangers heeded none,
But in her cottage worked away
Baking the brown loaves one by one
For the boys who fought on the hill that day.
When lo! as she worked, a rebel ball
Like an adder hissed through the open door,
And the stricken maiden tottered to fall
Lifeless upon her kitchen floor.
Never to know her soldier lover,
Corporal Skelly, light of her eye,
Joy of her young heart over and over,
Wounded, had lain him down to die.

Down where the Shenandoah River,
With current reddened, sought the sea,
Its bosom with war-sounds ever a-quiver,
As the battle-clouds their bolts set free.
When the Minnie balls sang through the thickets—
In place of the song-birds scared away—
After the bugle recalled the pickets,
And ere the batteries got in play.

When the skirmish line grew thinner and thinner
  And our army's edges were torn and frayed,
Ere the fight worked on to bass from tenor,
  The bullet flew hot that low him laid.
Laid him low, in life ne'er knowing
  His love in death on her hearth-stone bled,
From rebel bullet her heart's blood flowing;
  Neither to know the other dead.

This is the story of Jennie Wade
  And Corporal Skelly, her Boy in Blue!
Gettysburg's "Saragossa Maid"
  And her country's soldier brave and true.

The Old Grist-Mill.

HALF hidden by weeping willows,
  At the foot of a wooded hill,
In a setting of quiet beauty
  Nestles the old grist-mill.
Its roof is seamed and moss-covered,
  And tottering is its wall,
And silent and still is the water-wheel
  All compassed in Time's enthrall.

Slimy and green is the penstock,
  And covered with nettles rank ;
Weed-grown the winding mill-race,
  Crevasses cleave its banks.
The willow's coquettish branches
  Are kissing the glassy pond,
With its splatterdocks in floating flocks,
  And the thicket-lined shore beyond.

Back to the days of my boyhood
My thoughts fly on memory's wings,
I see the old mill in its glory;
What spray the big water-wheel flings!
As the buckets strike the water
With merry, pattering sound,
And what rattling peals the counter-wheels
Ring out as they whirl around!

Hark how the mill-stones rumble
As the golden grain runs through!
List to the clattering " damsel "
Shaking the agueish "shoe!"
Swiftly is gliding the belting—
The cogs reel round in a maze—
As with mute surprise in my juvenile eyes
I wondering stand and gaze.

There stands the miller musing
On the ups and downs of corn,
His form appears bowed down with years
And the weighty sacks he's borne.
Dust wraps him round like a halo—
Dented his mealy hat—
An honest old man is the miller I scan,
Though they say his hogs are fat.

Weighing out quarters of flour—
Measuring bushels of feed—
Plenty of grist work his dower—
Plenty of water his need.
Toiling from morning till even,
Grinding the golden grain ;
When death one day chanced over that way
And heavenward jogged the twain.

No longer the spectral miller
  At his onerous post is found ;
From his haunts he's missed, he's ground his grist,
  And the miller's grist is ground.
Well toled, they say, was his grist work,
  Well told were the yarns he spun,
Well tolled was the bell at his funeral
  After his work was done.

And now that mill is standing
  Cheerless and silent and old.
Owls and bats through the windows
  Are flying fearless and bold.
Time and the rats are gnawing
  At rafter and beam and floor ;
And soon the old mill, so silent and still,
  Will crumble to rise no more.

*　　　*　　　*　　　*

Oh ! what is the world but a grist-mill?
  Where Right is ground down by Power ;
Where Fashion is grinding its minions
  Into very indifferent flour.
Where Vice is crushing out Virtue,
  And the Rich grind down the Poor.
Where grists of Cares and Hopes and Fears
  Pass in and out at the door !

Oh, what is Life but a mill-stone ?
  Turning round once each day ;
Crushing us, tearing us, grinding us,
  Slowly but surely away.
Grimly, remorselessly gliding,
  Stilling the panting breath ;
Who is that ghastly miller?
  Who but the scarecrow—Death ?

A Lyric of the Cuttalossa.*

WHERE Cuttalossa's waters
  Roll murmuring on their way,
'Twixt hazel clumps and alders,
  'Neath old trees mossed and gray,
Just where across the valley,
  From the old, old grist-mill come
The water-wheel's low patter,
  The mill-stone's drowsy hum.

Here sparkling from its birthplace
  Just up the rifted hill,
O'er tiny cascades leaping,
  Comes down a little rill;
Till in a rude built fountain
  It pours its crystal tide,
Just where the road comes winding
  On the valley opening wide.

Here a Samaria-dweller
  Had brought a rustic cup,
From the milky cocoa fashioned,
  And there had hung it up.
A little gem poetic,
  From New England's Quaker bard,
With his name beneath, was graven
  Upon its outlines hard.

---

* On the Cuttalossa, two miles from its mouth, is a spring which has had much
printed notice from its romantic surroundings. It had long been utilized as a
place of liquid refreshment by placing there a water-trough and drinking-cup.
The latter, a cocoa shell neatly handled, had an apt inscription placed upon it.
A colored teamster from Buckingham bore the cup away for private use; but
brought it back on hearing that the road-master had posted up a notice threatening the abductor with suspension unless he did so.

Here through the sweltering summer
  The thirsty wayfarer stopped
To quaff this liquid manna—
  This nectar heaven-dropped.
There Dives in his phæton,
  There Jehu with his wain,
And the ragged, grimy tramper
  Met on a common plane.

Met in this Temperance tavern,
  With swaying branches roofed;
The bar-maids wanton Naiads;
  While Satyrs horned and hoofed,
Played hostler; while no landlord
  With bills the guests did vex—
They freely drained the cocoa
  Of Adam's XXX!

One sleepy, summer noontide,
  When all was still around,
Save when, like a tired bee's buzzing,
  A Pan-pipe's droning sound
Came drowsily from the meadow,
  Morpheus, the tricky elf,
Fast bound the fountain guardians,
  So the bar had to run itself.

That day a colored orphan,
  Of fifty years or so,
Just from a neighboring province,
  Stopped here his mules to blow.
He spied the pendant goblet—
  This "child-like" son of Ham,
Quoth he, "That palm-born cocoa
  Will soothe my 'itching palm.'

"Oh what a cup for cider!
    I'll put it to that use,
And drink from it genial bumpers
    Of beady apple-juice."
Then this colored man and brother
    Glanced warily toward the mill,
Low humming across the valley,
    And the farm-house on the hill.

Then spake, "One Whittier owns it;
    But I do not care a—clam,
Not one whit I err in taking,
    For wittier I am.
For wit I e'er was famous,
    In logic I bear the palm,
So away I'll bear the palm-fruit,
    And hie to the land of Ham!"
So he quick annexed the cocoa—
    His conscience gave no qualm—
Saying with tragic Richard,
    "This much for Buckingham!"

The elves awakening, seeing
    The spoiler had been there,
The Satyrs stamped their goat-hoofs,
    The Naiads tore their hair,
And fearing the wrath of Dian—
    She of the groves and fields—
The Naiads took to the water,
    The Satyrs took to their heels.

While this brother bore his treasure
    Homeward, and late that night
He tapped the frothing cider,
    With blithesome heart and light.
But oh, what horrors seized him
    When he to drink essayed;

Fierce spasms shook his muscles,
    He felt a nameless dread.
'Twas cider-phobia had him
    Within its awful grasp.
He sought his couch in terror,
    And many a thirsty gasp.

He prays aloud for Morpheus—
    His prayer naught avails;
His bed seems filled with chestnut burrs,
    His pillow with wrought nails.
These prick-like stings of conscience,
    He tosses to and fro,
Crying out, "No wretch so suffered
    On earth or down below.

" Not vulture-gnawed Prometheus,
    Chained to his lonely rock;
Nor Tantalus, ever baffled
    By the waters that him mock.
Not Ixion, ever turning,
    Snake-bound, upon his wheel;
Nor Sisyphus, ever rolling
    His stone up an endless hill.

" O is't what folks call conscience
    That makes this night a hell?
O for some incantation
    To break this magic spell.
O for some Afric sorcerer,
    Some grim magician's wand,
Some 'fetich' of my fathers,
    From far Apingi land.

" Come from the mountain, Dinah!
    Once chaste Diana called.

Come from thy haunts and tell me
What has my spirit thralled!"
Scarce was the prayer uttered,
When the Sylvan Goddess come,
And with her presence haloed
And glorified the room.

"Burnt-corked" her Grecian profile,
Her "Grecian Bend" curved high;
Crimped were her flowing tresses,
"Greek fire" was in her eye.
And thus she spake, "Oh, monster!
Who with sacrilegious hand
Stole a vessel from my altar,
List while I thee command!
Before to-morrow's noontide
Take thou that goblet back,
Or fiercer pangs than ever
Thy recreant soul shall rack.

"And traveler, be he tramper,
Or Dives with his chaise,
Or Jehu with his wagon,
Will curse thee day by day.
E'en now the roadway guardian,
A note has posted up,
The fate of Haman threatening
To the robber of 'Our Cup.'

"If peace thou wishest, promise,
Or by the fabled boar,
Ancestral curse shall reach thee
From far Zambesi's shore,
Of the arch-baboon Darwinian,
Our sire pre-Adamite—
Its Upas bane shall shade thee,
Life's fairest prospects blight."

Thus she; with teeth a-chatter,
  He promised. From the room
She rode off on a moonbeam,
  And left the place in gloom.
The chestnut burrs turned feathers,
  To down the nails were wrought,
He slept the just man's slumbers,
  Till day its duty brought.

Then he geared his long-eared comrades,
  And the cocoa shell conveyed
To the nook beside the roadway,
  Where the bubbling fountain played.
A weight was off his spirits,
  His whistle blithe and gay,
Rang out on the Cuttalossa,
  As he went his winding way.

The woodland sprites, exultant,
  In sportive gambols played,
Pan-piping a Bacchanal measure,
  Frisked up and down the glade.
While the goat-like prancing Satyrs,
  And the Naiads scant arrayed,
Keeping time to the pipes' wild music,
  Danced minuets in the shade.

Dickens.

I SEE his grand creations rise
  In troops from depths abysmal,
And file along before my eyes,
  With faces gay to dismal—
Gay like the jolly, jovial Mark,
  Perennially cheerful ;
In every shade of character,
  To Gummidge, always tearful.

Well to the front stalks Copperfield,
  Whose future ope'd so dreary
When boyhood's trials weighing down
  Made him of life a-weary ;

Till, hopefully, he trudged along
  When time made all things even,
And all his purgatorial paths
  Merged to an earthly heaven.

In thinking of his rival girls,
  With Pat I'd say : "Be gorra!
I'd taken Agnes at the start—
  Not waste those years with Dora."
You cannot find a nobler type,
  Through Dickens' women sorting,
But she should not have been slow,
  And done some livelier courting.

While David, burdened with his doll,
  Looked back with glances yearning
To that regretted point in life
  When Agnes graced the turning.
Close by Aunt Trotwood walks erect,
  As if naught would unbend her ;
And yet beneath that rugged form
  Were heart-throbs pulsing tender.

And here comes Peggoty, the nurse,
  With cheeks like russet apples ;
Her brother Daniel, rough but kind,
  Whose tongue such English grapples ;
And little Em'ly, at whose face
  Such lecherous glances leer forth
From him for whom Ham lost his life:
  The polished villain Steerforth.

And Tommy Traddles, Simple Dick,
  And more along come trooping.
I'll have to stop, they come so thick,
  And seek another grouping.

Ah! here is Pip in churchyard bounds,
    As day grows dim and dimmer,
Trying to con life's early tasks,
    With tombstones for his primer.

And convict Magwitch shuffles by,
    I hear his chain's harsh clangor;
While henpecked Gargery plods along,
    Lashed by his shrew-wife's anger;
And ponderous Orlick, holding tight
    His murderous blacksmith hammer;
And cautious Wemmick, and the "Aged"—
    His ears so proof to clamor.

And weird Miss Havisham appears,
    And convict-born Estella;
A shame she e'er should wed our Pip—
    He was too nice a fellow.
Another group: "Our Mutual Friend"
    Stands forth in outlines splendid;
Who gave up fortune—lived unknown,
    To test a wife intended.

And ox-like Boffin, with his mate,
    Who made such tilts at fashion;
And literary Wegg, who had
    For poetry such passion;
And Gaffer and Rogue Riderhood,
    With callings so unholy;
And bony Venus—Jenny Wren;
    The Jew so meek and lowly.

And Eugene Wrayburn! how could he
    E'er marry Gaffer's daughter?
Such fearful price for being pulled
    By her from out the water;

And Bradley Headstone, on whose life
  There seemed to dawn no morning,
Who shunned one woman's loving smiles
  To meet another's scorning.

Another group, and at its head
  Is Pecksniff's form appearing;
His speech so full of pious talk,
  His eye of carnal leering.
Here pass along twin storied dames,
  Whose gait the rest embarrass;
They are material Mrs. Gamp,
  And mythic Mrs. Harris.

Young Chuzzlewit, his servant Mark—
  That synonym for Jolly;
And poor Tom Pinch, whose dearest friend
  Made his love-yearnings folly.
Another group which Pickwick leads
  With legs abbreviated,
And Weller and his " widder " wife
  Who were so badly mated.

Another crew by Dombey led,
  I see, has just up-anchored;
And still another, led by him
  Who for some "more" so hankered;
And other chiefs lead other hosts,
  Till comes the grand finale,
When Death tears Edwin Drood in two—
  Half left each side the Valley.

What shall I say of him whose brain
  These passing forms created?
Did he deserve the praise bestowed,
  Or was be overrated?

Alas! I fear the crucial test,
  If placed upon him rightly,
Would show him of but mortal stuff,
  With blemishes unsightly.

We judge the writer by his words,
  To find at last our folly,
On seeing what a wealth of thought
  One private life can sully.
The snob and hypocrite for e'er
  His pen's point was impaling—
Pecksniff and Podsnap, merged in him,
  Their doubles were assailing.

Alas! whose pen could draw the tear,
  Wronged woman's woes portraying,
Should act Don Juan while the part
  Of household tyrant playing;
O'er novelists he lived enthroned,
  All rival kings unseating—
To die at last of too much drink,
  Combined with over-eating.

The Old Saw-Mill.

No MORE the glassy pond reflects
  The lithesome willows' play,
The walls which pent its waters up
  The floods have washed away.
Dead are the bright green water-plants
  That fringed its shaded rim;
The plow its arching furrows turn
  Where fishes used to swim.

Thick sown with briars and tangled weed,
  And sedge grass waving rank,
The head-race winds in dim outline
  Along the meadow bank.
Till crawling 'neath the turnpike road
  It nears the ruined mill,
With roof-tree sunken to the leaves,
  With voiceless wheels and still.

Its forebay sunken in the mud,
  Its walls but crumbling stone,
Its timber mouldering to decay,
  Its log-yard weed-o'ergrown.
Yet fancy needs but sway its wand,
  When full of busy life
The old-time scenes start up again
  With ringing music rife.

Again upon the brimful race
  The willow branches play ;
Again the dripping mill-wheel flings
  Aside the foaming spray.
Again I hear the rag-wheel's grate,
  And hear the rattling cog,
And see the rising saw-teeth send
  The white dust o'er the log.

I see the sawyer crouching stand
  With keen and single eye—
The other shut, that he may see
  If the mill-saw runs awry.
With swinging axe he "sculps" anon
  The dirt from off the bark;
He hears the saw a "hinge-hook" strike,
  With eyebrows frowning dark.

Anon with watchful glance he sees,
Slow moving down the road,
The low log-wagon, oxen drawn,
And creaking with its load.
He grasps the toilsome cant-hook tight,
With horny hands and brown,
And with the teamsters' added help
The logs come thundering down.

Through toiling years he wore away
His life upon that mill;
When death smote one he smote them both
And left them ever still.
He who uprightly walked the earth,
Full careless of its pelf,
Now in his plain-made coffin lay—
He sawed the boards himself.

He sleeps in peaceful rest beneath
The daisy-sprinkled sod;
No more to care for summer's drought,
Or spring-time's angry flood.
As neighbor good, as friend oft tried,
With large and kindly heart,
His life, well spent, this tribute earned—
" He acted well his part ! "

After-Thoughts.

Suns rise and set; moons wax and wane;
　　The seasons come, the seasons go;
Onward to the eternal main
　　The everlasting rivers flow;
From ocean's bosom mists arise,
　　Arise to fall to earth in rain;
The snow-flakes winnowed from the skies
　　Like Antæus touch to rise again.

Eternal mountains prop the clouds;
　　Eternal valleys stretch between;
The one enwrapt in snowy shrouds,
　　The other robed in endless green.
I ask, why should these elements
　　Live soulless on, while mortal man,
So filled with soul and God-given sense,
　　Meets death, when lived his little span?

We know the river flowing by
　　Will, heaven-descended, seek its source.
We know the shrubbery, bare and dry,
　　The spring will cover in its course.
But do we die, though know we not,
　　The scenes behind the curtain's fall?
If to our gaze it is not brought,
　　Is there no hope beyond the pall?

If light Divine illumine not
　　The dreaded haunts of the Beyond;
Is there not proof within the thought
　　Which in earth, sky or stream is found?

If death gives life to soulless tree—
    Clothes winter's icy slopes with green ;
Cannot our faith, from trammels free,
    Make our deaths turned to life be seen ?

And if the waters flowing by,
    All soulless, to the absorbing sea,
Can rise wind-wafted to the sky
    To drop to live in flower and tree,
Can we not know there is no death,
    That life flows on wave after wave,
And all unseen the parted breath
    Sighs and exhalts beyond the grave?

Can pulseless clods thus favored be,
    To grass and flowers and trees give birth,
And we, who live and love, must we
    Die only to enrich the earth?
If withered seeds can grow and reach
    In spreading splendor to the sky,
Must we yearn on in vain beseech,
    Grope heavenward, fall, and vainly die?

We want no voice of gibbering ghost,
    From gruesome graveyard taken flight,
To prove in death we are not lost—
    The future not an endless night.
Even he who doubts the Word inspired,
    In nature should not seek in vain,
To find the proof so much desired—
    We only die to live again !

The Wind-Up.

HAVING written one conclusion within the confines of this volume, it becomes an easy task to write another. In this one I am given opportunity to say that if readers knew how tired an author grows of his book by the time he sends his last proof to the publisher, they would not deem him an object of envy. What the writer looked upon in its preparatory stages as a labor of love, at last so wearies him that he is glad to get it out of sight. Reading the same thing over and over, as the proofs are returned for the correction of mistakes, makes him so tired of what was once a pleasure that he goes through it as mechanically as if it were the work of some one else, and feels that his readers should be under obligations to him for getting the words in readable shape. The worst of it is that repeated proof-readings so dull the senses that the overlooking of errors is rendered easy ; so that after the types are set and the forms struck off beyond recall, the author sees staring at him errors which in bitterness of spirit he reproaches himself for not seeing in time. These are repetition of words in such close connection that they mar the harmony of composition, and other mistakes equally unpleasant. I call attention to this, so that when the reader comes across anything bearing criticism, he will know I am aware of it also.

I may mention another source of annoyance. This is, when too late to remedy the matter, the author sees what fine things he might have inserted to enliven certain dull pages; but now, alas! impossible, since the book is printed and the cold, cold type distributed.

Thus commenting, I start off my Book with the old saying,

"What's writ is writ; would it were worthier."

www.ingramcontent.com/pod-product-compliance
Lightning Source LLC
Chambersburg PA
CBHW020234110726
47898CB00004B/1253